Echoes of Our Ancestors

Brenda Vicars

BLOODHOUND
— BOOKS —

First published in 2024 by Bloodhound Books.

The author and publisher are grateful to The Literary Estate of Robert Penn
Warren for permission to quote from the poem 'Bearded Oaks'.

www.bloodhoundbooks.com

Print ISBN: 978-1-917214-09-4

Chapter One

Philip thought he was alone.

He'd arrived too early for the nightly dinner special, so he waited with a beer at the small bar in the corner of the café. A whiff of cotton-candy perfume alerted him that someone was approaching. The scent triggered dread in his gut. His thigh muscles tensed ready to run. *Why this visceral reaction to a smell?*

Before his mind could form an answer, a barstool bumped the side of his own, and a slender woman in a satiny red shirt looped her purse over her stool's back.

He had no idea who she was.

She boosted herself onto the seat and pressed her arm against his side.

His shoulders stiffened. He held his breath to avoid her too-sweet scent and leaned away from her, but she was so close that each movement snagged his glance, and he eventually had to inhale.

She flicked long black hair away from her pixie-like face. Her eyebrows were straight charcoal slashes. Pushing her shoulder against his bicep, she said, *"Buenos tardes."*

He nodded once but kept his gaze on his phone. *"Buenos tardes."* She must have mistaken him for someone else, and he didn't want to add to her embarrassment when she realized her blunder. With his tan skin and thick black hair, people often assumed he was Latino.

She ran one long red fingernail under the edge of his short-sleeved denim shirt and whispered, "Are you happy I'm finally back... Philip?"

What the hell? Who is she? Searching her face didn't jog a recognition.

She tugged on his sleeve and whispered into his ear, "I thought about you every night I was gone. I remember everything you said. We're soulmates, so much alike, not close to our sisters, rambling from job-to-job." She squeezed his thigh. "My strong *hombre*. This will be the night we carry out our plan." Instead of waiting for him to reply, she called to the bartender. "Frank, where are you?"

Frank stuck his head in through the open doorway to the back room.

"May I please have a mojito?" Her girlish voice didn't fit her late-thirties appearance. She smoothed her cream-colored skirt across her knees.

"You bet, Carmen." He pointed at Philip's mug. "Refill?"

Philip shook his head, and Frank headed to the other end of the bar to fix her drink.

Carmen? Her name meant nothing. Philip straightened his back, getting ready to stand. He no longer wanted the dinner special.

She gasped. "No. You're leaving?" Tears welled in her eyes, and her cheeks flushed.

Philip's hand lifted to pat her shoulder as he would an injured child's. He stopped himself, freezing midway.

She sniffled and clutched his forearm. "What about our

Valentine's night promise?" She elongated *promise*, dragging the word into a sob.

His face heated.

Her words *Valentine's night* sledgehammered the barricade he'd built around that evening almost a month ago. He'd downed too many bourbon shots after his sister phoned about their father's cancer. Philip slid off his seat and stood on the side across from Carmen, using his now empty stool to block her. "Uh... Sorry... Must have been my mistake."

Still clutching his forearm, she scooted from her stool onto his and whispered, "You aren't worth my..." Her voice cracked with anger. "...*escarabajo*."

He frowned. *Escarabajo?* He thought it was Spanish for beetle.

Glaring, she rummaged in her purse. "Forget it." Her girlish lilt morphed into gruffness. "I changed my mind." She slapped cash onto the cedar bar so recklessly that a bowl of peanuts slid off the edge.

Frank, approaching with her drink, retrieved the dish and gaped as she barreled through the dining area past a couple of coffee drinkers. A deep frown creased his shiny bald head when he straightened up. "What's with her?"

"Not sure." Philip watched her stomp away with her long skirt swishing around her western boots. She yanked the heavy front door open and banged it shut behind her.

Resting his elbows on the bar, Frank lowered his voice. "What was she saying?"

Relieved that Frank hadn't heard, Philip settled back onto his stool. "It didn't make sense. I don't think I've seen her in here before."

"You know, you might not have. She's an expat, spends a lot of time in Mexico." Frank frowned. "She's been gone a few weeks, maybe ever since you started coming in."

"Expat?"

Muttering, "Damn. Peanuts everywhere," Frank reached for his broom before explaining. "Yeah. You know, an American with a home in Mexico." He bent closer and lowered his voice. "Her husband, an older guy, died a few years ago. She still stays down there a lot but comes back here for visits. Her sister's family lives here."

"Ah." Philip nodded.

The full realization that his Valentine's night bourbon blackout must have included Carmen, hit Philip as the café door opened again. Expecting her reentry, he spun around. But instead of Carmen, the hulking form of his boss, Al Wilson, entered. He spotted Philip, and headed toward the bar.

Frank straightened up and asked, "Why are you guys in so early today? Did you finish the power plant?"

"No," Philip said as Al approached. "I went in at two this morning, so I took off early."

Al clapped Philip on the shoulder. "Damn right he did. This guy saved my ass today. Everything he wants tonight is on me." Shoving Carmen's vacated barstool to a normal distance away, he added in his booming voice, "Now let's hear how the hell you managed to squeeze through that asbestos barrier in hazmat gear."

Philip shrugged. "Anyone could have done it."

"Nope." Al shook his large shaggy head. "Not true. When they called me at midnight, they were sure the power would shut down for the whole region." He faced Frank, who was finishing his sweeping. "No way could I get back from Dallas in time." He knuckle thumped the bar. "How about a couple of drafts."

The door opened.

Again, Philip tensed. But it was only a family, probably coming in for dinner.

When Frank set beers in front of them, Al took a quick drink, clunked his mug down, and with one elbow on the bar, faced Philip. "I hate to think how much money I could've lost on this job."

While Philip answered Al's questions about the repair, the café filled with diners.

Granny, the head cook, wearing her yellow-checkered apron, stepped out of the kitchen and called, "Dinner special is ready. Pot roast, mashed potatoes, and fresh green beans." She held two loaded plates of the meal. "With pecan pie for dessert."

Al, nodding at Granny, grabbed his beer and headed toward his regular table. "Those plates for us?"

Philip followed.

"You betcha." Granny, waddling a little, approached with the plates. "Heard your big feet stomp in." She set the plates on their table. "Well, Mr. Philip Richards, everybody's saying if it wasn't for you, we'd be without power."

"Thank you," Philip said, accepting a plate. "Looks delicious."

Al scooped a bite of mashed potatoes. "How come you're serving, Granny? Where's the waitress?"

"Up and quit on me. But this is an easy meal to manage." Watching Philip dig into the food, she patted his shoulder. "I thank you for your hard work while the rest of us was sleeping in our beds."

Throughout the meal, Al complained about change orders at his Dallas construction site.

Philip tried to focus, but Carmen's words, *Valentine's night promise*, nipped at the edges of his thoughts.

They were finishing the meal when a text from Philip's younger sister Lily buzzed in. "Call asap."

He stepped outside onto the long, railed porch, pressed call, and scanned the parking lot in case Carmen was still lurking around.

Except for the turquoise glow coming from the neon *Hilltop* sign above the door, darkness covered the lot. The *o* in the sign flickered as if deciding whether or not to stay on.

He started across the dusty gravel toward his motel room.

"Oh, Philip." Lily's stressed voice twisted his heart. "The doctor told me it will be days... maybe even hours, and Daddy's asking for you. There's something he wants to tell you."

Philip's stomach clenched so hard his steps halted. Every fiber within him resisted seeing the man, but Lily's need was compelling. "Text the address."

"Come tonight. He may not make it until..."

"Okay. It'll take a couple of hours."

At the hospital, Philip slowly pushed open the door for his first view of his father in almost twenty years. The old man appeared to be asleep, but loose skin hung so heavily that his lower eyelids drooped open, exposing half-moons of yellowish eyeballs. His once-sandy hair lay in thin white wisps over his pale, splotchy scalp.

Lily, wearing her trademark jeans and a black T-shirt with *Easy on Me* embossed in sky blue, wrapped both arms around her brother. From the time she'd been old enough to have her own phone, she'd always stayed in touch with Philip, keeping track of where he was working and making sure that the two of them met for dinner several times a year.

Over the top of her head, Philip scanned his father's body. Skeletal as it was, a bloated belly protruded under the sheet.

"Greetings, Philip." His older sister, Dinah, in a navy pantsuit, sat in the corner, her back rigid, legs crossed, a leather briefcase by her side. Her black hair was slicked back into knot at the base of her skull. Her foot, with its navy, high-heeled pump, rocked casually, out of sync with the tension in the rest of her body.

"Dinah," he said softly, stepping toward her. "I'm—"

She stood abruptly, turned her back, and put her phone to her ear to take a call.

He wanted to say what he wished he'd said long ago, *I'm sorry for what happened to you, sorry I didn't protect you.* He had seen her only once in the past twenty years, and that day he'd been too stressed to apologize.

Lily clasped Philip's arms and peered up, teary-eyed. "Daddy goes in and out because of the morphine. If he wakes, you may have just a few minutes before he drifts off again." Her sweet smile and her long dark hair, so much like their dead mother's, slammed him. "I know he has something important to tell you."

Ending her call, Dinah gathered her briefcase and approached, but she kept her attention on a text. "Well, he has nothing to tell me, so I'll be in the waiting room. I have a dissertation meeting in the morning, and I want to review my presentation." She evaded eye contact as she opened the door. "Text if you need me."

Philip stepped toward her. "Okay if I come with you? Can we talk?"

Dinah froze in the doorway and stared back at him as though waiting for an explanation.

"For just a few minutes?" he added.

She continued to stare with no expression. Silence stretched, punctured by their father's raspy breaths. Finally, Dinah tilted her head and said, "No." She held his gaze for a moment as if daring him to respond. Then she pushed the door open and strolled out of the room.

As soon as the door closed, Lily whispered, "I'm so scared she's not dealing with this, and neither are you. He's about to die and you two have shunned him for years." She tightened her grip on his arms. He started to pull away, but Lily stepped closer. "Daddy tried to make up for not being the best father." She angled her head in an effort to make Philip face her. "Look at me." She waited until he met her gaze. "Holding onto ancient grudges hurts you, not him. You'll be sorry later."

Her spiel caught Philip unprepared. Lily had been only four years old when the unthinkable happened. Even though she was a grown woman now, he didn't have words for the disgust his father stirred. "I'm already sorry."

"Phil, is that you?" Their father, raising one finger, pointed in their direction.

His voice.

His low voice, though weak, had its same old relaxed and confident tone, sucking Philip back into a childhood memory when he had hit the bull's eye while target practicing with rifles... Daddy saying, "That's my man."

And now in this hospital room, a forgotten place within Philip unearthed a traitorous yearning to hear his father's voice again say, "That's my man."

Lily rushed to the bedside. "Yes, Daddy, he's here. Are you in pain? Is there anything I can get you?"

Shoving down his feelings, Philip approached the bed.

The old man said, "Ready for this to be over." He sounded tired but clear. Then he looked at Lily. "Need to talk with Phil. Man's business."

Lily kissed his forehead. "I'll step out. Love you, Daddy." She left them alone.

"Where you been?" his father asked as if his son had been gone twenty minutes instead of twenty years.

Roiled emotions made Philip's voice rough. "With a general contractor up in Culmine."

"Worthless work. You need to stay around now for your sisters." He pointed to the little bedside table. "Get my keys out of that drawer. Go out to my house. In the attic above the northwest corner bedroom my trunk is hidden... has my will... never got around to getting a box at the bank... You get the house market ready. Split the money with your sisters like it says in my will... And there's life insur—"

"Stop." Long simmering rage that had driven Philip to leave home at fifteen shook his voice. "Answer one question? Why did you ignore what your old man did to Dinah? You pretended it didn't happen."

Pallid eyes glared for an instant then closed. "If you'd been in my shoes, you'd have done the same. You're the same as me."

With a sharp intake of breath, Philip's nostrils flared in revulsion. "But she was twelve years old and—"

A nurse entered. "Mr. Richards, ready for your morphine booster?"

He nodded and grunted weakly, keeping his eyes closed.

Lily came back during the injection, and almost as soon as the nurse left, their father started snoring. Lily touched Philip's arm. "What did he say?"

"Told me to get his will and life insurance."

"Now?"

"Yeah." Ready to escape the emotional weight in the room, he took the keys from the drawer. "Can you text me his address? I don't know where his house is."

The attic was simply a crawl space with a crude, pull-down ladder. Philip's phone light revealed mold streaks on the walls and scraps of insulation piled in a corner, a mess typical of his father to hide. The trunk was made of rotted, taped-together cardboard.

As he hauled it down the ladder, he huffed a single laugh. High on one side of the trunk was a crudely cut slot, the right size to slide papers through without having to open the lid.

Decayed tape took several seconds to detach before he opened the lid to uncover jumbled piles of papers, photos, newspaper clippings, and old greeting cards. The corner of an aged, blue cardboard stationery box jagged up amid yellowed photos. When Philip lifted the box, one side crumbled away, and an inch-thick stack of loose pages slipped out. Faded, handwritten lines caught his eye:

> Feevah never thought about loving a white man before Russell Richards. She first saw him while she was standing in the auction line sick with fear that her daughters would be sold away from her.

The lines in the middle of the page were a little dim to read in this poorly lit bedroom. But the bottom paragraph was clear.

> Feevah's scan of the buyers froze, and the fine hairs all over her flesh twisted because one man in the group was staring at her. Although she had never seen him before, she felt a sense of recognition, and for a moment there were no thoughts in her mind, but only awareness that his gaze was on her.

Puzzled, Philip lowered himself to sit on a crate and gather the pages. There were maybe seventy or eighty altogether. *Why would something about a slave auction be here?* His father had never been interested in history and had never read anything except blueprints.

While he straightened the stack, a folded bundle of nine or ten pages slipped out. Scrawled on the outside of the bundle in the same handwriting, "Dearest Reader, If you seek truth, read this preface." These few pages were less faded and fragile than the others. Philip unfolded the pages.

PREFACE Sabine Richards, 1935
    Was it because my arousal contortion forced my phallus backwards, rendering me a twisted mortal incarnate of Priapus?

Philip had no idea what this meant, but the fact that a backwards penis narrative was among his father's leavings to be perused by his sisters disgusted him.

He squinted at the strange name in the top corner: *Sabine Richards*

Setting the box aside, he shuffled through the trunk until he found a large envelope labeled *WILL/LIFE INSURANCE.*

A text buzzed in from a strange number. "Come back. Dinah." Lily must have given her his number.

Flinching as if Dinah, through her text, could see these Sabine pages, he stood. Where could he stash them until he could cull out and burn the *arousal contortion* part and anything else he didn't want his sisters to see? Climbing the ladder again, he tucked the pages behind a wooden beam where they wouldn't be noticed.

––––––––––––

"Is that the will?" Dinah snatched the envelope as soon as he entered.

He glanced at their father, still snoring. "Looks like it. What's going on?"

"No change." Dinah slid the envelope into her briefcase. "But I don't want Lily alone when he dies, and I've got things to do."

From a corner, Lily, wrapped in a blanket and curled up in a large chair, said, "Hello, I'm not a child. Duh. Twenty-four years old." She yawned and closed her eyes. "I'm fine by myself."

"I'll stay," Philip said.

Dinah pushed through the doorway. "Back by noon."

"Bye," he said to the already closed door.

Lily hadn't opened her eyes again, and fatigue pulled at him. It was almost three in the morning; he'd been up twenty-five hours. He dropped into a reclining chair near his father's bed, tilted back, and instantly fell asleep.

Chapter Two

"You do what I said?" His father's voice woke Philip.

He raised his reclining chair to an upright position. "Found the envelope."

Early morning sunlight filtered through the blinds of the hospital room, but Lily still slept.

His father grunted in approval. "Now, I want you to—"

Philip stood and bent closer. "Why do you have papers about a penis contortion? What kind of perverted trash is that?"

His father glared at him. "Don't know what you're talking about."

"In your trunk. Handwritten pages by Sabine Richards."

For a moment the old man's brows raised. "Sabine," he said with a surprised lilt, but he quickly reverted to a flat tone. "Nutjob great uncle. Never moved out of his mama's house." He wheezed then whispered, "Misfit."

"Why are his papers in your trunk?"

"Mama." And as if the word he himself had spoken was a shock, tears filled his eyes, and his chest shook with a sob. "Mama died."

Philip, unwilling to let compassion dilute his hatred for his father, glanced at Lily. If she were awake, she'd deal with this unexpected grief for their long-dead grandmother.

As fast as the sorrow had rushed in, it receded, and the old man resumed his detached attitude. "Most of those photos and papers were things Mama gathered over the years when people died. I never read any of it." He pushed his call button, and his voice weakened. "Don't know why people save stuff their whole lives to pass off to someone else and someone else and someone else." He sucked in a long breath as if he needed to be sure his next words came out strong. "Burn Sabine's lies."

In that instant, Philip knew he would read the pages.

A nurse came and injected the drip, and their father slept through the morning. Lily made calls to relatives around the state. Dinah returned from her meeting and worked on her laptop. Philip tried to keep himself out of their way... but available.

In the early afternoon, Al called, inquired about the patient then said, "I'm sorry as hell to bother you. I've tried to get someone else in here—power is down for the whole region."

"What?" Philip tensed, mentally ticking through the work he'd done. What had he missed?

"Not the ones you fixed. The second row of transformers is off now." He detailed the gauge readings.

"I see." Philip visualized that row, the entry points, the gauges, and the aging transformers that were probably jammed.

"Anyway," Al went on. "I can't find anyone to come before next week."

Philip gazed past his sleeping father at Dinah and Lily, both listening wide-eyed. "It would take a couple of hours to get there; two, three hours to repair. Let me check with my sisters." He relayed the situation to them while Al waited.

Expressionless, Dinah shrugged and returned to her laptop.

Lily approached and patted Philip's arm. "Of course. Go. We understand."

After the call ended, Lily gripped his arms and peered up at him. "It's okay for you to go. The important thing is you talked with Daddy. He was agitated before. Now he's peaceful."

The space around the second row of transformers was a little larger than the first had been, so it was easier to squeeze in and unlock the rivets. The power was back on within an hour.

But when he finished, there was a text from Lily. "Daddy died. He never woke after you left. Get a good night's sleep before returning. Love you."

Philip's fists tightened and he exhaled a disgusted growl. *So that's it. You'll never own what you did.* Mixed with resentment was his usual dose of guilt for not being with his sisters at a time of trouble. And his guilt transformed into shame because at his deepest core, he liked the distance.

Being alone was easier than being with Dinah.

After a shower, Philip—hungry, tired, and dehydrated—walked into the Hilltop with the hope that Carmen wasn't there.

Scanning the crowd and not spotting her, he settled into the chair Al had waiting.

Kenneth, an old guy with a walker, looked up from his dominoes at his regular table. "Well, there's Philip."

Two shot glasses of amber-colored liquor waited on Al's table. The inviting aroma of bourbon flooded Philip's senses.

Al raised one. "To flowing electricity."

As soon as their glasses were empty, Frank approached with

a bottle of bourbon. "Here's to the hero of the day." He refilled Philip's glass.

Al turned his own glass upside down. "Yep. That job took knowing old systems and the agility to get to the transformers."

Downing the second shot, Philip grinned. "Do I need a raise?"

Al's bulk shook with laughter. "We'll see about that."

Frank filled Philip's glass again. "What are you drinking tonight?"

"Tap beer. Thanks," Philip said.

"You?" Frank asked Al.

"That's it for me, but put everything Philip gets on my tab." Then to Philip, "Got a bid due in the morning. Need to go finish it so I can get another contract to afford your pay."

Frank refilled Philip's shot glass.

Al stood, and with his hand on Philip's shoulder, leaned down. "Take all the time you need with your old man."

Before Philip could force out words about death, Al clapped him on the shoulder. "Get some food in you. Never seen anyone hold liquor like you, but everybody's got to eat."

"Here you go." Frank set a beer in front of Philip and refilled the shot as Al left.

Kenneth, sliding his dominoes around to shuffle, caught Philip's eye. "Ready for a game?"

"Sure thing." Philip didn't love dominoes but hated to disappoint the old guy, so he drank his shot, picked up his beer, and moved Kenneth's walker aside to make room for another chair. Then he paused, frowning at the walker. "Woah, Kenneth, this hinge is almost worn through—looks like it could break on you."

Kenneth squinted at the hinge. "Yeah, got a new one on order."

"Good." Philip sat. "Bet you a double cheeseburger I can

beat you." The café was busier than usual, and a cheeseburger actually sounded good in case the dinner special had been depleted.

Kenneth finished shuffling. "You're on."

A new waitress—thin, gray-haired, and harried—approached. "May I take your order?"

At that moment a large group of noisy people, maybe four or five couples, surged in.

The waitress dropped her mouth open, her eyes widened, and her hand, poised with a pencil, trembled.

"That's okay," Philip said. "I'll order later."

"Thank you," she whispered, and a brief smile crinkled the corners of her eyes before she hurried to the newcomers.

Kenneth and Philip played steadily, interrupted from time to time by regular patrons commenting about the outdated electric plant. Fresh shots and mugs of beer appeared one after the other.

"All right," Kenneth said. "We're at 43 and 40. Getting serious now."

Philip downed a shot. "I feel luck coming on."

Philip's alarm woke him at 7.30 the next morning. He didn't remember finishing dominoes or walking to his room. As if a black curtain had closed on a movie screen, images and sounds had ceased. Where memory should have been, a void stretched.

Damn. Blacked out again.

His first blackout had been at the age of fifteen, and over the years, he'd learned that too much alcohol could prevent memories from moving into his brain's long-term storage. So, he'd been careful to never drink too much too fast, and until Valentine's and last night, he hadn't blacked out in years.

His phone showed no calls or texts after Lily's *Daddy died* message.

He shifted a curtain and was relieved that his truck sat where he'd parked it yesterday. A quick glance around the room revealed nothing out of place. His wallet and keys were on the table as usual.

In the bathroom he confronted his own dark eyes in the mirror. Two blackouts in one month. Both times had been after news about his father. *This stops now. He's dead. It's over.*

All the towels had been used. Had he showered again before going to bed? And, the towels were draped neatly on hooks instead of thrown into the tub the way he always left them for the maid.

His gaze dropped to the small trash can near his feet... empty except for two used condoms.

His gut churned.

Last night. Someone. Here. Who was she?

Chapter Three

The first row at the funeral was reserved for immediate family.

As Lily and Philip walked up the center aisle toward the open casket, he spotted Dinah's husband, Jack, rubber necking to scan the room full of people. Next to him Dinah sat facing forward, and beside her slumped her twelve-year-old daughter Jacqueline, focused on a phone in her lap.

During their obligatory pause at the casket, surrounded by perfumed white flowers, Lily blotted her face with a tissue. Philip patted her back and looked down at the corpse. *You're a dead human being. I should feel something.*

His father's words in the hospital came back. "Ready for this to be over." *For once we agree.*

A surge of anticipation bloomed in Philip's chest.

Clinamen.

Ever since he had taken a quantum physics course in college, the notion of unexpected change in the movement of atoms played like an imprinted melody wisping through his memory at odd times. His ideas about shifts in patterns didn't align with any particular philosophy or science. But the possibility that a swerve could happen, whether a major event like the Renaissance or a simple shift in a single atom's trajectory, gave him hope. His father's death could be a clinamen, a big swerve, a new start. Now the pattern of his and his sisters' lives would shift and start fresh.

Instead of awkwardly connecting with only Lily for an occasional meal in a restaurant, he could live nearby and have a genuine connection with both sisters. He could settle in this area permanently.

He had already spent the last three days working at his father's house. While Dinah and Lily made funeral arrangements, Philip had hauled off loads of trash and made lists of repairs.

For years he had worked lots of overtime, spent little, and maintained a healthy investment portfolio, so he had the cash and skill to flip the property quickly.

When Lily and Philip turned away from the casket and faced Dinah's family, an unexpected tsunami of emotion tightened his chest. Jacqueline, keeping her eyes cast downward, looked like Dinah had twenty years ago. Regret he'd felt that Christmas Eve made his heart race and sent heat to his face. Frustrated rage roiled because he had been useless to prevent Dinah's pain. Years of his shameful absence resurfaced and smothered his clinamen fantasies.

He composed his face while Jack, who was seated next to the aisle, jumped to his feet and hugged Lily too long. Philip shook Jack's hand then followed Lily to their seats next to Jacqueline.

During the sermon, with Dinah and her family in Philip's line of vision, he was pulled back to his fifteenth year when he left home.

That Christmas Eve, his family had planned to spend the night at his paternal grandparents' home about a hundred miles away. Visits were always tense because his grandfather, instead of being a quiet drunk like his father, had a mean streak that could turn violent. Philip had heard the whispered story about his grandfather's drunken rage when he took Grandma to bed and held a gun to her head all night.

Perversely, Philip liked being at his grandparents' house because he and Daddy would go to the pool hall that Granddaddy had bought after his retirement from construction. Philip played pool as much as he wanted and drank from the whiskey bottle under the cash register.

Later that Christmas Eve night, after they'd come home from the pool hall, Philip was asleep on the sofa. The voices of Grandma and Dinah from the kitchen woke him.

Grandma said, "You go on back to bed now. You'll be tired in the morning when your cousins get here."

It wasn't surprising for Grandma to be awake because she routinely stayed up late to bake. But something was wrong for Dinah to be up. Dinah's answer was too soft to understand, but suddenly she was crying hard, out of control.

Jolted, Philip started toward the kitchen. As he entered from one side, Mama, with Daddy behind her, entered from the other. Philip froze. In the bright light of the kitchen, Dinah shook and cried with her wild-eyed stare darting around the ceiling.

Mama slid into the chair next to Dinah.

Philip stepped back into darkness, and across the kitchen at the other doorway, Daddy retreated into shadows as well.

Dinah turned her face into Mama's shoulder, so her crying was muffled, and her eyes were covered. Now she sounded mournful instead of crazy and loud. "I was asleep and something woke me up." Between sobs she gasped like a baby who couldn't get her breath.

Mama, with her arms wrapped around Dinah, said, "It's

okay. You can tell me." Tears ran down Mama's face. "What woke you, Dinah?"

Dinah started in a whisper. "It was Granddaddy..." But unspeakable words cracked out loud, and blurred into hard sobs, "...kissing me and putting his tongue... his fingers... rubbing back and forth... poked into me..."

Philip stood in darkness ashamed because he was a man in a family where men did this. Ashamed because he'd heard from cousins that Granddaddy had a thing for little girls, and Philip, like a coward, had told himself they were joking.

Now, with Jacqueline's flesh and blood reminder of how vulnerable Dinah had been, Philip glared at the coffin and forced his breathing to stay even. *I'm glad you're burning in hell with your father.*

After the sermon ended, the attendees passed by the casket and greeted the family. An elderly lady with a cane, walked past Dinah's family without pausing. She stopped in front of Philip and leaned with both hands on her cane—Aunt Loraine, his father's last surviving sibling.

Her eyes were red and swollen from crying. "I can't believe my baby brother is gone."

Patting the old woman's shoulder, Philip looked over her head at Dinah, whose glare sliced into him. The memory of Aunt Loraine's role in the carnage of Dinah's young life flogged him. Comforting this old woman was betraying his sister again.

Dinah turned away from him.

It had happened a few days after that Christmas, while Lily was napping and their father was at work.

Mama had called Philip and Dinah to the kitchen table. "Granddaddy is a twisted man, but you don't have to worry because Daddy and I agree... we'll never see him again. He's out of our lives."

Dinah had stayed silent, but Philip said, "Good." He hoped

this meant their lives would get better. Maybe his father would become decent and quit drinking.

"I also want you to know I talked on the phone with Aunt Loraine on Christmas Day after she arrived at Grandma and Granddaddy's house." She pulled Dinah close to her. "Dinah, I'm going to tell you this in case your cousins ever mention it. I want you to hear it from me and be assured we know they're wrong."

Dinah's eyes had widened with fear.

Mama said, "Aunt Loraine told me she discussed everything with Granddaddy, and he doesn't remember anything Dinah claimed. He says she made it up."

Dinah's stunned face paled.

Philip stood so fast his chair toppled over. "That's bullshit." Dinah flinched as his chair clanked to the floor, and, hunching her shoulders forward, she pulled herself closer to her mother. Philip raised his hands in a calming motion. "Sorry." Then to his mother, "How could they say that? Did you tell them the truth? Did Daddy?"

"Yes. I did. And I told Loraine, we never want to hear that again. But it doesn't matter what she says because we're not going to talk about it again with them... ever. We can't make them tell the truth, but we can keep their lies out of our lives."

Philip righted the toppled chair. "Let's call the police. Get him locked up."

Their mother's eyes filled with pain. "I don't want Dinah to have to tell the story again and to deal with his lying. It's best this way. We're done with it. Dinah is safe."

But the next Sunday after lunch, Daddy scooted his chair back from the table. "Got to go out to the job site." He stood and tapped Philip's shoulder. "Come with."

A few miles later, when Daddy turned down an unmarked dirt road, Philip's stomach sank. They weren't going to the job site. They were headed to the cock fights. His mother would have objected had she known. Philip had been twice before and hated watching two animals fight to the death. Daddy loved it, especially the gambling among the spectators.

When they arrived, a crowd was already gathered near an old barn in the middle of a field. Men were circled around two red roosters, squawking and jumping at each other. Daddy grabbed a couple of beers from the cooler behind his seat, and they headed toward the fight. There wasn't an actual fence around the roosters. It was just a hard-packed circle of earth about twelve feet across. Spectators, flashing cash, made bets.

One of the cock handlers, using a small knife, cut his rooster's cone and blood streamed down the neck. Someone passed the handler a lime cut in half, which he squeezed to drizzle juice onto the cut and into the rooster's eyes.

Sickened, as the animal screeched in agony, Philip turned away and chugged his beer.

Then he saw him.

Granddaddy.

Walking up to them calling, "There you are. I got off on the wrong damn road."

Philip was shocked to see him, shocked to realize Daddy and he had planned to meet.

"Look at Phil," Granddaddy said. "God damn, he's grown since Christmas."

Philip's face grew hot, his fists clenched. Did Daddy believe Dinah lied? Or did he not care what Granddaddy had done? "What's he doing here?"

Both men ignored his question.

Daddy shoulder bumped his old man and said to Philip. "Go get us more beers."

Philip shook his head. "But he—"

"Hey, boy." Granddaddy, grinning bigger, held up a fifth of

whiskey and thrust it into Philip's chest. "You got off without your Santie present. Big guy like you needs a real drink."

That day was the first time Philip drank so much that he blacked out. He lost the end of the cock fights and the drive home. The next morning when his mother knocked on his door and called, "Time to get up," the memory of his grandfather at the cock fights sickened him. He couldn't face Dinah.

He pretended to get ready for school, packed clothes instead of books in his backpack, and left a note on his bed: "Dear Mama, I got a good job offer. Don't worry, I'll be back soon. Love, P." He had $80 and no job or any place to go, but he needed to get away long enough to figure out what to do.

Chapter Four

After the funeral Philip went back to Culmine, planning to stay the night and spend a few hours the next morning checking on his crew's progress before returning to work on his father's house.

As he stepped across the dusty gravel toward the long porch of the café, the turquoise sign with its flickering *o*, soft country music, and the aroma of nachos greeted him. He swallowed unconsciously, anticipating the dinner special, whatever it was. Tonight, unless Carmen showed up, he would unwind. The condoms in his trash can flashed in his memory... if she had come to his room... He refused to finish the thought. He wouldn't have. No matter what. Her strange vibes. Her neediness. Even drunk, he wouldn't have.

On the porch, a man thrusted a card into his hand. "I'm representing, Samuel Rogers for re-election as district attorney."

Philip extended the card back to him. "Thank you, but I'm not a resident of this county. I won't be here to vote in this year's election."

"Oh, too bad. Enjoy your dinner."

Inside, two couples were slow dancing in the corner, lit only by the glow from the old-fashioned jukebox, and a half dozen people clustered around the bar.

Carmen's slight build with long black hair was not there.

As Philip expected, Al sat in his regular spot at the edge of the well-lit dining area.

"Lookie what the cat dragged in." Al kicked out a chair for Philip. "How the hell are you?"

Philip dropped into the offered chair.

"Well, there's Philip." Kenneth looked up from his dominoes. "You still owe me a double cheeseburger. Don't be thinking I'll forget."

"You bet." Philip obviously had lost their game.

A faint, warm scent—lavender he thought—launched a hum throughout his body. He inhaled deeply and tilted toward the scent, and a gentle hand squeezed his shoulder. A new waitress, pad in hand, stood beside his chair waiting for his order. Small talk dried in his throat. She was shades of honey, her hair, skin, and eyes. One summer during high school he had worked for a beekeeper. Her slightly slanted eyes were the darkest honey from the rare years the black brush flowered. Her hair, a lighter tint, coiled into a tight knot at the back of her neck. Her face, with the hair pulled back, was naked and honest. Her skin, a shade darker than her hair, almost shimmered in the soft light.

"He'll have a draft on my tab." Al picked up the slack for Philip.

"Thanks." Philip grinned as she walked into the brighter lighting near the kitchen entrance. Her cherry-red uniform was loose on her small, curvy frame. The apron with its white bow in the back, cinched in at her waist.

"Ain't she something?" Al said. "But don't get your hopes up. Many a poor sap, even lookers like you, has tried to get it on with her and gotten nowhere."

"She works here now?"

She entered the kitchen.

"Nah, she's friends with the owner—just fills in sometimes. You know the owner's been gone for the birth of a grandbaby. So, how's your old man?"

"Dead. Funeral was this morning." The waitress came out of the kitchen. "Need to go back to help my sisters with his estate." He explained his plan to get the house market ready while the waitress headed behind the bar. "My room here's paid for another couple of months, so I'll come back two or three times a week to check on my crew's progress. And, stay and work as needed."

Al nodded and leaned back in his chair. "Now, what was it your old man did?"

"Construction, mostly industrial sites." The waitress stopped under the glow of the small hanging lamp in the bar's prep area. Frank said something to her, and her smile made Philip wish he was standing next to her, hearing her voice. "Then real estate after he got older."

The waitress, her uniform's embroidered name said *Myra*, moved toward him. Philip caught himself inhaling deeper while she was near. She placed his beer in front of him and crossed the room to the jukebox.

A couple of crew members dragged their chairs to Al's table, and Philip went to the jukebox and stood next to Myra while she selected Willie Nelson songs.

"Easy to see whose music you like," Philip said.

Her small, slightly tilted nose crinkled as she smiled and scanned the titles. "I love the way his slanted timing takes the lyrics to a new level."

"Yeah, hard to put into words," Philip said.

Her gaze, direct and warm, caressed him. "That thing you can't capture with words is what matters, isn't it?" She moved closer. He lowered his head sensing she wanted to say something private. Her whisper warmed the flesh on his neck. "I'm glad you got back before I leave." She paused a heartbeat as if to let him speak, but he stayed silent, struggling for a response.

Granny dinged the kitchen order bell, and Myra left to pick up plates.

An hour of talking and eating blurred, and the crowd thinned. Although Myra had an easy, friendly way with customers, she never clasped anyone else's shoulder as she had his.

With most diners gone and only a few guys left at the bar, Al stood. "Well, guess I'll get some shut eye." He bent close to Philip and lowered his voice. "Reckon you're gonna close this place down tonight. I seen you and the waitress eyeing each other." He sauntered out, and Philip signaled Myra for another beer. It would be only his second drink that night.

"All right." Granny stepped out of the kitchen. "I'm fixing to wash my pots and clean my oven. If anyone wants anything else to eat, I need to know about it right now before I take my hair net off." She turned toward Philip. "Dessert? It's that peach cobbler you like?"

"No thanks," he said. "You filled me up." All he wanted was to get to know Myra now that she wasn't so busy.

Granny tried again. "You sure? Last chance. I'm closing the kitchen early tonight cause the owner's coming back tomorrow, and I want everything spic and span."

"I'm okay, thanks."

Myra approached with his beer. Before thinking through what he was about to do, he stood and lifted his arms into dance position.

She slowed her pace, tilted her head, and seemed to be holding back a smile. She set his beer on the table and turned to face him.

With his arms still waiting for her, he made a slight bow.

She curtsied, silly and old-fashioned, with a deep-throated laugh that could have stopped him in the middle of a dive. She took his hand and stepped into his arms. Her warmth registered in every cell in his body as he led her in a slow two-step toward the darkened jukebox corner where the rough floor had been sanded smooth.

The song ended quickly, and he asked, "One more?"

She didn't pull away.

Ray Charles's run down the keyboard started "A Song for You." No steady beat, but she followed Philip even though his steps just slid along the melody with no pattern.

About midway through the song, they were swaying in place during a piano run, and she whispered, "The 'space or time' line is magic."

Moments later, Ray's voice released the words, "I love you in a place where there's no space or time."

"Phil!" a guy at the bar yelled.

The tang of electrical burn bit the air.

"Oh, Philip!" Granny shouted from the kitchen.

Philip released Myra and, with fast, long strides, entered the kitchen as Granny rushed out holding a towel over her nose. Thin lines of blue smoke crawled up the wall behind two refrigerators and a freezer chest. A wood-burn odor blended with the electric, so the source had to be near the wood floor. Luckily, the breaker box next to the back door had clear labels. None of the switches had tripped, so he cut power to all the appliances and pulled the refrigerators and freezer away from the wall. He immediately discovered that the frayed cord to the old chest freezer had been on the floor underneath the motor. The motor must have warmed the lint and dust on the wood floor over time, creating heat that ruined the cord's coating.

Granny, standing in the kitchen doorway, called, "Frank, it's okay, no need for the fire truck. Oh, thank God you was here, Philip. This old building would go up like a match box."

"It'll be fine," he told her. "Cord needs to be fixed before we turn the freezer back on."

Disappointment drooped Granny's face. "How long will it take to get an electrician in here? I don't have any place to put the meat, and we just stocked up."

"Don't worry," he said. "I'll get tools out of my truck. We'll have the freezer back on soon." He stepped out the back door saying, "Be right back."

For minutes, after he returned, everyone crowded into the kitchen. Myra talked Granny into going home, and one by one the customers and Frank departed until finally only Myra and Philip were left.

Thinking how lucky he was to be alone with her, he fixed the cord, tested it, and swept up the years of dust that had accumulated underneath the freezer.

With nothing left to do he said, "I should stay a little longer." The freezer was still pulled out from the wall. "It's important in the beginning to take time to make sure the splicing is good." He cocked his head toward the electrical cord, but he really meant the connection between her and himself.

She glanced at the freezer. "Okay. How about a drink while we wait?"

"Drink would be nice if you join me." He'd finished only one beer the whole evening. What was it about this woman that made him want to stay fully alert?

"Sure. Mojito? There's a pitcher Frank mixed earlier."

He nodded, but his breath hitched—Carmen's drink. Had Carmen come in during the evening? Had he been so distracted by Myra that he hadn't noticed?

Myra brought the pitcher and glasses, and they sat on a small bench in the kitchen.

31

Now that they were alone, he should explain that he doesn't remember her. Would she be familiar with alcohol-induced amnesia? Could he explain the difference between *pass out* and *blackout*?

She sipped and turned to him. "You're the hero tonight." Her smile reached inside him. "You've been in Culmine how long, about a month?"

He nodded.

She said, "Then you haven't met the owner?" He shook his head. "She'll be grateful to you."

Being this close to Myra turned his brain to sludge. He shrugged and tasted the mojito.

She filled the gap. "Why is it that even in the short time you've been here, people intuitively called your name when the smoke started? How did you become so resourceful?"

"Don't know." Resourcefulness wasn't helping him in this conversation.

"Are you comparable to your namesake?" she asked.

"Nah. Don't have much to do with horses."

She looked puzzled. "Horses?"

"My mother liked Biblical names. Philip was a disciple good with horses."

Swirling the straw in her drink, she nodded. "How about the father of Alexander the Great—tactical genius in battles—diplomatic—primed the world for Alexander's conquests."

"Nope," he said, thankful he remembered facts from his college world history class. "He was unlucky in love, plus he got murdered."

She laughed, took a drink, propped her legs on a five-gallon pickle bucket, and turned to him again. "You're right. You transcend past. You're pure presence. Maybe that's what attracts people to you."

Now was the time to tell her the truth. He reached for the pitcher to top up her drink. This was going to be hard.

She covered her glass. "No thanks, this is it for me. I'm driving back tonight."

To where? he wondered.

Checking the time on her phone, she groaned. "In fact, if the cord's okay, I should go." She took the glasses and pitcher to the sink.

Philip slid the freezer back and followed her while she turned out the lights on the way to the door. At the main entrance, he asked, "How long will your drive take?"

"An hour or so, depending on traffic in Austin, but I have an eight o'clock in the morning and still have some prep to do." She faced him in the darkened doorway.

What did she have at eight? What prep? Before he could figure out a way to pose questions without tipping her off that he knew nothing about her, their gazes met. She raised her face and moved closer to him. He lifted his hands, ready to slide around her back. He wanted to touch her, but he would wait until she touched him.

A slow smile lifted her lips, and he thought she was going to kiss him. Her breath feathered his mouth. Very softly she said, "It feels strange to part like this after our night together."

She must have read on his face the discomfort that her words had triggered because a slight stiffening in her posture signaled that she was about to pull away.

To recapture their closeness he said, "Myra, when can we see each other again?"

Shock erased her smile.

Her barely perceptible shift became a full, firm step away, and she pushed through the doorway.

His question hung, unanswered while she turned away

from him to lock the door. He lingered behind her, watching her twist the key. "Myra?"

She kept her back to him.

Her shoulders rose and fell with a slow breath.

Then she faced him with a heartbroken expression. "What game are you playing? You know that we already have a date scheduled, and my name is Edith." She watched Philip glance down at her embroidered Myra name label. "Remember, this is a borrowed uniform."

He reached for her but dropped his hands as she stiffened. "I'm sorry." This was a new place for him. He'd never before cared about time lost. In the past, other than worry whether he'd said or done something stupid, he never grieved lost memories.

"It's okay," she said sympathetically. "I'm afraid..." She sighed and shook her head. "...what you called our clinamen, our big swerve, was just... just a fluke... a one-night stand, and now we're back to reality."

In that moment the ground beneath him could have shifted and he wouldn't have noticed. He had never talked with anyone about *clinamen*... so he had thought. That he had called their time together a *clinamen*, told him how profoundly she had affected him.

Her disappointed gaze wounded him while she whispered, "To me our night changed everything." She turned away and started across the parking lot.

He didn't want to cause pain, especially to this woman he felt drawn to. "Edith, I'm sorry. I have no memory of meeting you before tonight. I'm a blackout drinker."

His words stopped her, and she faced him again. The turquoise light revealed tears brimming in her eyes.

He slowly walked toward her. "It sounds strange, and it doesn't happen often, but sometimes I blackout chunks of time. I don't remember you. I want to, but I don't."

"You... you don't remember us? Anything you said? What your grandfather did?" His stomach twisted to hear this beautiful woman recounting his family shame. "Rosa?" His ex-fiancé! He hadn't said Rosa's name aloud in nine years... he thought. He continued to shake his head. "Not even going to Kenneth's apartment?"

"Kenneth's? The guy with the walker?" Peeled open and reeling, he shook his head again.

She tilted her head as if trying to clear her thoughts. "But you didn't act intoxicated."

Even hollowed out, he came up with rote words about his blackouts. "In my case it's not about drunkenness. I... I can drink a lot... it's about alcohol's effect on my brain's memory functions."

"Will you remember tonight... now... this conversation?"

"Sure," he said too quickly. "I think it happened last week because I drank too much bourbon and beer. I'd just..." He paused, not wanting to bring up his father.

She stepped closer and finished his sentence. "...learned your father died after you left your sisters with him." She placed her hand on the side of his face, her eyes searching his as if seeking a lost connection. He shifted his face so his lips touched her palm. "You were kind to Kenneth and to me. You listened... understood... saw... really saw me." She traced her fingers across his lips, dropped her hand, and stepped back. "Thank you, Philip." She turned and started toward her car.

"Edith," he said to her back. "Can we see each other again? I want to know everything that happened."

Facing him again, she started to speak then stopped herself.

He froze, sensing she was struggling with whatever she was about to say.

She pulled out her phone. "I'll send you my journal entries —what I wrote about the night we met."

She slid into her car and closed the door.

His phone pinged as she drove away. And beneath the turquoise light, the text came in under *Edith*. They must have exchanged numbers. He opened the attached doc.

Edith's notes. 1.32am
    Essays graded
    Lecture notes ready
    Alarm set
    I should close this laptop and sleep.
Only seven hours until my class starts.
But my core is a tornado, more agitated
than when my marriage ended.
    Philip has changed everything.

Her words arrowed to his center while he read. *She must be a teacher or professor. Divorced. Our time together kept her awake.*

Edith's notes. 2.28am
    Night of dust.
    That night my feet raised gravel's
dust when I left my car and crossed the
dark parking lot.
    The café door swung open releasing
music, voices, and light into my night.
Bronze metal legs of a walker pushed out
at a bizarre angle, up into the air,
gripped by Kenneth, who like a toddler,
was carried by a stranger. We three
froze and stared at each other on the
café verandah.
    They smiled.

I gaped.

Kenneth explained: "domino game… broken walker… rescue by Philip."

The once-dusty air surged with fresh oxygen. Philip's gaze burrowed into my own while he carried Kenneth with ease.

We talked too fast, spilling over each other.

Kenneth: I can drive my car.

Philip: I'll ride along… take you inside… uber back.

Me: I'll follow and drive you back.

In Kenneth's sparse apartment, he served us bourbon—mine in a pint jar still wearing a faded peanut butter label, Philip's in a cracked green mug, and Kenneth's in his Las Vegas shot glass.

Philip and I perched on the twin-sized bed, Kenneth reclined in his only chair. Fresh intimacy of recent strangers plus bare simplicity of space prohibited shallow talk.

Kenneth cried for his son dead in Afghanistan and his wife lost in Alzheimer's. Philip confessed shame for failing to protect his sister. I released grief for my stillborn son.

Our shared dust transformed into something beautiful.

I drove Philip back toward the Hilltop parking lot, now nearly empty. As we approached, I asked, "Where shall I drop you?"

He pointed. "Head up this street and turn left." As I drove he told me about leaving home at fifteen, working in an okra field. "Next left, then go about two miles."

On the next stretch of dark road, I told him about my love for dancing, poetry, and teaching.

"Left again up here." His first love, Rosa, disappeared into Mexico, and he searched for her four years. "Left at the second light."

My story-book marriage lasted less than two years.

"Two more blocks then right." Earlier that day, his father died and he had not been there to help his sisters.

I shared that my mother worked at the Hilltop before she abandoned me as a newborn and vanished from my life.

"You can pull in up here," he said at last.

"Philip! This is where we started. We're back at the Hilltop parking lot!"

He leaned closer and smiled. "I stay at this motel. Wanted to be with you longer."

I touched his stubbled jaw. It was too soon, but I followed him into his room. We danced to slow pulsing music. Our clothes, the fabric dividing our swaying

```
bodies, went unnoticed at first. But
then his words and warm breath vibrated
in my soul; his work-rough hands and
elegant  strength  changed  my  pulse.
Fabric became a barrier to be broken.
   Later, our goodbyes promised a future.
```

Her written words made their hours alive at a level he'd never known... more authentic than an actual memory. Their hours in her words instilled value into a rare, unsullied place within him.

Still in the turquoise glow, he texted, "Thank you for your journal entries. They are beautiful. Can we see each other again? Sorry I don't know when we planned to meet, but if you tell me, I'll be there. Anytime, anywhere."

Chapter Five

Philip checked his phone the instant he woke the next morning. Still nothing from Edith. *But then why would she want to hook-up again with a blackout drunk?*

After several hours at the site making sure his crew had their work planned, he set out for his father's house. Thrumming miles of gray highway lulled the chatter in his mind. His thoughts snagged on Edith's face when she said one word: *Rosa.*

He met Rosa when he was fifteen, the same day he left home.

That morning he had headed south. Things were cheaper closer to Mexico, and there was lots of day labor with few questions about age or identification.

He walked several miles to the interstate highway where he caught a ride with a closed-panel truck. The driver, a young guy, started talking to him in Spanish.

"I don't know much Spanish," Philip said.

The driver grinned. "I am Lupe. What kind of Mexican are you—cannot understand Spanish?"

"I'm Philip and not Mexican. Cherokee grandmother on my mother's side."

"Your father is white?" After Philip nodded, Lupe said, "Ah! Mixed blood. Must be why you are so big. I am going to Vuelta to cut okra for a few days. Then Laredo to pick up tiles to sell to builders in Texas."

"Is this your truck?"

"No. Belongs to my boss. Hey, how old do you think I am?" Lupe didn't wait for an answer. "Check this out." He handed Philip a Texas drivers' license.

"Looks like you're twenty-two."

"Cool. Right? My boss give it to me, so I can haul his stuff. I am really sixteen."

Philip soon heard about all of Lupe's relatives and girlfriends. His father, an undocumented Mexican, was missing, picked up by border patrol months earlier.

Hours of stories later, Lupe pulled up to a huge okra field near Vuelta. "Want to work the rest of the day?" About a dozen men and women were cutting. "A buck for every bushel you put on the truck." He pointed to an old one-ton truck already half loaded with bushel baskets of okra.

"Sure," Philip answered. "But I don't have a knife."

"*No problema.* I got plenty knives. What about gloves?"

"No gloves either, but that's okay. I don't need any."

"You ever cut okra before?"

Philip shook his head.

"*Ayiee,*" Lupe exclaimed. "You crazy if you think you do not need gloves."

They took several empty bushel baskets stacked together and started at the end of a row cutting the okras and laying them in a basket. Fine prickles covered the plants and pods, stabbing his skin when he reached into the bushes. After cutting about a dozen pods, his hands itched. Lupe's mother, Soledad, who was stirring a pot on a grill set up on the side of the field, offered him a pair of gloves, but they were too small.

Philip attempted to use his ninth grade Spanish. *"Muchas gracias, está bien sin..."* He didn't know the word for gloves, but she understood.

Lupe had moved several feet ahead, so Philip hustled to catch up, but within minutes Soledad stopped him. She shook her head, speaking rapidly and pointing at the okra in his basket.

Not understanding her, Philip said, *"No entiendo."*

Lupe came to interpret. *"Aiyee*, Felipe. Why you saving the big ones?"* He held up one of the largest okras and attempted to pierce it with his thumb nail, demonstrating that the large okra was too tough. Then Lupe cut a shorter pod about three inches long and did the thumb nail test again. "This is your dick when it is little and soft, and it is the only kind we can sell. This big one is your dick when it is hard. It is good only for making new seeds. Leave the big dicks alone."

By this time Soledad had dumped most of Philip's cuttings and moved his stack of baskets back to the beginning of his row. Philip's skin burned, his basket was nearly empty, and he had no choice but to begin again.

Within hours, they had filled the back end of the truck, and Lupe's mother drove away with the load while another lady, who had been grilling tortillas, spooned beans and cheese onto them, clapped her hands, and called, *"La comida."*

While eating, the okra cutters settled on logs and posts arranged around the fire, near the side of the crude road. The road and cooking area was covered with caliche dirt, a fine-light mineral, that had probably been dumped there to prevent weeds from taking over.

The truck returned while they were eating, and Soledad waved Lupe and Philip to her. She held up long, peeled cactus leaves.

Lupe said, "She rub you with aloe vera."

Like magic, every place she rubbed felt cool and stopped

burning. After she smeared the peeled leaves all over his hands and wrists, she reached into the cab of the truck for a pair of large cotton gloves.

As the sun began to set, he and Lupe were near the farthest fence line, cutting on two parallel rows in an area where some cedar posts were lying on the ground between the rows. Someone had been rebuilding the fence. The boys continued to cut, stepping on the posts as it grew darker, and Philip wondered where he would sleep that night.

A sickening feeling punched his gut.

The *cedar post* he'd stepped on was not a post.

Instead, with a rubbery roll, it sank beneath his foot.

He'd stepped on a huge snake lying between two posts.

The distinct rattler sound vibrated a couple of feet to his left. And, to his right, where Lupe stooped over a plant, the snake's head shot up and began a panicked darting.

Philip jumped several feet forward.

Lupe yelled and tripped while backing away.

The snake, as wide and long as a fence post, tried to work its way out from between two posts. Lupe had landed on his back with his head raised to stare at the snake. It moved closer to Lupe. Mexicans ran toward them from every part of the field. Philip picked up a cedar post and brought it down hard on the base of the snake's head, trapping it. He wasn't prepared for the power with which the snake slammed itself into his feet as it swirled around trying to escape. Lupe scooted farther away while Philip kept the post pressed into the snake. He didn't know what to do now. If he lifted the post and ran, the snake might strike him before he could get out of its range.

Even after men reached them, there were long moments of circling and talking fast Spanish while Philip pressed down with the post. He could feel the snake working its way free. One man came closer with a large machete. Philip couldn't see what the man did behind his back, but he felt the snake reacting.

Finally, the snake's resistance died. Philip kept holding the post, afraid if he let go, the head might reflex back and the fangs could strike him. The machete man circled to the front of the snake's head. With one hand on Philip's post, he leaned down and plunged the long blade into the snake's open mouth. The fangs extended out over an inch, and as the man twisted the machete, a shiny fluid pulsed out of each fang.

Several men nudged the post and Philip apart then they all followed the machete man, who used the still-inserted blade as a handle and carried the snake in front of himself toward the cooking fire. The snake was close to six feet long, so its tail dragged along the ground.

The women were now adding wood to the fire as if they'd expected this event.

Although everyone else buzzed with talk, Lupe and Philip were silent. Near the fire, they sat on the ground. Several of the men were working on the snake's body stretched out on a flatbed trailer.

The women set up their grill and pot again. While they were chopping onions, the machete man, Hector, sat down beside Lupe and Philip with a pint of tequila. He was a lean, older man, who spoke in a low, intense voice and exuded an air of calmness.

Lupe broke their silence and slapped Philip's back. "You save my life! That snake would have killed me!"

By the time the snake stew was cooked, hunger and Hector's tequila had readied Philip's palate. The dark, chewy meat in broth thickened with leftover beans and okra was delicious.

Somehow the news spread. More vehicles drove up, and someone turned on a battery CD player—blasting Mexican accordion music in a polka rhythm. An older lady exclaimed,

"Conjunto norteño" as she danced through the caliche toward the fire. Immediately other people joined in, some dancing alone and some in couples. The clingy dust rose about a foot high, so by the firelight, it looked as if they were dancing on a cloud. Dancers were left with light-colored boots.

When the music changed to samba, people shouted, "Rosa, Lupe, Soledad."

Lupe shook his head. "Too tired."

The crowd kept at him, the other dancers parted, and in the middle of the caliche cloud, a beautiful, long-haired Mexican girl danced alone. Her arms, slow ocean waves, beckoned Lupe to come to her while her hips pulsated to the faster samba beat. Even though she was baiting him to dance with her, she seemed content dancing by herself. She wore jeans and a tank top like any high school girl, but her rhythm and motion were different from anything Philip had ever seen. How could Lupe resist?

"Okay, okay." Lupe went back to Spanish, *"Bailaré, pero Mama, usted baila, también."* Philip guessed Lupe was consenting to dance but wanted his mother to dance, too.

Lupe danced into the arms of the girl, and his mother danced by herself. After a while Lupe released the girl and danced with his mother. Even though Lupe and his mother were stealing the show with dips and spins, Philip couldn't pull his gaze from the girl.

When the polka-like *conjunto norteño* started again, Lupe sat beside Philip. "Mama and Rosa. All they want is to dance. My grandparents are dance instructors in Cuernavaca. The women got the dancing blood, not me."

"Rosa? She's related to you?"

"Yes, my brat thirteen-year-old sister I told you about."

After the dancers finished, Philip got into Lupe's truck, this time with Soledad and Rosa between them on the front seat.

Philip tried to ask if they were going into the town. "*Nosotros ire a Vuelta?*"

Everyone was silent. He wondered what he'd said wrong. Finally, Soledad, who was seated next to Philip, said, "Oh! *Iremos a Vuelta? Si.*"

Rosa and Lupe laughed at Philip's addition of the unnecessary *nosotros* and wrong verb form.

"Oh yeah," Philip said, "that grammar rule about changing the verb."

Rosa leaned forward to see Philip. "It is more than grammar." A sweet smile lit her face. "The going itself becomes a different thing when we go together."

Philip never forgot her words. Or her smile.

Lupe stopped the truck on a gravel street of small houses and pointed to an even smaller house behind the row lining the street. "Hector lives back there. You can sleep on his spare cot."

Residents along the street were outside, sitting on their porches. Through open doors and windows of houses, families could be seen moving around.

Hector's house was one square room about twelve-by-twelve feet. A cooking grill outside the front door was dimly visible in the dark.

Hector, extending his hand, welcomed Philip inside.

It was an honest house, everything had a purpose—a small table where he ate; a bookshelf with a few books, tools and some canned goods; a wooden chest for his clothes; no stove or refrigerator. There was a sink in one corner and a toilet in a closet, but the shower was outside and consisted of a garden hose wired up within rusted sheet-metal walls.

Philip said, "*Muchas gracias,*" over and over. Between Hector's limited English and Philip's ninth grade Spanish, Hector explained that Philip had "*corazón de coraje,*" heart of courage, for saving Lupe.

The next morning at a pay phone about a mile away, Philip called home. "I promise, Mama, I'm okay." She cried as soon as she heard his voice. "I've got a good job down south. You don't have to worry."

"Where are you? Where did you sleep?" she asked.

"I don't want you to know where I am. I don't want you to have a secret to keep. But I'm safe, with good people."

"When will you come home?"

"Soon... but I'm going to make... make... things change." He couldn't bring himself to tell her Daddy was still meeting with Granddaddy as though nothing had happened to Dinah.

He didn't know how to explain the way Daddy talked when Mama was not around or about nights like the one when he was ten years old and Daddy, leaving Philip in the locked car, had gone into a woman's house to do his "man's business." Philip was contaminated with years of depravities against his beautiful dark-haired mother and now against Dinah.

He wished his father could be like the men in his mother's family, who were honest and hardworking and innocent. "Mama, he's not who you think he is."

She made a soft groan. "Maybe you have a better chance of growing into a decent man if you can be away from your daddy a while."

So, she wasn't fooled. Maybe she could see through him.

Philip blurted, "Leave him. Take the girls and get out. I'll help." But even as he said this, he knew he couldn't support them.

"No," she said in a soft, resigned voice. "Don't worry about us. Daddy is keeping his word. We're never seeing Granddaddy again. It's different for daughters. They're more influenced by their mother. It's harder for a son."

"Bye." That was all he could say.

His mother had tried to make it okay for him to be away, but he hung up knowing he had to go back and stand up to his father.

And, he might have gone home then, but Lupe drove up with a bottle of tequila and plans to go to Laredo. Philip let going home slide.

Weeks with Lupe proved jobs, booze, and girls were plentiful until the day Lupe's boss got busted. Then Lupe had to go back to working in the fields full time with no more truck or fun trips to Laredo. Hector lined up a series of jobs for the boys loading hay bales.

Even with Lupe's diminished lifestyle, his spirits stayed high. On their first morning to work in a hay field, he pulled up to Hector's house in Soledad's little black Nova and said, "Aiyee, *es* Felipe the snake slayer! *Buenos días, hermano!*"

Philip was surprised to see Rosa in the back seat.

Lupe explained, "She is going to drive for us today. And she is the worst driver in the world."

Rosa rolled her eyes. "Shut up, Lupe."

"Rosa, the last time you drove, you make me run all over the field to catch up with the trailer. A good driver stops, so you can pick up the bales and put them on the trailer without taking a journey."

"At least I did not run you over."

"Only because I am fast on my feet!"

When they arrived at the field, it looked like at least seventy-five acres dense with bales. A farmer with a gasoline can was filling the tank of a rusted, half-ton pickup, hooked up to an eight-by-twenty-foot flatbed trailer.

"Morning, Lupe," he called. "You can unload the trailer in the pole barn first. When it's full, you can stack the rest up by the house and cover them with a tarp. I'm only paying a quarter a bale since I'm providing the truck and the gas."

Lupe was a negotiator. "Hey, *Señor,* I got Felipe here. He so strong he can pick up two at a time. He put those bales in fast so you do not have to worry about the rain coming on Thursday. Also, Felipe is a good packer. He get more in your pole barn than you think. That is worth forty cents a bale."

The farmer frowned. "Rain on Thursday?"

By this time, Rosa had started the truck. Black, stinky exhaust filled the air as she U-turned to line up with the edge of the field.

Philip gripped the steel handles of a pair of hay hooks and lifted the nearest bale out of the dirt. Like magic the flatbed trailer glided to his side, and the truck brakes squealed as Rosa stopped the trailer in the right spot for him to drop the bale. He took a few steps and hooked another bale. Again, the trailer halted exactly where he needed to drop his bale. Surprised, he glanced at the truck, and in the side rearview mirror Rosa's gaze and smile sent warmth through him.

Before the feeling could settle within him, her image was pierced by Dinah's face, drawn and tortured.

Philip wanted nothing more than to smile back at Rosa, but she was too young. He forced his gaze downward, and hoisted two more bales onto the splintered wood floor of the trailer.

That spring and early summer the weather let most of the farmers get two and three hay cuttings. Some weeks Lupe and Philip worked seven days from sunup to sunset picking up bales. By late summer the watermelons started ripening, so the boys transitioned into loading them. Hector would take only ten dollars a week for rent, saying Philip was covering the rest by helping him improve his English. So, Philip saved most of what he made.

He was planning to go home before school started, but one day while they were loading melons, a clean, unfamiliar car came down the dirt road. Tension buzzed through the field because no one recognized the car, and most of the workers didn't have legal IDs. The car stopped and two white men got out, leaned on the fence, and watched. Hector, standing on the edge of the field, talked with the men for a while, and several times Philip noticed them looking at him.

That night in Soledad's kitchen, Hector explained in mixed English and Spanish, with Lupe throwing in occasional translations.

"The men who came to the field said all illegal youths should come to school. Immigration will not pick up anyone at school. One of the men is the football coach, and he said Felipe should come next week to start football practice."

Lupe jumped up and gave Philip a high five. "Oh, bad, so bad!"

"But," Philip said, "I don't think you can enroll in school without parent consent."

Hector grinned. "The coach thinks since you live with me, you are my relative from Mexico. If you want to go to high school in Vuelta, I can get you a Mexican birth certificate and school transcript. You can enroll as my orphaned grandson."

Soledad had concerns. Lupe and Rosa went to school part of each year in Mexico, but during their months in Vuelta, they never attended because the whole family was illegal. Soledad was doubly fearful because her husband had been missing for months. She wanted to return to her home town of Cuernavaca, Mexico, but the last message from her husband instructed the family to wait for him in Vuelta.

Philip said, "Hector, if you can get papers for me, let me go to school first, and we'll see what happens. If I get picked up, I'll be okay since I'm a citizen. If no one bothers me, then Lupe and Rosa can enroll, too."

Philip pushed down his guilt about not going home, and on Monday he jogged three miles to the field house for the morning workout. The coaches already had his new name, Felipe

Moreno, on their roster. They gave the boys gym clothes and put them through several hours of calisthenics and drills.

There were three weeks of practice before school started. By then Hector had taken Philip's papers to school and enrolled him as a sophomore.

One morning about a month later, Lupe showed up in the school hallway flirting with a group of girls near Philip's locker. "Hey! Felipe, I am a sophomore like you. Rosa is in seventh grade. Mama finally consented thanks to you."

The men from the school had told the truth that day in the watermelon field. No one was bothered by immigration.

Chapter Six

The next three years went well for Philip. The first year he called his mother several times, but gradually he let his calls lag, and he never made the trip home to see his real family.

He stayed in athletics, going from football to basketball to track. He tried baseball, but never had the knack for it, and he could tell he wasn't adding value to the team. So, when track ended each year, he worked in the fields until football started again.

Even though Rosa grew more beautiful each year, Philip kept a distance from her until his senior year when Soledad threw a graduation party for Lupe and him at the church social hall.

Rosa walked in wearing a royal blue strapless dress, and when her gaze locked with his, Philip got the same feeling he'd had when she smiled at him years earlier in the rearview mirror.

As always when there was a gathering, they had *la musica*. For this celebration, Soledad had planned two choreographed dances for Philip, herself, Lupe, and Rosa. She'd made them practice for months, and she was far more demanding in her drills than the football coaches were.

The first dance was a fast-paced samba featuring Soledad and Philip. The patterns showed off her athletic abilities, and she needed Philip as a partner because she wanted a finale that required his strength. In the opening of the dance, they did basic samba patterns. Then she began to pull away from Philip and move toward Lupe and Rosa, who were also doing a basic samba. As soon as she sambaed toward them, Philip went into a double time pace of spins to gain her attention. She ignored Philip and danced around Lupe and Rosa. Philip gave her a fast shoulder lead into a complete turn and stepped her backward for three samba sets. As she continued to avoid Philip, he lifted her over his head, and with his free hand, on the first two beats, he gestured, "Give in?" Her body, remained in the same perfect pose she held when she was standing, and with the second two beats of the measure, she gestured, "No, no."

He continued to step the samba measures, and they repeated the question-and-answer gestures for three more rounds until the music slowed and she finally gave in. In the last section of the song, Philip lowered her and ended with a basic dip that Soledad took into a deep back bend.

After the samba they switched partners and did a tango. It was not as showy as the samba had been. And while dancing with Soledad was supporting a spicy, athletic little star, dancing with Rosa entailed a deep level of connection. She was always with him no matter how subtle his lead might be.

Later, after the performances, Hector and Philip stood on the side watching dancers. Rosa whirled by with a boy from her class.

Hector was never a big talker, so when he spoke in a low tone, it stood out. "She is a woman now. You have been respectful, but if you continue to treat her like a child, some other man will win her heart."

Hector's words were the nudge Philip needed. Rosa was old

enough, and the time had come for them to have something more than their brother-sister relationship.

The irony was he'd spent three years making sure they were never alone together, and now that he wanted time with her, he knew there would be no opportunity. While Lupe seemed to have no boundaries, Soledad was a hawk when watching Rosa.

When the party ended, Soledad organized Lupe, Rosa, and Philip into cleanup and packing crews. She ordered Philip and Lupe to take off their white shirts so she wouldn't have to scrub out the stains they might pick up while cleaning. Then she sent Lupe to the dumpster with bags of garbage and loaded Philip's arms with trays and bowls to carry to her car.

In the dark parking lot, Rosa was leaning over the open trunk arranging stuff.

Without looking up, she said, "Just set it on the ground. I'll pack it in."

He set it down and stood gazing at her bare shoulders. Without a word she turned to Philip, wrapped her arms around him, and put her face on his chest. Skin on skin. Holding her made his body sizzle and go numb at the same time.

And then, for the first time, she spoke to him in Spanish. He hadn't thought about it before, but she had always spoken to him in English. *"No quisiera que usted fuera lejos de mi."* She did not want him to go away from her.

"Rosa, my Rosa." He kissed the top of her head.

She raised her face, and they kissed full, long. The taste of her. The feel of her lips and tongue. Their legs stepped between each other's.

The door of the social hall opened, and Soledad and Lupe called to each other about where the church coffee pot was supposed to be stored. Rosa turned back to her packing. Philip dropped down in a squat to hand her pans he'd set on the ground and to conceal his bulge. Squatting beside her put his face in line with her pelvis. Philip must have groaned because Rosa looked down and grinned.

By then Soledad reached them. She rattled in Spanish, "Did you see my salad bowl, Rosa? Ah, there it is. Felipe, why are you down there?" She didn't wait for an answer. "Lupe, do you still have the church keys? Check all the bathrooms, and make sure the toilets are flushed and the lights are off. It is so dark out here. This church needs lights in the parking lot." By the time she tapered off and Rosa had the trunk loaded, Philip managed to get back to normal and climb into the car.

Later he was asleep on his cot on Hector's porch, where he slept sometimes in the summer when the mosquitoes weren't bad. He felt tugging on his arm and opened his eyes to Rosa's. He got up and walked with her a couple of hundred feet into a brushy area behind the house. They stayed back there until daybreak, mostly kissing. And that became the pattern of the summer. Almost every night she woke him and they slipped into the brush.

On his last night before going away to college, Philip gave Rosa his senior ring to wear on a chain. She was happy to have it, but they both knew once Soledad found out they were more than friends, they wouldn't have an easy time slipping out to be together.

"I have something for you, too, Felipe." She handed him a condom.

"Where did you get this?" Rosa couldn't have purchased a condom in Vuelta without causing a major stir.

"I stole it from Lupe," she answered, placing one hand on Philip's chest. "I want us to make love. I love you, Felipe. I want us to be one together."

The next part was hard. "I love you, too." He put his hand over hers, and his voice grew husky. "And I want you. More than anything." He kissed her, almost losing himself in her. But he pulled away, with a hand on each of her shoulders. "Our first time shouldn't be out in the brush." He didn't tell her the other reason. She was too young.

Rosa cried.

He promised her he'd keep the condom for them to use when the time was right.

For the next three years at college, he played football, majored in math, and looked forward to trips back to Vuelta to be with Rosa even though Soledad's relentless chaperoning made their nightly make-out sessions impossible.

On the spring break of Rosa's senior year of high school and Philip's junior year of college, he bought an old Ford Falcon for $750 saved from his part-time and summer construction jobs. Actually, Hector made the purchase. Philip's student green card status had never been questioned, but they weren't sure what would happen if he tried to register a vehicle. Philip planned to leave it in Vuelta because it was pretty old to be driving the 400 miles to college.

He also bought an engagement ring with a chip of a diamond.

Philip drove Rosa to a secluded spot near a creek. As soon as he stopped the car, they were all over each other, and she felt the ring box inside his front pants pocket.

"Felipe, what is this?"

"Open it and see."

He could barely understand what she said because her Spanish was so fast. When she finally settled down a little, he said, "Will you marry me, Rosa?" Then her fast Spanish started again, and he heard *si* several times.

"Now, look in my other pocket. There's something else for you." It was a condom. "A new one. The one you gave me dried up and cracked open." Within seconds they were both stripped and in the back seat.

The next morning Philip went to Soledad's and told her they wanted to get married soon. They would live in married students' housing during his senior year, and Rosa could get loans to attend college her first year. And after he graduated, he would put her through the rest of college.

That conversation was the last he had with Rosa and Soledad.

That night, after he returned to his dorm, he awoke to the smell of smoke. His roommate, who had disconnected the smoke alarm because it kept going off when he made popcorn, had left a pan of grease on a little cooktop he kept on his desk.

About the time Philip reached the burner, the pan burst into flames. He grabbed a lid to smother the fire at the same moment his roommate pulled the pan from the burner. Apparently, the handle of the pan was too hot for his roommate to keep his grip, and he slung the flaming grease toward Philip. Spatter burns sizzled all over Philip's upper body, but he and his roommate managed to extinguish the flames. While his roommate opened a window, Philip went to the bathroom mirror to inspect his burns.

"Man, I'm sorry." His roommate came up behind him. "I was sure I turned that off. Are you okay?" He sniffed. "You smell like barbeque."

"Yeah. Nothing serious." In his reflection, Philip scanned the scattered stinging burns on his chest and shoulders.

"Holy Jesus."

Philip looked in the mirror at his roommate's shocked expression.

"Look at your arm," his roommate said.

A downward glance at his left arm, hanging by his side, was like peering into a horror movie. His forearm had a path almost a foot long and two or three inches wide that looked like molten lava. Black streaks mingled with pink and yellow. He used his right hand to carefully lift his left arm, and a wave of nausea hit him along with the stink of sizzled flesh. "It doesn't hurt."

"Man, either you're in shock or your nerve endings are destroyed. We need to get you to the hospital."

Philip was admitted for two days to treat his fourth-degree burns. The day of his release, the Dean of Student Life summoned him to her office. Philip assumed the dean wanted to discuss how his injury would affect his athletic scholarship or his insurance and medical bills.

With no greeting, the dean asked, "What's your real name?"

"Philip Eugene Richards." He answered without hesitation. He had suspected this question would come sooner or later.

"What is your date of birth?"

"Same as the one on my Filipe Moreno birth certificate?"

"Are you Mexican?"

"No."

"Well, Philip, we routinely do random background checks, and I'm sorry. I have no choice but to follow up on this."

Philip simply nodded. His college career was over.

The dean handed him a statement to sign saying that he was withdrawing from East State because he had enrolled with fraudulent papers. "If you don't sign, you'll be expelled and served with criminal charges."

Philip signed, packed, and went to the bus station.

Not having a college degree was disappointing, but he and Lupe had worked at building sites during summers. He could make good money in construction. And there was one bright spot—he'd be back in Vuelta with Rosa immediately.

At about 4am, he arrived at Hector's and dozed on the front porch until Hector came outside to make his breakfast.

"Did Rosa call you?" Hector asked. Then he noticed the bandaged arm. "What happened?"

Philip told him and was surprised at how much it upset Hector.

"It is my fault for giving you Mexican papers," he said.

"It's nobody's fault. We all thought it was a good idea at the time. It got me through high school and almost three years of college."

Hector looked heartbroken. "So, you did not come home because of Rosa."

Philip's gut twisted. "What happened to her?"

"Soledad and Rosa disappeared after you returned to college."

"What?" His pulse sped up.

"Some of their things are missing from the house, so I hoped they followed you. Lupe hasn't seen them either."

"They wouldn't leave this close to Rosa's graduation." Philip paced.

"Maybe Soledad's husband came back, and they had to rush before the border patrol catch him again," Hector said.

"But immigration picks up people who happen to be in their path. They don't go out of their way to track one family." The story of Soledad's husband had never been clear. The short answer was he'd been deported and didn't get around to returning to Vuelta for the past six and a half years. But during Philip's time in Vuelta, illegal drug trade kept carriers passing through from Mexico to San Antonio. Philip wondered if Soledad's husband was involved in something criminal. He said, "I'll go to Cuernavaca." They both knew this was Soledad's hometown.

Hector said, "If you go into Mexico, you must take your real birth certificate because without it you will not be able to get back into the U.S."

On the drive to Gire to get his birth certificate, Philip wondered whether this gut clench—not knowing whether Rosa was okay—was what his mother and sisters felt six years earlier when he'd left Gire.

Dinah was the only one at home, and she didn't recognize Philip at first. After he told her who he was, she hugged him, but she was shy.

It was hard to relay the whole six-year story in a few minutes, but Philip tried. In all his phone calls home over the years, he'd left out details because he hadn't wanted anyone to have to lie about where he was. Now, there was no reason to hold back. In fact, from the moment he told the dean his real name, he was on a truth roll, and his need to find Rosa outweighed everything else.

Dinah got his birth certificate for him. "I believe..." she said after he stepped out the door to leave. The nervous sister he remembered was gone. Someone hard was in her place. Her eyes narrowed. "...I believe the college knew all along about your fake papers. You were of no use to them after your injury. They were finished using you."

Before he could answer, she shut the door.

On his way to the border, he bought a prepaid phone. He'd forgone having a phone because of the expense, but now he felt desperate for a way to communicate. In Nuevo Laredo he left his car at the transport station and caught a train for the 700-mile trip to Cuernavaca. He found a room to rent above an art studio within walking distance of the *zócalo,* town square.

Almost every night on the *zócalo* he found groups of dancers doing rumbas, waltzes, and tangos to live orchestra music. To anyone who would give him a moment, he showed two pictures from the graduation party: one of Soledad and himself and one of Lupe and Rosa.

After a month, his arm had healed into a slick brown, mottled scar, and he found work brick laying. He needed to earn money to get back to Vuelta after he found Rosa.

His cell phone didn't get service in Mexico, so each Monday morning, he went to a pay phone to call Lupe or Hector. Several months dragged by before Hector had news; Soledad had been seen in the border town of Nuevo Laredo, her husband's hometown.

Philip didn't know where to look in Nuevo Laredo. There were no town squares filled with dancing to attract Soledad. Instead, the public spaces were crowded with vendors, beggars, and prostitutes. His money ran low, and he couldn't find work.

For the next three years, Philip worked in south Texas for a few weeks at a time to save enough money to go back into Mexico to search for Rosa. He was in Nuevo Laredo one day when a little boy came to his rented room.

"*Señor Felipe?*" he asked. "*Señor Lupe dijo llamarle por teléfono sobre Rosa y darme pesos, por favor.*" Lupe had left a message—he had news of Rosa.

Philip ran past the boy, threw him some pesos, and phoned Lupe from a café.

Lupe said, "I got a letter from Mama. They are all okay. Mama and Papa had to hide, but they left Rosa in a church in southern Mexico."

"Where? When can I get her?"

"Felipe... Felipe, Rosa married and has two little boys."

"When can I get her?" He repeated before Lupe's words sank in.

He couldn't make what Lupe said fit with how he and Rosa were together. How could she have moved on with her life so fast... a husband and kids... while Philip was in limbo searching?

Lupe said, "I am coming to Laredo to pick you up. Stay on Highway 35. I will find you."

One day Philip had been a searcher, and the next day he was nothing.

Chapter Seven

Edith called.

"Edith," Philip said on her first ring. "Thank you... for calling me back."

"Hi. You're driving?"

"Yes. Going to Gire. From what you wrote, I must have downloaded my life story on you."

She gave a short, low laugh. "We were both pretty intense."

"I'd like to see you. My schedule is flexible. I can pick you up or meet you anywhere."

Edith took a long breath and when she spoke her voice was tremulous. "If we meet again, I want to be sure you understand... we won't be..." She hesitated, searching for the right word. "... simple. I'm not interested in a one-night stand. I think..." She paused. "I think you said it better than I can. You said that you and I bonded in a way you had never experienced before... as if your life began the night we met."

Her words, which were really his words, stirred in his chest —a mix of need and connection. The truth in the words he didn't remember saying found home within him. His voice

62

thickened. "Thank you for telling me. And thank you again for letting me read your journal."

She said, "We had agreed to meet tomorrow night at the Hilltop."

"What time is your shift?"

"Oh, I won't be working. Just visiting Myra."

"Myra?" Disappointment in himself reared up. He'd know who this was if he hadn't blacked out.

"Myra is the owner and a good friend of mine. I worked for her summers during high school and college, and now I go back and work sometimes when she's in a lurch. I'll get there around seven."

"I'll be there," he said. "Did you write about us again—last night?" He hoped she had. Hoped she'd share with him again.

"Yes, I did." She took a breath and with a tremor in her voice, said, "If you read and decide I'm too complicated, just don't show up tomorrow. I'll understand."

She clicked off without saying goodbye, and almost immediately her attachment pinged in. He pulled over and parked on the shoulder next to an open field.

```
1.00am
    The second night I met Philip, only a
mirage of our magic gleamed in his eyes.
A kiss, I thought, will reignite our
connection.
    But, then he called me Myra.
    He explained, "... sometimes I black out
chunks of time... I don't remember you. I
want to, but I don't."
    Google   search   of   alcohol-induced
amnesia:
```

National Institute on Alcohol Abuse—
"It can be quite difficult for an
outside observer to tell if someone is
in a blackout. The person could seem
aware and articulate, but without any
memory being recorded."

Health Magazine—"...the defining
characteristic of a complete blackout is
that memory loss is permanent and
cannot be recalled under any
circumstances..."

National Institute on Alcohol Abuse—
study participants "reported learning
later that they had participated in a
wide range of... events they could not
remember, including... sex..."

Philip knew all of this about himself, but seeing it from her
perspective stripped him. Fresh sorrow engulfed him for not
being able to remember all they'd shared, and he hungrily
continued to read.

He asked, "Can we see each other again?
I want to know everything that
happened."

He deserves to know that in his
vulnerable state, he spoke of horrible
family secrets he'd run from at fifteen...
of his dangerous compulsion to handle
rattlesnakes... of his own shame and
damage.

His pulse quickened. He groaned aloud. He had told her

about his years of handling rattlesnakes. What else did he tell her? He quickly read on.

> His act of letting me see his raw, laid-open heart made him beautiful and precious to me.
>
> Sadly, even when I give him the facts, he won't experience the truth as I know it.
>
> How can I make Philip know the communion we shared?

Edith, Edith, you have made me know. You have. He believed that he understood their connection better from her words than he would have from his own memory. In his glance at the last part, he thought it looked like a poem.

> In the early morning hours, I dreamed about Philip and me… LOGICAL causes of my passion for Philip march forward:
>
> Our first meeting disorients: he, carrying old man.
>
> Philip bares his shame, and for the first time I see my own.
>
> Our union melts and restores me.
>
> LOGIC shouts, Philip is…
>
> a drunk,
>
> floundering, job-to-job,
>
> stuck in quick-sand shame.
>
> FORGET HIM.
>
> I say, LOGIC, you fool,
>
> this beautiful man with his damage infuses my core.

```
Need for him, insistent as a magnet,
pulses with heartbeat.
LOGIC, you cannot control
dreaming mind
or
yearning heart.
```

Her shouts of LOGIC torpedoed him. He did drink. He was stuck in shame. But then her response, *this beautiful man with his damage infuses my core...* surround-sounded and drowned out everything else.

He shook his head in slow motion as if pushing away a fog collected around his face. He laid his phone back in the console and placed both hands on the steering wheel... he'd been breathing as though a clamp were around his chest. The radio's classical music, simple background filler for miles, was now too loud. He could hear each individual violin deep in the chorus cradling the brass melody. He turned off the radio, inhaled deeply and peered out his side window at the dry, bare field stretching back to a sparse line of mesquite trees. Each branch curved in its own pattern against the pale grayish sky. He'd not noticed the arced limbs before.

Without turning away from the window, he reached for his phone and called Edith. His voice was rough like that of a man who'd been asleep too long as he said to her voicemail, "I read your journal. You are my clinamen." He closed his eyes and almost in a whisper added, "No matter what, Edith. I'll be there."

Rattlesnakes. He'd told Edith about his snake handling.

It had started the day he found out Rosa was okay. He was in the midst of getting a new transmission installed in his old car, but now repairing it felt futile. He wanted out of Mexico. He sold the car for the price he'd paid for the transmission and caught a ride with a semitruck. As he rolled north, he shoved his emotions down and decided it was time to go home and reconnect with his mother and sisters. He'd mostly gone silent on them during his frantic Mexico years. When the trucker stopped for gas in the United States, Philip bought a bottle of bourbon, stepped around to the side of the store, and called home.

Lily, a teenager at the time, answered and started crying as soon as she heard his voice.

Her first words froze his heart. "Mama died."

He heard his own hollow voice repeat, "Mama died."

Lily spoke softly as if trying to make the blow less painful. "It was a bad wreck. Six months ago. We couldn't find you. I was afraid you were dead, too." She stopped for a moment, choking on a sob.

He couldn't remember the end of their conversation. After hanging up, he pulled out the bourbon, leaned against the building in the hot sun, and gulped the sweet, oily burn. Then he started walking north.

A couple of hours later, Lupe's truck approached from the opposite direction.

Lupe slowed and drove across the brown grass of the median, bumping up and down across the low barriers to make a U-turn. He pulled up next to Philip and opened the passenger door. "Get in."

"How did you find me?" Philip asked.

"I told you to stay on Highway 35. Remember?"

"Oh yeah." As soon as he climbed into the truck, rattlesnake musk was strong. "There's a snake in here." Philip expected him to react.

Instead, Lupe grinned and accelerated. "Hey, *hermano*, you part dog? I do not smell it."

"Stop."

"No, not for a little rattlesnake." Lupe put his hand over the back of the seat and shoved stuff around. Instantly, the distinct hiss of a small rattlesnake sounded.

"What the..." Philip reached toward the steering wheel, ready to force him to pull over.

Lupe blocked his hand. "It is in a cage. Chill."

Philip looked over the back of the seat, and right behind him was a small wire-mesh carton with a little rattler coiled in the corner. "Why do you have it in here?"

"I am stopping on our way to sell it to the snake preacher. He pays $20."

Philip turned and stared straight ahead.

"Preacher Carson. It is his religion." Lupe's face grew somber, and he reached over and clasped a hand on Philip's shoulder. "You okay? You do not look so good."

Lupe was like a brother, but even with their history, Philip couldn't say the words, *my mother died while I was looking for Rosa*. Instead, he slumped in the seat and stared at the photograph taped to the dash, Lupe's two little boys, one toddler and one infant. While Philip had been frozen in time, searching for Rosa, Lupe's life had moved forward.

Philip pulled his cap over his face and fell asleep.

He woke at dusk when Lupe stopped the truck next to a small, weathered farmhouse in the middle of a dried-up maize field.

Philip yawned. "Doesn't look like a church."

Lupe pulled the cage out of the back. "He has church in his

house to keep sheriff away. It is against the law to have rattlers in a public place. Coming?"

"No thanks." Philip stayed in the truck, finished his bourbon and dozed. When he woke again, thirsty and soaked with sweat, it was dark. Out-of-tune piano music and off-key singing drifted from the house through the lit-up, open windows.

He slid out of the truck and walked toward the house.

The front door stood open, and a skinny old guy with shoulder-length gray hair posed in front of the room full of about twenty people, his arms raised above his head.

He stared straight ahead with wild blue eyes seizing Philip's focus. "Taking up serpents is our path to redemption." He sounded like a woman trying to make her voice more masculine. Although the preacher's gaze focused hard on Philip's eyes, some abnormal energy lured Philip to break the gaze and peer upward. The preacher, with his arms stretched high above his head, held a rattlesnake about three feet long.

The old man nodded once, dropped the snake into a trunk on the crude altar and slammed the lid shut. The pianist started a new song.

With increased volume, the preacher spoke directly to Philip. "He will by no means leave the guilty..." He pointed at Philip. "...unpunished, visiting the iniquity of the fathers on the children and the grandchildren to the third and fourth generations."

Words nailed the fear Philip had always run from. He would never escape the ugliness of his father and grandfather. Truth washed through him. *Rosa's better off without me.*

The small congregation started singing, "Softly and tenderly Jesus is calling, calling for you and for me..."

With his eyes squeezed shut, the preacher, reached toward the people and spoke over their singing. "Now's the time, brothers and sisters. Come forward and give your life to Jesus. I feel His spirit. He's calling, calling for you and for me."

One by one people rose from rough wooden benches and went to the front to kneel while singing over and over, "Come home, come home. Ye who are weary come home."

Raising his hands toward the ceiling, the preacher shouted, "Jesus knows you are weary, but he's pleading, pleading, come home. He knows every hair on your head, every fear in your heart. Come home."

By now almost everyone, even Lupe, was up front kneeling. Only Philip and an elderly lady with amputated legs were left.

As if the preacher wouldn't be satisfied until the last person came to his altar, he shouted, "Look! See them black windows." He pointed to the open windows along one side of the room. "Sinner, get on your knees to the light, or the hell you'll find will be as black as them windows."

What a joke. Philip almost laughed. At twenty-five years old, he was already in hell. Mama dead, Rosa married, and he didn't need a preacher's theatrics to expose sins of fathers. He thought it would have been an act of kindness to pick up the legless lady and walk to the preacher. Instead, Philip sat on the back-row bench, unyielding.

The service ended and the room emptied except for Philip.

Some people drove away. Others were still outside talking. A detached calmness settled over him. He ambled toward the altar's metal trunk. Fear of what he was going to do clenched him. But the fear wasn't big enough to stop the doing. When he raised the lid, the stink gagged him.

Then, like his own bad breath, the rattler's musk disappeared. The snake eased around, flicking its forked tongue to gauge the closeness of human warmth. Philip's hands worked into the snake's layers to feel the rippled muscle, the scaly back, and the soft underbelly. The rattle buzzed, warning the intruder.

Footsteps approached from behind, and voices muttered, but the words were too dim to comprehend. Philip was outside of everything, more alive now that he could die at any moment.

He brought the snake out of the trunk and stretched his arms straight in front of himself, side by side, to give the reptile a base on which to coil as it pleased. Starting on Philip's palms, the snake looped around on his forearms, and moved toward his elbows. Veering onto his left arm, it worked its way toward his shirt collar.

Philip could no longer see the eyes that never closed. Instead, he felt its head work downward as if seeking to burrow under his shirt.

The fangs... near the pulse of his throat... could pierce the beat.

Mama was still dead and Rosa was still married. The shame for what happened to Dinah still haunted.

But for that one instant, the boulder of pain in his chest disintegrated and lifted in a way that surpassed the hours of numbing bourbon.

Then the snake, with some instinct of escape, crossed over to Philip's right arm and moved back toward his palms. Dropping to the floor, it crawled toward the darkness beneath the piano.

The preacher shouted, "Don't let it a-loose in here."

"What the shit, *mi hermano*," Lupe said.

Philip caught the rattler, laid it in the trunk, and dropped the lid.

Eyes popping and face reddening, the preacher said, "That wasn't taking up serpents for the Lord. That was Satan's work. You been cursed." He raised his right hand high as if demonstrating his own connection with heaven.

71

Brenda Vicars

Lupe clasped Philip's shoulder. "Let us get you out of here."
They walked out into the dark, hot night.

An urgent seed, ready to root and infest, formed within Philip.

He'd need to handle a rattlesnake again.

At its core, this need for risk was steeped in shame because in that moment when his life could end at the whim of a reptile, the adrenaline lifted him above all of his regrets. Snake handling was a cheap escape.

Chapter Eight

In spite of Philip's snake handling memories, Edith and her journals left his mood elevated.

Driving up to his father's place, the old dread was gone. Instead of focusing on the filth in the house, Philip saw beauty in 200 acres of slightly rolling land, covered with mesquites, post oaks, bluebonnets, primroses, and fire wheels.

The sprawling ranch-style house, although poorly maintained, was well built and spacious with six bedrooms and bathrooms. The property had potential.

Dinah and Lily showed up at dinner time with merlot and barbequed chicken.

Lily hugged with her usual exuberance. "I can't believe how much you've already done here. It's so fresh with the trash gone and carpets pulled out." She let go of him and spread both her arms wide, waving at all parts of the front room. "I love how you kept the few good pieces of furniture."

With the nearly empty spaces and light pouring in through the uncovered windows, the beauty of the outdoors became part of the room.

Covering the table with a white cloth, Dinah busied herself opening food containers.

Philip turned toward her, but Dinah kept her eyes averted. He stood awkwardly, wanting to connect but ever cautious of offending her. Since her glare after the funeral service as he consoled Aunt Loraine, Dinah hadn't made eye contact with him.

The silence was filled by Lily, chattering about colors and flooring.

Dinah poured three glasses of wine. She lifted one and nodded toward the other two glasses, signaling Lily and Philip to join her. "To my brother. May he make profitable progress on this..." She panned the room and rolled her eyes. "...project."

They drank. Then Lily raised her glass again saying, "To Dinah for finishing her Ph.D."

"Congratulations," Philip said, as they drank again. "And to both my little sisters. I'm lucky to be here with you."

Dinah slid into a chair at the table, and motioned for the others to sit across from her at the two places set for them. "Actually, Lily and I are the lucky ones. I picked up our father's files at his real estate office, and I learned we now own four other vacant houses." She reached into her briefcase and pulled out a large envelope. "Here are the addresses, keys, and appraisals."

"Oh, wow! Four houses," said Lily, alternating her gaze between Philip and Dinah. "That's a good thing, right?"

Philip nodded as he pulled out a chair for Lily and sat next to her.

Dinah continued without acknowledging the interruption. "Apparently, he had the habit of picking up bargains with the plan of renovating. Of course, he rarely followed through. I drove by the properties." Lily filled their plates while Dinah spoke. "They all need some work, but when they're sold, they could bring hundreds of thousands, if—" She abruptly turned toward Philip and smiled for the first time. "—someone renovates them."

Lily gasped and clamped a hand onto Philip's arm. "Oh, say you'll do it!"

"Sure," he said, glad his sisters valued his construction skills.

Lily jumped up and did a silly jigging dance around the table. "Yes, yes, yes! We'll keep you here for ever and ever."

Dinah ignored her and, looking directly at Philip, said, "I'm assuming you're qualified for this project."

"Yes, I am. I've had lots of experience in renovations." He could have added that most of his recent work was far more complex.

"What's your licensure?"

He pulled out his phone and showed her screenshots of his resumé, Texas electrician's license, and contractor's registration with the Texas Residential Construction Commission. "I started in high school with carpentry and apprentice electrician courses. Took other courses while I worked. Passed the state exams. I'm bonded."

Dinah took his phone, texted his screenshots to herself, and passed his phone back to him. "I'll open a checking account in all three of our names, and I'll deposit the life insurance checks and commission payments still coming to us from his last real estate sales. We can't officially split the money until probate is complete, but as executrix I can use funds however I want to manage his property."

"You're executrix?" Lily asked. "I thought Daddy wanted Philip to take care of all that."

"It is odd in view of our father's paternalistic bias that he named me, but he probably suspected Philip wouldn't show up." She glanced at him. "But surprise, surprise... here you are."

If her words were meant to wound him, they worked.

Dinah, without missing a beat, continued, "You can debit the account to buy materials for the repairs and to pay yourself for your time and to pay any laborers you hire. Just maintain records and give me original invoices and receipts. After the property is sold, and his final bills are paid, we'll divide the money and pay our inheritance taxes. The end."

Philip said, "I like renovations. I'll inventory the houses tomorrow, make a list of materials, and post some work bids if it looks like we'll need to."

"Yes, let's toast our plans!" Lily said, raising her glass.

Dinah hadn't touched her food and she only pretended to sip from her glass. "To our plans." She placed her napkin beside her food, and pushed her chair away from table.

To keep her there, Philip said, "I can't believe you have a Ph.D. What are you now? A superintendent?"

Both Dinah's hands fisted on the either side of her plate. "I'll never be a superintendent. In public education, eighty percent of us are women, but only ten percent of the superintendents are women." She sounded as though she was giving a speech. "I researched this for my dissertation. What's worse is women superintendents on average make lower salaries than men. According to the U.S. Census Bureau, the superintendency is the most male-dominated CEO position in the country."

"How can that be?" asked Lily.

"Simple. Sexism. If you haven't figured it out, Lily, unless you have balls, you get screwed. And not just professionally." With the last words, she slowed down. Her sharp voice softened, and her face drooped into lines of exhaustion. "I can attest that it happens personally as well."

"Would you feel better..." Lily reached across the table toward Dinah. "...if we talk about your marriage?"

"Oh, Lily." Dinah stood, sending her chair scraping backwards.

"You truly sound like a social worker, and you haven't even finished your certification. But sure, let's talk." Erect and rigid, arms hugging her own stomach, she spat her words fast. "Jack started working in New Mexico two years ago. He said he would be there less than a year. That was a lie. He said he would come home once a month, but until this funeral, he hadn't been home in six. Another lie."

Her bitterness took the breath out of the room. "When his secretary moved to New Mexico, I asked if they were having an affair. He said I had a dirty mind to think such a thing. She's a sweet person, too young for him, and if I knew her, I would never suspect her of having an affair with a married man." Lily, tears welling in her eyes, approached Dinah and touched her tensed arms. Dinah shrugged away and shook her head. "My life is a cliché."

Lily said, "If you think he's having an affair, why don't you have him followed?"

"I don't know."

The stark pain on Dinah's grown-up face took Philip back to the nightmare that broke apart their lives, and in a moment of clarity her mournful, "I don't know," made him see the truth. *Dinah's accustomed to living with lies. She doesn't recognize that she's stuck in the pattern.*

Dinah picked up the napkin from the side of her plate, unfolded it, and dropped it onto her untouched food. "Well, we've covered our business plan and dissected my marriage, so I'm out of here."

"Wait, you haven't had a bite," said Lily. "I'm afraid it's happening again. You're getting too—"

As palpable as a slap in the face, Dinah's glower stopped Lily mid-sentence.

After an edgy silence, Lily changed the topic. "We've got so many years to catch up on." She turned toward Philip. "You must have a girlfriend or something we can talk about." She looked at him expectantly. "Right?"

"Yes, I do." He surprised himself because he'd never before been open about his feelings. But he wanted to talk about Edith, and he wanted to connect with his sisters. "I just met her. And she's the one."

Even Dinah looked intrigued.

"Oh good, tell, tell," said Lily.

Philip grinned at their eagerness. A cool breeze blew through the open windows, and tension flowed out of the room with it. "Okay, sisters, I could use your advice. I don't want to mess this up."

He'd opened a trunk of treasure that they couldn't resist exploring. "I met her the same day you texted about our father wanting to see me." After years of aloneness, this novel sister confiding felt right.

"Sit, sit." Lily ushered Dinah back to her chair and poured another splash of wine into their still full glasses. "Go on." She nudged Philip as they sat.

"Her name is Edith. She's beautiful. She's a poet and a professor. Lives in Austin, but I met her in Culmine at a café where she helps out for her friend, the owner. I don't want to say much more about her because she should tell you when she's ready. But meeting her was life changing. We talked about everything that matters to us." Philip spoke steadily and maintained eye contact with first Lily then Dinah, then back again. His words flowed as if Edith's written words had somehow strengthened his own communication abilities. "We shared on a deep level, even our flaws. Things I'd never told anyone before. Meeting her is a turning point for me."

Everything was still. Even the breeze died down. "I told her about my years of searching for Rosa." Dinah knew there'd been a girl who'd disappeared in Mexico because she'd been at home when Philip came for his birth certificate. But neither sister knew he'd wanted to marry her.

"I also told her about my phase of handling rattlesnakes."

"What," Lily gasped. "What did you say?"

"I handled rattlesnakes for a couple of years."

Lily stood, turning her head from side to side. "Wait. What do you mean—you handled rattlesnakes?"

Seeing her shock and Dinah's pale face, he quickly downplayed. "Yeah, the first time was in a church. I did it on a whim. The preacher had been handling a snake, so I just did it."

Both sisters gaped.

"Then after that I went to a few roundups, learned the tricks of handling and—"

Dinah cut him off. "Are roundups still legal?"

He was glad that her interruption gave him a moment to veer away from memories of the adrenaline rush, the uplifting moments of escape that handling a deadly snake had given him. "Yes, they're still legal, but now hunters are prohibited from using gasoline to flush them out." While his sisters chattered about their horrors of roundups, he took deep breaths and remembered his months when seeking rattlesnakes, not only at public roundups but alone in the forest, became an obsession. The compulsion distracted from his grief over his mother's death, his failure to find Rosa, and his unending shame about how the men in his family had desecrated Dinah. Probably, he thought, it was like heroin. The first high was amazing, but after a while, the high was never as good. His sisters chatter fell silent and he said, "But the shows got boring. After you learn all the tricks, it's not much of a challenge."

Lily finally sat back down. "You don't do that anymore, do you?"

"No," he assured them. "Outgrew that hobby."

As he talked about his background, one thing stayed untold: his blackouts. He wouldn't remind Dinah of their grandfather.

Lily said, "You need to invite Edith to dinner, here to meet us. Meeting family is the best way to win a woman over."

"You can keep trying if you want," Dinah said. "But keep in mind you barely know her, and the whole attraction could just be pheromones. They fizzle as fast as they flare." She stood. "I have to pick up Jacqueline." Her plate was still covered with the napkin, the food uneaten. Her wine glass was still full, and she was dashing toward the front door.

Lily said, "Well, let's all do this again soon. Maybe next—"

Dinah jerked the door open. "I hate this fucking door. It always sticks."

Philip stood. "Thanks for the food and wine."

Before his sentence was finished, Dinah had slammed the door on her way out.

Chapter Nine

Enchilada aroma reminded Philip of the regular dinner special when he walked into the Hilltop an hour early. There were a couple of dozen people eating, a young couple doing *salsa* in the jukebox corner, Frank with several customers at the bar, but no Carmen.

Philip had intended to stay in his room and read until seven. He'd brought the old Sabine manuscript from his father's crumbling trunk, determined to get through it soon. But he couldn't focus knowing Edith would be walking into the café within the hour.

Leaning against the cashier's counter, a sixtyish woman, wearing the Myra uniform, zeroed in on him. He nodded at her and headed toward a small table.

The woman reached his table almost as soon as he did. Up close, she had light brown and gray hair. "You must be Philip." Her unsmiling face and steel gray eyes sharpened her words.

"Hi, Myra, glad to meet you."

"Well, now that I see you—" She tilted her head and cracked a lopsided grin. "—I understand how you got my old freezer with a hundred pounds of meat in it away from the wall.

I hear you saved my place that night. I thank you." Her slender well-lined face was warm. She didn't wink at him, but something about the tilt of her head and her smile made him feel like she had.

"Glad to help, but anyone could have done it."

"No one else could've done what you did." Not waiting for him to reply, she gestured toward a chair. "Please, have a seat. Edith said you might be in tonight."

He pulled out the chair but stayed standing. "Thanks, I'll sit here until she arrives. But if you need this table just let me know." He glanced around the dining area. "You're pretty busy tonight."

"She's already here." Myra cocked her head toward the jukebox. "I called and asked her to come early to help my grandson."

Philip followed her glance toward the music. There was Edith.

With two long braids hanging below her shoulders, she looked as young as the skinny boy she was dancing with. She wore a snug light blue T-shirt that stopped at the waistband of her low-riding jeans. In Philip's quick scan for Carmen's long black hair when he first entered the café, he hadn't noticed Edith's face.

Myra beamed when the boy executed a turn with Edith. "He's going to *salsa* at a *quinceañera* in a couple of weeks. You know, a big traditional celebration for his fifteen-year-old girlfriend."

With Edith's arm lifted during her spin, the bottom of her shirt rose and revealed taut, golden skin above her waistband.

"Looks like he'll be ready," Philip said, letting his eyes drink in Edith. Watching her move to this music exposed deeper nuances and woke every cell in his body. Her voice on the phone came back... *you and I bonded in a way you had never experienced before... as if your life began the night we met.* She had opened an untried pathway between them, and now her physical presence tugged like a magnet.

Myra nodded and shoved her hands into her apron pockets. "He's quite a boy. I'm sure proud of him."

"I see why."

Edith's back was to him and her hips, bound in faded denim of her snug jeans, swayed to the *salsa* beat. His body wanted her. And knowing he'd had her but couldn't remember their time together made his wanting urgent. He must have cupped—

"What can I get you while you wait? It's on the house... least I can do after all you did in my kitchen."

Philip pulled his gaze off of Edith. "Thanks, but I'll wait until she's done."

"All righty, but if you change your mind, just let me know." Myra strolled back to the cashier counter.

The *salsa* music stopped. Edith released her student, and moved to his side showing him some subtle foot movements and spin patterns before she restarted the music.

When the music stopped the next time, Edith patted the boy's shoulder. "You've got it! Let's go through it once more..." For the first time she raised her eyes to see Philip. Her smile brightened, and she skipped a beat in her sentence. Even the boy followed her gaze. "...just for practice." Then she started the music and drilled him again.

The boy, his lips moving to count his steps, went through the spin sequence.

When the music stopped, they and Myra came to Philip's table. Their chatter jumbled in his mind when Edith clasped his bare arm, right below his elbow. She gazed up at him. "You came."

"Said I would."

Her smile lit something inside him.

"Yes, you did, but I was afraid after you thought it over—" She stopped herself, as if remembering they weren't alone, and turned to the boy next to her. "This is Sean, an awesome *salsa* lead."

Philip pulled his gaze from Edith and shook the boy's hand. "Looked great."

Sean, face reddening, mumbled something about Edith being a good teacher.

Edith's hand stayed on Philip's arm.

Myra talked about the upcoming *quinceañera*.

Standing this close to Edith in the flesh, inhaling her scent and feeling her hand, Philip thought about dark cave allegories. He was the man who'd lived in darkness now experiencing his first glimmer of light. He could never again look away.

Finally, Myra and Sean left.

As soon as Philip and Edith sat, she pressed her knee against his thigh. An involuntary exhale pushed out of him. He looked down at her mouth. His breath must have swept her because gooseflesh stood on her neck and chest.

As if acknowledging their heat, Edith said, "We should take this slowly."

"We can do whatever you want." His voice was low.

A glass of red wine appeared in front of Edith. Frank popped his head between Edith and Philip. "Got a new one for you to try."

"Thank you, Frank." Her voice sounded breathless. She lifted the glass, closed her eyes, and took a deep inhale. Faint freckles were scattered across her cheeks. She opened her eyes, raised the rim to her bottom lip and tilted the glass. She closed her eyes and nodded. "Entangled... gentle... a little angular." She looked up at Frank. "I feel it throughout my body."

"I knew it." Frank bobbed his head and grinned. "I knew

you'd go for this one. It's a new Argentine Malbec our distributor just brought."

"You were right." Edith moved the glass toward Philip. "Want to try?"

His fingers brushed hers when he took the glass and sipped from the same spot she had. "Good." He had nothing against wine but rarely drank it.

"What about you, my man?" Frank asked Philip. "Beer?"

"No, I'll have what she's having."

Edith's knee still pressed against his thigh.

"Coming right up." Frank turned back toward the bar.

"No rush," Philip said to Frank's retreating back. "I'll come get it when we're ready."

Tango music started from the jukebox, a Julio Iglesias classic. Sean and a teenaged girl, with Myra instructing, were practicing in the dance corner.

Edith ran her finger up and down the stem of the glass. Her knee shifted against his thigh in rhythm with her finger movement. She turned her gaze to Philip. "I know you won't touch me first."

"How do you know?" The truth in her words, words he'd never consciously articulated, shocked him.

"How's Dinah now?" Edith answered his question by leaping over his family's nightmare and fast forwarding to the present moment.

"Brittle," he said, surprising himself with this one-word summary.

Myra approached. "You two want the enchilada special?" The tango dancers gave up, laughing at themselves as they left the café.

"Thank you," Edith said. "I'd love it."

Philip nodded. "Same."

"Will do," Myra said over her shoulder, heading toward the kitchen.

Philip lowered his voice and leaned closer to Edith, their faces inches apart. "You think your mother worked here?"

Edith nodded slowly. The movement of her knee stilled, but she continued to press into his thigh. "She and Myra were both teenagers then." Edith looked around the room as if imagining her young mother there. "Her name was Susan. She was blonde, light blue eyes, very pale and small, new in town. Myra's parents, who owned the place then, sensed she needed help and let her work for a few months. Back then letting someone work for cash without legal ID wasn't uncommon."

Philip nodded, remembering all the day labor he'd done in south Texas with no ID.

"Susan's pregnancy became obvious. One day she stopped coming to work, and a couple of days later I showed up, a newborn in a box, at the Lutheran parsonage. At first, the pastor and his wife took me on as a foster child. Eventually, when no parents could be found, they legally adopted me." Edith smiled. "They already had four boys, so I grew up a little princess with a perfect life... except for the mystery of my biological parents."

"Makes sense why you keep coming back." Her hand slipped into his under the table. "How did you find out about your mother?"

"My adoptive parents told me." She caressed his hand with both of hers. "Being here makes my mother feel real, keeps her story alive."

Tango music restarted. Philip stood and gestured toward the now-deserted dance corner.

She tilted her head. "Tango?"

"Edith, may I have this dance?" He offered his hand.

She slowly rose and took his hand. "Uh, I don't tango much."

"That's okay, just follow."

He took her onto the floor, and wrapped her into the tango pose. He could tell she wasn't used to the body-to-body contact or to having her face lying against her partner's chest. For several measures, he held her in place and swayed to the music, letting her adjust to his lead. He edged his feet closer to hers until their shoes were touching, then with the upswing of the music they moved into the patterns. He gave a silent thanks for Soledad's relentless drills. Near the finale, he held Edith in a deep back bend for a few seconds.

As he spun her up into a final embrace, she surprised him by whispering, "Thank you, Soledad, wherever you are, for this man who tangos."

When the music stopped, their locked gaze was broken by applause. Everyone in the restaurant had stopped to watch.

Philip, scanning the crowd, instantly regretted making a display of Edith and himself. *Is Carmen here now?* But he saw only friendly, smiling faces.

Myra came closer. "Oh my gosh!" She flapped both hands, fanning her face. "Takes me back to that movie, *Scent of a Woman.*"

Edith said, "Myra, can we get those dinners to go?"

"Sure thing. You two must have been practicing," Myra said over her shoulder.

Philip whispered to Edith, "Where're we going?"

She squeezed his arm and stood on tiptoes to speak into his ear. "Your room."

Chapter Ten

Philip and Edith walked at a fast pace across the dark parking lot toward his room.

He asked, "Could you define *slow*?"

Still walking, she cut her eyes toward him and tilted her head in question.

"You said we should take this slow," he clarified. "I want to respect what you say."

She braked as if she'd hit a wall. "I did say that." She faced him squarely. "You're right. I said that, and I meant no sex tonight." Her words were sharp and decisive.

"Okay." He willed his body to accept her plan.

"But," her voice rising, she clasped both his arms, "I changed my mind. I'm sorry to—"

His lips took hers. He let the bag of enchilada dinners drop to the ground. He lifted her. One arm across her back, another supporting her butt. Her arms clasped his neck and shoulders. Her legs wound around his waist. He was almost a foot taller than Edith, but they fit.

Unwilling to lose her legs clamped around him, he walked, still carrying her, to his door. He let her feet slide to the ground while he pulled out the key. She kept her body flush against his with her arms around his chest while he unlocked.

Inside the room he kicked the door shut and lifted her again.

"Philip," she murmured.

His mouth covered hers. The taste of her radiated throughout his body.

With a regretful sigh, she pulled out of the kiss. "Wait."

He forced himself to freeze. "Yes." Struggling to make his voice calm, he let her slide down and move away even though he grieved the loss of her contact.

"Enchiladas... in the parking lot."

Relieved by her wide-eyed reminder, he pressed a quick kiss on the top of her head, slung the door open, and rushed out to retrieve the bag.

When he returned, she stood next to the desk, squinting at the old manuscript in the dim light of the clock radio. The pages, yellowed and brittle with worn, uneven edges, exuded a slightly musty scent. And even in the dim light, the spidery hand-writing whispered of a past era.

Frozen, as if holding her breath, she whispered, "What is this?" Her voice was full of wonder.

He dropped the bag onto the desk. "Not sure, found those among my father's papers. Guessing they were written by an ancestor. I want to read them."

"May I read them, too?"

"Sure," he said. "Now?"

Gently, she laid the pages on the desk. She turned her gaze to him and pulled her T-shirt up and off. Pushing her body against his, she reached around him into his back jeans pocket, and pulled out his wallet. Stepping back, she lifted the little flap covering his condoms and pulled one out.

She grinned. "Glad you restocked."

He had his shirt off by then and was unbuckling his belt. "Did that after I read your journal."

For a moment she gazed at him. Then with a condom between her teeth, she caressed his length. He groaned and stepped out of his shoes and pants. Then he unzipped hers and slid them down. When nothing was left between them, he pulled her to him again.

If he entered now, it would be over too soon, so he carried her to the bed and laid her on her back. She reached for him to put the condom on.

He stilled her hand and looked at her until she gazed back. He took the condom and laid it on the bedside table. "Please, let me... know you first."

Questions in her eyes prompted him.

"I want to see, touch, taste every part of you." His hands ran down the sides of her body. "I want every secret you have." One hand traced from her neck to the center of her chest.

Reverently, he explored her, read her. Her breathing, occasional gasps, increasing moisture, and the movement of her flesh beneath his touch communicated to him. He loved that this woman with a body so responsive to his touch was also a person who understood him better than anyone he'd known.

She pulled his face up to hers and kissed him as if she could never get enough. She reached for him and tried to guide him in. Somehow her excitement and release had calmed him. He pulled back to sheathe. He entered slightly, but stopped and gazed into her eyes. She nodded, touched his face and said his name, softly, over and over, as his full length slowly found home.

Afterwards, he brought her a glass of water and then spooned against her, wrapping his arms around her and entwining his legs with hers. He wanted nothing more than to lie flesh to flesh and hold her for hours.

"Philip?"

"Mm?"

"Yes," she said in a clear voice.

"What do you mean—*yes*?"

"You asked if I want to read it now."

He laughed, got up, retrieved the papers, and turned on the bedside lamp. A glimpse of the first line about a *secret arousal contortion*, revived his dread. He didn't want to learn his other ancestors, such as this Sabine, were as depraved as his father and grandfather. "Promise you won't hold whatever this says against me?" He handed the manuscript to her.

She kissed his forearm resting on her chest as she positioned herself onto her side to read. "Who am I to hold anyone's ancestors against them?"

He relaxed back into his place behind her to read over her shoulder. "I'm planning to cull out some parts before my sisters read this. Dinah shouldn't be exposed to any more filth."

Edith laid the pages down and turned to him, caressing his cheek. "I think you and your sisters are already... wounded by everything in your family's past. You just may not know the weapon that wounded you. If Dinah reads this, whatever will be exposed to her is something that's already a part of her. Something dark that could now be in the light."

Chapter Eleven

Sabine Richards' manuscript. Preface, 1935

Was it because my arousal contortion forced my phallus backwards, rendering me a twisted mortal incarnate of Priapus? Was it because my stubborn German mother would not hear, let alone answer, my endless probing into the reasons behind our family's suffering? Was it because my father's unpredictable rages filled my childhood with terror, which was relieved only by his mysterious death when I was twenty? Which, if any, of these eventualities compelled me to write about Feevah, the alluring slave who turned my father's life down the pathway of misery?

Perhaps all three of these factors spawned my avoidance of intimacy, my incessant need to escape into books, and my laborious travail that brought forth this written history.

Unlike most working middle-class men of Anglo-Saxon origin in central Texas, who marry, raise children and build homes, I remained single and lived with my mother until she died. Although my outward vocation was by the brawn of my back delivering furniture, my leisure time was filled with reading, escaping this world and searching for an answer to my private, tortuous deformity.

On the evening of September 23, 1920, when the census takers came to our home in Waco, and I heard my mother report facts about our family, facts far more evocative than the census takers had sought, my relentless longing for answers was finally mollified. My mother liberated long-sequestered secrets that led me to the story of Feevah.

The night of the census takers began as many of our family birthday celebrations. Because the dates of our births were a week apart in September, my mother and I celebrated together. On this evening my brother, Neville, and his wife and children had joined us for dinner. Afterwards, while the children chased fireflies, we four adults drank several glasses of my mother's wine; winemaking was a practice as natural to her as breathing. Any excess fruit or honey that she acquired eventually found its way into a mixture of water, yeast, and sugar.

Ordinarily my mother's drinking precipitated no noticeable effect upon her. Perhaps this night she had exceeded her typical measure, or perhaps she was extraordinarily reflective on this, my fifty-fifth and her sixty-ninth, birthday week. Shortly after Neville and his family had departed, as Mother and I sat on the front porch savoring a final glass, three census takers arrived and asked their simple questions about our family: names, birthdates, places of birth, death dates, job titles, and ability to read.

Thus, with her German accent intensified by wine, my mother stated her full maiden name, Tennessee "Tenny" Madelyn Schmidt; then she recounted events that I had never heard. The census takers, an elderly woman and two weathered men, were transfixed by her words. Until this moment, I had reluctantly accepted that my parents' history was a locked chest, so I scarcely breathed rather than risk interrupting her flow of information. Somehow the government census takers with their structured questions and official book spurred the release of my mother's story.

"I was just thirteen when we hear Yankees were coming. Our farm was a half day from Chattanooga, and folks rode by saying Yankees took town and be here soon. Mama began to cry and pack;

she loaded the wagon with barrels of wine, food, blankets, and goods that Yankees would steal. She shook Papa and cried, 'We must go. Yankees steal everything and have their way with Tenny.' Papa just lay there. I think Mama knew it was hopeless for him to escape. He was bedridden with broken shoulder and brain swelling; he and I had fallen off the barn roof a few weeks earlier doing repairs. Mama was crying as my brothers and I helped load the wagon.

"I don't know what Mama would have done if our neighbor, Russell Richards, had not come running up on foot to borrow a horse. Then his crippled slave, Seth, came running after him. Mama said, 'Take wagon, take my Tenny, too. If she stays here, Yankees ruin her. Take her and hide; take wine for payment.' Russell, Seth and I rode away; I never saw Mama or Papa or brothers again."

The census takers and I sat in silence. I had an urge to refill Mother's glass and offer our guests wine, feeling I must keep this fountain of information replenished. In spite of that urge, I was struck mute imagining my portly mother as a thirteen-year-old and my father, who must have been twenty-four at the time, running up to her home out of the darkness.

Finally, the female census taker, who had been writing steadily in her thick ledger, halted her pen. "Mrs. Richards, what was the year of your marriage?"

"I don't know," my mother answered. "I didn't know we were married until we were in Texas, and I heard Russell tell a man passing by, 'This is my wife, Tenny.'"

All attention converged on my mother.

The vulnerability in her eyes, as her own words pulled her back in time, broke my muteness. "That question does not seem to be on the official census form, but if you must know my parents were married in 1864," I stated sharply, voicing the assumption I had made my entire life. "Do you require additional information?"

My voice seemed to drive my mother back into her customary silence. As the census takers continued their official duty, I cited the rest of the information they needed. They left us on the porch, and shortly we heard them knocking at the house next door.

After they had gone inside the neighbor's house, I revived a weak voice. "Mother, did you ever learn what happened to your family? Did my father own more slaves? Did he fight in the Civil War? What happened to the crippled slave?"

Mother resumed her stoic demeanor and pushed herself up from her chair. She grumbled as she lumbered toward the kitchen, "I have to finish my pecans. If I don't shell and roast, they'll turn rancid. No time to talk."

Her slow, heavy steps halted and she turned back toward me for a moment. "Seth came to see us once. Came driving up late one evening in a carriage." The moment Mother said this, a dim memory emerged: I stood, as a small child, in the front yard of our home. A dark man from a carriage, softly called my name and watched me. "Last I know he was living in a hut by railroad tracks near the town now called Temple. If he ever died, I didn't hear about it."

On the following Sunday, as soon as I delivered my mother home from church, I changed clothes and headed back out to the automobile. Mother did not ask me where I was going, but, she said, "Take this bottle of wine, and if you find Seth, tell him I sent it. He loved wine. Mine was the first he ever had."

I drove south toward Temple. I had taken this same route often throughout my life and had likely passed the very house I was seeking. Until this portentous day, the colored shacks were of no relevance, and I had always focused on the homes of people who purchased furniture. However, now with my mission to find the former slave who had known my father, I took note of the details of each dwelling, appreciating how the inhabitants had made efforts to personalize their homes with an abundance of flowering plants.

To my astonishment and delight, I found him within an hour. As if the universe orchestrated our encounter, he was sitting outside in a rocking chair, blowing into a harmonica. It was a familiar melody, similar to "Amazing Grace" from the service I had attended with Mother earlier that day. However, he was infusing half tones that lent a primitive flavor. I slowly approached, dismounted, and stood several feet away listening to his song.

His long, angular face was very dark and deeply lined in a hard way. He did not have the soft, sagging look many elderlies acquire; instead, his appearance had the quality of a mahogany carving. It was the only moment in my life when I regretted not having the talent to paint portraits. Although his music tempted me to simply feel the flow without intellectualizing it, I was striving to analyze his technique when he reached the end of his song.

"You got to be Russell's boy, Sabine."

Before I comprehended his words, my core shifted in response to the sense of familiarity his tone and accent touched within me. His voice, though deeper than my father's had been, was similar in quality. It left me vulnerable and incapable of speaking anything other than the purest truth.

"Yes, I am."

He stood and we shook hands.

When he offered me a chair under the awning, I remembered the wine. "Mother sent this for you."

He seemed shocked. "For me? Tenny sent this? Are you sure?" Shaking his head, he slowly set it on a small, rough wooden table near the two chairs. "I'll just get us some glasses." With a cane he shuffled into his small house and presently returned with two glasses; accordingly, I pulled the cork and poured.

To this moment I can close my eyes and recall the light, the breeze, the taste, and the words of that long afternoon. My constant hunger that had pushed me searching all those years was perfectly complemented by Seth's need to release his story.

Seth was a man who had survived being maimed by his father and scapegoated for his white half-brother. We began a long and rewarding connection, passing every Sunday afternoon together until

Seth died seven years later. With his deep voice and his unspoiled language, Seth took me back to my youthful father's innocent love for his slave, and the events that eventually twisted Russell Richards into the monster whom I knew as my father.

Out of my need to understand the truth of my ancestry and out of deep respect for Seth's wish to share, I have done my best to render the story of Feevah in the language of her moment. I liken my attempt to tell her story with stark language to Seth's harmonica music. When I finally inquired whether the melody he had played as I approached him that first day was "Amazing Grace," his simple answer astonished me.

"My song ain't 'Amazing Grace.' It just 'Grace' cause them that knows grace, knows there's no need to put 'amazing' in front of it."

As you have learned, until my mother's revelation with the census takers, I was a fifty-five-year-old bachelor living with my widowed mother, and I was struggling to understand the factors that had led to my wretched existence. My surviving seven brothers and sisters had long since married and established independent lives. Although all of us had suffered from my father's rampages, the others had escaped our home. Of course, the reason I remained a bachelor, living more in books than in the real world, is that I have a contorting phallus.

I was normal until I was sixteen. Up until the night my father clubbed my erection with the barrel of his rifle, I had for several years awoken each morning with a pleasant and painless stiffness pointing upward. Additionally, unknown to anyone in my family, I had on one occasion spent several hours alone with the beautiful Amelia, a young widow, who took me into her bedroom to help her hang a heavy mirror. When I delivered her new washstand and mirror from the furniture company, and she asked me to come in and determine where to hang it, I knew she could discern the appropriate placement without my assistance. Nevertheless, I entered eagerly, aware that being invited into a lady's bedroom was an extraordinary privilege.

I had long admired her beauty from afar and daydreamed of comforting her in her lonely, young widowhood. It began to rain while we were marking the wall. Each time she pointed to a place, I held the mirror up and briefly leaned in close enough to inhale the scent of her skin and to see the cream-like flesh on her chest leading down into her bodice. A loud clap of thunder startled her. She placed her hands on my shoulders and said I must stay until the shower passed; she had heard recently of someone being struck by lightning while walking during a summer shower. I was pitifully inarticulate, nodding mutely in response to all of her requests. Her hands moved up and down my arms, and suddenly they were on my face.

Amelia said, "Sabine, you have no idea what a dear man you are. You have no idea how these lines that crinkle at your eyes when you smile touch a woman's heart."

"Well, thank you, Miss Amelia," I managed to say as she brushed the sides of my temple with her thumbs.

"You have no idea how the width of your shoulders, the profile of your face, and the muscles in your back warm a woman." Next, she kissed the side of my face, kissing in circles that grew smaller until she was kissing the corner of my mouth. My paralysis ended, and I took her mouth with my own, tasting her sweetness while letting my hands partake of the soft flesh down her sides and back. Our garments, like useless winter tree leaves, dropped away, and soon we were on her bed; she guided me into her hidden cove. I was scarcely inside, scarcely understanding the warmth, when quick, joyful spasms overtook my being.

She laughed softly and said, "Stay. Don't pull out." We remained together and kissed again and again. I wanted to kiss her forever, kiss every part of her. As I was kissing her neck, she stopped me. "You are the dearest man. You have a wonderful touch."

After a while I felt myself harden again, and we began the rhythmic dance as I moved in and out. Each increment of movement made me feel closer to her, more a part of her. I thought if I died in the next moment, I would be at peace because I had truly lived. At the same time, I desperately wanted to live forever in this room, in this woman. I was thinking nothing, nothing on earth could be more wonderful when I heard her whimper and realized I, Sabine Richards, was giving her pleasure. Though I believed I had already experienced the most wonderful sensations imaginable, when her body began to squeeze me, my ecstasy soared. Her sweet cove caressed me spasmodically until I felt my eruption building again, this time exceeding the length and depth of the initial spasm.

Philip groaned and interrupted Edith's reading. "Looks like this sex interlude goes on and on."

Edith smiled and turned to him. "I think a too-long sex scene is exactly the sort of thing you'd find in the manuscript of an entitled older man with literary pretensions who steals a narrative from former enslaved people."

"Okay. Let's skip it."

Edith silently scanned to the end of the scene and started reading aloud again.

Two days later my father delivered the blow initiating my horrible contortion.

He had come home late; we were all asleep. I awoke hearing him enter the room he shared with my mother.

"Tenny, wake up. I'm ready for you, girl. Wake up."

She murmured reluctant sounds of drowsiness. Even though no one in our family would have ever discussed coitus, I knew my mother did not want to awaken for him. Drunk, he would thrash at her for hours, hopefully achieving the satisfaction needed to lull himself to sleep but more likely getting angry, banging with frustration into everything in his path.

I dozed while hoping, for my mother's sake, he would finish

soon. When I roused sometime later, my father was in our room. My younger brothers slept next to the wall; I was nearest the door.

My father had opened the door and, holding up a candle, said, "Which one a you worthless shits has been into my tools again?" Almost every time he came home drunk, he proclaimed someone had moved, stolen, or damaged his tools.

Maybe I had been dreaming of Amelia; I was lying on my back, and my manhood was erect.

My father noticed my rise through the covers. "You piece of chicken shit. Thinking you got a big pecker." He threw the candle down and grabbed my rifle, the one bequeathed to him by his own father. Proudly, I had kept it propped against the wall by my bed ever since Father handed it down to me on my twelfth birthday.

He swung the barrel hard into my phallus. I gasped and covered myself with my hands, afraid he would swing again. Instead, he stood over me for a moment, aiming the weapon at my heart. We both knew the gun was worthless, not fit to shoot any more, and not loaded in years. I kept it only because he had carved my name and birth date on the stock when I was a baby. "You're the sorriest excuse for a son any man could have. I wish you'd never been born." He dropped the gun to the floor, retrieved the dead candle, and left the room.

With my back to my brothers, who were silent and frozen, probably in fear of our father's wrath, I gently prodded to detect damage. I was a little numb but otherwise seemed unchanged.

At dawn I felt soreness comparable to that of an over strained muscle. Each day, although the soreness seemed to subside, erections became more uncomfortable, and instead of rising upward, began to pull downward.

This incident, of course, prevented me from returning to Amelia.

Sadly, I never became normal again. Over the next few months, I was free of pain except when stiffened. Then my phallus bent more and more backwards, pushing down into my testes, with a curious blend of pain and comfort. As time went on, the size and muscle tone changed, becoming narrow and stringy when stiffened.

Initially, my passion for reading developed because I journeyed great distances, searched libraries, and devoured medical books and journals hoping to find a cure for my deformity. The closest medical explanation I discovered was in a detailed history of Louis the XIV's staff, in which a note alludes to Francois de la Peyronie's treatment for a disorder of the phallus in 1743. This discovery led to my speculation that a physician might possess updated information. With hope, I secured at great expense an appointment with a surgeon in New York City shortly before I turned thirty. He declared, with visible repugnance at my malady, that there was no cure, and the only victims of Peyronie's disease are men past the age of fifty. Others who suffer from contorted erections are simply pleasuring themselves too vigorously. I was too disheartened to recount my father's assault that had precipitated my condition.

After that disappointing verdict, I gave up hope of finding a cure in medical books and journals. At this time, I began my journey into the world of fiction; the easiest way to deal with the pain of my aloneness was to lose myself in stories. I lived a life of thought conceived through British and American authors whose books found their way to Waco.

However, after I met Seth, the enticement of the world of fiction diminished in comparison to the powerful attraction of the history he detailed. In spite of the hundreds of Sunday afternoons Seth and I spent together, those hours never lost their allure, and they became the focus of my life.

After the first year and Seth's initial chronicle had unfolded, I began to wonder if an inevitable time would dawn when Seth would no longer have the capacity to elevate my understanding of my father's history. My fears were groundless; each week there would be yet another jewel illuminating a new perspective. Although he occasionally digressed from this important history so that he could

101

detail his futile years of searching for his own people after the war and his subsequent marriage, I patiently indulged his meanderings and then politely guided him back to the significant discourse.

Often while we were talking and the capacity of mere words had been exhausted, Seth would play his harmonica, and our enlightenment grew through our submission to music. I purchased him a booklet explaining the technique with which he played expressive tones: bending. I disclosed to him the significance of his accomplishment, cleverly developed on his own with no formal training.

"Seth, the way you bend normal tones to produce a richer, more expressive note is the way your speech bends normal American dialect."

Revealing the full measure of his innocence, he responded, "Why you say your talking and notes is normal? Why wouldn't you say my talking and notes is normal, and the white folks bend from normal?"

Oddly, he then picked up his harmonica and played "Amazing Grace" in an exact replication of the standardized version without bending. After the final note, he said, "I can change my playing as well as my speaking."

One Sunday afternoon in the winter of 1927, I arrived at the regular time to find his front door boarded over. I suspected, and a nearby neighbor soon confirmed, that Seth, who must have been about eighty-seven years old, had died.

Weekdays became painful as I attempted to continue my outward life selling and delivering furniture. The constant drivel of the customers was unbearable. My only relief came when I could be at home alone while Mother was away at her new occupation as a cook at the Waco hospital.

Even though she had taken this position for a negative reason— her complaint that my reduced hours of employment did not bring enough money into the house—the work was beneficial for her. She had other people to listen to her monologues, so she had fewer hours to torment me. Nevertheless, when she was at home, her constant refrain that I should work more and her steadfast refusal to discuss Seth's history with me were infuriating.

Her accident happened early on a Monday morning as she was preparing to leave for the hospital. I had asked her once again to tell me what she knew about my father's death, and again she claimed all she knew was he had been away for several days when deputies on horseback came to the house and dumped his body in front. My head was pounding because in recent years the wine she made was poorly fermented and often made me ill. I explained to her that truth, only truth, would give us both the peace we needed to move forward.

"Truth!" she said. "I tell the truth, but you don't hear!"

I put my hands on her shoulders firmly, thinking I could help her understand what my words alone could not communicate. I was shocked by how pulpous she felt! I had not touched her in years, and though she appeared stout, my fingers sank into malleable flesh. I reflexively pushed her away from me, and because she was again attempting to ignore me, she lost her balance and fell off the three-foot high porch.

Landing fully on her back with a solid thud, she was silent and still. For a secret moment, her muteness seemed appropriate revenge against a person who had stubbornly refused to speak the truth to me for my entire life. However, I flew to her side and ascertained that she was still breathing. Then I ran to the neighbors and begged their assistance in taking her to the hospital. Within minutes, the backyard was full of people; someone covered her with a blanket; another waved a fan over her face. Neighbors speculated she may have had a heart attack.

The nurses and doctors at the hospital were courteous and helpful; because Mother cooked for them, they all knew her affectionately as Tenny, and they kindly offered me their supportive encouragement. She lingered for several days, drifting in and out of consciousness. On her last day she was alert for more than an hour. By now the doctor had diagnosed both hips were broken; while she was awake, he asked her how she had fallen. She began to explain her preparation to leave for work. She paused and looked at me.

"Tenny," the doctor asked again. "How did you fall?"

Still looking at me, she said, "My shoulders." I almost gasped thinking she would describe my grasping of her shoulders before she fell. But she merely muttered, "Pain."

"Your shoulders?" he asked. "Could it have been your chest, your heart?"

She closed her eyes. "My heart."

She never spoke again.

My dear reader, for years following Mother's death, I continued to struggle with my search for truth, until, I believe, I reached the same precipice on which Seth had balanced in his final years. Just as his need to impart the history informed my understanding of how my hateful father had begun his life as a kind and caring soul, I pray that Seth's story of Feevah will contain a ray of truth that will enlighten you. I further pray whatever prejudices you may have opined against me, based on the frailties revealed in this preface, will be set aside because this story you are about to read is the one pure and valuable legacy I have to share. Let not your judgment of me prevent you from receiving the beautiful truth of the love between my father and his slave as recorded in the following pages.

In earnest prayer, I, Sabine Richards, close my preface to this chronicle in the year of our Lord, 1935.

Chapter Twelve

Edith gently turned over the last page of Sabine's preface as if making sure they'd reached the end of it. The next section began with Feevah standing in the auction line. "Do you think this preface is true?" She rested her hand on the top page. "Or was Sabine a novelist?"

"Don't know. My father called him a nutjob." Philip was quiet while Edith thumbed back through the pages they'd read. Finally, he added, "I hope it's not true."

She placed the manuscript on the bedside table. "Why?"

"If it is true, Sabine's mother was raped as a child—she must have been fourteen when he was born. Worse, he's a wine sot who literally killed his own mother. And he was disrespectful to Seth... saying his part of the story didn't matter. Those years after the war must have been hell for Seth, and Sabine referred to them as *meanderings*."

"True." Edith stroked his face. "Sabine's an unreliable narrator when he tells about his drinking and his mother's death and Seth's struggles." She moved her hand down to Philip's chest.

He stroked her back, tracing her spine down to her buttocks. "I wonder if any alcoholic is ever straight about his drinking."

"You are. You told me about your blackouts. I don't think you're hiding your problem. But I think Sabine lies and believes himself."

Carmen. He should tell her about his blackout with Carmen and the *Valentine's night promise.*

But she raised herself up on one elbow and reached again for the manuscript, flipping through pages. "And I believe Sabine when he says the goodness in his father was destroyed. Listen to this part again: 'With his deep voice and his unspoiled language, Seth took me back to my youthful father's innocent love for his slave, and the events that eventually twisted Russell Richards into the monster whom I knew as my father.'" She placed the pages back on the table. "I also believe Sabine longs to understand his own family history, and he suffers pain, both physically and emotionally. But what I can't wait to read is how he tells Feevah's story. According to his preface, he spent seven years with Seth, learning the story of Feevah. How will he portray her life? Will it be accurate or tainted by his own biases?"

She kissed the curve of Philip's collarbone then sat up in the bed letting the sheet fall away. She began speaking faster, with excitement. "We could search the Waco 1920 census for their names. Sabine reveals birth years of his mother and himself, so we could also search genealogy sites to see if they're listed. And Peyronie's." She slid off the bed and pulled her phone from her jeans pocket. "Is that a real thing?"

Her bare flesh, when she plopped back beside him, made it hard for him to focus. He managed to say, "Not sure."

She sat with her thigh pressed against his chest.

"Yes. Look." She showed him her phone. "Peyronie's: it's exactly what Sabine says. Another element of truth." She pulled away to put the phone on the bedside table. "Such irony. I've searched my whole life for any clue of my genealogy, and you have this rich story." She slid back under the sheet and moved close to him. "I've done every DNA test on the market, just trying to link up with anyone who might be related." She turned her face so they could make eye contact and her hand slid down his belly. "Thank you for letting me read this."

"Edith, you can have anything of mine." Face to face, they gazed into each other's eyes. He grasped her buttocks and pulled her closer. "I'll hold nothing back from you." *Except Carmen.*

This time their lovemaking had the comfort of the familiar.

Later, when they were both spent, Edith said, "I need to leave. I have class in the morning."

"Will you have time to see me tomorrow—after you teach?"

"No. It's the English faculty quarterly meeting. They usually don't end until after ten. But the next night, I'm free."

He kissed her. "Just tell me the time and place. I'll be there."

"I'll text you." She got up and started pulling on her clothes. "Shall I take this manuscript and make copies? The old paper is so fragile for us to be handling it. I could get three made so each of your sisters could have one." Before he could answer, she shook her head. "No. What am I thinking? You shouldn't give this incredibly precious manuscript to a near stranger."

"Edith. You can have anything... anything I own. The only thing in my life that is precious is you." He watched her dress and missed her already.

Chapter Thirteen

At first, Philip ignored the *thump, thump* coming from inside a nearby car while he crossed the dark parking lot to go to his room.

It was almost ten, and he wanted a good night's sleep because the next day, he'd see Edith. At this moment he had one goal: bed.

Yawning, he pulled out his room key.

A muffled voice groaned.

Slowing his pace, he scanned the lot. No other people outside. Quiet, except for music seeping from the café. As usual, vehicles near the entrance were illuminated by the turquoise sign. Several other cars were parked farther away in the unlighted corner.

He froze to silence the noisy crunch of gravel beneath his boots.

"Please stop." A young woman's plea jolted him. "No. Don't."

Sprinting toward her voice in the dark corner, he didn't think about Dinah, but his ever-present, undercurrent of shame about her was as much a part of him as the burn scar on his forearm. Jagged, slick, ugly. Numb in places. Hypersensitive in others. A flaw always there.

He drew closer to the groans.

A flicker of motion stirred inside a battered, tan SUV. The sole of a bare foot pressed against the backseat side window. A narrow foot, a small woman's, pale in contrast with the car's dark interior. When he reached the car window, a naked butt hovered over the back seat... over the girl.

Philip jerked the handles of the back and front doors. *Locked.* "Let her go."

She cried out again. "Help me."

Philip grabbed a sharp-edged rock from the border of the parking lot and slammed it against a window. The blow did nothing. And the man inside, as if oblivious to sound, kept his rhythm going.

A roar exploded from Philip's chest as he struck harder, crumbling a section of glass so he could reach inside, unlock the door and yank it open.

The man shifted off the girl. "What the—"

Philip, straining hard, jerked the average-sized man out and hurled him into a bare-butt slide across the gravel.

Then, shoving down his rage to make his voice gentle, he bent to look in at the girl. "Are you okay?"

She had gathered herself into the far corner of the seat, with her knees drawn up under a loose skirt. Her head bowed over her phone, and her straw-colored hair almost hid her hands, but through the strands, he could see her thumbing something.

911, he thought.

But she started shaking too hard to wait for an answer to her call. The phone dropped to the floor.

The man groaned in pain. A zipper sounded.

Careful not to get too close to her, Philip leaned farther into the backseat. "I won't let him get you."

A shocking blow crashed onto Philip's back. He spun around and knocked the sharp-edged rock out of the rapist's hands and punched him in the ribs.

"Oomph." The man slumped forward but stayed on his feet.

Philip drew his fist back to bash again. Adrenaline fueled an overwhelming impulse to batter. *Stop. I have to stop.* He forced a deep breath, unclenched his fist, and pivoted the rapist around to clasp his wrists behind his back.

"If you touch her again, I'll kill you." Never before had Philip been in a fist fight, injured a person, or uttered a threat to kill.

Wheezing squeaks, along with the reek of stale tequila and onions, emanated from the man's mouth.

Pow.

A gunshot made both men flinch. The bullet had hit the ground a few feet away, broadcasting stings of gravel and dirt.

Standing near the open back door of the SUV, a woman aimed a Glock at the ground in front of the men. "Let him go," she whispered in a cigarette-rough voice, controlled and commanding. With her back to the dim light shining from inside the car, her face was shadowed.

Philip, still gripping the man's wrists, jerked his gaze from the woman to the backseat of the car, now empty. "Where's the girl?" But before the words left his lips, he realized the girl from the backseat had to be the woman now holding the gun. The same loose skirt billowed a little with the breeze. The same straw hair hung below her shoulders.

Voices drifted from the front of the café.

"That was gunfire."

"Call 911."

The woman stepped closer, holding the Glock steady with both hands. Her voice, louder this time, scratched like a match right before the flame bursts. "Let him go."

Philip said, "It's okay. You don't have to shoot him. I've got his hands."

The rapist tried to wrench free. "Damn you."

Now the woman raised the gun, clearly aiming at Philip's heart.

Realizing she must be in shock, Philip released the wrists and held out his hands, palms down in a calming gesture.

The rapist lurched toward the gun. "Give me that."

Philip kicked the man's legs out from under him, sending him face first into the gravel. With quick strides, Philip reached the stunned woman and grabbed the gun. He backed several feet away. "Don't move." It was the first gun he'd touched in twenty years. The heft of it released sickening memories of target practicing with his father.

The woman brought her hands to her face and lowered her head, and the attacker, who'd been trying to stand, slumped back to the ground and lay on his side. Distant sirens screamed.

Sweat broke out all over Philip's body. *The police will think I'm the bad guy, holding a gun on a crying woman and injured man. Nothing to do now but wait.*

Voices from the front of the café continued to hum with occasional phrases reaching him.

"He's got a gun."

"Someone's on the ground."

An ambulance stopped in front of the café. Seconds later a police car pulled into the same area and beamed a spotlight that scanned the parking lot, settling on the three. Philip slowly laid the gun on the ground and raised his hands high, bracing for loud-speaker orders, but nothing came. More sirens sounded in the distance.

The man on the ground raised up on one elbow. "Shoot this maniac. He tried to kill me." His face, now well-lit by the spotlight, was lopsided. Blood flowed from his nose, and his jaw

111

jutted to his left as if pointing out something. His eyes, a pale blue or gray, caught Philip studying him, and for the briefest instant, the rapist grinned as if this were an embarrassing joke.

The police will check my background. Thirty-five years old. No criminal record other than a DUI in his twenties. A permanent address that wasn't his own—he moved so often he used Lily's address for his driver's license and bank accounts. That wouldn't look good. There would be hard questions, but the police would understand after his story lined up with the victim's.

Three more squad cars skidded in. Doors flew open and officers approached, pointing guns at Philip. The woman dropped to the ground and pressed her forehead onto her drawn up knees.

Three officers circled Philip. The one facing him pointed a gun at his chest. The other two grabbed each of Philip's arms and shoved him face down to the ground. The urge to explain was strong, but everyone's adrenaline was too high. He'd wait. A foot pressed on Philip's back while someone cuffed his hands. Then someone put a plastic bag over his hands. He'd read enough crime novels to know what the bag meant. They'd find no gun powder residue on his hands, but they would find it on hers.

The ambulance pulled in closer and blocked his view of the couple, but he could still hear his moaning and her crying.

Two officers walked away from Philip, but the third one, who could have passed for a teenager, stood with his gun still drawn. "Don't move an inch."

The tension in the young man's voice kept Philip still. It would be stupid to get shot as a result of a nervous kid's reaction, especially when all of this could be easily cleared up.

Peering underneath the EMS van, Philip could see the rapist flat on his back, and the woman sitting on the ground beside him, her body visible from the shoulders down. A female officer squatted next to her, and a male EMS worker adjusted a stretcher.

Philip's breath hitched.

He blinked.

He couldn't believe what he was seeing.

The woman he had saved minutes ago had her hand resting on her rapist's chest.

Competing voices overflowed from EMS people, café customers, and police with their staticky shoulder-mounted radios.

Through the babel, the woman's shrill gasping words pierced Philip's gut. "That big guy was raping me, but Ralph fought him off. Then he shot at Ralph." Her voice rose to a thin scream. "He would have killed us if you hadn't come."

The man, still on the ground, whined, "That's right." Then he panted as if out of breath. "I went into the Hilltop just for a minute, and when I come out, he'd broke the window and was raping her." His speech was oddly slurred, and he continued to pant between words. "Right in the back seat."

Someone asked, "What about the gun?"

"I told him to get on out of here." Ralph slurred a couple of words then sped up and spat out syllables like rapid-fire bullets. "You can't rape my wife's own sister. And he said to me, 'No, you get out of here.' Then he pulled a gun. Shot right at me but I ducked just in time."

The woman said, "I begged him not to shoot us. I told him..." She gasped, childlike. "I told him Ralph has three children who need him. I said, 'Please, you can do anything to me, just don't shoot us.'"

The officer said, "Then what?"

The question hung unanswered as she wept, but finally, she

said, "We heard people from the café. I said, 'You can't shoot us now. People will see.'"

Philip's mind scrambled to rationalize her words. *She must be afraid of this guy... Ralph.* But the gun would be the flaw in their story. Philip had never owned a gun, so it would be registered to one of them. And her hands would have gunpowder residue.

The officer said, "Why were you two out here?"

"Ralph got a ride to my house after work so he could hook up my new window air-conditioning unit. My trailer gets so hot. And I made him some frozen margaritas in my blender, but I didn't drink because I knew I'd drive him home." Her voice, a little calmer, still trembled... and now sounded familiar. "When we came through town, he saw his neighbor's car parked here, and he said to stop so he could get a ride the rest of the way home. Ralph's thoughtful that way."

"That's right." Ralph still panting and slurring his words. "I didn't want her to drive all the way out to my house, so I said wait right here while I check to see if he's inside. I said lock up the doors so no one bothers you. I made sure they was locked before I left." He let out a loud howl, gasped several times and said, "I got broken ribs."

"How did your ribs get hurt?" an EMS worker asked.

A new officer approached Philip before Ralph's mumbled answer could be deciphered.

The officer tugged Philip's arm. "Let's go."

Philip, getting to his feet, leaned farther around the front of the ambulance to see his accusers. He'd never gotten a look at the woman's face.

Carmen.

Same thin face and charcoal slashed brows. But her hair was no longer black.

Nudging Philip in the opposite direction, the officer said, "We're going to that car."

When the officer opened the car door, Philip said, "They're lying."

"Everybody lies. Get in."

Philip ducked into the backseat. "Will you question her without the guy being there? She'll have a different story. She was calling for help when I stopped him. She must be afraid of him. And will you test her hands? She's the one who fired the gun. I took it away because the guy was trying to grab it."

"We'll get your statement at the office." The officer started the car.

Another officer got into the passenger seat, twisted his face toward the back, recited the Miranda rights, and emphasized, "You're under arrest for assault, rape, illegal use of a gun, and vandalism of property."

They pulled out of the parking lot past a group of Hilltop regulars congregated near the porch. Al's tall form stood out—shaking his head and waving his arms.

At the small jail, a few blocks away, Philip went through a long intake process including fingerprints, mug shots, DNA cheek swabs, and an adhesive gun powder residue test on his hands. A jail attendant gave him an orange jump suit and paper shoes to change into before escorting him to a cell. Bed, toilet, sink, cinder block walls painted light green. No windows.

A thin pillow on the bed was dented with the imprint of a head. Clearly the sheets had not been changed since the previous detainee had lain there. The cell across from his was empty.

"When you get a statement from the woman, will you come tell me?" Philip asked.

"Up to the sheriff," the attendant said, turning to leave.

Philip shook out the sheets, flipped the pillow over and lay on the narrow bed. By now, Edith had probably heard. And his new life with her may have already ended.

Hours later a couple of officers strolled in. "Okay, Mr. Richards. Your attorney is here."

Attorney? He hadn't called one, didn't even know one, but he followed the officers to a room with a glass door, which had embedded bars.

Inside, a tiny elderly woman and Al sat at a metal table in the center. Al, in rumpled khaki shirt and jeans, approached and clapped Philip on the back. "Damn, I'm sorry we couldn't get anything done sooner. Hate you were stuck in here all night."

"Thanks for coming."

The woman, in a stiff black suit and snowy white shirt, offered her hand without moving away from the table. "I'm Nelda Perkins, retired district attorney, and I'm offering to represent you." Her clear, firm voice clashed with her frail appearance.

Philip stepped closer to shake her hand, and Al explained, "Nelda's friends with my uncle. And she got things moving." Al grinned like a schoolboy and rocked on his feet. "She knows everyone in the county system."

Nelda nodded once. Her gray hair in its tall updo gave her nod an assertive air. "Do you accept me as your legal counsel?"

"Yes, ma'am." Philip wondered, should he tell her only what he'd told the police or should he also talk about his bar conversation with Carmen—when she had black hair?

"Good. Sit. Let's get started. We have a few hours before your arraignment." Uncapping a pen and adjusting her yellow legal pad she called in a surprisingly loud voice, "Oscar, take Al

116

out while I consult with my client. I'll call you when I want him back."

The guard opened the door, and his and Al's footsteps echoed down the hollow hallway.

"Start from the beginning."

For the next half hour, they covered every minute after he walked out of the café. Nelda picked at details and took copious notes, but she never asked if he'd been connected to Carmen before the incident, so Philip didn't mention his bar encounter. Whatever Valentine's grudge Carmen had harbored, he was innocent of anything illegal last night in the parking lot.

The room went silent after Philip finished. He was about to ask what happens next when Nelda seemed to anticipate his question and went into rapid-fire recitation.

"At the arraignment, we'll plead not guilty. They'll let you out on bail. They have a flimsy case. They'll probably charge you with something like assault and vandalism of property, but I think they'll hold off on rape until they get the SANE report."

"SANE?" Philip asked.

"Sexual Assault Nurse Examiner report. They took her to Austin last night, has a hospital with one of the best SANE departments in the state. It might be a couple of weeks before they get the results. Since they have other charges against you, they'll wait and decide about rape later." Without missing a beat, she ratcheted up her volume. "Oscar, bring Al back."

"Yes, ma'am," came from a distant voice.

Then for the first time, she smiled. "I don't want you to worry about a thing." She tapped her index finger on her notes. "You were in the wrong place at the wrong time just trying to do the right thing. Their story doesn't even make sense. You'll be freed in a few hours. Then we'll strategize on getting the charges dismissed."

Al came in as she finished talking. "Damn right." He clapped a large hand on Philip's shoulder.

Nelda scooted her chair back. "You'll need clothes to put on after the arraignment. They might keep yours for evidence. Want to give Al permission to go to your home? Or to purchase what you need?"

"I'm doing a monthly rental at the Hilltop," he said to Nelda. Then to Al, "Will they let you in my room? Number six."

Al shrugged one shoulder. "Probably. If not, I'll pick some stuff up. Size?"

"Thirteen-and-a-half shoe, XL shirt, thirty-six by thirty-four jeans," Philip said.

"Same as me except..." Al laughed a single *ha* and patted his large belly. "...ain't seen thirty-six in many a year!"

Nelda stood and took Al's arm. Her towering hair reached just above his elbow.

Philip's load lightened for the first time since this nightmare began. He looked back at his unlikely rescuers while the guard waited by the door. "Thank you both for everything."

Al talked the maid into letting him into Philip's room to get clothes, and everything in court went as Nelda had predicted. Philip was released on $15,000 bail, which he paid in full without going through a bondsman. Nelda said the only reason he wasn't released without bail was that he moved around a lot and was living in a motel. By three that afternoon, he was free, and Al drove him to his room.

Philip phoned Edith as soon as he was alone in his room. As he expected, she'd already heard about the incident. He explained what happened just as he had to Nelda, but this time while he told the story, his stomach clenched with guilt and fear. Guilt for not mentioning his first encounter with Carmen and fear that Edith would back away from him now.

She was silent after he finished.

Trying to make it easy for her, he said, "If you don't want me to come today, I understand. If you want to wait until this is cleared up, it's okay."

She exhaled and stayed silent. He was about to repeat his offer when she said, "I'm so sorry this happened to you, but it changes nothing between us. More than ever, I want you to come. Now. Bring an overnight bag. Stay the weekend with me in Austin."

Chapter Fourteen

Edith's one-bedroom apartment was full of books—stacked on the floor, shelved to the ceiling, and scattered on tabletops.

"I like books," she said in a small voice. "Maybe too much." She looked around her living room, as if seeing it anew.

He pulled her into his arms and kissed her. He loved the way she crawled up his body each time they came together. More than he wanted his next breath, he wanted to be inside her again. He wanted her flesh against his. And from the way she pushed against him, she was ready as well.

Still holding her, he found his way to the bedroom. This time there was little preamble. Their bodies were ready for each other.

Later, Edith said, "Hey, are you really okay?"

"Now, I'm more than okay."

"But that awful scene in the parking lot—the night in jail."

His body tensed. "My biggest concern... I don't want anything... to affect what we have."

She pulled him close and peered into his eyes. "It won't. I promise. I just want you to be okay. I hate that you've been accused."

He kissed her, then whispered, "How did I get so lucky to meet you?"

"We're both lucky." She kissed him back. "Want to eat now?" He let her go reluctantly as she slid from the bed and grabbed a robe. "I froze our enchiladas from the Hilltop, and I'll pour some wine while they microwave."

Philip pulled on his jeans and followed to her small kitchen area, where he settled on a bar stool. He braced himself for more questions about the parking lot incident, questions that would lead to Carmen. He was ready to disclose his blackout mystery of a Valentine's promise.

But while she turned on the microwave and opened a bottle of wine, she talked about the manuscript. "I'm sorry but I couldn't wait to start reading the story of Feevah. It seems real, as if it actually grew from years that Seth spent with Feevah and later relayed to Sabine."

"You think?"

"Why do you doubt it?"

Philip raked his fingers through his hair. "I can't stop remembering... this whole story is coming from Sabine, who rationalized killing his own mother and blamed his behavior on 'poorly fermented wine.' Why should I believe anything he wrote?" *Any more than I believed my father or grandfather.* "He could have twisted Seth's story. Seth could have told Sabine that Russell beat and raped Feevah. I think Sabine would have left that out."

"You know," Edith leaned with her back against the counter and faced him, "that's exactly what classic American history is—a chronicle reported by white men who see things through their own lenses." She turned away and took wine glasses from a cabinet. "Actually, we all see things through our own lenses."

The microwave pinged, she pulled away to check the food,

and then gave it more time. She poured red into their glasses. "Hope this is okay—it's all I have."

He kissed her hand and took the glass. "It's perfect."

She smiled. "You haven't even tasted it. Are you sex smittened? Enough sex you'll agree to anything?"

"Nope, not sex smittened." He took a drink and set the glass down. He slipped one hand inside her robe and rested his open palm on her heart. He lifted her chin. For a long moment, with their gazes fixed on each other, he held still with her heart beating into his palm. "I'm Edith smittened."

After eating, they crawled into bed like a couple accustomed to sleeping together. Philip, lying on his side, curled around her.

Loosening her braids with her fingers, she said, "Okay if I read to you? The part I've already read?"

Dread filled him. "I remember the first line... doesn't make sense. A slave standing in an auction line wouldn't be thinking about loving a strange white man."

She snuggled with her back against his chest and held one of his hands against her breast. "We'll have to decide whether Sabine twisted Seth's story." With that, she began to read aloud the next section of the manuscript.

Chapter Fifteen

Sabine Richards' manuscript. 1859

Feevah never thought about loving a white man before Russell Richards. She first saw him while she was standing in the auction line sick with fear that her daughters would be sold away from her.

The day before, Robin, her mate of eleven years, had been sold to the railroad. She had been both relieved and terrified. Relieved, because as much as she depended on Robin, she was more afraid of him than she was of the masters. Robin was a pus-filled boil of rage needing a place to spill out, and most of the time that place was on Feevah and their two daughters. But with her relief to be free of Robin's beatings came terror that her daughters might also be sold away from her. The auctioneers had sold Robin with no mention of grouping him with his family.

Now, the next day, waiting with over a hundred other slaves, mostly women and children, she furtively watched buyers gather on the other side of the busy Chattanooga street. The railroad buyers were gone along with the strong, young men they had purchased the day before. Most of today's crowd looked like farmers and families. She prayed for a kind family who would want a strong, hardworking woman with two young daughters.

Feevah's scan of the buyers froze, and the fine hairs all over her flesh twisted because one man in the group was staring at her. Although she had never seen him before, she felt a sense of recognition, and for a moment there were no thoughts in her mind other than the awareness that his gaze was upon her.

The dirty, bone-thin old woman in chains standing next to Feevah pointed at him with a shaky finger and whispered, "That's Russell Richards. He's the young one that ain't mean." She had been ranting nonsensically most of the morning, so Feevah wasn't sure whether these comments were reliable, but the words were enough to yank her back to reality.

Feevah forced her eyes away from him and knelt down to whisper to her daughters, "Remember, stay beside me with your faces cast down." The girls, with serious expressions, nodded. "And speak only if the masters speak to you. And answer with 'masser.'" Still kneeling, she pulled them both close to her and mouthed, "Please, God, please let us stay together."

Ten-year-old Dorcas, with eyes of fear, was too much aware of the evils in the world, and she kept her body attached to her mother. Four-year-old Grace, usually full of antics, was serious but not fully aware that this bright, sunny day could become the darkest one of her life.

A deep voice broke into their embrace. "Is this Feevah?"

Feevah raised her eyes to find Russell Richards standing over her. At first, she was too startled to answer, but even in that moment, a part of her was calm with the sense that she had known he would come to her.

"Are you Feevah?"

"Yes, Masser." She quickly stood.

"I've heard good things about you." He smiled directly into her eyes.

In a rushing stream of words, she said, "I'm a hard worker. I can do housework as good as any woman and field work as good as any man." Feevah was close to six feet tall and was able to speak directly into Russell's face. "And my two girls are good helpers. They don't eat much and do more work than most grown hands."

A worried expression erased his grin. Russell looked down at the little girls as though he hadn't been aware of them.

"You won't be sorry, Masser, if you buy all three of us." Each of her hands grasped one of the girls' shoulders. "I swear to God it will be the best buy of your life."

She thought she saw kindness in his eyes when he raised them up from her girls, but she feared her desperation was making her see something that wasn't really there. How could he have heard "good things" about her? Feevah knew she was smart and hardworking, but it had never occurred to her that masters might recognize her qualities and talk about her.

"Russell, honey, come on. They're about to begin." A creamy-skinned, dark-haired young woman, resembling a child playing dress-up in a bright yellow frock, called to him from the buyers' area.

His gaze still locked with Feevah's, Russell raised a hand in acknowledgment to the child-woman. He nodded once to Feevah and turned away.

In rhythm with his retreating steps, the old woman in chains began to chant. "He gonna be the death a you, he gonna be the death a you, he gonna be the death a you."

Feevah's oldest daughter began to cry.

Feevah pulled Dorcas closer and whispered to the old woman, "Shut your mouth, you're scaring my girls."

"He gonna bed you and be the death a you."

"That's crazy. Even if he buys me, look at those pretty young girls all around him. He'll want nothing from a rough, hard slave like me except work."

Throughout this interchange, Russell spoke with the auctioneer who looked in Feevah's direction. There was no doubt. The two men were talking about her. Russell passed something to the auctioneer, who slipped whatever it was into his pocket.

The auctioneer called out, "Feevah, Dorcas, and Grace. On the block."

The overseer in charge of the lineup approached and grabbed Feevah by the arm. She quickly scooped up Grace and held Dorcas's hand. The three of them were instantly on the block.

The auctioneer shouted, "Feevah, about twenty-five, cooks, sews, barn work, field work. Dorcas age ten, Grace age four, all bred on Fuller Plantation in east Tennessee. Don't need no chains. Who'll open the bid at $200 for this group?"

After a flash of a hand signal from Russell, the auctioneer said, "$200... Who'll give me $210?" The buyers standing in the auction area were quickly shuffling around, getting their bearings to take part in the auction. "Two hundred, once, twice. Sold to Russell Richards."

Disapproving murmurs arose from onlookers. "Hold on a minute, we ain't even ready," someone complained.

"Auction was supposed to start an hour ago," the auctioneer retorted. "Sally, on the block."

Feevah's eyes brimmed with tears of relief as she whispered to her daughters that they were not going to be separated.

"Are you sure, Mama?" Dorcas asked.

"Yes, baby, we get to stay together."

The overseer grabbed Feevah's arm and steered her and the girls to a table wedged against the side of the livery stable. "Wait here."

A man sitting at the makeshift office was writing in a ledger. Russell quickly arrived and counted out money.

"That was slick." The ledger man chuckled. "Just like how your daddy does business. When he wants something, he gets it one way or the other."

"That's right," said Russell as he held out cash.

"But your daddy's gonna tan your butt for buying them kids. You know they're just gonna slow things down." He paused to fill in the ledger. "Your daddy ain't gonna like what you done, and I wouldn't want to be around when he finds out."

"You know him well." Russell wasn't laughing at the prediction nor did he seem to regret his own actions. In a straightforward manner, he acknowledged the truth in the statement and waited for the ledger entry to be completed.

Finally, the ledger man laid down his pen, took Russell's money, and said, "Well, I guess that's what he gets for leaving a kid in charge of the place while he's wheeling and dealing back in Virginia. How long's he been gone now?"

"Almost a year," Russell said as he took the bill of sale and folded it. "Is that it?"

"That's it. They's yours now."

Russell turned to his new slaves. "Feevah, come with me." He pointed toward an unhitched wagon nearby.

"Climb in," he said when they reached the back of the wagon, which was already loaded with several large bags labeled *flour*.

"Yes, Masser." Feevah quickly boosted the girls in and then followed. The five-by-eight-foot wooden wagon, although open at the back, had sides four-feet high. When the three sat down, the outside world was unseen.

"Wait here," Russell said as he walked quickly back toward the crowd. Dust puffed up with each step he took.

"Yes, Masser." Feevah peeked over the side. The child-woman in yellow, accompanied now by two other young women, stepped away from the crowd to meet him. The three were giggling and chatting, and Russell grinned from one to the other. The child-woman clung to his arm, and he covered her hand with his own.

The sound of crying drew Feevah's eyes across the street to the line of slaves where she and her daughters had stood a few minutes earlier. A little boy was being sold away from his mother. The overseer, carrying a wide leather strap, approached the boy to keep him on the block. The mother fell to the ground where she was tied to a post.

"Mama, look!" Grace had licked her pointing finger and was drawing designs in the fine layer of flour dust covering part of the wagon's wood floor.

Even Dorcas started drawing her own designs.

Feevah felt herself relax so much that she laughed aloud at the girls' creations, and she wished the wagon had a back closure, so their little world could be completely private.

Dorcas suggested to Grace that they draw a house and garden in the flour. Grace, eager for any game, watched as Dorcas drew the rooms in the house and explained what was in each room. Using two fingers on each hand as legs, the girls imagined themselves in the house walking with their fingers from room to room, carrying out various chores.

Feevah remembered the biscuits wrapped in a cloth inside her pocket. A kindly cook had slipped them to her the day before. "These is for the children to eat along your way," he'd said. Feevah had been saving them for an emergency, but this moment called for celebration. She took off the shirt she was wearing over her dress. Using the shirt as a table cloth, she covered a flour bag and placed two biscuits on top. Grace squealed with delight at the unexpected treat. She and Dorcas scooted over to the "table" to eat the biscuits.

"Aren't we lucky, Mama?" Dorcas said.

"Yes, the Lord is good to us." Feevah gave silent thanks, and arranging a flour bag to work as a pillow, she lay on her side with her back to the opening, so the girls couldn't fall out of the wagon, and no one could get in without alerting her. For the first time since they had been taken from the Fuller Plantation, she let herself relax. She fell asleep to the sounds of the girls' gentle voices playing house in their world sketched in flour on the wagon floor.

As darkness fell the girls lay next to their mother and the three of them slept for hours until Grace woke fussing with the need to relieve herself. Feevah peeked over the side and saw no one. Faint voices and light drifted from a saloon far down the street. She helped the girls out of the wagon, and the three of them squatted in the darkness on the side of the livery stable. Next, Feevah lowered a bucket into the well in front of the livery stable. The water smelled and tasted good, so they washed their hands and faces, and using their hands as cups they drank as much as they could hold.

Chilled by the water and night air, Feevah found two blankets under the driver's bench of the wagon. She worried that Master might not want her to use them, but keeping her daughters warm was worth the risk. She also discovered a tarp near the front of the wagon bed. It was the right size to cover their five-by-eight world. She smoothed the tarp over the back of the wagon to provide a roof in case they were still in the wagon when dew formed. When the three positioned themselves back into their bed, Feevah covered them with the blankets.

As the girls slumbered, Feevah lay awake, staring up at the tarp. The noise from the saloon died down, and she could hear a woman wailing with grief for her sold child. Feevah wondered what had become of Russell. She had never heard of a man abandoning a wagon load of property, but after the ledger keeper's warning, had Russell decided to resell her and her daughters? Maybe he was searching for a buyer for her daughters.

And, Robin, in this dark night, where was he? Would God punish her for being relieved that she was no longer with him? Her relentless worries, the crying mother in the distance, the hard floor of the wagon kept her awake as her girls slept against the front of her body.

Shortly before dawn she woke Dorcas and Grace so they could relieve themselves before daylight took away privacy. This time at the well she soaked the rag she kept tied around her waist, and the three of them walked into brush bordering the animal pens in the back. They washed with the wet rag. Feevah broke off pine needles from a tree and instructed the girls to clean their teeth. Even though it was dark and damp, the children enjoyed the adventure, but as they started back to the wagon, they smelled bacon frying. Grace began to cry with hunger.

Feevah had one biscuit left, so she lifted the girls into the wagon and gave each of them half. She seated the girls on the back end of the wagon with their feet dangling while they ate. She straightened the wagon by folding the blankets and putting them back under the driver's bench, accordion folding the tarp back to the front of the wagon bed, and tying her wet rag on a nail head to dry. Next, she straightened the girls' clothes and retied the kerchiefs on their heads. Then she sat next to the girls and told them stories as the sun rose.

As daylight brought the town into full view, Feevah continued the stories, and she tried to keep the girls from looking in the direction where they had been lined up for the auction because the skinny old woman was asleep on the ground, still chained to a hitching post near the auction block.

"Good morning." Russell approached quickly from behind them. "Who's hungry?" He handed Feevah a flat pan covered with a cloth. He raised the cloth to show sliced bread with scrambled eggs sandwiched between the slices. Several fat strips of fried bacon were beside the sandwiches. "Can you girls eat this?" he teased with a friendly wink.

"Yes, Masser!" exclaimed Grace. Her feet were kicking back and forth in such excitement Feevah placed her hand on the child's knees to prevent her from propelling herself off the wagon.

"Good!" Russell laughed. "I'll be back later. Enjoy your breakfast."

"Thank you, Masser," Feevah said as he turned to leave. For a moment he grinned, and his clear blue eyes met hers. Then Feevah rediscovered that it wasn't only her fear drawing her to him. He was a beautiful man.

While they ate, Russell readied the wagon for the trip. He set two buckets of water in the back. Next, to the girls' delight, he delivered a two-foot-square cage containing about twenty chirping chicks. Then he brought a bag of chick feed, and said, "I wonder who can feed these chicks?" Finally, he led a pair of horses out of the stable and hitched them to the wagon. Both girls' excitement mounted with each exuberant pass Russell made.

After they finished eating, Feevah stood beside the wagon and waited to hand the cloth and now-washed pan to Russell when he might be ready to return them to their owner. He approached her with a small cloth bundle. "These are cookies for the children to have on the ride." He nodded toward the girls. "Let them sit in the front end of the wagon, and you sit up on the driver's bench." By this time the wagon was fairly full, but there was an open space large enough for the girls in between the baby chicks and the driver's bench.

He took the pan and cloth from her and walked down the street. Several people stopped and greeted him. While Feevah helped the excited girls get into their assigned place, she surreptitiously observed his interchanges with the town's people. They respected him and sought his opinions even though he was very young. By the time Feevah climbed onto the driver's bench, Russell was bounding toward the wagon with a link of rope. He went to the back and doubled the rope across the end to secure any of the load from shifting during the ride.

Before he finished tying, the child-woman from the day before joined him. Feevah was turned toward the couple while talking to her daughters, and she overheard bits of their conversation. The girl, in the morning light had a sweet, delicate face, and she wanted an exact statement as to when Russell would be returning to town. He teasingly evaded her questions, and finally, when he finished roping the rear of the wagon, he led her to the side of the stable.

He lifted her off her feet and kissed her full on the mouth. Feevah heard him say, "Don't worry, Francine, I'll be back as soon as I get Grandma settled in with the new help." Then he set her down and turned toward the wagon.

He climbed onto the seat, readied the reins, and signaled the horses to move. In a few minutes, they were out of town heading west. The girls rode contentedly, poking their fingers through the wire cage to touch the yellow fluff.

Feevah felt alive. They were going to a new place with a young man who seemed kind and full of positive vitality. A young man who had a grandma.

On the narrow bench, their bodies were close, but he seemed not to notice the places where their thighs and shoulders touched and the way his arm pressed against her at times as he guided the horses.

Russell stopped the wagon shortly after they were out of town. "I need to adjust the harnesses and check one of the hooves."

Her eyes followed the lines of his prominent thigh muscles as he moved around the horses, squatting and bending to examine hooves and harnesses. He had muscular shoulders and arms, but more noticeable were his powerful legs. He was taller and fuller bodied than most men.

She forced her eyes back toward her daughters.

For a time after he finished with the horses, they rode in silence, and he seemed to be watching closely to see whether the horse was showing signs of favoring a leg. Feevah understood why Francine and the other young women were attracted to him. His blond hair brushed back from his face, curled down to his collar, and his strong profile stood out with a curved nose and prominent forehead.

As they rode in silence, Feevah reflected that she had never felt this pull toward Robin. She had been about thirteen when they were paired on the Fuller Plantation. He was the best young man on the plantation, and until he started beating her, she was happy to be with him. She had wanted to please him and have his children, but she had never noticed a man as she was noticing Master. She wondered, "Dear Lord, what is Your reason for making me know this beautiful man?"

The old woman's words came back to her. "He got a hold on you." Feevah determined that she would keep her eyes from settling on Russell Richards.

"Well, I think we're set for the ride," Russell assured himself. "Now, Feevah, let's talk about you."

His sudden comment ambushed her, and she turned to see him smiling at her in his direct way. Her resolve of moments earlier to keep her gaze from settling on him was broken. Each time he smiled, she was struck anew by the warmth in his eyes.

Russell continued, "Brother Tune told me about you. He said on all his rounds, he'd never seen a woman more capable of running a house and caring for folks than you. The last time he stopped by to see Grandma, he told me Fuller was about to sell you, and you'd be just the one to take care of Grandma."

Brother Tune Wesley Stone had visited the Fuller home many times over the years. However, she was surprised to know he had noticed her capabilities, and even more surprised that he would think to recommend her.

"How long were you on the Fuller Plantation?"

With her many years of living inside the Fuller home, Feevah was comfortable talking to masters. Other slaves often called upon her to be a spokesperson, and it was easy for her to tell her history. But even with her comfort, she tensed, knowing her next words would be the start of her relationship with her new master. She could choose to speak in his language, or she could restrain herself to the vernacular slaves used with masters. With her stomach knotted, she weighed the choice. Somehow, she sensed this kind young man would not punish her for speaking in his language.

"I was born on the Fuller Plantation and was raised to work tobacco until I was about fifteen."

"Is that when you started running the house?" Russell asked.

"No, Master." She had easily slipped away from the expected pronunciation, *masser*. "I was moved into the house then, but I didn't run it at first. I had been paired with Robin and had just given birth to Dorcas when Mrs. Fuller had her first baby."

Her voice had a soft strength and truthfulness that held a listener's attention. "Mrs. Fuller was frail and had no milk. A few days after her daughter Ruth was born, Master Fuller brought Dorcas and me into the house to help feed baby Ruth."

Russell, as if thrown off balance, stayed quiet with his eyes straight ahead. For the first time since she'd met him, his easy demeanor seemed humbled.

"Mrs. Fuller was weak, but she wanted to be near her baby, so she had us moved into her bedroom. For the first few months, she watched as I nursed Ruth. Over time Mrs. Fuller became attached to Dorcas and me. After Ruth could have been weaned, Mrs. Fuller still kept us in the house."

Feevah hesitated before telling the next part, weighing whether this new master would value or resent what she was about to reveal. Again, she decided to risk the truth.

"Mrs. Fuller taught me how to read and do figures, so she could give me directions for running the household and the garden. Some days when she was too tired to get out of bed, she would have me read aloud to her for hours."

Russell had continued to look straight ahead while Feevah spoke, but now as though he felt her concern about revealing these skills, he turned to her and smiled.

"When Ruth was almost three, Mrs. Fuller gave birth to a baby boy, but she was even weaker during this confinement. Jeremiah was born too early, and the midwife, thinking he was dead, told me to take him away."

Feevah paused and looked back at her daughters. As she had expected, they were attentive, ready to hear again about Jeremiah's miracle. Russell, with a questioning look, glanced back at them as well. Then all three sets of eyes focused on Feevah.

"Jeremiah was so small you could hold him in one hand." Feevah held out her hand as if she were holding the baby. "It broke my heart to see such a tiny, helpless, perfect baby with no life in him. I began to rub his little body, hoping he would feel comfort in this world after leaving his mama too soon. After a while he moved as I touched him. At first, I wasn't sure he was really alive, but he began crying and kept moving."

Russell, caught up in the story, turned back to the girls, smiling this time. Again, all three sets of eyes fixed on Feevah, lit with the moment of joy.

"To feed him I took a glass tube out of one of Mrs. Fuller's fancy lanterns. I squeezed my milk into the tube and dripped it into his mouth drop by drop. As little as he was, he was always ready for milk. After Mrs. Fuller understood that her baby was struggling for life, she again had us moved into her room. His first bed was in a bread-loaf pan lined with cotton next to his mama. For most of his first year, I stayed in her room and cared for her and Jeremiah."

Russell spoke with a low, husky voice. "I can see why they valued you so much."

"After this second birthing, no matter what we did for Mrs. Fuller, she grew weaker. On Jeremiah's third birthday, she told me she was at peace with whatever happens because I would be caring for her babies. When my second baby daughter was born, I asked Mrs. Fuller to allow me to name my baby after her."

"That's me!" Grace piped in.

Dorcas gasped and looked fearfully toward Russell. Feevah also had a moment of discomfort hoping Russell would not chastise Grace for speaking out.

But Russell threw back his head and laughed aloud. "So that's you! Are you sure?" he said.

"Yes, Masser, that's me!" Grace replied, standing up in the back of the moving wagon, almost losing her balance. Everyone laughed as Dorcas steadied Grace and helped her sit back down.

Feevah said, "So, my Grace became her namesake." She didn't

like telling the next part. "Mrs. Fuller passed in her sleep when Grace was a month old." She stopped, and everyone stayed quiet as if paying tribute to the young mother who died.

Russell asked, "Is that when Fuller moved you out?"

"No, sir. Mrs. Fuller died almost four years ago, and I kept running the house and caring for the children until a few months ago."

"So, you ran it for about eight or nine years?"

"Yes, sir." Feevah wasn't sure what Brother Tune had told Russell about why they'd been sold, but she decided to offer an explanation. "Master married again, and his new wife brought her own housemaids. Two weeks ago, Master came out to the quarters with men from the auction company and said he was going to sell Robin, Dorcas, Grace, and me. He very kindly allowed each of us to take a bundle of possessions and to wear good boots and layers of clothes.

"We walked with the auction company for more than a week picking up more slaves along the way. We arrived in Chattanooga three days ago. Robin and most of the men were sold to the railroad company on the first day. And, Master, you know the rest. I am most thankful that you purchased us, and I promise that you will be glad. Whatever work you have for us, we will do with gratitude."

Feevah liked to tell stories and believed a story's strength came not from the teller but from the ring of truth. But even her value of truth was not strong enough to allow her to tell everything. She left out her suspicion that the new wife's rejection of her was only part of the reason for their sudden sale. Feevah knew Robin's rebelliousness was becoming more apparent to everyone. A few weeks earlier, Feevah had stepped outside the quarters to pick some mint, and she caught Robin in an angry, dangerous act. Mr. Fuller had apparently given him some directions about packing the tobacco; as the master turned his back and walked away, Robin, with his face enraged, kicked hard at him. For a moment Feevah was sure Robin was about to kill Fuller. She gasped and almost screamed, but she stopped herself when she realized the kick didn't connect, and Fuller didn't see it. Feevah didn't notice anyone else watching, but she knew that anyone in the household near a window might have seen Robin's hateful pretense.

Feevah remained silent, hoping Russell would assure her that she and her girls would get to stay together, that they would have a safe place, and that the mean daddy would not be a threat. However, as comfortable as she was in speaking to masters, she knew such questions would be inappropriate.

For a while the only sounds were the horses' hooves, the rumble of the wagon wheels turning, and the soft peeps of the chicks.

Feevah's story seemed to leave Russell in an unfamiliar place, but finally he spoke with new somberness. "Your job will be to run the house and take care of my grandmother. Our place is smaller than the Fuller Plantation, only 140 acres and seven field hands right now. Grandma used to run the house and garden by herself, and she's still strong and healthy enough in body, but the doctor says she's..." He paused, frowned, and rolled his shoulders as if trying to nudge something off. "...feeble-minded. You won't have to worry about feeding the field hands; Seth takes care of them. You'll just take care of the house and Grandma. Sometimes she's her old self, sometimes she's like a child, and sometimes she cries for hours." He faced Feevah. "I just want her treated well and kept safe."

The ride to the Richards' farm took half the day, and when they finally turned down a road leading up to a two-story stone house, Feevah was amazed by the orderliness and by the fact that several white people, including children, were out working in the gardens. The house was surrounded by neat outbuildings, white fences, animal pens, beehives, and irrigation ditches leading to orchards and gardens.

Russell said, "That's the home of the Schmidt family—Germans—our nearest neighbors. They only have a few acres—do all the work themselves." Feevah took that to mean they owned no slaves. "A nice thing about our place is unless you know where our right-of-way is, you'd probably never find it." His tone turned almost regretful. "The only people who ever come to us are those who've been shown the way."

They passed the Germans' house and slowed down when parallel to the barn; instead of staying on the road, Russell veered to the right down a narrower lane, almost hidden from sight by thick grape vines hanging from arbors.

"We give the Germans the profit from an acre of tobacco each year to allow us right-of-way."

Beside the lane, a child about nine or ten years old lugged a thick shoulder pole with two large buckets of water hanging from it. The buckets were so deep, they almost hit the ground as the child trudged from one grapevine to the next, watering the roots.

Feevah gasped softly. "What a heavy load for such a small boy."

"That's not a boy. That's Tenny, their only daughter."

After they passed the grape arbor, Feevah looked back at Tenny who was now standing in the middle of the lane, watching them with a blank expression. Feevah smiled and raised one hand in a wave, but the girl only stared with stony eyes that made Feevah shiver and feel inexplicably sad.

The horses sped up as if sensing they were nearly home, and in minutes the Richards' house became visible in the distance. Russell pointed out the locations of the fields, curing houses, barns, and slave quarters. A woman sat in a straight armchair on the front porch of the one-story, unpainted house, framed by sparse elm trees on either side.

"That's Grandma sitting on the porch. I guess Mrs. Schmidt is inside. She's a relative of the Germans, who stays when I have to leave."

Russell waved at his grandmother, but the old lady stared toward a point far beyond the wagon and didn't respond to the wave. Her body was thin to the point of emaciation, and her long gray hair hung straight down on her shoulders. She wore no shoes, and even from the distance, her loosely fitting, pink print dress appeared faded and dirty.

"Hey, Grandma, I'm home," Russell called to her and waved again as they came closer. There was no response. Mrs. Richards sat still, her hands resting on the chair arms, her gaze unwavering. He waited a few moments and called to her again. This time she gave a startled grunt and began to wail loudly. She became so agitated her chair shook.

"It's all right, Grandma, I'll be right there. Just hold on."

Feevah gasped. The old woman was tied with cloth ropes around both ankles and wrists. As the wagon rolled into the yard, Mrs. Richards jerked the chair with such ferocity that it seemed likely to fall over with her. The instant Russell reined in, he and Feevah leapt to the ground and bounded up the porch steps to steady her. While Feevah untied the ropes at her ankles, Russell freed her hands. The old woman stood, wrapped her arms around her grandson, and wept, turning her face from side to side against his chest. Feevah quietly edged back to the wagon.

Mrs. Schmidt came out onto the porch. "I know you don't want her tied, but I have no choice." Her heavy German accent made her words difficult to understand. "She keep running off. At first, I thought she wanted to go after you, but twice she call out, 'Thomas,' so she thought it was your papa who left."

Mrs. Schmidt's monologue intensified Grandma's agitation, and several times she raised a fist and yelled, "No, no. Get her out of here."

Russell motioned for Mrs. Schmidt to be quiet as he called out, "Seth, where are you?"

Seth, a smallish adult slave with a dragging, crippled gait, was already waiting by the wagon anticipating Russell's plan. Feevah had lifted her daughters and the chick cage from the wagon. She placed the cage under a shade tree near the porch.

When Seth caught Russell's attention, Russell said, "Oh, there you are. Take Mrs. Schmidt home."

Mrs. Schmidt went into the house to gather her belongings. By the time she came back, Seth, using only his right hand, had placed a stool on the ground next to the wagon, so Mrs. Schmidt could easily step up to the bench. As he scuttled to the other side of the wagon and climbed up to take the reins, he clearly had only partial use of his left arm and leg.

With the wagon rolling away, Mrs. Schmidt yelled back to Russell, "I couldn't get her to eat nothing, and I couldn't get her to take bath, and I find dirty clothes hidden all over house, and she didn't sleep more than two hours last night, and yesterday morning I catch her outside without a stitch on."

Russell did his best to get his grandmother's attention onto the newcomers. "Look, Grandma, look what we've got." He nudged her toward the chicks and the girls.

Mrs. Richards' alert glance and her direct nod to Feevah indicated that she took them all in, but she had something else to tend to before getting acquainted. In a quick move of surprising dexterity, she stomped into the house. With Russell, Feevah and the girls following, Mrs. Richards ran through the front room, looking angrily from side to side, as if checking to make certain all of her belongings were in order. Not finding anything amiss, she rushed into the kitchen. On the kitchen table was a pan of biscuits and some ham slices on a plate. Mrs. Richards grabbed the plate and tossed the contents out the window.

Russell moved toward her, trying to calm her, but she spotted a wash tub where Mrs. Schmidt must have been working on dirty clothes. With a high-pitched, angry drawn-out grunt, Mrs. Richards began jerking the clothes out of the water and throwing them around the room. The four onlookers dodged to avoid the propelled clothes, but everyone in the room was wet with flying water by the time the wash tub was emptied. Next, Mrs. Richards poured the remaining

140

water out the back door. Giving a curt nod and a loud, "There!" she slammed the wash pot down near the back door.

With everyone still recovering from the water barrage, Mrs. Richards walked straight back toward the front room and side stepped close enough to Grace to scoop her up. Grace froze and stared back at her mother while Mrs. Richards carried her into the front room. Feevah and Russell caught up with the two, ready to rescue the frightened child, but Mrs. Richards quickly set Grace on the sofa, picked up a large book, seated herself next to Grace, and began to read aloud. Her bright, expressive voice seemed to have a different origin from her previous wailing and grunting. For several minutes Russell, Feevah, and Dorcas stood still. Little by little the tension left the room. Feevah relaxed as she sensed Mrs. Richards' tirade was over and she meant no harm to Grace.

Dorcas was drawn to the story in *Pilgrim's Progress* about Christian, on the Hill of Difficulty and the page with the large sketch of Christian showing his gratitude at finding the House Beautiful. Dorcas walked slowly to the sofa, where she sat cautiously on the other side of Grace. Feevah and Russell both tensed, ready to intervene, but it was unnecessary. Mrs. Richards, without interrupting her flow of reading, simply reached across Grace and patted Dorcas on the knee.

Feevah glanced at Russell in relief and was surprised by the emotion she saw in his eyes. Feeling Feevah's glance, he whispered, "I didn't think she could still read." The kindness in his voice drew Feevah so powerfully that she had to hold herself back from leaning into him. He quietly walked outside.

Feevah would have liked to gather the wet clothes from the kitchen floor and check the pantry and garden to see what she needed to do to prepare supper. However, she was afraid that taking liberties with Mrs. Richards' home might offend her as much as Mrs. Schmidt's work had. After Russell went outside, Mrs. Richards paused in her reading and smiled at Feevah.

141

Feevah said, "Mrs. Richards, thank you for reading to the children. You are very kind and we are grateful. Would you like for me to clean up the kitchen and fix supper?"

"Yes," she replied with a direct, warm smile much like Russell's, and then she began reading the same page she had just read. Grace looked up and started to comment, but Dorcas placed her hand on Grace's arm. At the same moment, Feevah caught Grace's eye and signaled, *no*. So, the girls listened as Mrs. Richards reread the page.

With one eye constantly on her girls, Feevah tidied the kitchen, discovered dried beans soaking that Mrs. Richards had missed when she cleared out Mrs. Schmidt's work. Feevah stoked the fire, started the beans, and looked around for other ingredients to add to the soup. For nearly an hour, as she learned her way around this new kitchen, the girls sat on the sofa listening to Mrs. Richards read.

Russell came in and invited the girls and Mrs. Richards to join him outside and help get the chicks situated. They went to an area in the back where Feevah could watch from the kitchen window. By now Seth had returned, and he stood with the grandmother watching as Russell allowed the girls to place the chicks one by one into their new pen; then he showed the girls how to feed and water them.

The rest of the day passed peacefully with Seth clearing out a storage shed near the house. Feevah and her daughters were to sleep in the shed close to the house rather than out in the quarters with Seth and the field hands.

By supper time the girls and "Grandma," as Russell had instructed them to call Mrs. Richards, had fallen into a routine of reading, checking the chicks, and stopping by the kitchen to talk to Feevah. Each time they came in, Feevah asked Grandma for instructions using questions that could easily be answered with *yes* or *no*.

There were a few tense moments when Feevah began to serve Russell and his grandmother their supper. The girls had gone out to the shed, and for the first time since the fracas with Mrs. Schmidt, Mrs. Richards got agitated.

She backed away from the table firmly saying, "No, no."

Feevah and Russell both attempted to understand what was bothering her. Feevah asked if there was something amiss about the food or the table setting.

Russell walked to the back door. "I think I know what she wants." He called outside, "Dorcas and Grace, would you come in here? Feevah, set two more places. Grandma wants the girls to eat with her." Russell set chairs for them on either side of his grandmother. The two surprised little girls, in a day full of new experiences, sat down to supper for the first time in their lives with their masters. Mrs. Richards supervised their plates as if they were her own children. Feevah was proud her girls had learned proper table manners in their years with the Fuller children.

By the time Feevah finished in the kitchen and covered the fire, so the embers would be ready for breakfast, she was eager to take her daughters to their room and try their new bed. Mrs. Richards and the girls were on the sofa with Dorcas looking again at *Pilgrim's Progress* and Grace collapsed in sleep against Mrs. Richards' other side. As Feevah walked over to gather Grace, Mrs. Richards smiled broadly and motioned for everyone to be quiet because Grace was sleeping.

"Good night and may God bless you both," Feevah whispered as she lifted Grace and led Dorcas out through kitchen.

When they stepped out the back door, Seth approached them with a candle. "Good evening. Your room is ready." Seth, with his lopsided gait, walked along beside them holding the candle ahead. The little shed had been built to contain tobacco racks, but when the Richards family started using curing barns, most of the racks had been trashed or sold, and the shed had become a catchall for tools and supplies. "I hope you will feel comfortable in here. Lucky the nights are not too hot right now. There's no windows."

Seth had cleared out the clutter and set up a bed and two wooden barrels for tables. "There's a night pot by the bed. And I left the old rack hooks along this wall in case you might like to hang clothes." He'd placed a pitcher of water and a bowl on one of the barrels, so they didn't need to go to the well in the darkness. "You don't have to worry about rain. It stays dry in here, and if you have any trouble during the night, just holler 'Seth' and I'll come in a snap."

"Thank you, Seth. This will be a fine room." Feevah had worked Grace's boots off, dropped them to the floor, and laid Grace on the bed. "I saw you working all afternoon to fix it." She straightened and stood with her hands resting on Dorcas's shoulders.

"My pleasure, Feevah."

"How long have you been here?" She kept her voice low.

"I was born here the same year as Russell." He also spoke low, almost in a whisper. "My ma and pa were here too, but they passed, and Master Thomas took my baby brother back to Virginia with him about a year ago. He left me to take care of the field hands."

"Does Russell whip our folks?"

"No, ma'am. He never whipped anybody and he never got whipped himself because he's a bleeder. But his daddy is as mean as they come. No man, outside of Russell, escaped his whip, including his own sons."

"How many other sons are there?"

"Three, all older, back in Virginia."

"When is the daddy coming back?" This question preyed on her mind.

"Don't know, never I hope."

"What's a bleeder?" Feevah thought she'd heard about this condition, but she wasn't sure what Seth meant.

"Russell can't get cuts. When he was little, he almost bled to death many times just from a little cut. That's why he escaped the hard work and beatings his brothers got. He got to stay in the house with his mama until she died. Then Grandma took care of him, and he still never had to do the work of the other boys, and his daddy never whipped him for fear Russell would bleed to death."

Feevah's mind filled with questions, and she sensed Seth would be a good friend. "I am blessed you are here and can guide my girls and me so that we please Master."

Seth set his candle on one of the barrel tables. "I'll do my best. Good night," he said on his way out.

"Good night and God bless you," Feevah replied before she released Dorcas and shut the door.

"Mama, why can't Seth use both of his arms and legs like we do? What happened to him?" Dorcas asked.

"I don't know and it wouldn't be polite to ask," Feevah answered. "If he wants us to know, he'll tell us."

Feevah and Dorcas washed and slipped off all of their clothes except the sleeveless shifts they wore under their dresses. Then Feevah lifted Grace while Dorcas turned down the quilt. The fresh, clean quilts and the soft, straw-stuffed bed were wonderful after their two weeks of sleeping on the ground or in the back of a wagon. Even though Feevah's mind was teeming with ideas about how to keep Mrs. Richards content, and every piece of her body was energized with her feelings for Russell, she felt herself yielding to the bed and fell into a deep sleep.

"Noooo, don't, don't. Thomas, Thomas, where are you? Noooo, let me find Thomas." A screaming voice shocked Feevah and Dorcas awake.

"Screaming. What now, I wonder?" Philip said, yawning.

Edith laid the pages on the bedside table. "Maybe this is a good place to stop. The *screaming voice* episode may take a while to get through, and it's late." She clicked off the light.

Chapter Sixteen

The next morning when Philip opened his eyes, the first thing that he saw was Edith's hair—big hair, not the tight knot or the braids she had worn before. Her face resting next to his chest was blocked by long, wild honey curls. She stretched and started waking.

His hook-ups had always ended before morning. This was a new feeling to wake up in her bed next to her body. He tightened his arms around her and buried his face in her curls. "I like your morning hair."

She shifted to face him, and her smile went all over him. "I like your morning scruff." She explored his overnight growth with her lips, moving over his face until her mouth settled on his before pulling away and going into the bathroom.

He was afraid she'd come out dressed. Instead, she returned quick, still nude with her loose hair pushed back from her face as if she wanted nothing in her way. She offered him a glass of water.

He propped up, took a drink. She went to the foot of the bed and began to rub his feet through the sheet.

She slid the sheet away and ran her fingers around his

146

ankles and calves—gentle at first, then deeper, exploring the long calf and thigh muscles. She worked her way up his legs. She had him ready, but that didn't seem to matter to her. She savored her time. She hummed as she moved over him— sometimes so softly he could barely hear.

She had a tight body, but even though her muscles were toned like a gymnast's, there were fine white lines on her belly from the stillborn son she'd mentioned in her journal. She had one long surgical scar below her navel. Her arms and her shoulders were dotted with sun freckles. The full light of day laying open the life story of her body made her beautiful and honest... and touched him in an unexpected way.

She worked her way up to his face. When he thought she was finally ready, she nudged him over so he was lying on his stomach, and she began the same careful work starting at his ankles again.

It was hard being face down unable to touch her, but it was also hard to pull away from the way she was touching him. When she worked her way up to his shoulders, he rolled over to face her, unwilling to wait longer. She crouched between his legs and began kissing circles around his center, pushing him to the edge.

All he could see was her hair fanned out. It gently slid around on his belly. Her tongue brought him so close that he was sure he wouldn't last another second. Her legs flexed against his. Her humming intensified.

Then it happened. Something shifted for Philip. It was not a climax. It was not just her hands and mouth on him. Feeling and hearing the vibration of her humming, something primal he couldn't name pulsed through him. Warmth. Comfort. Connection.

He started thinking again when she moved back to his face, kissed him, and reached for a condom. As he entered, she stopped being the driver and responded to his rhythm. Even though there'd been times during the long beginning when he thought he'd reached his limit, their movement was slow and deep. He loved her flexing—first strong then quick and fluttery. He loved it a while later when he felt her intake of breath and her stillness. She was feeling him in the same way he'd felt her.

She made breakfast for them. Scrambled eggs with cheese wrapped in a tortilla. "Okay if we hang out and read this morning? I want to find out what happens in the middle of the night." She'd already picked up the pages and found the place they'd stopped. "Who's crying out and waking everyone."

"Sure." He sensed this story was going to scrape into deeper layers of ugliness about his family. But he'd do anything for this woman.

Chapter Seventeen

Sabine Richards' manuscript. 1859 (continued)

"Noooo, don't, don't. Thomas, Thomas, where are you? Noooo, let me find Thomas." A screaming voice shocked Feevah and Dorcas awake.

"Mama, what is it?" Dorcas wrapped her arms around her mother.

"Nooooo, please let me go," the voice wailed.

Feevah picked up Grace, opened the door, and peered outside.

Seth was standing outside their door. "It's just Grandma having a bad night," he said. "She'll be fine."

"I'm going to help." Feevah hurried with her girls in through the back door of the house, leaving Seth by the shed. As she and the girls came into the kitchen, Russell entered through the front door of the house carrying his grandmother like a baby. She was weeping, struggling, and begging him to let her go. Feevah stepped into Mrs. Richards' bedroom, laid Grace on the bed and instructed Dorcas to stay there with her.

Russell, with a tired, worried face, had managed to work his way into a sitting position on the sofa with his grandmother struggling against him. As Feevah approached, Mrs. Richards cried, "Please make him let me go. I've got to find Thomas."

"Grandma, he's going to let you go just as soon as it's safe. There are dangerous things outside in the dark. Master Russell needs to keep you safe in the house."

Mrs. Richards had paused momentarily, but halfway through Feevah's assurances, the wailing and struggling started anew. Russell had one arm across her chest with both of her wrists clasped in one of his hands. He had the other arm across her legs to prevent her kicking or running, and all the time he was softly saying, "It's all right, Grandma, just rest. Everything is fine."

Feevah tried rubbing her shoulders and stroking her hair, but touch seemed to make things worse. Finally, Feevah began singing, "Swing low sweet chariot, coming for to carry me home, swing low, sweet chariot..."

"No, no, no," Mrs. Richards screamed louder than ever.

A soft, tentative voice caught Mrs. Richards' attention, and she froze, listening. Russell and Feevah, seeing her reaction, became silent as well.

"Are you washed in the blood, in the soul cleansing blood of the lamb? Are your garments spotless, are they white as snow, are you washed in the blood of the lamb?" Dorcas softly sang from the bedroom where she lay with Grace... a new hymn they had learned from other slaves on their long walk to Chattanooga. Mrs. Richards began to hum along with Dorcas. Russell released his hold, and Feevah took her arm and led her to the bedroom. In the dim light, they could see Grace sleeping on her stomach like a little frog with her seat up in the air. Dorcas lay beside her on her side looking toward the door and singing softly.

Smiling now, Mrs. Richards put her fingers to her lips signaling for Russell and Dorcas to be quiet. Next, she crawled into the bed and covered the two girls and herself with a quilt. She patted Grace and Dorcas on their heads and whispered, "Pretty, pretty, pretty."

Feevah and Russell stood silently, hoping the peaceful moment would last, and the three would sleep. Russell nudged

Feevah toward a trunk by the bedroom door and motioned for her to sit with him. It was then that Feevah let herself notice that Russell was shirtless, wearing only his trousers. She was wearing only her shift.

He gave her a grateful smile.

Feevah felt as agitated as Mrs. Richards had been a few minutes earlier. She allowed her bare arm to rest against Russell's, and in the dim light, she allowed her eyes to roam over his body. She imagined running her hands over his chest and shoulders. They sat on the trunk for nearly half an hour, waiting to make sure everyone was asleep.

"I think they're sound asleep now," he said, interrupting her thoughts.

"Yes, Master."

"Let's go."

When they were in the living room, he added, "Once or twice a week, she wakes up and takes off for the road."

"How long have the two of you been awake?"

"I guess she slept for about an hour, and since then she's been trying to leave."

"Master Russell, I wish you had awakened me. I could have cared for her and you could have slept." Feevah realized while she had been sleeping for hours, Russell had been trying to calm his grandmother. It was then that the light confirmed what she thought she had noticed in the dark bedroom: Russell's upper back, shoulders and chest were covered with fingernail scratches. "And, sir, please let me tend to your skin. Human scratches can turn to pus."

"She doesn't mean to scratch. It just happens when she's trying to get away."

Feevah remembered Seth saying Russell was a bleeder, and she wasn't certain whether she should risk making him bleed or risk leaving the scratches alone.

Russell added, "They've never gotten sore before, but I guess you know best."

"Yes, Master, let's clean them with water and put honey and lard on them. I'll get them and a wet cloth from the kitchen."

As she hurried to get the supplies, she felt a stab of shame. She was aroused by the anticipation of touching him. When she turned to go back to him, she found that he had followed her into the kitchen and was seated at the table, waiting. In spite of her self-chastisement, Feevah relished in the touching as she cleaned each scratch and gently rubbed the honey and lard mixture onto his chest. His chest was broader and more muscular than she had imagined, and he was hairless except for the tuft below his navel pointing down into his pants. His hairless chest made him seem more naked than other men. As she rubbed his skin, she allowed her breath to fall into his rhythm. After she tended to his chest, she started on his back.

"That feels good," he responded as she worked on the few scratches on his back. "I guess my muscles are tight from the struggle with Grandma. Funny how it doesn't seem to bother her at all. You watch." He chuckled. "In the morning she'll be fresh and spry."

Feevah began to massage his back and shoulders. "Yes, sir, you are tight." Out of his line of vision, she leaned her face as close as she dared, and breathed in his masculine scent.

"Well, I thank you," Russell said, standing. "Do you want me to carry the girls back out or do you want to let them sleep in here?"

"Why don't I sleep on the floor near your grandmother's bed," Feevah suggested. "If she awakens later, I'll keep her from running outside again."

Facing her and placing both of his hands on her bare arms, he said, "Brother Tune was right when he said you would take good care of Grandma. I'll go get the mattress off your bed. We can put it on the floor." He released her and headed out the back door.

When he moved away from her, she felt a physical pull in her chest, as if part of herself were leaving. She wanted to follow him, to close the door to the shed, and stay with him. As he headed out the back door, she watched his proud profile, then his strong back. A glimpse of his expression told her he was completely unknowing of the powerful feelings that were shaking her. He was innocently intent on fetching the mattress and making sure everyone had a comfortable bed for the night.

Feevah looked out into the darkness waiting for him to reappear, and she saw Seth leaning on the side of the shed, almost hidden in the night shadows, watching her. Knowing Seth had seen the interlude in the kitchen startled her conscience. "Dear God," she prayed to herself. "Help me be free of my lust." But even as she prayed, her truest part revolted. This most beautiful and compelling emotion was too precious to pray away. She had never felt more alive.

She held the door open for Russell as he returned with the mattress. He carried it into the bedroom, where the three continued to sleep peacefully, and laid it next to the bed.

Feevah followed him into the bedroom. He nodded to her as he left, and she closed the door behind him. She leaned briefly over each of her sleeping daughters, kissing their heads.

The next morning Grandma was cheerful as if the rampages of the previous night had never happened. She and the little girls fell into an easy rhythm of reading, playing with handmade dolls, tending to the chicks, and helping Feevah with chores. The three were always nearby, and both of the girls had a natural affinity for avoiding anything that might upset Grandma. Dorcas, with her gentle singing, and Grace, with her silly antics, held the elder's attention.

Feevah stayed busy with her chores, and many times when Russell was near, she forced herself to cast her eyes in another direction, rather than look at him. After lunch Russell and Seth left to inspect the fields where the hands were cultivating the young plants. Feevah decided this would be a good opportunity for her and her three charges to wash their hair and bathe. Grandma with her long, unkempt hair and general dirtiness struck a chord of compassion in Feevah.

After Feevah gathered clean clothing for the four of them, she said, "Grandma, the girls and I need a good head scrubbing and bath. Would it be all right if we get cleaned up while Master Russell and Seth are out in the field?"

The girls stopped their play with their button-eyed dolls and waited to see the reaction.

Grandma looked at the girls and smiled back at Feevah. "Let's give the girls a bath!" she said energetically.

Before Feevah could begin to execute her own plan for setting up the large washtub in the kitchen, Grandma, took each of the girls by the hand and headed out the back door to an area between the shed and the clothes lines. "Get the blankets, towels, buckets, and soap," she called to Feevah.

Feevah scurried to follow the order and catch up. Mrs. Richards instructed the girls to hang their clothes on hooks attached to the side of the shed. As they were disrobing, Feevah hung blankets for privacy on the clotheslines surrounding a six-feet square area next to the shed. The ground had been covered with white smooth stones, so bathers would not have to stand on dirt. Grandma directed Feevah to place buckets of water on a bench within the enclosure. This would be more of a shower than a bath. Feevah scooped water over the girls' heads and began to work up lather, alternating from girl to girl. Grandma quickly took over Dorcas's hair, and left Feevah to work on Grace.

After scrubbing and rinsing the girls, Feevah said, "Grandma, I think you and I should have a wash, too."

Mrs. Richards nodded and followed Feevah's example by

removing her clothes and hanging them on the hooks. At first when Feevah worked on Grandma's hair, there was a moment of tension in which it seemed she would object. Fortunately, Grace, ready for water play, was giggling and flicking water at everyone. Grandma, entertained by the play, forgot for a while that Feevah was shampooing and bathing her. Each time Grandma became annoyed with Feevah's efforts, Feevah would simply turn her scrubbing to one of the girls. Little by little, all three of her charges were scrubbed from head to toe. After Feevah had helped the three to get dried and dressed, she asked them to sit on a bench while she bathed.

With all the noise and splashing, they had not heard Seth and Russell return.

While Seth unhitched the horses, Russell went into the house looking for the women and girls. From the kitchen window, he could see Grandma sitting with the girls, still toweling Grace's hair. He could also see Feevah's head and shoulders above the clothesline blankets as she bathed. It was the first time he had seen her bare shoulders and her head without a kerchief. Instead of her usual downcast posture, her head was high, and her neck long and elegant.

Edith put down the manuscript. "Sabine has changed viewpoints here. Now he's narrating from Russell's viewpoint instead of Feevah's."

"Yeah, he has," Philip said, turning the unfamiliar concept over in his mind.

"It's just not something a professional writer would do," Edith added. "But I guess that's not shocking: Sabine wasn't a professional writer."

Philip nodded slowly. "The scene I keep questioning is the one in which Feevah works on Russell's scratches and cleans them. The notion that she's trying to prevent an infection doesn't fit because during the Civil War era, I think knowledge of infections was non-existent. That's why so many soldiers died of infections."

"Gosh. I didn't think of that, but you make sense. Let's continue..." Her eyes scanned the page. "The next part looks... uncomfortable."

Grandma stood and announced, "It's time to fold the blankets." She headed toward the blanket hanging on the clothesline, concealing Feevah's nakedness. Russell could have moved away from the window. He could have called out to Grandma and asked her to wait.

Feevah, with her head tilted back, was holding a bucket high and slowly pouring the water over her face and hair, using her free hand to work the water through her short, cropped hair. Grandma took the blanket away and carried it back to the bench to fold.

Russell saw the beautiful woman in the full sunlight with her head still held high and tilted back, her arms raised above her head. Although he'd seen the rich color of her face and hands many times, her full naked body made her darkness seem intensified, almost gleaming. Her body had an intrinsic strength combined with a womanly softness. At any moment she could have recognized her exposure and covered herself, but after she emptied the bucket, she continued to bathe the rest of her body with the water in the second bucket. He watched her move her hands over her the smooth flesh of her thighs and hips. He couldn't pull his eyes away.

A loud clang alerted Feevah that they were not alone. She quickly pulled a towel from the hooks, and she covered herself.

Russell did not have to look toward the barn to know Seth had struck the old iron pipe they used to signal workers. From Seth's vantage point, he could see Russell spying on the bathers.

Russell turned away from the window, went back out through the front of the house, and sat on the steps of the front porch. He stared toward the road.

When Seth came limping around to the porch a few minutes later, they both stayed silent. Russell must have known Seth had done the right thing by alerting Feevah to their presence, and that Seth was disgusted with him. Russell, solemn and still, seemed to be an older man than he had been when he walked into the kitchen a few minutes earlier, and Seth, breathing heavily with new deep frown lines between his brows, was an angrier man.

After a while Grandma and the girls came out onto the porch. Grandma sat in a chair and instructed Grace to sit on a low stool in front of her. Together, Dorcas and Grandma began to braid Grace's hair; as each braid was finished, they tied a colored ribbon at the base and at the end. Little by little, Grace's hair was transformed into a profusion of colors.

Feevah came out of the house and, standing behind Grandma, she gently brushed the old woman's long silver hair, forming a braid on each side. Seth and Russell, who'd been watching Grandma, turned to the road again with their backs to Feevah. The memory of her nakedness was still vivid in their minds.

Grandma muttered, "Pretty, pretty, pretty," over and over as she worked on Grace's hair. After a while, Feevah quietly returned into the house.

When the men heard Feevah's retreating steps, they looked in her direction, and saw Grandma in a clean, blue dress, with her shining hair braided and coiled into a neat bun at the base of her neck. She was different from the unkempt woman she'd been in recent years. Grandma looked up at both of them with her blue eyes brightened from the color in her dress. "Pretty, pretty, pretty," she said as she continued to work on Grace's hair.

Russell stayed outside with chores until several hours later when Dorcas came to tell him supper was ready.

Feevah, with her layers of loose clothing and her kerchief tied low on her forehead, served their food. Grandma and the girls continued their comfortable chatter.

Russell looked like a man trying to sort out a puzzle. Finally, in a blurt that silenced everyone, he said, "I'm going to Chattanooga tomorrow. I'll be gone for several days. Feevah, if you need supplies for the kitchen, give me a list."

With all four of the females watching him, he backed his chair away from the table. "Well, I'm going to go to bed now, so I can get an early start." He was already out of the room and closing the door as the women responded.

The next morning when he came into the kitchen, Feevah had his breakfast ready and a list of supplies waiting. With her eyes cast down, she wished him a good morning and asked, "Will you need anything else, Master?"

"No, thank you," he responded.

"Then I'll go out to garden. Have a safe trip."

Shortly after she went out the back door, Seth called from the front door to tell him the wagon was ready. Next, Grandma and the girls awoke and came to the table. Grandma was in her nightgown and the girls were clad in long, old shirts. Russell couldn't help laughing at Grace. With her head still covered in the ribbons, yawning so big that her eyes were closed, she walked right into Russell.

Dorcas went to the back door, and called, "Mama, we're awake."

After bumping into Russell, Grace turned and bumped into a chair.

Laughing, Russell stood and picked her up and put her in a chair at the table. "Miss Grace, you might need to wake up before you go walking around."

Grandma said, "Let's have eggs." She took her seat. "Come to the table," she directed Dorcas who was still standing by the door waiting for her mother.

Russell cracked several eggs, dropping them into the frying

158

pan; he found the bacon and biscuits Feevah had left on the stove, and he was placing them on the table when Feevah came back in. He stood awkwardly between the stove and the table as if uncertain whether he should finish the eggs or turn them over to Feevah.

Reaching for the spoon in his hand, Feevah took over.

Russell backed out of the kitchen. "I guess I'll be going now. I'll be back in three or four days, five at the most." He paused, glanced at Feevah, and opened his mouth as if to speak again. He turned toward Seth who was still near the open front door waiting to hand off the reins. There was a long moment of silence while everyone in the room watched Russell's face redden. Abruptly, he turned and rushed out the door.

"Have a good trip," Grandma said cheerfully.

"Goodbye, Masser," the girls said.

As Feevah spooned the eggs onto their waiting plates, she kept her eyes downward. But as soon as Russell went out, Feevah walked to a window in the living room and watched him ride away. He was different this morning, but she couldn't say why. Watching his back grow smaller, she felt a pull as if a part of her were leaving, but she also felt relief. She would be more able to focus on her responsibilities with him gone.

That night after Grandma and the girls were asleep, Feevah returned to the kitchen to do some final cleaning for the night. She expected Seth to come in; she had sensed he was ready to talk to her in more depth about the household. So, when she heard the soft knock at the kitchen window, she wasn't surprised.

Feevah sat at the table and motioned for him to join her.

Seth dragged his way to the chair. "Please be careful. Russell is a good man, but he has an uncommon need to raise the skirts. He's had most of the girls in Chattanooga. And I'm afraid he'll be coming after you." He shook his head and shifted his gaze from her to the candle flame in the center of the table. "He saw you bathing yesterday; he was watching you through the window. That's why I hit the signal, to let you know."

A surge of warmth rushed through her, but she kept her face calm. "With the attention Master Russell has from all the pretty young town women, he won't want anything from me except work." She used the moment to ask a question she'd been thinking about. "I wonder why Master Russell hasn't taken a wife."

"Master Thomas says Russell needs to wait until Francine grows up so we can be family with tobacco buyers." Seth raised his eyes to meet hers. "But I think Russell doesn't want to be tied down to just one woman. He never stays with one very long before he's off to another one. I heard him say he had to wait to marry until his daddy comes back. I heard him tell someone else he couldn't marry because Grandma gets agitated if there's another woman in the house. But I think those reasons are lies."

Feevah smiled. "Well, judging from Grandma's tirade, that reason's true." She laughed and recounted the efforts to undo all of Mrs. Schmidt's work.

Seth didn't deny Feevah's assertion, but he still scowled.

Feevah asked, "Has he lain with our folks before?"

"Not that I know of, but there haven't been any women here in a long time. I heard his daddy and granddaddy laid with them all, even the women that already had a man and children. His daddy locked the men and children up at night, had iron bolts on the quarters. He made the women sleep in here in this very kitchen."

"Seth." A shift in her tone made him know she was about to say something she meant for him to take to heart. "I thank you for your warning. But I don't want you to worry about me." She put her hand on his arm. "If you show anger toward him, it could cause trouble for all of us. Now that you've told me about your fears, I want you to put them out of your mind. There is nothing else you need to do." She folded her hands in her lap and leaned back in her chair. "I'm praying since Grandma is happy with my girls and me, Master Russell will want everything to stay as it is."

"I hope you're right," Seth responded darkly.

"I am. And if you show anger toward him, he may get rid of you." Feevah went on to tell Seth about her privileges at the Fuller Plantation, including the privilege of learning to read and write, and how she believed Robin's angry outbursts with the masters led to him being chained and sold to the railroad.

The next few days passed peacefully. Feevah and the girls gauged Grandma's moods and distracted her if she seemed restless or unhappy. Feevah carefully sorted through clothes and secretly burned the ones too stained to get clean. Feevah was also figuring out which foods Grandma would eat. The faded, dirty old woman, tied to her chair on the front porch less than two weeks ago, was gone.

On the eighth day after Russell's departure, everyone in the household seemed on edge. Russell had promised to be home in five days at the most; since his deadline had passed, they expected him soon. Late in the morning Grandma began to get restless; the usual singing, trips to the baby chicks, stories, and dolls didn't distract her.

Feevah said, "Grandma, I've never heard anyone play your piano. Do you play?"

Grandma sprang up and headed toward the tall, upright piano. "It's time for music!" She beckoned the girls to follow. She slid out the bench and motioned for the girls to sit on either side of her. She carefully rolled back the key cover, and sat staring at the keys.

Dorcas stood and reached for a book on top. "Is this your music book?"

"Yes, thank you, dear. This is my music book." Grandma opened the book and sounded a deep, grieving moan.

Alarmed, Feevah rushed to her side.

The moan grew louder and turned into weeping. Grandma

161

covered her face with her hands and cried, "I can't remember. Why can't I remember?"

Feevah tried to comfort her. "Don't you worry, Grandma. It doesn't matter. Here, let's read instead." She led Grandma to the sofa and tried to get her interested in a book.

But Grandma's weeping continued, and she rocked herself back and forth.

Feevah wrapped her arms around the thin shoulders and rocked with her. "Let your mind be peaceful, Grandma. We love you so much for all your kindness. Don't you worry about anything."

Dorcas began to cry. "Why can't Grandma remember? Help her, Mama."

Before Feevah could reply, Grace wailed, "Where's my daddy?"

Feevah felt helpless.

Seth, never far away, came into the room alarmed. After he understood the nature of the weeping, he assured them, "Grandma just does this sometimes. She gets sad and has to cry. She'll be better in a while."

Feevah's mind raced to think of some way to distract her when Seth, glancing out the window, said, "Well, here comes Russell."

"Grandma, Russell is home!" Feevah hoped this would cheer her up, and for a moment there was a break in the crying, but by the time Russell came into the house, Grandma and both the girls were weeping again.

While he patiently comforted Grandma, Feevah felt her own spirits sink. What a disappointment she must be to him. She had been so hopeful of keeping Grandma from ever again having such a bad moment, but the first time Russell left her in charge, he came home to find everyone distraught. Feevah led the girls into the kitchen. It was all she could do to keep from weeping herself.

A few minutes later, Grandma came into the kitchen beaming. "Look what Russell brought from town." She carried four nightgowns. Each gown was floor length with lace around the collars and ribbons streaming down the front. "Pink for the girls, blue for me, and white for Mama," Grandma said, handing out the gowns.

Seth and Russell came in next carrying kitchen supplies. Tears were forgotten in the hustle of sorting through the food. The rest of the day passed peacefully, but Grandma's crying stuck with Feevah. She could not let go of the disappointment in herself for allowing the old woman to reach such despondency, and she worried that Russell would wish he had purchased a different slave.

At bedtime, Grandma wanted everyone to wear the new nightgowns. The girls had never had such pretty sleepwear and were too excited to fall asleep quickly. After the usual stories and singing, Feevah waited until she was sure all three were asleep. Then she crept into the front room to close the piano and replace the music so, hopefully, no one would notice it the next day and be reminded of the disaster. Being near the piano brought back all the feelings of the afternoon, and she allowed the disappointment to wash over her. Silent tears rolled down her face. She walked to the sofa, and with her hands on her face, rocked herself much as Grandma had done earlier.

She didn't know Russell had entered the room until he sat beside her and wrapped his arm around her shoulder.

Startled, Feevah said, "I'm sorry, Master, if I woke you. I wanted to straighten up the piano, so Grandma won't notice it tomorrow. I'm so sorry she got upset. It was all because I asked her to play the piano. I promise not to do that again..."

"You don't need to be sorry. You're doing good work with her, and I'm grateful to have you here. The doctor says she is going to have bad days from time to time."

Feevah had leaned into him, and as his words of reassurance quieted her fears, his body answered a stronger need. He leaned back on the sofa drawing her close to him. "Now, is that better?"

She wasn't sure what he meant, but everything was better, and she nodded, her face pressed against his bare chest. He continued

163

to hold and comfort her. With her cheek against him, she was intoxicated by the scent of his skin and began to gently move her face against the comforting warmth of his chest. His hands moved across her back pulling her closer. As he leaned farther back on the sofa, their legs became a part of their embrace. She wiped her tears from her face then placed her hands on his chest.

The embrace that started as one of comfort flowed into the gentle, primitive rhythm. He lifted her face so he could kiss her. While kissing her he opened his pants; he brought her hand to his manhood. When she touched him, she felt the deepest part of herself respond, as though he were already inside. While she continued to caress him, he quickly lifted her gown up over her head and off; then he slipped out of his pants and entered her.

At one point he paused and looked down at her. "Feevah," he said. Nothing else, just her name. Even as she gave herself over to powerful feelings, she was aware that her own sounds and movements were new to her. When he finished, she wrapped her legs around him, holding him inside as long as she could.

Although fulfilled, she became cautious. She did not want to assume he would want to stay near her. Robin had wanted to be alone, untouched after. As much as she would have liked to continue caressing, she forced herself to be still and wait for his lead. He remained collapsed on top of her for long minutes. Finally, he kissed her again and said, "Feevah, Feevah, what am I going to do with you?"

She wanted to say, *Love me every night, just like this.* Instead, she laughed softly. "Whatever you want to do, Master."

He slowly unwrapped their arms and legs, stood, and said, "Come with me." He led her to his bed, and they lay embraced until he fell asleep. Feevah watched his face in the darkness and wondered at her fortune to have this night.

The breeze that had steadily blown across the bed, stopped. Leaves rustled outside the window even though the wind was still. A

plaintive tone, like an unusual bird song, made the hair all over her flesh rise. She flinched and Russell drowsily said, "It's all right."

The tone continued, in a melody too humanlike to be from a bird. The sound was something she'd heard before, but its lengthening distance away and its echo in the quiet night left her unable to name the source.

"What is that?" Feevah whispered.

"Just Seth, playing his mouth organ."

Soon Russell started breathing heavily as if in deep sleep, but Feevah listened to the mournful melody until it grew too faint to hear.

Before dawn Feevah awoke, gathered their clothes from the front room, slipped back into her new gown, and looked in on her daughters and Mrs. Richards. She was considering returning to her own bed when Russell appeared, still nude, standing in the doorway of his room. Even in the dimness, it was clear that he was ready for her, and she went to him. Unable to stop smiling at his naked hunger, she embraced him and asked what he would like for breakfast. He responded by drawing her close and sliding his hands up and down her body. Gently pushing her down onto the bed, he stood and looked down on her. As she gazed back up at him, she lifted her gown.

"What a lucky, lucky woman I am," she whispered as he filled her again.

When they finished, she kissed him goodbye, closed his bedroom door, and crept back to her own bed.

She lay for a few minutes reliving the night. When she rose and started breakfast, she couldn't stop herself from smiling. As the others woke, her happiness seemed contagious. Mrs. Richards and the girls were more cheerful than usual.

Dorcas said, "Mama, you look different this morning."

"How do I look different, baby?"

"I don't know. You just seem lighter somehow."

When Russell came into the kitchen, he was exuberant. He kissed and tickled Grandma, lifted Grace squealing and giggling onto his shoulders. After he set her down, he said, "Now it's Dorcas's turn!" Gentle Dorcas smiled at him sweetly; she knew he was teasing her and would not lift her as he had done Grace. Finally, he came over to the stove and leaned close to Feevah's ear. "Are you all right?"

"Yes, sir, I am more than all right this morning." She smiled, gazing directly into his eyes.

"Me too." He grinned back to her. "Me too, Feevah."

As she turned her gaze back to the stove, through the window she saw Seth leaning against the shed behind the house staring at the two of them. His dark expression pierced her mood, and she knew the thin walls and open windows of the house had not concealed their love making.

Chapter Eighteen

Edith closed the manuscript. "I think this story is true. I think Russell was your ancestor, and he fell in love with Feevah."

Frowning, Philip looked away from her. Each passing hour in this saga left him rawer and more exposed. "Love?" He shook his head. "He's using her. Taking advantage of his power over her." Russell reminded him of his grandfather.

Edith said softly, "I think Russell truly loves her, but he's young."

Philip stood and walked to a window. He knew he was taking this old manuscript too seriously. It may not even be true. It may be some poor sucker's attempt at a novel. But he couldn't stop himself from saying, "I've always known something shameful ran through my father and grandfather. Now it's like it also ran through my ancestors."

She came up behind him and wrapped her arms around him, her face against his bare back. "I get it. It's natural to worry about what traits run through your DNA." He turned to embrace her. With her face against his chest, she said, "I sometimes wonder if my father was a rapist—if that's why my mother was alone and pregnant."

"None of that stuff matters." He rested his cheek on top of her head. "Us. Now. That's what's real." He wanted his words to be true. His life could be perfect with this woman. He treasured his future.

"You're right. And maybe by the end of Feevah's story, it will all make sense. Hey." She gazed up at him. "Let's get dressed and get out of here—take a walk, have lunch. There's a park nearby and lots of cafés."

She led him to a path bordering a pond. There were nooks with benches along the trail. "May I tell you some things while we're not alone and naked and I can concentrate?"

Alarm sizzled through him. "Sure." Was she having second thoughts about his blackouts and his new legal mess?

Something in her voice was new. "I was planning to tell you this before we got so... so... connected, but..." she grinned sheepishly, "...we sped through my timeline." They kept walking on the path. "So, I'm sorry if I've misled you. I told you most of this that first night."

He nodded, worried. She might want to end their connection.

"I met my husband Garrison when we were both working on our Ph.Ds. Our marriage was troubled from the beginning." She gazed downward. "My pattern was predictable. Abandoned baby grows up, finds a man who can't be faithful, and sets herself up for more abandonment. After our divorce I had two relationships within a year, and both turned out to be similar to my marriage. I realized I was choosing men who didn't have the capacity to maintain a monogamous relationship."

She stayed quiet while a family passed close by on the trail. Then she started again. "So, I've spent time becoming conscious of what I'm about, and I haven't had a serious relationship in a long time. I'm no longer the woman seeking to be abandoned."

"No, you're not that," he murmured, relieved this was not some bombshell about not wanting to see him again.

She started talking fast. "I'm thirty-eight years old. When I start reading a good book or writing a poem, I sometimes have to stay up all night to finish. I get cranky if I don't dance or exercise every day. I have no money or property. I cannot get pregnant again—my uterus was removed to stop me from bleeding to death..." Her fast talking slowed. It had cost her to say the last part. He placed his hand over her scar, cradling this place of pain and loss. She took a breath to begin again, but she couldn't speak.

He picked her up, cradling her, walked to a nearby bench, and sat with her curled in his lap, her head against his chest.

After a silence, she said, "I guess I'll never master saying goodbye to my stillborn son."

"We have time, all the time you need."

She curled tighter against him. "Losing him was the pit of my life."

"What did you name him?"

"Love. Just, Love. I didn't want him to have a regular living name. I wanted to call him what he was to me. Love." She laid her hand on Philip's heart. "You're the only person who's ever asked me his name." She lifted her head and put her hands on the sides of his face. "Thank you for listening."

"You don't have to thank me."

She kissed him and held him close until they stood. Then she looked into his eyes. "I want to finish now—telling you all the negatives, no surprises." She took a breath. "I don't want to have casual sex, I want to always dance with lots of men and go home with only one, I want a monogamous relationship with you. If there's anything I just said that you don't like, we can end

169

this on an honest note with no regrets." She grinned impishly and peered up at him. "But please wait until we finish reading the Feevah story."

"Okay."

"Okay what?"

He placed his hands on her shoulders. Then he stroked one side of her face, and his gaze trailed all around her head and shoulders and face, trying to find language to express his feelings. His words were halting. "I've had a string of quick hook-ups over the years with lots of nice women, but nothing lasting since Rosa." His eyes locked with hers. "What has happened between you and me is unlike anything I've known." His cadence slowed. His eyes never strayed from hers. "I don't have words for it... Edith... The air is different when we're together. You see me. Hear me. And you make me understand myself better. You touch me in ways I didn't know existed." He leaned in close so his lips brushed hers as he spoke. "And more than anything I want... no I need... to see you and hear you and know you." He grinned, relieved to get his serious speech done.

Her eyes brimmed and she bit her lip as if trying to process all he'd shared.

He nudged her lips with his own until her teeth released their clamp on her bottom lip. Then he straightened again. "So okay, I'll keep coming back no matter what. Everything you said makes me want to be with you more. So..." He leaned down and kissed her, long and slow. "So, okay."

When they parted, she said, "Let's go back and finish reading."

"Yes, ma'am. Whatever you say."

Chapter Nineteen

Sabine Richards' manuscript. 1860

After several weeks of bundling tobacco, a load was ready for the journey to Chattanooga. Russell was quiet about the plans, murmuring that he didn't want to set out if rain was coming. The air was warm and close and still for the most part but the occasional gust of cool air brought the smell of rain that was falling somewhere else.

Feevah knew this trip would include a reunion with Francine, and Seth brought that reality to the surface late one afternoon. Russell and the hands were out at the drying barn, making sure all of the tobacco would be protected from the threatened rain. Feevah had left the girls with Grandma in the house while she took laundry off of the line. The air filled with tension as the sky darkened.

Seth leaned against the shed, apparently anticipating Feevah's plan to take in laundry. He approached her with the same dark look he had worn for weeks and said, "Feevah, you know when he goes to Chattanooga, he'll poke Miss Francine."

Feevah had been waiting for Seth's silence to break. Although he had never commented about her new relationship with Russell, his defeated, slumped posture shouted his unhappiness.

Feevah laid her armload of clothes across the line, turned,

clasped Seth's shoulders, and faced him. "Seth, don't hate Russell. If you go on like this, it will cause trouble. Don't hate him. Hate me if you must hate someone. I love Russell no matter what he does in Chattanooga. I have never loved anyone the way I love Russell. I used to think I loved Robin, but now I understand that in a way I did love Robin, but it was only if he would give me children and only if he would be faithful to me and only if he would keep our quarters up. With Russell there is no loving *only if*. There's only love."

Seth looked as if he had been slapped, and he slumped back against the shed when Feevah released her hold and turned back to the clothes. He seemed smaller and more crooked than before.

During the next week, with Russell gone, Seth gradually regained his normal humor. Most nights he came into the kitchen after Mrs. Richards and the girls were asleep as if drawn to know Feevah better. Feevah, too, wanted to be closer to Seth; in their world of uncertainties; together they could share their stories and feel safe.

One night, as they sat shelling beans at the kitchen table, Seth asked why she had been given the name of Feevah. She had not thought about the childhood legend of her birth for a long time, and as she resurrected the story, she felt an old closeness to her mysterious mother.

"My mama, they say, was a beautiful, strong woman who could sing like an angel. She birthed her babies easy, but a few hours before I was born, she ran a fever. They said I was hot when I pushed out of her and sure to die, so they called me 'Feevah.' It was a surprise to all our folks a few days later when we both rallied, but by then the name of Feevah stuck, and I've been Feevah ever since."

"Did you get to be raised by your mama?" Seth asked.

"The Fullers did let mothers raise their own, but Mama didn't live. When I was one month old, she started to bleed like she had given birth again. Only this time the life bled out of her. I missed her my whole life. My auntie said when I was a baby and cried in the night, folks could hear Mama singing to me."

They sat in silence with only the click of the beans rhythmically dropping and the chirps of crickets coming in from the darkness.

Seth said thoughtfully, "Feevah, you had your mama for one month, and it seems you know more about her than I know about mine who lived until I was half grown. I barely saw her. She worked in the kitchen, and I was in the fields with my brothers and the other hands. When I was about seven, we took a load of tobacco to some buyers. We were gone overnight and when we came back, someone said Mama got sick and died while we were gone. I never even knew where she was buried."

Feevah's understanding of Seth's hard life intensified. "I don't know how masters could be so heartless to let a woman die without even giving her folks the chance to bury her. And how they could send a child with your affliction off to work like all the other hands?"

The sudden freeze of Seth's posture showed that she had opened an old wound by mentioning his deformity. He said in a low tone, "I wasn't crippled back then. I was born to be a whole man. It wasn't until Russell and I were about eight years old that I was hurt."

Feevah stopped shelling and laid both hands on Seth's arm.

"One night Master Thomas came home late; when he got off his horse, he hollered, 'Russell, you and Seth, get in the stable and take care of my horse.' We loved playing in the horse barn. We'd throw the saddles across a rail and sit on them and pretend we were riding.

"While I was rubbing the horse down and giving her some grain, Russell threw his daddy's saddle across a rail, jumped on his play horse and started kicking and shaking the reins. I jumped on another old saddle, and we were riding like two renegades. That's when Russell found his daddy's liquor in the saddle bag. He pulled out this little bottle with a cork stopper and held it up. Looking at me through that golden stuff and making a big, full-faced grin, he pulled out the stopper, took a swig, and shouted like a wild man. I tried to hush him, but he just grinned at me and kept on swigging. He jumped off his

173

saddle and ran the bottle over to me. 'Seth, have some. This'll make you frizzly headed!'

"I pretended to drink, but I was scared to really swallow any. I said, 'Russell, get quiet. Your daddy will come out here and whip us both.' Soon as I said it, I remembered Russell never got whipped because he was a bleeder. Russell took the bottle back and was swigging again when Master Thomas came in from the dark.

"'Where the hell is my cane? I'm gonna beat the shit out of you, wasting my good whiskey, messing with my good saddle.' I was hoping he would go look for his cane when his hand lit on a shovel leaning by the doorway.

"Before I could leap from my saddle, he swung the shovel..." Feevah gasped and brought her hands to her mouth. "...so hard that a crazy thought flashed through me, 'Master's going to break his shovel across my back. Then he'll really be mad.' At first the pain was worse than anything I thought a person could feel, but after the second whack I didn't feel the shovel hitting. Just heard the thuds. Next thing I knew, I was on my belly on the ground. My dark blood puddling into the straw and dirt on the floor and the shovel flying up and down."

Feevah had no words. She rose from her chair, and standing next to Seth, wrapped her arms around his head, cradling him next to her waist. Quiet sobs shook her body.

The feel of her weeping gave Seth a relief, and he found himself ready to share more details. In his lifetime no one had spoken of his long, after-drag of surviving.

"I lost time... I figure maybe half a year went by without me knowing it. One day a fogginess cleared enough for me to be seeing the ground with speckled sunshine showing in the dirt. The sun was shining through the leaves of that elm tree near the door of the old quarters. I was looking at the speckled shadows of the leaves moving across the dirt. Propped up, sitting with my back against the wall.

"I was feeling a pushing on my leg, and a skinny dog was lying next to me, licking my leg like that was his only job in this life. There were places on my leg where I could feel his licking and places where even though I saw his tongue, I couldn't feel anything. For the longest time, I watched the speckled shadows moving and wondered why that dog didn't get tired of licking.

"Then I was hit with a shameful feeling because my bottom was barely covered by rags tied around me. When I tried to cover myself, only one leg and arm worked, and they were shaky. My other side was mostly dead, and that dog was doing his best to lick it back to life."

Feevah sat but kept her hand on Seth's arm while he continued.

"Back in those days there was still women and children here among our folks, and many days, I'd hear the little children playing and talking around me. Micah, my baby brother, was usually nearby. And he was always giving me something to eat or drink.

"I'd hear his voice saying, 'Come on, Seth. Take a little bite,' and I'd feel a poking at my mouth. I'd open my eyes to see him looking real serious right at my mouth. I guess Micah and that licking dog kept me alive.

"Most days Grandma talked to me or read to me. One day she was calling to me, 'Blow, Seth, blow. This'll make you stronger.' She pushed a mouth harp to my lips. Then she put it to her own lips and played 'O Susanna.' She made me use my good hand to hold it.

"At first, I just blew sounds—no tunes. In time the tunes came to me, and I've been playing ever since." He paused and his voice shifted into a rough whisper. "Tell me, why does God let these things happen? How come He lets me hunger to be free and whole in a life when I can never be either thing?"

Feevah shook her head. "When my mistress knew she was dying, she watched me nurse her baby and run the house and care for all the children. One morning as I nursed her baby, she lay on her bed watching him suckle and hold onto my finger with his little hand.

175

She was so thin you could see the bones in her face. Her skin had lost its pinkness and looked like ashes.

"She said, 'Feevah, how can God be so cruel to leave me lying here with the hunger to hold and nurse my boy. I will die before he is old enough to know his mama.'

"I thought about all I had learned from reading the Bible to her from cover to cover and answered, 'Mistress Fuller, God knows you're broken, just like Jesus was. And somehow in ways we may not be able to see, He sent Jesus to heal the broken world.'"

With a deeper connection between Feevah and Seth, the days went smoothly. But on the fourth day of Russell's absence, in the blinding midafternoon sun, they spotted a lone rider approaching, dressed in black on a dark horse. Except for the rider's large, pale face, he looked like a crude, charcoal mark moving slowly toward them.

"Stone," Seth said under his breath.

Feevah nodded and moved around the living room, straightening. The circuit preacher Tune Wesley Stone had visited the Fullers many times over the years.

While she prepared a tea tray, she watched him through the window steadily change from the curious mark on the horizon into the man.

Seth stepped out of the house and waited at the hitching post to take the preacher's horse.

Grandma and the girls, unaware, were sitting in the front room reading when his heavy steps, pounded on the porch.

Grandma stood and said, "Well here's Brother Tune come to visit us! Let's set an extra plate for supper. Come on in."

Dorcas retreated into the kitchen and hung closely to Feevah, watching the front room but not returning. Dorcas had always been quiet when Preacher Tune came to Fuller Plantation. Feevah told herself it was because he was so tall, in fact, probably the tallest man they had ever seen. At first glance he was handsome, but something about his mannerisms made him appear foolish.

Brother Tune came into the front room and sat briefly, but he seemed uncomfortable. After a short time, he stood and talked loudly to Grandma. "Well, Miss Richards, I see you got a fine nigress and two little pickaninnies." He paced in cadence with his words. "And it looks like you is so happy you is fit to be tied. Did Russell tell you it was me that told him about Feevah?"

Mrs. Richards smiled vacantly. "Amen."

"I been watching this nigress, Feevah, for many a year at Fuller's. I seen that she could cook and run a household good as any white woman. I seen that Fuller was fixing to get rid of her and that no-count Robin, and I seen what needs you and Russell's got here."

The preacher paused with his feet spread wide and his arms outstretched, turning his large head from side to side as he looked around the room. "I says to myself, 'Now why would the Lord show me this exceptional nigress, and why would the Lord show me the Richards' needs, and why would the Lord put me in just the right place at just the right time to know that this here nigress is about to be sold?'"

He paused long enough for Grandma to say, "Amen."

"And the Lord told me, 'Brother Tune, you need to give this message to Russell; you need to share the bounty of your travels with your flock.' Now, I just want to pass that word over to you. I discovered her and the Lord told me what to do with her. Now, just remember that."

Grandma knew from habit how to welcome guests and how to speak to preachers, but his words had no meaning to her. "Praise the Lord," she said. "And please set yourself down."

"I'll set down directly. Now how is little four-year-old Grace, who was born on July 17, 1855, exactly thirty-one days before her mistress and namesake passed over unto the loving arms of the Lord?" He paused with his hands on his hips and his body tilting downward toward her. Brother Tune claimed to know the full name and date of birth of every person he had ever met. He cited dates as if they had a mysterious significance. "Is you enjoying your new home? I seen you at the Fullers'. I'm the one that discovered your mama. I'm the one that got you here to this fine new home. Now, just remember that."

Without waiting for a response, he stood straight again and began pacing about the room. "And where'd Dorcas get to? Seems like she's always hiding behind her mama. Maybe she's scared she'll die like her namesake. She shouldn't be scared, because Dorcas was raised from the dead by Postle Paul. But you, little one, you is a brave one." He turned quickly toward Grace and pointed his long arm, finger extended toward her. "Now, where is your mama?"

Feevah, who had been listening from the kitchen, stepped in. Brother Tune repeated his speech, still pacing and saying again and again, "I just wanna pass that word over to you."

Finally, when his speech was finished, he asked, "Now tell me where does everyone sleep?" As he asked, he walked to the door of Russell's room and pointed. "Who sleeps in here?"

Grandma said, "Amen."

Feevah said, "This here be Masser Russell's room."

"Uh-huh, and who sleeps in here? And why's there so many beds?" He had paced over to Grandma's room.

"This here be Grandma's room. Masser done told me and the children to sleep with her cause she get scared in the night and run off. We watches her and keeps her company."

"Now you mean to tell me Russell got you and your pickaninnies sleeping in this here room with his granny?"

"Yes, suh."

"Well, I swannie." He paused, grinning with his hands on his hips, his head bouncing in a nod. "Was I right? Was I right? You know, it was me that discovered you. I just wanna pass that word over to you. Here you is safe from the ruckus that Mr. President

178

Abraham Lincoln, born February 12, 1809, is making everyone crazy with mancipation ideas. Just remember Mr. Lincoln's mama didn't even give him a middle name. You's better off out here safe from such fool notions. To everything there is a season, and this here is the season for you to be in this place. Just remember that."

"Masser, you be wanting some coffee whilst Feevah fix supper?" Seth asked.

At first, Brother Tune ignored his question. He had paced back to the door of Russell's room and posed with his weight on one leg. "This night I be sleeping in this here bed," he said. "I be right there. Now, I promised Russell to pray with his granny, and my horse been favoring her bad leg, so I'm gonna be needing to rest her a bit, so I be sleeping right here tonight. It wouldn't do for me to risk my life and go on down the road with a horse that might go lame." He glanced at Seth. "No, I don't need no coffee. I need to wash up after my long ride to come here to bring the Word. Just remember that. Now, I need Seth to get me some water ready and take care a my horse."

"Amen," Grandma said.

"Yes, suh," Seth said as he shuffled toward the doorway.

"Well, Seth, I sees you still a cripple," said Brother Tune as they walked out. "Just remember, it's the Lord's Way. So, you needn't be a thinking of a healing for your crippled body. It don't matter that the Lord sent Seth to replace Abel."

During supper, Tune's words and repetitions that had seemed harmless at the Fuller Plantation, left Feevah uncomfortable. Dorcas didn't eat.

When prayers and all the evening rituals were done, Feevah ushered her daughters and Grandma into their bedroom, and closed the door on Brother Tune with relief. She didn't go back out into the kitchen as usual. Instead, she fell asleep next to her children.

For a few moments, she didn't realize who was rubbing her leg; her first instinct was to check the girls and Grandma. She instantly

179

noted they were sleeping soundly. In the same instant she realized Brother Tune was rubbing her thigh. She was on her feet moving toward the door before speaking, hoping to guide him out of the room, so no one else would awaken. She wanted to move Tune and herself away from her daughters, so they would be safe.

"Now, you just come on in here and lay in this bed," he said as soon as they were out of Grandma's room.

"Masser Tune, I's in my monthlies." Feevah wished she were in her monthlies and knew she should be in her monthlies but suspected she was pregnant.

"You ain't unclean. I knows your smells and I knows when you is and when you ain't. You ain't unclean. The Lord brought you to me clean. If'n you was unclean, it would be an abomination." He led her into Russell's room. "Now, you gotta understand that I'm the one that discovered you. I seen you many and many a year ago. I seen you with that no-count Robin, and I seen how Fuller didn't understand your fine qualities. It was me that discovered you. The Lord put us together."

By this time, he had led Feevah into Russell's room and closed the door. He dropped his pants and stood before her with outstretched arms. "Now you seeing the real Tuney. You seen the Preacher Tune that the world sees. Now, you seeing the real Tuney." He placed his hand on himself and said, "This is for you. The Lord put you before me. Just remember that."

Feevah knew she had no choice but to lie with him; she wished he would shut up and get it over with. "Now, let's take this off," he said as he lifted her gown. "Every woman has a different smell. I love your smell. Did you know that? I love your smell. There will never be another man to tell you that."

Finally, he lay on top of her and entered. Surprisingly, he talked as he thrust, talked loudly, going through the same speeches he had given earlier. After more than half an hour, he slowed down and fell asleep, still inserted and stiff. Feevah tried to slip away, but he awoke and started thrusting again. Eventually, his stiffness limped, and he rolled away from her. This time she slipped out of the room and returned to her own bed.

The next day was endless. Brother Tune announced at breakfast that the Lord had told him to stay another day to deliver more of the Word. Seth struggled to contain his rage; Feevah struggled with despair. They hoped Russell would be early, but bedtime came, and he was not home.

This night Feevah rose from her bed as soon as Brother Tune entered the room. When they were near Russell's bed, Brother Tune said, "Now, you didn't see me at my best last night. When a man has to be working to spread the Word and goes without a woman, he can't perform like he should. Just remember that. It been two years and three months since I been with a woman, so it's a natural thing for me to have a little trouble."

With no further words, they stripped and lay on the bed; he quickly entered her, and as he had done the night before, he talked loudly in rhythm with his thrusting. "Isn't that something? Isn't that something? I love your smell..." Finally, he said, "Is you ready, girl? Is you ready? I'm going to give you my love, but you got to say you is ready."

"I ready, suh."

With loud grunts, he ratcheted up his thrusting, "There! There! I done broke my two-year and three-month dry spell! And you done it, gal. You done it! You said you was ready for my love, and the Lord heard you and broke my dry spell!"

Feevah stood and started toward the door.

"Now, where do you think you're going to?"

"Suh, I has to stay wi Grandma. Ifen I don stay wi her, she run off in the night. Masser Russell be mighty mad if she run off agin."

"No. Now, you just stay right here in this bed. I'm a gonna open this door just a bit and if anyone moves in this house, I'll know it. I'm

181

Brenda Vicars

a light sleeper, nuthin gits past me. Now, you just lay right down here."

"Suh, I's feelin sick. I has to go to the outhouse."

"Well, all right, you go on; then you come git back in this here bed."

She slipped outside through the kitchen, closing the door behind her. She took a couple of steps, keeping one hand anchored on the wall of the house. With her eyes closed, she leaned against the house and slid down to the ground into a sitting position with her forehead on her knees.

Seth lowered himself next to her. "I'll kill him."

"No, that would make things worse. He'll be gone soon enough." She stood and walked toward the outhouse; Seth followed and waited outside.

When she came out, she crumpled at Seth's feet. "I'm sick. I think I peed blood. It burned. I don't know what to do, Seth. I've got to take care of my girls and my work; Russell has been gone too long; Brother Tune makes me feel..."

Muttering comfort, Seth sat next to her until they heard Tune's loud snoring. "Let's go inside now." Seth led her to the sofa and made her lie down. He brought a pitcher of water, poured a cup. "Feevah, drink this. I know you don't want it, but you have to drink. You feel hot. We need to cool you off."

She drank and then leaned back on the sofa. He brought in a clean chamber pot from the shed, a clean rag, and bucket of water. Kneeling next to her, he dipped the rag into the water, and sponged her face, arms, and neck. She dozed fitfully for about an hour, and Seth woke her again and coaxed another cup of water down her. "Feevah, you need to pee out the sickness. The pot's right here. I'm going to help you." Like someone half alive, Feevah stood, lifted her gown and squatted on the pot. She cried out with pain.

"I must be dying."

182

"No, you're not dying. It's just going to hurt a while." He helped her back to the sofa.

Tune's snoring broke, and he started talking to himself. He made his way into the living room as Seth was lighting a candle and looking into the pot. "Now, what's goin on here? What are you two doin out here in the middle of the night?"

Feevah lay back, beyond caring.

Seth picked up the chamber pot and held it toward Brother Tune. "This what goin on. Feevah peein blood and burnin up with fever."

"Oh, well, now." Brother Tune looked into the pot. "Is that catchin?"

No one had noticed Mrs. Richards enter. "Seth, make her drink a cup of water; then go find some asparagus roots and greens to boil. She needs to drink the brine."

Feevah drank the water and went quickly with Mrs. Richards into the bedroom, closing the door behind them.

As Seth shuffled toward the back door, still carrying the pot and candle, Tune repeated his question, "Now, you gotta tell me is this here sickness catchin?"

Seth said over his shoulder, "Course it catchin. Kills most men that catches it."

"Well, now." Tune started back toward the bedroom to gather his belongings. "I best be going to Chattanooga to see Doc Brown. He always takes care of me. He understands my body. It wouldn't do for me to be getting sick and dying. I gots too many folks depending on me."

Seth shuffled down the trail leading to the little creek where wild asparagus grew. With candlelight he found a good handful. On his way back to the house, he pulled mustard and turnip greens from the garden. He was back in the kitchen waiting for a pot of water to boil when he heard Brother Tune talking to his horse, riding into the night.

He boiled the asparagus and greens as Mrs. Richardson had instructed; even though much of the time she was not fully present,

Seth trusted her memory of the cure. After it boiled until the brine was green, Seth strained it into a pitcher to cool down. He sat at the table and waited with the pitcher and cup for Feevah to awaken.

At dawn Feevah came into the kitchen. "Where is he?"

"Headed to Chattanooga. He won't be back this way for a long time. Drink this, it's what Grandma says will cure you."

Feevah sat in the chair next to him, drank a full cup, and leaned her head against Seth's shoulder.

Another week passed before Russell returned. The sun was close to setting when Feevah and Seth saw Russell's wagon coming toward the house.

Seth said with a glum face, "Here he comes. Happy as a child with none of the bads you suffer."

They watched Russell approach, and Feevah said, "Seth, we can hold onto bad and let it walk with us every step, or we can turn away from bad and make every step the best it can be. Let's just love this minute for the joy we can get from it. I'm carrying Russell's child now, and there's going to be a world of bad things I can't shield my children from."

Seth nodded slowly.

Feevah added, "I don't have to punish them now with bad that is already gone from here."

"Masser!" Grace, jumping up and down like a spring on the front porch, had spotted Russell's wagon. "Masser! Masser!"

Laughing as he drew nearer, Russell jumped from the wagon almost before it stopped and, picking up Grace first, he quickly made a round to everyone, hugging Mrs. Richards then Dorcas with his free arm, slapping Seth on the shoulders, and finally, in the full light of day, he kissed Feevah long on the lips.

Russell was different, surer of himself. With his strong, straight shoulders, he seemed to stand taller.

"I missed you," he said, looking straight into Feevah's eyes, and kissed her again. "Now, who's going to help me unload?" He looked at Grace and Dorcas.

"I'll help!" Grace shrieked, wriggling to the ground, so she could run over to the goods Seth was already setting into stacks.

"Pretty, pretty, pretty!" Mrs. Richards said over and over as she watched the unloading of the packages, mostly food items.

As soon as there was a moment in the unloading when Russell could take Seth aside, he said, "Come sit with me for a minute." Seth was stilled by Russell's new tone of voice. "Seth, I know you feel protective of Feevah, and I know you think I've been using her in a bad way. And until I was gone these past two weeks, I believed you were right. But I want you to know I'm a man now. I realized while I was gone that everything I want is right here on this farm. Feevah is the only woman I need."

"When your daddy comes back, he'll kill you for acting this way."

"I know he won't like it, but I'm not a kid or a bleeder anymore. I'll stand up to him. Besides, there's a war in Virginia. It's too dangerous to travel right now. And while I was in Chattanooga, I heard that in New York and London and Paris, coloreds are living like whites. Feevah can read and write. She runs this house as well as Grandma did, she keeps Grandma well and happy, and she is my woman. When Daddy sees Grandma is fine with Feevah, he will accept us. I won't give him a choice."

Seth shook his head, and his voice was low and threatening. "You believe what you're saying, but you're no match for the meanness in your daddy. And you can't know you're not a bleeder because you haven't been cut since we were kids. I saw you almost bleed to death many times. Besides, you know your daddy's always been set on you marrying with Miss Francine so we'll be family with buyers."

"That's over, Seth. I'm just going to be with Feevah."

"You'll get someone killed talking like this. Who else did you tell? Miss Francine?"

"Francine should know I'm not coming back to her again, and no one else is going to worry about what is going on out here on my farm. We're too far out, and everyone is distracted with Lincoln's foolishness up in Virginia. We'll be left alone, and we're going to get better prices for tobacco because the Virginians are too busy fighting to get their crops in. We'll be rich! This was all meant to be."

"What do you mean Francine *should* know you're not coming back to her again? She knows it or she doesn't know it. Which is it? And since when is this your farm? Your daddy never signed anything over to you."

"Seth, look at what I brought you." Russell carefully unfolded a leather wrap from a small rectangular shape. "It's a Hohner harmonica all the way from Germany, just made in '57. It's the most modern there is, way better than that free reed Grandma gave you."

When the small instrument touched Seth's palm, a knowing beyond language filled him. This harmonica would bring rich, new music. Even so, after Russell turned back to the women unloading the goods, Seth said again, "You believe what you say, but you're no match for the meanness in your daddy."

Chapter Twenty

Sunday morning Philip woke with instant awareness—Edith wasn't beside him. They'd read the manuscript late into the night and fallen asleep together.

Even though they'd slept together only two nights, the bed was an empty cavern without her body. As he got up to find her, another troubling awareness settled over him—*if this manuscript is true, my ancestor impregnated his slave.*

Edith must have heard him moving about. "I'm in the kitchen."

Finding her at the bar with her laptop, he nuzzled her neck and wrapped his arms around her waist, saying, "I didn't like waking up to an empty bed."

The swiveling bar stool let her turn, wrap her arms around him and kiss him. "Ummm." When he stepped closer and wedged himself between her legs, she whispered, "Oh, I could come back to bed."

Immediately, he lifted her from the barstool so that her legs wrapped around him, and never breaking their kiss, he carried her to the bed.

After their reunited bodies were spent, she placed her

hands on both sides of his face and peered into his eyes. "I love mornings with you. I could never get tired of this."

Settling into a cuddle, Philip, absentmindedly smoothed her hair, letting the wild curls coil around his fingers. "I hope not, because I don't think I could ever let you go."

Her hand rested over his heart. "Coffee's ready. Would you like a cup in bed?"

Stretching, he sat up and slid on his briefs. "I'll get it."

"I'm coming, too." Pulling on her robe, she followed him toward the kitchen. At the bar she shook the mouse and tilted her laptop screen toward him. "I woke early and, as promised, I went online through the university's research system. Look."

A photocopy of a handwritten page of 1920s census from Waco displayed before him. There in careful script were the names *Sabine Russell Richards* and *Tennessee "Tenny" Madelyn Schmidt Richards* just as the manuscript had described.

The actual handwritten record from 1920 made Philip feel as if ghosts had entered the room. He envisioned the night Sabine and his mother sat on their porch and talked to the three census takers. These had been real people. The old census page in front of his eyes meant the story was real. His ancestors did these things.

Pulling up other diminished pages, Edith said, "Look— 1930, 1940. Mother and son were both still there. Then..." She displayed the last page. "...in 1950—only Sabine." She opened another site. "I haven't found other Richards people yet, but Tenny's family shows up in Tennessee records." She showed a page listing a Schmidt family with seven children. The fourth one was Tennessee Madelyn Schmidt born 1851.

Stunned, he stared at the screen.

She slid out a tablet with a hand-drawn chart starting with *Thomas Richards* and ending with *Philip*. "So, if Sabine, the son of Russell, was your father's great uncle, then that would make Russell and Tenny your great-great grandparents." Edith, noticing Philip's silence, wrapped her arms around him and peered up at his face. "You okay?"

He took a slow breath and returned her embrace, but his gaze stayed on the screen. "Yes. Yes, I am." His words came slowly, like boulders being excavated from the ground. "This makes it true."

"It's staggering, isn't it? You know this level of detail about your ancestors. Somehow the old manuscript made its way into your father's trunk."

"It's worse than I thought."

She moved away from him to fill coffee mugs. "What do you mean?"

"This..." He struggled for the right words. "...this true story shows my father's and grandfather's filth went back generations. Russell talks a pretty talk, but he's using Feevah. Using his power over her. And, Tenny... She was the little girl watering the grape vines. She must have been fourteen when Sabine was born. How did she become Russell's wife?" He scrolled through the screens again and settled on the 1920s census page.

Edith placed a mug in front of him. The air had thickened making it harder for him to breathe, speak, or move. Philip turned away from the screen, and his gaze met hers. Still perplexed, he said, "Fractal."

Edith put her hands on the sides of his face. "I guess a family tree can seem fractal—things ripple from one generation to the next. But, think of the value in this manuscript. It lays bare the truth for you. When truth is uncovered, you can learn and heal from the mistakes of previous generations."

He nodded again, taking in the massive implications of everything he'd experienced the last two nights: connecting with

Edith and learning his family history. The world was a different place now. In a husky voice, he said, "Thank you."

"Me? I did nothing. Thank you for letting me be a part of this."

"You did everything." He stepped closer. "Not sure I would have ever read this far if you hadn't been here." In fact, he knew he wouldn't have read this far, and he wanted to hang onto Edith's positive spin even though the story troubled him. "And it would have taken me months, if I even could, to process the significance you've given it." Clasping her shoulders, he spoke slowly. "But also thank you for these two nights—with or without the manuscript." He lowered his lips to hers.

When their kiss ended, she kept her eyes closed and spoke softly, "Until now I've been living a half-life." She moved close enough that their lips touched as she whispered, "I must be dreaming."

He ran his thumb down the side of her face. "No, this is real."

She hugged him. "I made breakfast tacos and coffee. Shall we eat and then read the rest?"

Chapter Twenty-One

Sabine Richards' manuscript. 1861

When the baby was born, it was Seth and Dorcas who helped Feevah. Even though Russell now made fewer and shorter trips to Chattanooga, he was away at the time of the birth. It was Seth's good arm that guided the golden baby boy from Feevah and Seth who cut the cord. By the time Russell returned, the mess of birth was scoured away, and Feevah was moving about the house, almost with her normal energy.

The first person who Russell saw when he came home was Mrs. Richards rocking the baby. "Pretty, pretty, pretty." She chuckled from time to time.

With golden skin and Richards' facial features, there was no question the baby was Russell's child. Russell knelt beside the two and gently touched the baby's cheek. Mrs. Richards extended her arms, and Russell took his baby. "Pretty, pretty, pretty," she said.

Feevah came and stood beside Russell, and he put one arm around her.

With his eyes on the baby, he said in a husky voice, "I will be a good father to her."

"It's a boy—Solomon Jedidiah," Feevah said.

As the girls and Seth came in from the garden, Russell laughed.

Brenda Vicars

"Hello, Solomon, I'm your papa." The room was hushed with tears starting in everyone's eyes.

"Pretty, pretty, pretty," Grandma said.

And as if on a signal, the others joined in, laughing and saying, "Pretty, pretty, pretty."

Solomon was a healthy, good-natured baby from the beginning. He rarely cried, and Mrs. Richards was content to rock him all day. He was a living, breathing baby doll. It was a golden life for a golden boy.

During the war years, it was not as easy to sell the tobacco crops, but the family had enough resources to eat well. Russell kept the hands busy drying and storing the tobacco he couldn't sell. He believed he'd have an opportunity to market it later. And he used tobacco to barter with the Germans for honey, flour, goat's milk, and pork.

Although Grandma was slowly declining, she enjoyed hours of puttering in the garden and watching the children play, and she tucked in happily each night to sleep between Dorcas and Grace. Some days she didn't speak at all, and other days she talked almost normally, but most days she only muttered, "Pretty, pretty, pretty."

Sabine Richards' manuscript. January1865

A few months after Solomon's third birthday, Mrs. Richards was sitting on the front porch watching Solomon play with the spinning top Seth had made. "Well, here's Brother Tune come to visit us! Set an extra plate for supper. Come on in."

"Mama," Solomon called. "Grandma is talking!"

Feevah and Seth were already standing at the door looking toward Tune; Seth sent Grace running to the field to get Russell.

Still fifty feet away from the house, Tune started speaking as if he had planned his speech during his solitary ride and couldn't wait another moment to begin. "Well, there goes a running nine-year-old,

Grace, who was born on July 17, 1855, exactly thirty-one days before her mistress and namesake passed over unto the loving arms of the Lord. And here I see is fifteen-year-old Dorcas turned into a mature woman, old enough herself to be giving birth. And here's Seth, still crippled, I see. And this young 'un must be Feevah's bastard," he said as he reined in and dismounted. "And from the looks of that belly, Feevah's carrying another. I needs to know this here boy's name and birthday, so I can save him out of purgatory."

When Feevah stated Solomon's full name and birthday, Brother Tune scowled at her as he stood at the base of the porch with his Bible in his hand. "You're a bold nigress. God's wrath will smite you down for giving this bastard that name. Bathsheba gave birth to Solomon Jedidiah after she and David were married. It is blasphemy for you to give a bastard that name. You was never married by a legal preacher. Broom jumping don't mean nothing in the eyes of the Lord Almighty." He raised his arms toward heaven and increased his volume as if preaching to hundreds. "Purgatory! You have doomed this boy to purgatory! You needn't be thinking just cause Yankees have filled up the towns that you can get by with blasphemy out here. Won't matter what the Yankees do, you still be a nigress with bastard young 'uns, and they never gonna be nothing else." Then he turned to Mrs. Richards. "I just want to pass that word over to you."

"Amen." Grandma nodded vacantly.

Tune, still preaching, paced away toward the field in the direction Grace had run.

Feevah knelt down to Solomon and jerked Dorcas down with her. "Dorcas, don't get out of my sight while he's here. And both of you don't pay attention to his talk about purgatory. I read the Bible from cover to cover. Nowhere does God say that a wedding must be performed by a white preacher. And nowhere in the Bible is the word *purgatory*. Those ideas are not from Holy Scripture but from men who twist the Word. Do you understand?"

Solomon nodded wide-eyed; Dorcas looked sick with fear.

"Brother Tune is dangerous, and you must both try to stay away from him. When he talks to you, you put your head down and say, 'Yes, Masser.' Solomon, do you understand me? Solomon, what are you going to say if Brother Tune speaks to you?"

Solomon had never seen his mother so angry. "Yes, Masser."

"And what are you going to do with your head?"

He looked puzzled. She slapped him hard and shook him by the shoulders. Mrs. Richards started crying. Solomon gasped in shock, and Feevah slapped him again. "I told you, put your head down... down!" He lowered his head. Seth approached and with his good arm, pulled the boy to him.

During the years of Solomon's life, their existence had been so isolated that Feevah had failed to prepare him for the behavior he must exhibit around whites.

Tune's approaching voice stopped them all. "And here comes Russell, the happy masser and bridegroom to be. Your daddy told me to get ready to have a quick wedding for you and Francine. We can't have her coming to her time before the nuptials."

"When is he coming?" Russell asked as he dismounted.

"Oh, he's a-coming as we speak, him and one slave he's got left. And he's a angry, angry man, near lost his faith with—"

"When and where did you see him?" Russell interrupted.

"Well, now let me see, don't be rushing the word of the Lord."

Russell started toward him, and Tune quickly said, "He was near Knoxville about a week ago. I don't know how long he'll be there. He was resting his horses a bit from his run across Virginia. But don't you worry none. He'll be here soon enough, Lord willing."

Feevah froze as the words sank in. The three children were silent behind her; Dorcas had picked up Solomon and was holding Grace's hand. Feevah's gaze locked on Russell's face. She didn't notice Seth beside her until he started guiding her, saying, "Come on, Feevah, let's go inside."

Terror settled over her. "This can't be true. I'll talk to Russell," she said, grasping Seth's shoulders as if convincing him would convince Russell. "He'll take us out of here before his daddy gets back. He won't leave us here. He won't leave Solomon and the baby I'm carrying."

"Feevah, where's he going to take you? There's no escaping, and Russell is no match for Thomas. Russell will do what his daddy says."

"No, you'll see. Russell won't let this happen. You'll see. Dorcas, take the children out to the quarters and stay there until I send for you."

Feevah worked in the kitchen, hoping to be able to talk to Russell alone. But he and Grandma stayed in the front room listening to Brother Tune tell news about battles and changes going on throughout Tennessee. Hearing their rambling, it almost seemed as if Tune's earlier revelations weren't real: Thomas on his way, a wedding impending, Francine's time coming.

Seth stayed close to Feevah.

Finally, Tune made his way to the door. "Well, I best be going up the road back to the Germans."

"I'll get your horse saddled," Seth said.

After Tune left, Seth brought the children to Grandma's room. Russell and Feevah had managed to calm her, but she was agitated by the disrupted routine. Dorcas handed Solomon to Feevah, and then the girls took their regular places on either side of Grandma. Within minutes they were settled for the night.

Feevah walked into the kitchen and sat at the table holding Solomon, who as he fell asleep, regularly made the after-gasps a child does after a long cry. Seth stood behind her, with his good hand on her shoulder.

Russell talked too fast. "It's amazing how Grandma depends on Grace and Dorcas. I had forgotten what a hard time she has without them. This is the first time she's been upset in years. I guess having company plus not having…" He slowly wavered off and the room became silent until Solomon gasped again.

Russell asked. "Is he sick?"

"I guess his heart is sick," Feevah answered. "I slapped him, twice on his face."

"Why?" Russell had never seen her strike anyone.

"So, he will remember how to respond to a white man." She let Russell think about the answer, praying he would say he's going to take them somewhere safe.

Russell didn't speak, so Feevah said, "Are you having a baby with Francine? Are you going to marry her and leave us here with your daddy?"

"No, that's not true. Tune is crazy. The war makes everyone crazy."

"What are you going to do when your daddy gets here? What will happen when he sees how we're living? When he sees your son?"

"I'll take care of it," Russell said without looking at anyone.

Feevah pressed close to him. "Let's leave before he comes."

"Where would we go? We don't have money until I can sell the stored tobacco. We're going to have to wait at least until…"

"Listen," Seth interrupted them, "that's a wagon coming." He put out the candle, and he and Russell walked to the front windows to peer out. Feevah held her breath and clutched her sleeping boy.

"Hello? Seth? Masser Russell? Mrs. Richards? You in there? It's me, Micah."

"It my own baby brother. It's Micah!" Seth said as he went to the door. "Micah, you're alive!"

Seth and Micah, who was a taller and fuller man, embraced.

"Are you alone?" Russell asked.

"Yes, Masser, your daddy gave me this pass and sent me to tell you to come to Chattanooga with money and a wagon to bring back his goods. This wagon is too damaged to carry his load." Micah handed Russell a folded paper, and Russell lit the candle to read.

"This is Feevah and Solomon," Seth said as Feevah came forward, still carrying the sleeping Solomon. "Micah, to be my baby brother, you've grown into the biggest man of the family."

"Hello, Micah," said Feevah. "You look so much like Seth. I am blessed to meet you." Seeing Seth beside his strong, full-bodied brother was a reminder of the man Seth would have grown into had he not been stunted.

"My own baby brother," Seth said, clapping him on the back again.

Russell said, frowning at the letter, "Seth and Micah, go out to the quarters and have the wagon and a couple of hands ready to go first thing in the morning. I'll head out early."

After the brothers left, Feevah laid Solomon in his small bed near Russell's room. When she and Russell were finally alone, he held her close and said, "Feevah, I promise you, I'll make things work. And I promise you there is no truth in what he said about Francine. Tune's caught whiff of some rumor grown out of our daddies' old idea that we'd marry."

The next morning as soon as Russell and the two hands left, Seth and Micah came into the kitchen. This was the first time Micah and Dorcas met, and their smiles hinted there would be something special between them. Grandma grinned and pointed from Dorcas to Micah, back and forth, saying, "Pretty, pretty, pretty."

After introductions, Seth asked Feevah to come outside alone to talk with Micah and him. "Micah and I worked out the best way to get through this. Micah says President Lincoln is whipping the rebels, and soon the war will be over and we'll be free."

"Praise God!" Feevah said.

Micah said, "Some Negroes are already living free in New York City. They have jobs and houses and can read and write. And the government is going to give all freed slaves forty acres of land and a mule that they'll take away from the Confederate slave owners."

"My children will live free!" Feevah exclaimed.

"But," Seth went on, "the coming days will be rough because Thomas is running scared. He lost his place in Virginia, and all his slaves ran off except Micah. Micah stayed just to come back here to me."

"Micah, you're a good man," Feevah said.

"Seth may be my only family left. I had to come back here."

Seth continued. "Feevah, you and Dorcas need to start dressing covered over again. If Thomas sees you in white woman clothes, he won't like it and worse, he'll get the notion to poke one of you. And we'll keep Dorcas and Solomon out in the quarters. Thomas might see them from time to time, but no use having them right in the house under his nose especially with the way Grandma calls Solomon by Russell's name sometimes. We don't need Thomas fretting over Russell being Solomon's daddy. We'll let Grace stay in the house to help you, and the two of you stay with Grandma at night. And we just all lay low until the war's over, and we're free."

"Bless you both," Feevah said as she embraced them. "It's a good plan, and we'll do it."

"Feevah," Seth said. "I have to tell you something... Micah heard Thomas tell Francine's daddy that Russell is coming to marry her quick before their baby is born."

Feevah's jaw tightened. "No, Russell promised me that's not true. You'll see."

Seth let her denial pass. "We'll try to wait until the war's done, but we've got to be ready to run. Feevah, listen to me." He waited until she met his gaze. "If Thomas takes over here and Russell is gone, you and the children won't be safe. Micah knows a place we can go to be safe and free."

Feevah closed her eyes and shook her head. "I'm not leaving without Russell."

"I'm not saying we leave now... just get ready, set aside supplies for the journey, get the old wagon set up..."

"You mean to steal the wagon? No, then we'd be outlaws."

"We wouldn't take anything we haven't earned."

"Russell won't forsake me or his children."

The argument was left to rest, and everyone worked on getting ready for Thomas's arrival. By evening the kitchen was stocked with cooked meat and baked bread, the yard was swept clean, and Feevah and her daughters were dressed in layers of loose clothes with tight kerchiefs on their heads. Seth and Micah kept the four remaining hands busy in the fields, and the place looked as if no war was going on.

The only person who didn't seem bright and hopeful was Grandma. She grew more somber as the day went on. And instead of chuckling, "Pretty, pretty, pretty," she mourned, "Russell, Russell, Russell?" No one knew whether she was missing Russell, gone to Chattanooga, or Solomon, gone to the slave quarters, because often they were both Russell to her.

The argument between Feevah and Seth about when to leave lost its urgency as day after day passed, and neither Thomas nor Russell showed up. Finally, one day shortly before dusk, Thomas came riding up to the house alone.

Seth observed, unseen, from the corner of the house. Even if they had not been expecting Thomas and Russell, Seth would have known from a distance this was Thomas. His twisted walking cane jutted out at an angle. No one knew for sure why Thomas carried the cane because he'd never seemed to be lame.

Micah met Thomas and took his horse. "Masser Thomas, what happen? Where's Russell?"

"God damn it." Grayer and more shriveled than the last time Seth had seen him, Thomas stomped onto the porch. "I don't know where that worthless piece of shit is. Did you tell him to come like I told you?" Thomas's hard voice filled Seth with dread, far deeper than he'd felt in the past because now he was also afraid for Feevah and the children.

Micah tied the horse to a post. "Yes, Masser, he left more than a week ago."

Thomas pounded his cane on the ground. "Well, I don't know where the hell he is—probably laying low with one of his whores. I never seen him—had to leave all my goods hidden in a ditch—probably looted by now—all I got is what I could carry on this horse." He came into the house, stood in the middle of the front room, and threw off his jacket.

Seth, thankful that at least Dorcas and Solomon were out in the quarters, rushed to the back of the house and entered the kitchen where Feevah was already browning onions and potatoes in bacon grease.

Thomas, banging his cane on the floor for emphasis, called out demands to no one in particular. "Bring my stuff in here. Get me something to eat." Sniffing the aroma, he gazed toward the kitchen. "When I get ahold of him, he's gonna wish he done what I said."

"Yes, Masser," Micah said and started removing the saddle with its overstuffed bags.

Mrs. Richards and Grace were sitting in the front room; Grace had been reading aloud from *Pilgrim's Progress*. Grace silenced her voice and lowered her head, patting the old woman gently and turning the page to hold her attention.

"Well, Mama, look at you! Ain't you looking good. And what a pretty little darkie you got a waiting on you." Thomas bent and kissed his mother's cheek, but she continued to gaze at the pages. "And what's your name, young 'un?"

Seth stepped in from the kitchen. "Welcome home, Masser Thomas. Her name Grace, but she can't hardly talk, and your mama don't talk too much anymore either. She been poorly."

"I can see she ain't doing good. Don't seem like she even know her own son. Get me some supper." He peered past Seth. "Who's that in the kitchen?"

"That be Feevah. She the housekeeper and the mother of Grace. Feevah don't talk much neither, but she making you a fine supper."

Thomas pushed Seth aside and walked into the kitchen. With one loud cane thump on the floor, he said, "Damn." He paused and appraised Feevah. "That's a tall gal. No wonder Russell bought her. Get over here, Feevah."

She'd had her back to him stirring the vegetables, but moved the pot off the flame and turned toward him with her head bowed low.

Thomas clamped her jaw with his rough hand. "Let me see your teeth, open up." He twisted her face from side to side, peering in. "Good, looks like we can get another eight or ten young 'uns out of her." He rubbed his hand over her belly. Feevah froze. "And we gettin' a brand new one here in another two-three months. Good. We gonna be needing to restock cause I lost most of my hands." He propped his cane against the wall, ran his hands under her clothes and lifted her breasts. "Good udders." He leaned in close to her face with both hands still under her clothes. "You like that don't you, Feevah. You like Masser rubbin you right there, don't you?" He pulled his hands away as if tired of a game and shoved her. "Go on, get my supper now." While she backed away, Thomas grabbed his cane and headed to the table. "Seth, we need to keep her busy breeding. Who you got her bred to?"

Seth choked on his powerlessness.

Thomas plopped into a chair, let his cane clatter to the floor. "I said, who you got her bred to?"

"Big Noah. He the strongest hand you got, he make the best offspring."

"I'll take a look at him tomorrow. I might wanna breed her with someone else next."

Feevah placed a plate of ham, cornbread, and vegetables in front of him and backed away from the table.

"This looks good. You're right, Seth, this one can cook. And we gonna figure out what else she can do, ain't that right, Feevah?" He grinned at her.

Feevah, her head still low, returned to the stove. Seth, now behind Thomas's back, clenched both fists.

After Thomas finished his supper, he went back into the front room and sat with his legs stretched out. "Grace, git over here and yank off my boots."

Grace followed his order then started back toward Mrs. Richards, but Thomas said, "No, now don't go back over to Mama. She done fell asleep in her chair. You stay here and let me check you over." He grabbed her skirt. "Let's see, you got so damn many clothes on, I cain't tell for sure if you's a male or female." Grace stood frozen as he ran his hand up her leg. "Yep, you's a juicy little female all right."

Feevah gasped, and holding the long knife, still smeared with ham fat and speckled with cornbread crumbs, started toward Thomas.

Seth grabbed her arm and pushed it downward, so the knife was hidden by her skirt. "No."

Thomas's eyebrows shot up and his gaze darted from side to side as if he was deciding where to send his focus—Grace or Seth. A crash of breaking glass on the front porch diverted his attention.

Micah said, "Oh, Masser, I's sorry, I done dropped your bottle. I's sorry, Masser. Please forgive me."

"God dammit, you stupid fool, I can smell my spilt whiskey," Thomas raged, stomping barefooted toward the porch where Micah cowered. "I wisht I'd a sold you when I had a chance. You been nothing but a waste your whole life. You gonna pay for that whiskey with your hide." Thomas raised his cane and began to beat Micah, now slumped over. "Git over here closer where I kin beat you without stepping in that glass." Micah moved forward and stood still until Thomas finished. "God dammit to hell, clean up this mess before I lose my head and kill you. Seth, bring in the rest of my stuff. And don't drop my other bottles. God dammit, the one thing I cared about that I brung with me was my whiskey, and now a whole bottle is wasted."

When he came back into the house, Grace and Feevah were leading Mrs. Richards into her bedroom. "You gals come back in here after you put her to bed. I ain't through with you. Seth, I need a bottle in here right now."

Feevah and Grace delayed in Grandma's room, and soon after Thomas drank some of his whiskey, his full belly and tired body had him snoring.

Seth ushered Feevah into the kitchen and whispered, "We've got to leave tonight. If Micah hadn't got Thomas mad about that whiskey, there's no telling what would've happened to Grace. There's no use in waiting for Russell." Feevah silently clutched her stomach. "Micah and the hands are loading the wagon now."

Her face wet with tears, a whisper scraped out. "What if Russell is hurt somewhere. We've got to find him. Maybe he never made it to Chattanooga. Please, send someone to look for him."

"We'll look for him on our way," Seth said. "We're going tonight."

Feevah seemed frozen so Seth nudged her toward the pantry. "Come on, Feevah, let's find food to take, so we don't starve. With all the soldiers around, there's no rabbits or squirrels to be had."

A strangling sound struggled deep inside her throat, and tears flowed from her eyes, but she moved with Seth.

"Seth," Micah called from outside. "I found Russell." Micah came into the kitchen carrying Russell slumped over his shoulder. "I found him outside. He's been crawling."

Feevah rushed to them. "Put him in his bed."

Micah carried him through the front room, past snoring Thomas and into Russell's bedroom. When dropped onto the bed, Russell groaned but didn't speak. Seth and Feevah checked him over and found, though battered and scraped, he seemed to have no serious injuries.

As soon as Feevah lifted Russell's head and offered him water, he opened his eyes and said one word. "Feevah."

"Let him drink, and let's get out," Seth said. "His daddy can take care of him. We have to go."

"No," said Feevah. "Now that Russell's home, he'll protect us. We'll stay until he's stronger and can go with us."

"Feevah," Seth said with exasperation. She ignored him while she eased Russell's boots off. "Listen to me. If you never listen to me again, hear me now." She finally faced Seth. "Russell is no match for his daddy. We have to go now."

"No." Feevah turned back to Russell.

Seth shook his head at Micah who waited in the doorway.

Micah whispered, "It's a mistake to stay. When I found Russell, I saw escapees heading north. They say the South is winning. Everybody's escaping to New York City. With the Yankees whipped, it will be worse than ever here. This may be our only chance."

Seth sighed. "Go on out and tell the hands to stay ready but unhitch the wagon. We'll go soon, just not yet."

With Micah gone, Seth closed the bedroom door and approached the bed. "Where you been? What happened to you?"

Russell gazed at Seth as if in a stupor.

Feevah said, "He's too weak to talk now."

Defeated, Seth left the room and went to the old tobacco rack storage building where Feevah and her daughters had stayed before they moved into the main house. From there he could see the house as well as the slave quarters. Throughout the night he watched to see how Thomas would react when he woke to find Russell.

Before dawn, Feevah slipped out of the house and told Seth that Russell had revealed that retreating rebels took away his horse, wagon and two slaves, and gave him a beating. Russell had hidden for a couple of days to be sure all the Confederate troops had passed through. As soon as the rebels stopped coming, he had to wait for Union soldiers to pass. By the time Russell was able to come out of hiding and walk home, he was so weak the journey took days.

In the morning Thomas showed some compassion for Russell, and there was an uneasy silence in the house while Russell stayed in bed. But by the third morning, Thomas ran out of sympathy, and he ranted at the open door of Russell's room, pounding his cane for emphasis. "You nothing but a chicken shit. Look at you lying in bed like a baby. If you had any guts, you woulda kicked their butts and kept my wagon and done what I told you to do. You lost a good wagon and two horses."

Feevah, Grace, and Seth stayed nearby but attempted to be as unobtrusive as possible, trying to escape Thomas's attention.

Thomas rested a while in the rocking chair. Then he pushed himself up and again stood at Russell's doorway with more complaints. "You got everybody in Chattanooga pissed because you knocked up Francine. You didn't even fight in the war. Just been hiding out here when you weren't carousing in town. You probably ain't even a bleeder no more."

He started toward his chair then stopped, turned back toward Russell, and added, "I seen your white nigger boy and his mama this morning out at the quarters."

Feevah gasped, realizing Thomas was now aware of Solomon and Dorcas in spite of efforts to keep them out of sight.

Seth clutched her arm and whispered. "They're okay. Micah's made sure."

Thomas, caught up in his rage, didn't notice Feevah and Seth. "It's a good thing Mama don't have the sense to see what you're up to. You're a disgrace to the Richards' name."

Russell closed his eyes and stayed silent.

Feevah was so distracted trying to keep Grace away from Thomas and trying to find private moments to talk with Russell that she never went out to the quarters to see Dorcas and Solomon. She trusted Seth when he said Micah was guarding them, but she didn't know how important Micah had become to Dorcas.

One afternoon Seth approached her as she sprinkled white flour across her bread-making board. "Feevah, Micah and Dorcas have married themselves."

Feevah dropped her dough onto the flour. She nodded, seeming unsurprised. She spoke with resignation. "Dorcas has become a beautiful woman, and Micah is a strong, protective man. In normal times I'd get them to wait, but in this struggle, I accept their union." She opened the oven door and jiggled a leg on a baking chicken, testing for doneness.

Seth took a breath and mustered up as much conviction as he could. He whispered, "We're all getting out of here tonight—I can't hold the hands back any longer. Once Thomas sees they're gone, he'll be meaner than ever. We're leaving tonight after Thomas and Russell and Grandma go to sleep."

"Yes," said Feevah.

"Yes?" Seth expected her to argue.

"Yes," she said again.

Later while Thomas and Russell ate their supper, Seth sat on the front steps and played his harmonica. He had also set a full bottle of whiskey near Thomas's preferred rocking chair. Seth hoped music and whiskey might lull him to sleep soon.

Mrs. Richards, who'd been refusing to eat since Thomas came home, was intrigued by the molasses sweetened milk Grace was spoon feeding her. The two sat quietly with the book on Grandma's lap. A hush fell over the house with the harmonica melodies floating in through the open windows and doors.

For the first time since he'd been home, Russell came into the front room and pulled up a chair near Thomas. Thomas reached for the whiskey bottle and poured two glasses. Feevah brought in a candle, and for a long time, the men sat in silence in the flickering, dim glow, listening to Seth's music.

Thomas spoke in a mellow voice. "Remember that Christmas when your cousins from Virginia came and we danced in this room. Remember Uncle Charlie showing us the jig?"

Russell smiled and gazed at the room as though seeing the memory, and soon the men were laughing as if the hateful words of the morning had never happened.

Seth noticed Feevah watching the two men, and he whispered, "Don't be fooled by Thomas acting nice. He'll switch back soon enough. Devil in him never stays down long."

Thomas and Russell, alternating between war tales, tobacco sale predictions, and family memories, finished the bottle shortly after Feevah and Grace took Grandma to bed. With Thomas snoring in the front room, Russell staggered to his bed and flopped down with his boots still on.

As soon as all three white people were asleep and the wagon was loaded, Seth came into Grandma's room. The plan was for Seth, Feevah and the children to ride in the wagon while the men took turns running alongside. The old wagon couldn't handle all the passengers at once.

Feevah and Grace followed Seth to the quarters. But after Grace climbed onto the wagon, Feevah turned to Seth. "I'm staying."

Seth shook his head sadly. He'd been afraid she'd do this. "Feevah, they'll kill you."

"No, Russell will protect me and his baby I'm carrying. Micah told me where you're going. Russell and I will find you. I'll saddle the horse you're leaving and tie him behind the barn, and I'll hide in the barn until you have time to get away, then I'll wake Russell and get him to make a plan for us to join you." She saw Micah approaching the wagon. "Micah, come here."

He came closer and stood before her.

"You're a good man, and I love you like a son." She gripped his shoulders. "Dorcas is blessed to have you, and I trust you to take care of all three of my children. I'm asking you to promise me one

207

thing. Don't ever hit Dorcas. If you hit her once, you'll crack your goodness. And the next time you're mad, you'll have to hit her harder. Don't ever hit her the first time. Do you promise me?"

His eyes met hers. "Yes, I promise."

"Mama, please come with us," Dorcas cried.

"I'll be with you soon." Feevah stepped up on the wagon and hugged Grace and Solomon. "Dorcas is the mama for now." She climbed back down and turned to Seth. "Go. Don't waste another minute; you need to be moving." She turned and walked toward the barn.

Micah gripped Seth's shoulder. "Get in the wagon."

Seth placed a hand on Micah's arm. "I can't leave her. You go, brother. I'll come later with Feevah. Nobody will hurt a cripple and a woman about to give birth." Seth turned and dragged his tired body back toward the storage shed.

Within seconds the wagon was gone. Seth stepped inside the shed, and from the shadows by the door, he watched the house in case Russell or Thomas came out before Feevah made her move.

"Russell, Russell," Mrs. Richards mournfully called. Seth froze, dreading what would happen when Thomas and Russell figured out Feevah and Grace weren't with Grandma. "Russell."

Thomas, dozing in the front room, woke first. "Feevah, where the hell are you. Get in here and take care of Mama. Russell, get up, Mama's calling you."

"Russell, Russell," Mrs. Richards continued to call.

While Russell tried to settle her, Thomas grabbed his rifle and headed out to the quarters. "Seth, Micah, where are you? Where's them bitches? Mama needs 'em." Thomas, winded, came back into the house. "Russell, all the slaves is gone—so's the wagon and the horses. They's all gone! Run to the Germans and borrow one a their horses. We gotta find them black sons a bitches."

Russell was trying to keep Mrs. Richards in bed. "She'll run off if I don't keep her here."

Thomas dropped his cane, and gripping the stock of the rifle with both hands, slugged Russell across the shoulder with the barrel. "Go, I'm telling you. I'll keep her in here."

Russell ran into the darkness toward the Germans' place. Seth, from his hiding place, didn't call out to Russell because he didn't want Thomas to realize he and Feevah were still there. Instead, with his lopsided gait, Seth tried to catch up to Russell.

When Seth finally got to the Germans, he was surprised the house was lit up and the family was moving around. A loaded wagon with four hitched horses stood in front. As Seth dragged into the light, he could hear children crying.

The German mother wailed, "Yankees coming. Take wagon, take my Tenny, too. If she stay here, Yankees ruin her."

"Where?" Russell asked. "Where do you want me to take her?"

"Hurry. Your house. Yankees won't see right-of-way. Take her and hide. I stay with babies and Papa."

A gunshot rang out, too close. The war had finally come to their remote area. Seeing Russell and Tenny climb onto the wagon bench, Seth pulled himself up into the back.

"Russell," he said as the wagon turned down the hidden right-of-way toward the Richards' farm. "Everybody ran off except Feevah and me. She's hiding behind the barn, got a horse, waiting for you to save her."

Russell turned and gaped at Seth. "Feevah? The barn?"

"Yes, we got to get her and catch up with the others."

Russell shook the reins hard, and the four strong horses and the sturdy wagon traveled quickly through the darkness.

"Slow down," Tenny ordered. "You'll wreck this wagon. No need to get us killed just going to your house. It isn't that far." Seth had seen Tenny, who was probably thirteen, many times over the years. She was one of the children still living at home; the older brothers had gone to war. Short and stout, Tenny had one arm splinted and in a sling. She was dressed in boy's clothes, probably to hide her

209

gender from Yankees. "I said, slow down! You want me to drive?" she bossed.

Russell slowed a bit.

Seth added, "Russell, you have to escape from your daddy. He'll kill Feevah and me when he finds us. Keep him out of the barn away from her."

Russell muttered, "I won't let him near her."

As they got closer to the barn, the horses reared and the wagon lurched to a hard stop because Mrs. Richards was standing in the middle of the road in her long blue nightgown. "Russell," she cried. Russell reined in the horses and leapt down to get her. Seth used the opportunity to run into the barn to tell Feevah what was going on.

Approaching, he heard movement inside the barn. "Feevah?" he called quietly, his eyes adjusting to the darkness. He noticed a rifle propped by the doorway. "Feevah?" he said again. He heard a shuffling sound, and squinting into the dimness he made out Thomas struggling next to the old dried-up stock well. "Masser Thomas, is that you?"

Seth's body knew before his mind understood that Thomas was grunting and pushing Feevah's limp body into the well.

"Feevah!" he shouted and lunged forward. He tripped over something in the dark and fell to his knees. He pushed himself up with the rifle he'd grabbed as he fell forward.

Thomas shoved her body over the edge—a solid thud sounded when she struck the bottom. "Don't worry." Thomas was breathing hard from his effort. "This dumb bitch is dead. I heard the horse and come out here—caught her trying to steal it. If I hadn't a stopped her, she'd a taken off like the rest of 'em. She weren't much good anyway."

"Feevah," Seth said again, and he raised the rifle as if there might be a way that he could use the gun to save her.

"Now, Seth, don't be pointing my own gun at me. You gonna

need me to take care of you like I been doing your whole life. Put that gun down."

"Feevah," Seth said again, pointing the rifle at Thomas, starting to understand Feevah had been left alone and Thomas had killed her. "This can't be," he said under his breath.

"Now you can't shoot me, Seth. I'm you own daddy. You can't shoot the one that give you life. You mama was my best woman, specially after my wife died. Put that gun down." Thomas started crouching behind the stock well.

A blast filled Seth's ears. Thomas's head burst, and the red blood flew all around. On some level, Seth knew Russell must have come in and shot Thomas, but wonderings flitted through his mind. "Did I shoot without knowing I pulled the trigger? Did Yankees shoot him?" The rifle he was still holding glistened with spatters of blood.

Something propelled past Seth, so hard he almost fell again. Russell leapt forward to pull a length of rope down from the rafter. He secured it to a bull pen near the well and threw the end down. In an instant Russell climbed down into the well.

When Seth reached the side of the well, he got a last glimpse of Russell's head as he scaled into the black pit. There was no lantern or candle, no way to see if Russell and Feevah were alive or dead.

"Russell, Feevah, do you hear me?" Seth called out.

Silence.

Seth tugged at the rope. It was loose. He didn't know if Russell had fallen or had let go.

"Russell," Seth called louder. "Answer me."

An unearthly howl rose from the well. In the first instant, Seth didn't recognize the sound as human. But Russell's one long agonized word—"Feevah"—told Seth she was dead.

Chapter Twenty-Two

Philip stood, shaking his head. "Jesus. Let's stop. Don't read the rest."

Edith froze. "Okay," she mumbled, but her eyes were still on the last line. She slowly turned the manuscript over and picked up the remaining unread pages. "There're only ten or fifteen pages left." She looked at Philip and added softly, "Maybe there's redemption by the end."

"There's no redemption for murder. Thomas murdered Feevah, and Russell executed his own father." He stepped toward the window and gazed out.

Edith laid the pages down and hugged him from behind. *"Ages to our construction went, / Dim architecture, hour by hour."* Her voice was so low, he held his breath to be sure he heard her words. *"And violence, forgot now, lent / The present stillness all its power."*

He waited for her to say more, but she stayed silent, still with her face pressed against his back. Finally, he said, "Is that one of your poems?"

"No. Robert Penn Warren. The lines remind me of how small our lives are in the scheme of time and the universe. How much of this moment was created in a past we're not even aware of."

Nodding, not sure what to say, he caressed her arms that still encircled his chest.

Still hugging him, she slid around to his front. "I also like the closing of his poem: *We live in time so little time / And we learn all so painfully, / That we may spare this hour's term / To practice for eternity.*"

With one arm around her, Philip said, "I like that, too... *this hour's term.* Like, that's all we really have." He pulled her closer. "Let's live for now and look to the future. We've looked at these old papers—got the gist. Maybe someday when we're bored, we can look at them again. But for now, it's enough."

"Deal," she said.

He kissed her, and close to her lips, he said, "We don't have much time left today. I don't want you staying up all night to get ready for classes tomorrow. What time is it?" He'd turned his phone off Friday night. Pulling it out to check the time he said, "Can't believe I ignored my phone for two days."

"Are you saying I'm a distraction?" She gazed up at him with an impish grin.

He kissed her. "For sure."

His phone powered up with missed calls from Al, Culmine Police Department, Nelda, and Lily. "Something's happened."

He called Lily first.

"Oh my God, Philip." She sounded near tears. "Are you okay? We've been trying to reach you since Friday night."

"Sorry. Had my phone off—just now powered up. What's wrong?"

"The Culmine police phoned looking for you. Then yesterday afternoon two local deputies came by my house wanting to know if you were here. I let them in to see for themselves—even took them out to Daddy's house." Her voice quavered. "They wouldn't say why. They went to Dinah's, too. I called and called you."

"I'm not sure what they want, but I'm sorry you had to go through that." He reassured her as well as he could and promised to let her know as soon as he had news.

Next, he called Nelda and explained he'd had his phone off but was headed for Culmine now.

"Okay, I think they just have some new questions for you and got rattled when they couldn't reach you. I reminded them your bail agreement gives you statewide rights. I'll let the sheriff's office know we're coming in."

On Philip's drive back, Al called.

"Hey, buddy, you okay?" Al's booming voice sounded alarmed. "One of your crew called, said there's police tape on your room door."

"Yeah, headed back now to talk to the police."

With his good-natured optimism, Al reassured, "Don't you worry. Nelda will kick their butts. Everybody knows this whole case is rigged."

"Hope you're right."

"Course I am. They'll be lucky if you don't sue them before this is over. Hey, not to change the subject, but you remember a Mexican from Vuelta—Lupe Hernandez?"

Warmth enveloped Philip. "Yeah, knew him and his family well—like a brother when I lived in Vuelta."

Al's voice had a smile in it. "That's exactly what he said about you—*mi hermano*. Said you'd vouch for him. Gotta tell you, I like the little guy."

"Where'd you run into him?"

"I'm setting up a temporary branch office in Vuelta—just got two big jobs down there—demolition and renovation. Need an office manager who knows a little about construction and lot about local labor. Need someone who knows the people and can speak Spanish. Lupe applied."

"Hire him. He's a hard worker. Ingenious. If he doesn't know something, he'll figure it out. He'll get your job done, whatever it is." *Lupe... back in Vuelta.* They hadn't been in contact since Rosa was found, and at that time Lupe lived in San Antonio. Philip hadn't sought him out, not wanting to dredge up his four-year search and Rosa's marriage.

When Philip arrived at the sheriff's office, Nelda was already set up in a conference room. She greeted him, pointed to a chair, and shouted, "Stanley, tell Renfro we're ready."

While they waited, she explained, "The sheriff himself is taking the lead on your case. I'm glad because I worked with him for years when I was DA. He's an honest man. I trust him to do the right thing."

Philip expected to see another elderly person shuffle in, but Renfro was tall and fit, wearing jeans and well-scuffed western boots. He looked like a tanned rancher who could put in a full day's work in spite of his iron-colored hair.

"Joshua Renfro." He shook hands with Philip and turned to Nelda. "Good to work with you again. We miss you as a DA." Then back to Philip. "Thanks for coming in, Mr. Richards." Not waiting for an answer, Renfro pulled a small electronic device from his pocket, gave the date, named the attendees, and said, "Mr. Richards, in all your moving around, have you ever done business in Houston?"

"Yes. Lived there almost two years. I worked on an apartment construction project there about seven years ago."

"Have you been there in the past three years?"

Nelda put her hand on Philip's arm and shook her head. "No more answers. What's this about, Renfro?"

Renfro nodded. "Gun Mr. Richards was holding when the police arrived is registered to a Houston resident. Stolen three years ago."

"Totally irrelevant. Mr. Richards' statement clarifies he took the gun from the two reprobates in the parking lot when they were squabbling over it. Mr. Richards most likely saved several lives that night."

Renfro's expression revealed nothing. "I need to know what activities Mr. Richards has had in Houston during the past three years."

"Nope." Nelda gave him a dismissive shake of her head. "You're not getting that information and you know better than to ask. I want to see the full discovery before you waste any more of our time." She dropped her yellow pad into her bag.

Nelda stood fast, sending her chair scooting backwards. "Philip Richards is an innocent man. His only mistake was trying to help a woman who was being raped in the backseat of a car. He did exactly what you would have done, Joshua Renfro. And as someone who values truth, you know it. He stopped the rape. These people have some hidden agenda."

She jabbed her pointing finger at the sheriff. "You need to be investigating them, not harassing my client. Furthermore, I've not been advised whether the prosecutor is going to have a preliminary hearing, go to grand jury, or drop the case. It's been four days since this absurd arrest. The case is cut and dry. If there's no inkling by this time about what the prosecutor is going to do, the case should be dropped. This delay is keeping a shadow over an innocent man's life."

Chapter Twenty-Three

"Insane," Edith proclaimed on the phone after Philip relayed the gun questions. "I can't believe they created such an uproar. Where are you now?"

"Pulling up to my father's house. Lily and Dinah are meeting me here. I've got some explaining to do. I hadn't mentioned my arrest to them."

"And the manuscript? Are you going to tell them about it?"

"Yeah." Dread washed through him.

"I bet they will be amazed. You left the copies here. I'll also print the genealogy info for them."

"That'd be great. Thanks."

"I believe this will be a turning point for your sisters. After you left, I kept remembering your mention of fractals and I did some reading about the impact of transgenerational events within families. Getting this family record will put their own part of the story into perspective. It will be healing... especially for Dinah."

He wanted to believe her positive take on the ugly story. "Thank you for everything." He paused and his voice lowered.

"Miss you." He hung up wishing he had better words to describe the emptiness he felt without her.

Fractals had run through his thoughts since college. A math professor had explained how a single quadratic equation could produce an endless, self-similar pattern, similar to patterns in nature. Calling it a miracle of math that replicates nature, he'd held up a picture of the Mandelbrot fractal. The students gaped at this strange figure with a Buddha-like black center and baroque designs spiraling out. The moment stood clearly in Philip's memory.

"Is that a bug? A heart?" one of the girls in the class asks. "It looks weird."

Another student says, "It's not a bug. It's Buddha!"

Someone whispers, "Psychedelic. Did I just drop acid?"

The professor is ignited. "It's a miracle," he says. "The spiraling patterns remain infinitely similar. Mandelbrot coined the name fractal because the Buddha-shaped core conveys a sense of something that is fragmented and fractional." He magnifies a single spiral to show it going on endlessly in similar patterns.

"Like broccoli!" a girl says.

The class laughs, but the professor nods. "And mountain ranges and growth patterns in the rain forest and ocean waves."

Unlocking the front door of his father's house, Philip thought about all the changes since he'd locked this door. Even with his parking-lot arrest and the gun questions, he felt lifted by his connection with Edith. Energized, he was eager to finish the property improvements and move forward with Edith. He scanned the front room, ticking off the renovation steps he'd do this week.

Lily and Dinah drove up, so he approached their car.

Smiling, Lily rushed forward and hugged him. "I'm so glad you're okay." She released him, and distress streaked across her face as her eyes cut toward Dinah who zipped past them heading toward the house. "I was so scared something awful had happened."

Philip acknowledged Lily, but his focus, like Lily's, was snagged by Dinah's angry energy. She went into the house and sat at the table with her arms folded over her chest and her back ramrod straight, facing Philip with no expression on her face.

He'd prepared for outrage, even crying, but her flat expression crawled inside him and took him back to the day he left home at fifteen. He had so badly wanted to make her life better.

But now things were worse.

He pulled out a chair for Lily. "I apologize for what both of you went through with the police. I haven't told you about the Culmine incident I'm involved in because it's a bogus charge and everyone, including my lawyer, says it will be dropped." He paused, waiting to see if Dinah or Lily had a response. Lily leaned forward nodding, but Dinah stayed frozen, her gaze boring into him. Slowly he sat. "It happened Thursday night." He related the whole story of the attempted rape in the parking lot. Throughout his account, Lily made a few sympathetic comments, but Dinah stayed silent.

After he'd told it all, he said, "Again, I'm sorry police came here looking for me. It's the last thing I wanted to put you through."

Dinah's hard voice commanded the room. "Finished?"

"Yes, unless you have questions," Philip said.

Dinah slowly shook her head. "I had to explain to my twelve-year-old daughter why the police were looking for her uncle. And you sit here and tell us you've been arrested for rape." The slightest smile played around her mouth. "But everyone knows you're innocent."

219

Like everyone knew Granddaddy was innocent. She didn't say it, but her tone left no doubt.

Her lip curled into a snarl and her voice took on a hissing quality. "Then you spent the weekend with a woman you've known less than two weeks. And we're supposed to say, 'Poor brother.'" Her eyes narrowed and her face paled. "You know what, brother, I want you to finish the work you promised. Then I want you to disappear like you did when I was twelve." She stood. "Only this time don't ever come back again." She started toward the door.

Lily reached for her. "Oh, Dinah, you don't mean that. Let's talk some more."

Philip said, "I don't blame you." Dinah was almost to the door. "Wait, please. I need to tell you about something else I've kept from you, something I found in our father's trunk."

Dinah faced him. She seemed thinner than the last time he'd seen her a few days earlier. The bones in her face were more pronounced. Or maybe it was her anger defining her face.

"I found an old manuscript, maybe eighty or ninety handwritten pages by our great-great uncle Sabine Richards. When I first ran across it, I hid it in the ceiling because the opening lines were vulgar, and I didn't want you two to have to deal with them."

Both sisters stared at him, shocked.

"I read part of it this weekend with Edith, and it's a true story about our great-great-great grandfather Russell Richards. It's an ugly story, but I think it will be good for you to read it. It shows why our family got so messed up, why our father and..." He hated to say the next words to Dinah. "...our... grandfather were the kind of men they were."

Dinah's face blanched like a raw pink thing dropped into boiling water.

Lily said, "Where is it?"

"At Edith's. She made copies so you can each have your own to read. I forgot to bring them."

"What were the vulgar lines?" Lily asked.

Philip tried to think of a way to convey it honestly but to also soften the impact. "It opens with Sabine talking about his arousal contortion."

Dinah started laughing. Her maniacal sound and crazed facial expression froze Lily and Philip.

Before they could react, she stopped, turned her gaze to Philip. "You dare to come back into our lives. Take property that is equally ours. Share it with this stranger... this Edith. You are truly your father's son."

She reached for the door. "Mama always defended you, saying you had to leave us to save yourself. She said we shouldn't blame you. But you fooled her just like Daddy did." Her voice dropped into a whisper. "I'm glad she can't see you now."

Philip stood stunned as she walked out. Lily touched his arm and whispered. "I rode with her, so I'll go too. But I'll call you later. She'll cool down."

And then he was alone.

Now in the nearly empty room, his father was more present than he had been when alive. And, Dinah was suffering as much as ever.

He'd honor her request. Get this house and the four others renovated fast, so she wouldn't be forced to see him. He pulled out his phone and checked the sites where he'd posted job bids. He needed a roofer, landscapers, masonry workers, painters, and carpenters for sure. Each site he pulled up had the same result. No responses.

Pocketing his phone, he started toward the door to go to the local hardware store where he'd left notices posted on a bulletin board. The vibration of his phone stopped him.

It was a strange number, and a voice from the past surprised him. "Hey, *mi hermano!* How are you, man? It is me... Lupe. Got your number from your boss. How are you? You sound just the same."

"Lupe." Philip, his face breaking into a smile, sat in one of the chairs at the table. "Oh man, it's great to hear from you."

"I must tell you." Lupe's voice was as upbeat as ever. "I had given up on you. Tried for years to find you, but you are slippery. Not on Facebook, Insta, X, or TikTok."

Philip laughed. "Are you on Facebook, Insta, X, and TikTok?"

"No way. But I had my kids try to find you. I figured a cool guy like you would be on social media."

"Holy Jesus. Your kids? The last picture I saw of them, they were babies."

"Three now and another on the way. My oldest is thirteen. Hey, thanks for the recommendation. Big Al just called and offered me the job. Starts in about three weeks. It is a fortunate opportunity for a small town like Vuelta. *Muchas gracias.*"

"That's great. I thought you lived in San Antonio."

"*Si.* Many years. Lots of construction work. Good money. But we wanted the kids to go to school in Vuelta. Hey, you need to come see us soon. Meet *mi familia.*"

"Yeah. Sounds good. Listen, I'm looking for some workers here in Gire... got five houses to renovate... need to do it fast."

"Al said you inherited houses."

"Yes. Promised my sisters I'd get the houses ready to sell. Know anyone here in Gire looking for work?"

"Of course. Well, not in Gire, but I have good guys lined up in Vuelta. We can come to Gire if you can find a cheap place to stay."

"I've got a free place to stay." Philip gazed down the long

hallway where six empty bedrooms waited. "This house I'm staying in has plenty of room. When can you come?"

"*Mañana*," Lupe said in a heartbeat. "We're free until my new job with Al starts."

After Philip described the work to be done, Lupe said he'd be in Gire the next day with five guys ready to start.

As soon as they hung up, Philip started pulling trash out of the bedrooms. The dumpsters he'd ordered had been emptied, so he loaded them again. He put his father's cardboard trunk into the closet of the bedroom he was sleeping in. He'd let his sisters decide what to do with the old photos and documents. He didn't want to make the same mistake he had with the manuscript. By nightfall he'd removed the trash and old mattresses and made a list of stuff he'd need to buy the next morning to set up sleeping quarters for Lupe and his workers.

Tired as he was by the time he crawled into bed, he hungered for Edith. They talked before going to sleep and decided the weekend was too far away. Philip would go to her apartment and spend the night Wednesday.

The next morning Philip was unloading the camper cots and pillows he'd picked up when the rumble of a diesel pickup came up the long driveway. It was followed by a small black car. Three men rode in each vehicle.

Lupe leaned out the open window of the pickup and slapped his hand on the outside of the door. "Felipe! *Buenos dias!*" Mexican music blaring from his radio, Lupe braked to a stop and jumped out leaving the door open. He had aged well, a little thicker around the middle but still slight and spry, with a head full of black, thick hair.

He slammed into Philip. "You are still a giant! But I can still outwork you!" Short but strong, Lupe clasped his arms around Philip's middle and lifted him off the ground.

Philip threw back his head and laughed. "Still crazy."

The five other Mexicans piled out, and Lupe, after he made introductions, said, "Now, let us get these houses fixed." The six guys, full of energy and Spanish chatter, settled in quickly then toured the four other houses. By late afternoon, with Lupe supervising and Philip picking up the immediately needed materials, work was underway.

Chapter Twenty-Four

Lily's jaw dropped when she pulled up to her father's house. She was still gaping when she stepped out of her car and approached Philip, waiting for her in the front yard. "OMG, Philip, I thought I was at the wrong place. I can't believe all the changes you've made in two weeks."

"Not me. Lupe's landscaper. He's an artist." Philip and Lily hugged. Then he followed her as she dashed to the house to inspect the new stone-lined courtyard. "I've given him free rein, and he's working magic at all the houses."

"I can't wait until Dinah sees."

It won't make a difference. She'll still hate me. "Take a look inside." He swung the door open.

But Lily stalled outside and ran her hands over the antique barnwood lining around the entryway. "Where did this aged wood come from?"

"Found it in the horse barn. We're replacing the exterior barn walls with weather-proof material that will be better insulated and easier to keep clean. The guys are finding places to use this old wood in a couple of the houses."

Lily continued to gaze. "The color streaks are amazing.

Priceless." She finally stepped inside and sniffed. "Yum, are you cooking? Cumin?"

He shrugged. "Nah. Not me. Lupe and the guys cook their meals here. That's probably their lunch slow simmering."

After she toured the house, Philip pointed to three large envelopes on the dining table, two labeled *copy* and one labeled *original*. "Here's the old manuscript I told you about. Edith suggested keeping the original separate and using the copies for reading. The old paper is fragile in places. She also printed some genealogical info she found."

Lily picked up the envelopes and grinned. "So?"

Philip frowned. "So?"

She dropped the envelopes back onto the table. "So, Edith. How is it going with her? Progressing?"

"Yeah." He smiled. "Going great. I'm meeting her parents next week."

"What? Already! OMG. Isn't it quick to be meeting the parents? You guys must be really getting serious."

"We are serious. But her parents are missionary volunteers in Haiti, and they're only here every six months. That's the main reason for the timing."

"When do I get to meet her?"

"I hope soon."

"I'd love that, and I bet Dinah will, too. Let's plan something here at the house, a celebration of completion. When do you ever get to see Edith? Looks like you've been working nonstop." Before he could respond, she noticed the deck outside the kitchen and headed toward the back door. "The deck. You've painted it."

Philip followed her out. "We work about twelve hours a day. Mostly seven days a week. Although, the guys sometimes take a day or partial day to see their families. But they want to get in as many hours as they can before their next job starts."

She bent over to inspect new shrubs bordering the deck. "Will they have everything done by then?"

"Just about. Whatever's left, I'll finish after they leave."

Lily gasped. "Is that a big patio?" She started down the new stone path that wound through mesquite trees to a large square concrete slab surrounded by a low rock wall, just the right height to sit on.

He followed her. "It's a slab. Looks like someone planned to build something here and never finished. We converted it to a patio. With all the trees around it, it's well shaded."

"I love it. Did you build that barbeque pit, too?"

"Nope. It was there all along, covered by brush and trash."

"Gosh. Have you run across any rattlesnakes out here?"

"No. But now that it's getting so hot, they'll be moving. We're always watchful."

She sat on the low rock wall. "So does Edith come here?"

He lowered to sit next to her. "She hasn't been here yet. I go to her place two or three nights a week."

She leaned a little closer. "I hate to bring up a bad subject, but is there any word on the Culmine charges?"

He shook his head. "But the DA is supposed to take his next step within thirty days, and that'll be up soon. So, unless they get some kind of extension, it'll close." His stomach clenched. *Eleven more days. Something will happen one way or the other.*

Lily squeezed his arm. "Fingers crossed."

Before he could say anything else, vehicles pulled up and the voices of men speaking Spanish flowed out.

"Want to meet Lupe and the guys? It's their lunch break."

Lily started back up the path with him.

Philip added as he opened the back door, "Gotta warn you, Lupe is a flirt... but harmless."

Someone turned on a radio and Mexican *conjunto norteño*

music filled the house. One guy peered into the pot on the stove, and another pulled salad fixings from the refrigerator.

"Felipe!" Lupe strolled into the kitchen. "Who is this beautiful lady?"

Philip started to make introductions, but a call came in from Nelda. "I've got to take this." He stepped back onto the deck.

"Congratulations," Nelda said. "It's over."

Relief surged through him. "The rape charge is dropped?"

"All charges are dropped—assault, illegal use of a gun, and vandalism of property. You were never charged with rape. Even though the officer said that when they arrested you, they never included it in the formal charges. Turns out she refused a rape kit. Your $15,000 bail will be reimbursed within ten days."

Philip's first urge was to hang up and call Edith, but nagging unknowns bothered him. "So, what happened? Did the woman tell the truth? That it was that guy, Ralph?"

Nelda was quiet a moment. "That I don't know. I think they just didn't have a case against you. Whether or not they're going to arrest Ralph, I haven't heard."

As soon as Nelda hung up, Philip texted Edith the news. He knew she was teaching a class, but he wanted her to know immediately. The nightmare was over.

Whatever had transpired between Carmen and him, whatever she had meant when she whispered, "...Valentine's night promise," whatever it was, it was over.

Back in the kitchen, one guy was spooning a bean and meat mixture onto tortillas, and the others were setting the table and chopping lettuce, tomatoes and jalapeños for the tacos. Lupe, leaning close to Lily, was showing her pictures of his children on his phone.

For a long moment, Philip stood inside the doorway watching and relishing the relief of no longer having charges.

The guys' Spanish chatter together with Lupe and his sister smiling flooded the kitchen with warmth.

Lily, snorting at an antic Lupe was relaying about his youngest son, noticed Philip. "Hey, what's up. You're glowing. Win the lottery?"

"All charges... dropped."

Lily squealed and ran to him. "Yes!" She hugged him then jumped up and down like a happy child. "Okay. Now for sure we'll have a celebration. Saturday after next. Here at the house. Lupe, you and your friends..." She swept her hand around the kitchen to include the workers. "...and all your families are invited. And Edith and her family. We'll have a big cookout."

In a low voice, Philip asked, "Will Dinah come?"

Lily beamed. "I think she will, now."

A call came in on Philip's phone. "It's Edith." He headed out to the deck.

Edith's voice was choked and tremulous. "Oh, Philip."

"Are you okay? Are you crying?"

"Happy crying. This ordeal is over."

He leaned against the rail of the deck and gazed out at the pasture and barn. "The whole world looks different now."

"We need to celebrate."

"Funny you say that. Lily's here and just said the same thing. Wants to have a big gathering here a week from Saturday. She wants your family to come. What do you think?"

"I'd love to."

"That reminds me, Lupe invited you and me to go to Vuelta this Saturday to meet his wife and sons. I told him I'd better stay here and get in another day of work, but now with the charges dropped, I don't feel as pressured to finish. Would you like to ride down there, meet Lupe and his family?"

"Of course. I want to know everyone in your life. Will Rosa be there?"

"No. She lives in Mexico."

"Still?"

"Far as I know. Lupe hasn't mentioned her." He paused. "Edith." His voice grew rough.

"Yes?" she answered, questioning.

Almost in a whisper he said, "Thank you for not giving up on me through all of this."

"Philip, I'll never give up on you. Never."

He almost groaned. "God. I wish you were here right now."

"You're still coming tonight? Right?"

"Yes, leaving here soon. I'll text when I'm on my way."

Chapter Twenty-Five

Saturday, driving into the outskirts of Vuelta, Edith said to Philip, "This town looks like an old movie—maybe from the sixties."

"Yeah, about the same as it was nine years ago except there used to be a Sears where Walmart is. The Sonic is new."

Lupe's street hadn't changed except Hector's house was boarded shut. Philip pulled up in front of it and opened the truck door. "Not sure which house is Lupe's. If you want to wait in the truck, I'll knock on a door and ask where he lives."

"Sure," Edith said.

Philip was halfway across the street when he heard Lupe's voice.

"Aiyee... *es* Felipe, the giant snake slayer." The screen door of a house swung open, and Lupe, wearing cut-off jeans, stepped out onto the porch. "Hey, *mi hermano*... you come to kill more rattlers?" Lupe turned back toward the house. "Josie, Felipe is here! The hero who saved my life in the okra field!" A pretty pregnant woman and three children came out onto the porch. "Felipe, this my wife and my three children. Felipe, Juan, and Felicia."

"Aw man, they're beautiful," Philip said, clapping him on the back.

"Felipe! Come here, *mijo*." He motioned to the taller boy on the porch. "This is the man you are named for. He saved my life, and he was the best football player in Vuelta's history. He took the team all the way to win state championship. And he made sure your papa get an education. He went to school and risked INS arrest so I could go to school. Then he taught me how to get work in the construction business."

In a heartbeat, Lupe revised the sad, defeated picture Philip had carried of his years in Vuelta.

Ancient tightness in his chest loosened.

A fresh-faced, wide-eyed boy, with one hand stuck in his pocket, looked up at Philip.

"Wow, this is great." Philip's gaze swept Lupe and his wife and children. "You have a beautiful family. Edith..."

Philip turned back toward the truck.

Edith had gotten out, and Rosa, Soledad, and a small girl were standing beside her. Soledad, with hands flying, was talking a mile a minute. Edith had stooped down to talk with the small girl.

Rosa.

Rosa was gazing at Philip.

She was as beautiful as she had been years ago in the hay field smiling at him in the rearview mirror of that old truck. Softer and rounder now, but with the same dark eyes and sweet face, she was ignoring all the commotion around her, focusing on Philip. She was still except for the breeze lifting her long black hair.

Philip might have continued to stare, but Lupe bounded toward the car, hustling his wife and children along with him. Rosa's eyes stayed on Philip, and years flashed through his mind:

their first kiss in the dark parking lot, their time together in the backseat of the old Ford, his years of searching.

Edith kept talking to the little girl. Rosa didn't stop staring at him.

"*Señorita, el gusto es mío,*" Lupe said to Edith, "I am Lupe..." Lupe got everyone introduced as he continued to glorify Philip's years in Vuelta.

Philip watched Edith, but she wouldn't make eye contact with him.

Lupe led them into his house, which looked a lot like Soledad's house had years ago, with space organized so lots of people could fit in. Everyone sat around in the front room, and children, including a few extra neighborhood kids, ran everywhere. Only young Felipe remained still and close, eying his namesake.

Over the next half hour, they learned that Soledad lived up the street with Rosa and her husband and children. Soledad's husband was missing again. Hector was living in Cuernavaca. He'd gone down for a visit, met a widow, and never returned.

"Can you believe. Hector is legal, but he is staying in Mexico. Just goes to show we will do anything for the love of a woman." Lupe grinned at his wife.

Philip worried he'd made a mistake coming here. Rosa's little girl had crawled into Edith's lap, and the two of them were having a discussion about three dolls. The little girl kept reaching up to touch Edith's hair, pulled back in a low knot. The girl seemed intrigued with the curly tendrils loosening around Edith's face.

Lupe continued. "Rosa has three boys, and finally she has this little princess, Marisol, with all the dolls on your *señorita's* lap, and Marisol is just like Mama, the boss of everyone." Marisol and Soledad both rolled their eyes at Lupe. "Rosa, where are Guillermo and your boys?" Lupe asked.

Before she could answer, Soledad passed around a platter of *empanadas*. Philip hadn't eaten the triangle-shaped fried pies since he left Vuelta. "Pork and pumpkin." Soledad pointed out two different stacks.

Lupe passed around beer and kept the conversation lively while everyone, except Rosa, dug into the offerings.

Rosa watched Edith and Philip.

After a while Soledad said she was taking the children to her house.

Philip thought this might be the right time to leave. It had been good to see everyone, and he'd invited them all to Gire next Saturday, but Rosa's silent staring made him uncomfortable. He tried to get Edith's attention while Soledad corralled the kids.

Before he could ask Edith if she was ready, Lupe, peering out a window, said, "Finally, here comes Guillermo! Felipe, now you get to meet Rosa's talented husband, the *artista nagual*, and her three handsome sons! But you must be careful—Guillermo can read your mind!"

Rosa's three boys, ages twelve, ten and eight, reminded Philip of Lupe when they first met. The boys went through the introductions, shook hands, smiled at Lupe's repeated story of the giant snake and the football heroics. After a few minutes, Soledad took all the children down the street, except for little Marisol who refused to leave Edith.

Guillermo, lean and dark with nearly black eyes, had been quiet during the introductions. He had a calmness about him, but at the same time, his eyes were always moving as if memorizing everything he saw.

What does he know about Rosa and me? Does he resent my being here?

Guillermo took a step forward. "I am happy to meet you, Felipe. You were an important support to Rosa, and I am grateful." His accent seemed Toltec, typical of indigenous people from deep southern Mexico. He had a low, gravelly voice. He could have been old because his black hair was steaked with gray, but his intense face was lean and young.

"Thank you, Guillermo, Rosa's family helped me. I'll always be grateful."

"And, Edith, welcome to our *calle*."

"Thank you." She grinned mischievously. "May I ask, *nagual*, are you a shapeshifter?"

Guillermo returned her grin. "Ah, you know your history, *señorita*."

"I took a course in Mesoamerican religions."

"I see," Guillermo said. "Alas, I am not a shapeshifter. I am trapped in human form. *Artista nagual* in my culture is one whose work is believed to be a gateway between flesh and spirit."

"So, you message through your art?" Edith asked as everyone settled in the living room again. Guillermo nodded. "Do messages come to you in verbal form? Or appear as images on the canvas?"

"Too ephemeral to articulate, but definitely not verbal," Guillermo said softly.

Edith appeared hungry with more questions, but Rosa straightened her posture, folded her hands on her knees, and faced Edith and Philip. As if Rosa's silent signal reached everyone in the room, all eyes shifted to her.

"Philip and Edith, I would like to tell you why Mama, Papa and I left Vuelta so abruptly." This was a new Rosa. Even though she looked much the same, she had a different intensity —calmness, confidence.

Guillermo, still standing, nodded and backed a couple of steps away. By this time Philip noticed Guillermo watching Edith.

Rosa gazed directly at Philip. "After spring break when you returned to college, Papa came home. On the first day, he thought he would be able to stay with us in Vuelta. However, in the night, one of his friends came and said members of Mexican Mafia were coming to kill us all. The mafia wanted to make an example, and Papa was the chosen. We had to leave and tell no one our plans because we did not want to endanger anyone else. We hid in the nearby pasture for days because Papa thought the assassins would expect us to flee to Mexico immediately."

Captivated, Edith and Philip froze.

"I saw you, Philip, with your bandaged arm, the night you slept on Hector's porch. I begged Mama and Papa to let me come to you, but they said I could not risk it because you and I might both be killed. We crossed the border at Del Rio, and Papa's cousin took us to Asilo, a small village in southern Mexico."

Philip followed her glance toward her husband. Guillermo had picked up a large sketch pad, and he was drawing Edith. His focus on her was intense.

Rosa observed this silent interchange and said, without a break in her flow, "Edith, Guillermo would like to sketch you if you do not mind." Edith smiled and nodded. Edith might have said more, but Rosa continued, "When he sees a beautiful woman, he must capture her." Guillermo and Rosa exchanged a comfortable, silent acknowledgment and held eye contact, but Guillermo never stilled his hand.

Rosa turned back to Philip. "When we arrived in Asilo, we took refuge in the church, and we thought we would be safe there, but after we went to sleep, police officers stormed in. I was sleeping in a closet, next to Mama and Papa's bed, and I think the police did not know I was there because they took Mama and Papa but left me behind. I stayed in the closet for many days and nights, too frightened to come out."

Lupe sitting next to her leaned forward with elbows on his knees and shook his head.

Rosa gave him a sympathetic glance. "I thought Mama and Papa might be dead, and I did not know how to contact Philip or Lupe. After days passed the priest found me. He urged me to eat, but I was not able to. He became frightened I would die in the church. So late that night, he led me to Guillermo's home to be cured."

Guillermo stilled his sketching hand and spoke directly to Philip. "Rosa had come to me in a dream, and I had painted her portrait before the priest brought her. When I told the priest to leave her with me, for eight days of clarity and recapitulation, he resisted at first. But when he saw the painting of Rosa I had done from my dream, he shared my belief that she was supposed to stay with me."

Rosa gazed at Guillermo and said softly, "He saved my life, and opened my understanding in ways I had never imagined."

Guillermo studied her silently. "As soon as I promised Rosa that Felipe, Lupe, Mama and Papa were alive and she would see you again, she could take food. When the priest came back after the eight days, Rosa returned to the church with him."

Rosa nodded. "I worked in the village with the nuns for several months, but each week I visited Guillermo. Over time I realized that my path was with his." She smiled at her husband. "I proposed to him, and after the third time, he finally said yes."

Guillermo smiled back at her and seemed to blush.

"That is wild... right?" Lupe, grinning, shook his head. "When I finally found out where Rosa was, I went down there to kick his butt. But Rosa convinced me they belong together plus they already have two babies, and I see Guillermo is a good husband and father. So, I crated up some of his art and brought it back to San Antonio. After I sold a few pieces, one of the galleries liked his work so much that they helped him get a green card. Now he is legal and making money for *toda la familia.*"

Edith said, "Guillermo, may we see your art?"

Lupe jumped up. "You bet. I got most of it out in the shed. We are about to pack some for a show next week. Come with me." Everyone except Guillermo followed Lupe to the shed where there were about fifty paintings and sketches. Some were stacked for packing. Some were already wrapped. But there were about twenty on the walls, mostly paintings of Rosa. In some of the pictures she looked young as she was the last time Philip saw her. In the later pictures, there was new light in her face. A couple of pictures looked like Rosa as an elderly woman.

There was a hush in the room until Edith whispered, "They're alive."

"Yes," Rosa agreed.

Guillermo came in carrying his sketch of Edith. He went to a work bench, grabbed an aerosol can and sprayed the picture. He handed the sketch to Philip. "A gift for you, Felipe."

In the center he had sketched Edith's face with the rapt expression Philip saw when they made love. And even though on this day she was wearing her hair tied back with a scarf, in the sketch her hair was free. In a strange way, her hair merged into the background that looked like fractal waves.

"Thank you, Guillermo, it's... amazing," Philip said. "These background lines remind me of Mandelbrot."

"Yes," Guillermo replied. "They do look fractal." Philip was surprised Guillermo knew that. "But these lines, from the ancient Toltec timeline pattern, predate Mandelbrot by thousands of years. I am happy you taught Rosa about fractals because I have learned much from Mandelbrot's ideas."

Edith had been quiet, focused on the picture. "I see that this is Philip, but..." She pointed to a small silhouette in the fractal-like waves that extended from her hair. "...who are the other people?"

Philip hadn't noticed the figures.

"This must be Felipe, your center," Guillermo said, pointing to the largest silhouette that was in the central location. It was a simple, primitive figure with few lines that grew out of the timeline pattern, but it replicated Philip's shape. Its arms were reaching toward Edith with palms up. "This one you lose." He pointed to a small fetal positioned infant. Finally, he pointed to a female figure, barely noticeable. "This one, I think, seeks Philip." This last figure was darker than the others.

Philip, after the figures were pointed out, could see them. But he wasn't sure he would have noticed them on his own. The primitive shapes, blending into the background and Edith's hair, were mirages that might disappear if he glanced away.

"Who is she? Did she seek him in the past or will it be in the future?" Edith asked.

Rosa answered for Guillermo. "When Guillermo draws objects in the Toltec timeline, he cannot define past and future because the ancient lines do not differentiate. Past and future run simultaneously, they are not sequential. Guillermo as an artist captures the present moment, but as *nagual* he must include the past and future."

In a low voice, Guillermo said, "Rosa is correct. But I do see deep pain in the one who seeks you."

All eyes were drawn to the black jagged lines just behind the figure of Philip. *Carmen?* Philip wondered.

Rosa broke the silence and looked toward her husband, "I will now finish telling Edith and Philip the story."

"Yes," Guillermo replied and nodded to Rosa.

"In the beginning of our eight days, I was bitter that you and I, Philip, had made plans for our lives that would never come to pass. You can see the bitterness in this painting." She pointed to a young, haunted picture. "With clarity and recapitulation, I learned the purpose of our days together had been to prepare for our new paths."

"Recapitulation?" Philip asked.

Rosa nodded slightly. "A Toltec process that helps one heal from traumatic experiences. You reshape the pain to find a heightened awareness." She pointed to another painting showing her face at peace. Rosa caught Philip's gaze again. "You taught me many things that have added value to my life and prepared me for Guillermo. And now I am deeply blessed to know Edith. She is the intuitive one with a higher purpose who Guillermo saw with you."

Philip said, "I'm not sure I understand 'intuitive one with a higher purpose.' She's a poet. Is that what you mean?"

Guillermo said, "You can answer your own question. Your Benoit Mandelbrot was an intuitive one with higher purpose. You are drawn to his work just as you are drawn to Edith. They are both beyond their earth time."

Lupe threw up both arms. "Do not worry, you do not have to say anything. They talk like this all the time, and they do not mind if you think it crazy. They are used to it. All I can say is they are good parents, and we are making good money on his art. So, I like Rosa and Guillermo even if they are weird."

"Shut up, Lupe," Rosa said with the same tone she had twenty years earlier when he griped about her driving in the hay field.

"Now, Rosa, do not be telling me to shut up! What if I am an intuitive one with a higher purpose? Huh! You telling me to shut up and I might be about to recapitulate a message."

When they stopped laughing at Lupe, Edith said, "Fascinating... recapitulation, your art, your beliefs." By now little Marisol, still in Edith's arms, was asleep with her head collapsed on Edith's shoulder. Philip had rescued the three dolls as they dropped one by one from drowsing hands.

While Edith went with Rosa to lay Marisol in her bed, Lupe and Philip waited near the truck. Through open windows of the little houses, families could be seen moving around. Mexican music played from a radio in the distance.

Philip said, "How are you doing, really, Lupe? Must be hard supporting a family in Vuelta."

His eyes narrowed and flashed in the dark, and the Lupe who stayed hidden under the jokes said, "*Los lobos están fuera de mi puerta cada noche.*"

With his switch to Spanish, it took Philip a moment to catch his meaning—*wolves outside my door every night.*

Back in English, Lupe said, "But I am not like Papa. I will not get into his business, will never put Josie through what Mama lives with." He looked down at the ground then said, as if telling himself as well as Philip, "My children are legal and getting an education." Then he looked back at Philip. "They will go to college and have choices like you did. That is all that matters." Edith approached and Lupe flipped back into his upbeat tone. "And now thanks to you, I have a good job working for Al for the next two years."

After Edith and Philip drove a few blocks away, he pulled over and stopped. He turned toward her and pulled her close. "I had no idea Rosa would be there... not sure why Lupe never mentioned her. Are you okay?"

She kissed him. "I'm more than okay. Today could not have gone better. How about you?"

He nodded. "It's good to know why Rosa left and how things have turned out for her."

"What did you think of Guillermo?"

"I can't decide whether he's a genius or crazy," Philip said.

"Maybe a true artist has to be a little of both."

241

Chapter Twenty-Six

On the day of the party, Philip was in awe to see so many people celebrating both the completion of the house and his liberation from the bogus charges. He didn't do a head count, but there were at least fifty people there, and over half were children. He'd anticipated the children from Vuelta, but each of Edith's four brothers also had children.

Lupe's oldest son had set up his sound system on the patio and kept music pulsing, everything from traditional Mexican polka, *conjunto norteño,* to the latest hip hop. Rented tables and chairs covered the deck and backyard, and the kitchen counters and dining table were loaded with catered food as well as multiple dishes guests brought in. Lupe had started a fire in the barbeque pit early, and it had burned down to a bed of coals where two of Edith's brothers, with Myra supervising, were grilling chicken. All the windows in the house were open to the cool spring weather, so music, barbeque aroma, and children's laughter drifted through the rooms.

The biggest surprise of the day had been Jacqueline when she arrived early with Lily. At the funeral Jacqueline's demeanor had been disinterested and almost sullen, so he was delighted when she walked in carrying a three-month-old golden retriever. Beaming, Jacqueline had said, "Hi, Uncle Philip. Look at my new puppy... Buster." Golden fluff vibrated with excitement as Jacqueline thrust him toward Philip. "Wanna hold him?"

As he took the squirming puppy and dodged its eager tongue, he wondered if this change in Jacqueline was because of her new pet or because Dinah hadn't arrived yet. Lily explained that Dinah was coming later because she had to finish a report at her office.

Philip had been afraid that Jacqueline might not feel comfortable with all the strangers here, but she fell in with the other kids and seemed at ease. Children of all ages ran in and out of the house and barn and through the wildflowers in the pasture.

Lupe's son started *cumbia* music, and soon Philip and most of the crowd were lined up, arm in arm, circling the patio to the simple *cumbia* beat. Guillermo and Edith's father, Gene, sat in lounge chairs under a shade tree discussing the merge of Christianity with indigenous cultures. And Bess, Edith's mother, relaxed nearby holding a sleepy baby.

Bess and Gene sort of resembled each other. Both were fit and wiry with short white hair and freckled skin suggesting they might have been redhaired when younger. They both wore faded green Peace Corp baseball caps and khaki slacks.

The music changed to hip hop, and Edith's nieces started teaching their moves to anyone who would try. Lily, Jacqueline, and Edith, all three wearing pastel sundresses, joined in. Philip backed off the patio and watched, wishing Dinah were here to be a part of this.

Lily grabbed Philip's hand. "Come on. Hip hop with us."

"Yeah, Uncle Philip, come on," Jacqueline echoed.

Grinning, Philip backed farther away. "Nope. You've got this."

He sat down next to Bess, who said, "Coward, I see."

Philip nodded. "You bet."

She gazed at the dancing crowd. "You know, Philip, I can't remember a happier occasion. This is a remarkable, loving group of people."

"Thanks, but you and Gene have to take credit for a lot of the people here. How many grandchildren do you have?"

"This sweet girl makes number thirteen." Bess looked down at the sleeping baby. "And I think I'm going to lay her in her porta crib."

Philip stood with her. "I'll go in with you." He opened the door for her and followed her inside and up the hallway to a corner bedroom where the crib waited.

After she laid the baby down, she said, "I'll sit in the living room so I'll hear her when she wakes."

Philip pulled up two chairs. "I'll sit with you."

"You don't have to do that."

"I want to." He huffed a short laugh, angling his head toward the window. "Safer in here away from hip hop." From where they sat, they could see the dancers on the patio and a group of smaller children on the deck playing with the puppy.

Bess laughed with him. "I was just watching my grandchildren, and I couldn't help thinking how ironic life is. The darkest hour of my life was when I learned I could never have children of my own. I grieved to be denied the thing I wanted most in the world. Now, I can't imagine my life without my five adopted children."

"How'd you find your boys?"

"The first two we adopted from an orphanage in Haiti. Gene and I were missionaries there right after he graduated from seminary. The boys, Jake and Sam, were both three years old—didn't know any English and had never been out of the compound. We brought them home with us and thought this would be our family, just the four of us. But then a few years later when Gene was pastor at a church in Oklahoma near the Chickasaw reservation, we heard about Ethan and Louis. They're brothers, and their mother was in prison, so we took them as foster children. Their mother's out now, and they visit her on the reservation."

"Edith told me about the mystery of her birth mother—what little she knows."

"Yes, we'll always wonder what became of her. I can still picture Susan—quiet, pale, small and so young. I'll always believe she picked Gene and me to be Edith's parents."

"How did you find Edith?"

"It was a weekday night... we had been in bed a while... thought we heard the front door close." She shut her eyes at times as if seeing each moment that she was describing. "We never locked the doors, and sometimes members of the congregation came by the house to leave us something or to talk with Gene. He got up... checked... no one was there... came back to bed. A little later the phone rang, so I went into the living room to answer, and as I picked up the receiver, I saw a small box on the floor."

Lupe shouted from the patio. "Mama is going to teach *salsa!*" The music changed, and Lupe and Soledad flew into several measures. Then they corralled some kids and the willing adults and started leading them in the basic steps. The threesome, Edith, Lily, and Jacqueline, danced in the middle of the kids. Even Myra joined them.

Edith caught his gaze as she laughed with his sister and niece. Her pale turquoise sundress drew his focus like a magnet in the crowd. He pulled his attention back to Bess. "So, there was a box on the floor?"

"I saw immediately it was a baby. I dropped the phone back into the cradle, and the moment I picked her up, I fell in love. The rest is history." She chuckled. "I was reading Edith Wharton novels that summer, hence her name."

Philip grinned. "Well, that was kind of prophetic since her work revolves around literature."

"Yes, it was."

They were silent for a minute, watching the dancers and the children with the puppy. Bess turned to Philip. He sensed a shift in her expression. "Philip, I must tell you, Gene and I have never seen Edith in a better place than she is now. With you, all the pieces of her puzzle have come together."

Philip felt himself go to a deeper level. "I'm the same way about Edith. I never expected the connection we have."

"We're grateful you've come into her life. We grieved for her over the loss of her baby, and we sensed she protected us from the depth of her pain. We were afraid she'd never find happiness in this world. But now with you—"

The front door flew open, and Dinah stepped in. She looked distracted, almost as if she expected to enter an empty house and not a lively party. It had been a month since the last time Philip had seen her, and his first thought was that she must be unwell. She was thinner than ever, and her skin was pale and gray. And, for the first time, she was dressed in dirty clothes, an old gray sweat-stained T-shirt and jeans with grease spots down the fronts of the legs. Her hair was twisted in a careless knot at the base of her neck.

"Dinah," he said softly as he approached her. "Glad you made it."

"I would have come with Jacqueline and Lily, but my quarterly report was rejected yesterday, and I had to resubmit this morning." She shoved the door hard, and it would have slammed but Philip caught it and eased it shut. "There are four associate superintendents in our district, three men and me, and, of course, I, the only woman, am the one assigned to the section of the district with all the Blacks and Hispanics."

Bess stood.

"Dinah. This is Edith's mother, Bess Strickland."

Dinah gave her one slight nod, tossed her purse into the coat closet and turned back toward Philip and Bess. "So naturally when I submitted my report, my data looked like crap compared to the three men's. My Blacks and Hispanics have lower test scores, more special ed placements, three times as many disciplinary removals, and more absences."

Philip, noticing silence had fallen over the deck, saw that the children, their attention caught by Dinah's loud, angry voice, were looking toward the window. He gestured toward the patio. "Did you see Jacqueline outside dancing?"

Dinah ignored his comment and spoke even louder. "So, overnight the system spat my report back with an error message, and I had to go back in and reenter all the data point by point with an explanation about each item." The *salsa* came to an end, and the silence that had started on the deck spread out to the yard and the dance patio. "The superintendent is pissed off because the district's overall data was looking great until my section, with all the Blacks and Hispanics, came in."

"Dinah," Philip said in a whisper. "There's a baby sleeping down the hall."

She lifted both her hands in frustration and jerked them in time with her next words. "Like I'm supposed to fix the Black and Hispanic students' performance. They simply do not perform as well as whites. We can endlessly theorize about reasons why, but until those minorities get over whining about the past and get their acts together, they'll just continue to underperform. Shit, I even wrote a damn federal grant to get the

Ally Program for my students and implicit-bias training for my teachers. What else am I supposed to do?"

Jacqueline's pink sundress flashed past the window as she approached the kitchen door.

He lifted his hands to alert Dinah and whispered, "Jacqueline's coming."

"Mom?" Jacqueline said.

Lily and Edith trailed behind her.

A group of children also wandered into the kitchen, and a small girl approached Bess. "Gram, where's the water."

Bess murmured, "Come, Shayna, I'll help you."

Dinah's gaze traced first Lily's daisy covered sundress, then Edith's pale turquoise. Her eyes narrowed as she settled on Edith for awkward seconds.

Jacqueline interrupted Dinah's inspection. "Mom, have you gone cray-cray? Everybody heard you, and what are you wearing?"

Lily took Dinah's arm and said, "Let's go back here." She gestured toward the master bedroom. "Philip, come with us, please. Jacqueline, go check on the puppy. He's probably hungry. I put his food out in the barn."

Philip took Edith's hand, and together they followed his sisters. He didn't know what Lily had in mind, but whatever it was, he wanted Edith with him. He wanted her involved in every aspect of his life.

In a bedroom with a view of the deck and patio, Lily guided Dinah to a corner and whispered, "Look out the window. Look at the people, at the children, here."

Dinah peered out at the diverse skin colors in the crowd, clearly representative of the groups she had just called out. Her pale face grew splotchy.

The four of them watched the crowd silently while another

salsa started, and Soledad and Lupe prodded the dancers into action.

Lily, still in a low voice, said, "Dinah, we heard everything you said."

Dinah, shaking her head slowly, slumped back against the wall and covered her face with her hands. "I fuck up everything. I always have." Her shoulders shook with silent sobs.

Lily embraced her. "That's not true. You've worked harder for the children in the district than anyone. That's probably why you have the assignment where there's the greatest need. But the things you said were hurtful. Maybe you could apologize, explain."

Edith whispered to Philip, "I should go back outside."

He shook his head and held onto her hand.

Dinah uncovered her face. "Edith?" She said the name with a questioning lilt. "We meet at last. I'm sure you're not surprised by what you've seen of me." With a half smile, she narrowed her eyes. "Philip must have already told you how disgusting I am."

Edith, sympathy in her expression, said, "No. He never said anything like that."

Stunned, Philip focused on Dinah. "Why would you assume I would say something like that?"

She rolled her eyes and shushed a sarcastic sound. "You, brother, you left home because of me." Her voice was so low, they had to strain to hear her. "Daddy was bad enough. He ignored me, pretended I didn't exist, but you... you couldn't stand to be around me, so you just left. Now Jack wants a divorce. He's not happy with me."

Reeling at her words, Philip said, "First, I'm sorry about Jack, but I'm here for you. I won't desert you again like I did when you were twelve. Second, I didn't leave because of you."

Dinah rolled her eyes and shook her head, disagreeing with him but looking too exhausted to argue. "It doesn't matter."

"It does matter." Philip's voice, low and intense, pulled her attention. "I want you to know the truth. I was ashamed I hadn't stopped our grandfather from raping you. Our older cousins had joked about how he liked little girls, but I shrugged off what they said, tried not to believe it. I should have guarded you. I should have defended you. I never knew what to say to you... how to help you... So, I did nothing. Said nothing."

The three women were riveted by his words.

He stepped closer to Dinah, holding her gaze. "Later, when the relatives acted like it never really happened, I should have stood up and made them admit the truth. Then when I found out our father and grandfather were still hanging out together at cock fights like nothing had ever happened, I couldn't stomach being around them."

Dinah still leaned against the wall, but her whole body took on an alertness.

"I left because I hated them, and I felt like I reminded you of them. I intended to come back and make them do the right thing, but coward that I was, I let life lead me in other directions. Then after I heard you had married, I figured it was all ancient history, and you'd done fine without me, so I stayed away. But I shouldn't have. I wish I could do it all over."

He stopped talking. Dinah's gaze stayed locked with his. Edith still held his hand. Lily stood paralyzed.

Philip said, "Dinah, I'm sorry for what our grandfather did to you when you were just a little girl. I'm sorry everyone pretended it didn't happen. And I'm sorry I wasn't the brother I should have been to you. And, I'm sorry if telling all of this now is hurting you more. But I don't want you to think I left because of you. It was because of them that I left."

A profound stillness held the room. All gazes were pulled to Dinah. Her eyes brimmed and her skin flushed. Philip feared he'd reopened a wound in her that should have stayed closed.

But a slow smile took over her face. He realized he'd never seen her genuinely smile before, at least not since she was a child. Dinah stepped into his arms and rested her head on his chest. She whispered, "Thank you, Philip. Thank you."

A choked squeak from Lily grabbed everyone's attention. She trembled so fiercely that all three reached for her. Her eyes darted from Philip to Dinah, back and forth. She whispered, "Did you say Granddaddy raped Dinah?"

Dinah, calm now, said, "I was twelve. You were four. I guess you never knew. No one talked about it later."

Lily whispered, hoarsely, "Why didn't anyone tell me?"

The question hung unanswered.

Lily straightened her shoulders as if pushing something away. "Why did I just ask that?" She took a deep breath, and raised her chin. "I know the answer, sociology 101. People don't talk about shameful events within families." She turned to Dinah and clasped her arms. "I'm so, so sorry that happened to you. Are you sure you're okay now? Victims can feel disempowered when someone else tells their story."

"I'm okay. It's a relief to understand Philip's perspective."

Edith spoke for the first time. "Dinah, I'm so sorry. I'm intruding in a private, family moment."

Dinah shook her head. "Not your fault. I saw Philip pull you in.

"And..." Lily shifted her attention to her brother, "...I think you're taking too much on yourself. You need to let the guilt go."

Edith stroked Philip's back and whispered, "Good advice."

Dinah let go of Philip and squared her shoulders. "Okay. We need to recess this family therapy session." She looked at Edith. "Looks like we have fifty or so guests I need to apologize to, starting with you, Edith. I'm sorry for the way we met."

Edith smiled. "Nothing to apologize for. I'm honored to meet you. And I love Jacqueline already."

Dinah put her hand on Philip's chest. "Thank you for telling me why you left."

Philip nodded, not trusting himself to say anything. His regrets would never go away, but seeing the hatred leave Dinah's face soothed his demons.

"Mom," Jacqueline called as soon as they started toward the living room. "I can't find Buster. We've looked everywhere." She gazed out the window where children and adults were searching.

Philip said, "We'll help. Did you look in the house? Under beds?"

They scattered to search all the rooms. Dinah, staying close to Philip, said, "The house and grounds look amazing, by the way. Thank you."

"We've enjoyed the project," Philip replied. "And we're almost done with the other houses."

They looked under beds in a bedroom the workers used.

Dinah quickly peered into a closet "What about the bills? You haven't written any checks. This must have cost a small fortune."

Back in the hallway, Lily, coming out of another bedroom, said, "I think we've covered the house—he must be outside."

Seeing Edith and Jacqueline going toward the barn, they headed out, too, and Dinah asked again, "What about the bills—materials, salaries?"

"Paid," said Philip.

"But you haven't used the account I set up."

"I'm paying the bills myself."

"Wait. That's not fair to you." Dinah stopped and took his arm. "How can you afford that?"

Scanning the grounds to decide where to look next, Philip said, "I have savings accounts and investments—I've done a lot of overtime over the years and I live cheap. I've always had in mind that someday I'd be able to help out you and Lily. This is the day."

Dinah stared at him as if she'd never before seen him. "I've misjudged you."

"Mom, Edith found him!" Jacqueline, beaming, called from the barn door. "He's asleep."

Philip called to Lupe who was directing searchers in an expanding perimeter around the house, "Found him."

Lupe raised a victory fist and motioned the searchers back.

Inside the barn Philip walked up behind Edith and watched while Jacqueline slowly approached the puppy.

"Watch," Jacqueline whispered. "I can pick him up without waking him."

The puppy was curled up next to a stack of folded paint tarps.

Philip's whole body jerked and he shouted, "No. Jacqueline, don't—"

He'd spotted one tiny section, less than an inch long, of the distinct diamondback rattlesnake's pattern at the edge of the golden fluff. The snake was underneath the sleeping puppy.

Jacqueline, bending toward her pet, glanced at Philip, but she was too far into her motion. She scooped up the puppy.

Edith, now spotting the danger next to Jacqueline's sandaled feet and glitter-pink toenails, screamed, "No!"

Philip's body slammed onto the floor as he dove forward toward the snake. He jerked it upward by its rattle end. It was about a foot and a half long. At the same moment, Edith lifted Jacqueline, one arm supporting the girl's back and one underneath her too-long legs.

Philip, in a calm voice incongruous with his tense body, said, "Look around—there may be another one." His eyes darted through the barn, as he sprang to his feet, still clasping the squirming snake.

Edith, weeping, stepped back and seemed to be trying to lift Jacqueline and the puppy even higher.

One with the reptile, Philip's experience in snake handling kicked in. He instantly let the snake's head touch the ground while he kept the body and rattlers straight up. This position triggered the reptile's natural inclination to try to gain purchase of the ground and crawl away. In this position, the snake was momentarily incapable of striking. In a heartbeat Philip used his free hand to grip the snake at the base of the head. Then Philip extended his arm, holding the trapped snake away from everyone, and with his free hand, he clasped Edith's shoulder. "It's okay. I've got the snake. It can't hurt anyone now. You can set her down."

Dinah rushed forward and wrapped her arms around Edith and Jacqueline, who were both weeping now. "It's okay. We're all okay. Philip saved you."

Edith, as though trapped in fear, stared at Philip and the now-protruding fangs so close to his flesh. She nodded but didn't stop weeping and didn't set Jacqueline down.

Lupe sidled up next to Philip with a large empty jar. "*Mi hermano.* Drop him in here, and we will find him a new home far away from annoying snake catchers and baby dogs."

Philip carefully lowered the snake into the jar, and Lupe edged the lid over the opening until only the head, still in Philip's grip was uncovered. Philip raised his brows in question to Lupe. Lupe nodded. In a heartbeat Philip released the head, and Lupe slid the lid over the remaining opening.

Lupe held up the securely covered jar. "*Señoritas*, no need to cry. I have rescued the snake from Felipe."

Dinah, her arms still around Edith and Jacqueline, laughed with tears in her eyes. "That you have."

Philip embraced Edith's trembling body from the opposite side, and whispered again, "It's okay. Everyone is safe."

Dinah's and Philip's gaze met as they each stood holding onto the frightened pair.

Dinah whispered, "Looks like your years of snake handling paid off today. Thank you." She paused, then whispered, "*Mi hermano.* Thank you."

Together Philip and Dinah gently pried Jacqueline from Edith's hold. Edith nodded, still not speaking, but her legs buckled beneath her. Philip supported her, holding her close.

Dinah said, "Edith, everyone is okay. Philip and Jacqueline are both safe." With one hand still on Edith's arm, she turned to her daughter. "Jacqueline, tell me why this experience is valuable."

In a voice younger than minutes earlier, Jacqueline sniffled. "Mommy, I'll never get surprised by a rattler again. Because of this, I'll always be on the lookout."

Dinah nodded and pulled her closer. "You are wise, my beautiful daughter."

Jacqueline set the now wide-awake puppy onto the floor. "And you know what else? I should've listened to Uncle Philip. He started telling me something, but I just rushed ahead."

"That's right," Dinah said, again looking over at her brother. "We should all listen to Uncle Philip." Then she faced Edith. "You have given me a gift today..." Her voice broke. "When I saw you get between Jacqueline and the snake and lift her. You protected her as fiercely as I would have."

Lily, who had followed Lupe out with the snake, came back into the barn, frowning. "Police cars are pulling up. Two."

"Police or ICE?" Philip asked, alarmed for the Vuelta guests. He was sure many of them were illegal.

"Police," she said. "One car has *Culmine* on it."

He followed Lily out. By now all the guests were back in the area close to the house and deck, talking about the rattlesnake. Lupe stood in the middle holding the jar up so all could see.

Four police officers rounded the corner of the house and met Philip near the deck.

One officer stood in front of him, and the other three circled him. "Philip Richards, you're under arrest for the rape of Carmen James in room six of the Hilltop Motel, Culmine, Texas, February fourteenth." His insides turned to liquid. There were gasps around him.

Silence fell over the crowd. Even the children were still.

The puppy whined once.

Without a word Philip put his hands behind his back to be cuffed. Maybe he should have been shocked, but the sense of dread he carried about Valentine's night had been waiting for some awful truth to come out. Without looking back, he followed the officers to one of their cars and ducked into the back seat.

Chapter Twenty-Seven

When the police officers had surrounded Philip and announced his arrest, Lupe had expected Philip to offer some explanation. Stunned by his silence, Lupe had approached one of the officers. "This is a mistake. He is innocent. He did not rape anyone."

The officer, never slowing his pace, had raised his arm in a blocking motion and told Lupe to back off.

Now, Lupe froze as the squad car drove away. Then he turned to the shocked faces of a few people who'd followed them around the side of the house. Myra had her arm around Edith, and Edith's parents were on either side of them. In the backyard Guillermo and Rosa had guided most of the children back toward the barn where Rosa was trying to hold their interest in the snake. Other adults were in tight huddles, whispering.

One of Lupe's workers approached him, asking, *"Que paso?"*

Lupe shook his head. He didn't see Philip's sisters anywhere, so he rushed into the house and caught up with Lily, Dinah and Jacqueline near the front door.

Dinah fished her purse out of the coat closet. "Let's go." She swung open the front door.

"Wait, please," Lupe said. "What is going on?"

Dinah turned to him as if he were a cockroach she didn't want to deal with. "It's obvious, don't you think? My brother is a rapist." She took Jacqueline's arm and guided her toward the doorway.

"It is a mistake." Lupe held his hands palms up, imploring. "There is some mix-up." He looked from Lily to Dinah. "I know him. He would not do that. Never."

Lily, her face blotched with tears, stared at him blankly.

Dinah, with her eyes narrowed, gave a sneering grin. "Right." She pushed Jacqueline, carrying the puppy, out the door in front of her. Then she turned and grabbed Lily's arm. "Lily, come with me. It's time you face the truth."

Lupe followed them out. "Do not worry about the house. I will clean and lock up. And I will keep two men here this week to finish the other houses. I know Felipe's plans."

"Thanks." Dinah stopped and pulled out her phone. "What's your number?"

Lupe recited it while Dinah punched at her phone.

"I sent you my contact info. Send me your bills." She ushered Lily and Jacqueline toward the cars. None of them looked back at Lupe as they climbed in and drove away.

"Lupe." A soft voice called from inside the house. It was Edith with Guillermo and Rosa behind her.

Edith's eyes filled with the same bewilderment he felt in his own heart. Curly tendrils of her hair, that had been in a tight knot at the base of her neck, had worked loose around her face. "It isn't true. I know him. He would never rape anyone. It isn't in him to force a woman." She gazed down at the tissue clutched in her hands. "I've been with him even when he's drinking." She met Lupe's eyes again. "He didn't do this."

Lupe clasped her shoulders. "I believe you. We will figure out what has happened. Do you know this woman the police named?"

"Not really but, I think Carmen James is the woman he rescued in the parking lot."

Lupe said, "That whole story is strange. I will go to Culmine and find out what is going on. Okay. We will clean up the party. Edith, you should go home with your family, and I will call you as soon as I learn anything."

Edith shook her head. "I'm going to Culmine. I'll ride back with Myra, and stay with her until he's released."

After Edith and Myra left, Rosa said to Lupe, "Guillermo and I will come with you. Mama will take the children home."

Lupe frowned. "No. You guys go home. You don't need to get mixed up in this. This woman could be dangerous."

Rosa glanced from Guillermo to Lupe. "Philip saved your life the day you met him, and he improved our lives by helping us go to school. He spent four years searching for me in Mexico. We will not desert him now."

Chapter Twenty-Eight

It was the same cell. Windowless. Sparse. The pillow even seemed to have the same head dent. This time Philip didn't bother to flip it over before lying down. For the first time since he'd met Edith, he craved the glow of bourbon that infused strength and led to numbness.

During his arrest for the parking lot incident, he'd known he was innocent. He'd believed the facts would exonerate him. But this time, he knew from the manuscript that he was descended from killers, rapists, and drunks. He had no memory of Carmen on February fourteenth. As much as he couldn't believe he raped her, with his memory blank, he couldn't claim innocence.

Worse, if he'd asked Carmen that night at the bar what she was talking about when she said *Valentine's promise*, he could possibly have prevented this nightmare from materializing. And there would have been no need to keep that secret from Edith and his sisters all these weeks. His waiting and hoping Carmen would just go away made the truth even uglier now. He'd done the same thing with her that he'd done at fifteen with Dinah's desecration. He'd run.

This time instead of escaping his pain with booze or snake

handling, he'd suckered himself into a fantasy that his life had turned around—made the big swerve. He'd envisioned himself breaking the fractal chain that linked him to his ancestors.

He felt a detached sense of acceptance. He'd always known there was an intrinsic ugliness about himself. He'd known something had happened with Carmen James on Valentine's night. Now everyone knew it, and his feelings were strangely numbed. This day had started out as one of the best of his life. Edith by his side. Dinah forgiving him. Lily and Jacqueline happy. His friends celebrating. Charges dropped. Even Myra and Edith's family, her whole family, with them.

At least, he thought, his crime would not slither underground to be uncovered generations down the road. It would all be over now, in the present.

"I'll see my client, Philip Richards, please." Nelda's strong voice echoed down the hallway.

He turned his face to the wall. He shouldn't waste her time, but he needed a lawyer to sort his finances and make things easier for his sisters and Edith.

Soon a guard escorted Philip toward the same conference room Nelda had used the first time. As he passed windows, Philip noticed it was growing dark. He must have been here several hours. Nelda, crisp as always, was seated at the table looking over half a dozen papers spread before her.

As soon as the guard left, she said, still gazing down at the papers, "They've already handed over discovery."

Philip caught a header: *Victim Statement, Carmen James.* For an instant he thought if he never read this, he'd never have to know what he'd done. His night with Carmen could stay lost in the dark matter of his brain. But the instinct to look at a train wreck was too strong. He slowly sat.

Nelda flipped the sheet around and slid it to him. "These

first pages are just routine forms." She pulled out a single sheet. "This is where she states in her own words what happened."

I met Philip Richards at the Hilltop bar on Valentine's night. We were both alone. And he was nice at first. Told me about himself. No serious girlfriend. Moves around a lot. Sisters he's not close with. Mother dead. Hates his father.

We had so much in common. My mother died, too. I was eight. For years I lived with my father. He stayed out late and didn't come home some nights. Finally, he remarried and things got worse. Their new baby was their princess. When I was a teenager, I left home just like Philip Richards did.

At the Hilltop we talked a long time until I decided to go home. He followed me out and grabbed my arm in the parking lot and dragged me to room six. He shoved me onto my knees on a brown chair and butt fucked me. He pushed my face hard into the back of the chair to keep me quiet.

When he finished, he said if you tell anyone, they won't believe you. So, I kept it bottled up inside.

Then that night in the parking lot when he broke in on Ralph and me, I thought, this is how I can get Philip punished. People will believe me now. But it didn't work. I'm sorry I lied about the parking lot. I was too traumatized to think straight.

Without a sound, Philip stood and barely made it to the trash can in the corner before he vomited. Then he faced the wall next to the trash can, and bracing himself, he closed his eyes and pressed his forehead against the rough cinder block surface. He could maybe convince himself that she was lying about Valentine's night, but the line, the one line that sickened him the most was... *he said if you tell anyone, they won't believe you.* He'd learned when he was fifteen that she wouldn't be believed just as Dinah hadn't been believed. The guard came in and, seeing what was going on, took Philip to a restroom.

A few minutes later when he returned, Nelda said, "It will be okay." She slid a canned cola toward his side of the table. After the guard left, Nelda asked, "Ready to finish reading?"

The next page was labeled *Witness Statement, Frank Turbino, Hilltop bartender.*

Valentine's night Carmen James was at the bar in a red dress with some guy who works, I think, out at the bottling plant. I noticed them because she gave the guy a Valentine's card. You know the old-fashioned kind with a big heart on it that puffed up when you opened the card. I didn't realize the guy she was with had gone until I noticed her crying. And the card was ripped to pieces next to her drink. I came over to see if I could help and she just shook her head and covered her face.

That's about the time Philip came up. I could tell he noticed her crying and I whispered to him that I think some guy had just been rude to her.

Philip sat down next to her and started talking. I didn't get much of what they said. It being Valentine's night, we were pretty busy. Anyway, she perked up. Laughed a lot. They both had more drinks. They talked a long time, a couple of hours. Maybe longer.

Then they left. A little before closing time I think, maybe ten. We close at ten thirty on weeknights. I didn't notice if they left together or just at the same time.

If you get her talking, she'll tell you anything. Any secret. She likes to talk. Likes to be listened to.

Philip turned the pages upside down and folded his hands. Any lingering fantasy that Carmen was lying about being with him Valentine's night shattered. Frank wouldn't make this up. Philip felt dead inside. "What else?"

"Here's the physical evidence." Nelda spread several more pages with a close-up photo of the brown chair from his room. Clear teeth marks dented the vinyl across the back of the chair. The other sheet was a DNA report showing traces of Carmen James and Philip Richards on the chair. A forensic statement said the teeth marks were Carmen James's.

Nelda gave him time to read then said, "That's it. Their whole case. This will go to trial, but I can rip her credibility on the stand."

She gazed at the Victim Statement then shifted her attention to the DNA report. As if talking to herself, she said, "Also, we know for a fact it's easy to get into your room. Al got in to get your clothes the first time you were arrested just by asking the maid. I checked out the motel layout. The maids clean two or three rooms at a time, leaving doors open while they clean."

She looked directly at him for the first time. "So, Carmen could have gone in and left her DNA and teeth marks easily. Of course, your DNA would be on the chair because you lived there." She brought the fingertips of each hand to her temples and closed her eyes. "There's got to be a connection here. Why would Ralph drop the assault charges when you openly admitted hitting him? And what about the gun at the scene being stolen from someone in Houston three years ago? Somehow, all of this must fit together."

She folded her arms in front and leaned toward him. "What do you think? Why is she accusing you again?"

Philip, his face expressionless, cleared his throat. "No reason to probe. It won't go to trial." His tone was flat. "I'm pleading guilty. You don't need to work on this anymore." He tapped the pages of discovery. "But I do need you to take care of other things." He spoke rapidly as if listing routine tasks. "I want to transfer my rights to my father's estate to my two sisters. Transfer my bank and investment accounts to Edith Strickland. And give my tools and truck to Lupe Hernandez. Can you take care of that?" He didn't give her a chance to answer. "Al can get you in touch with Lupe, and Lupe will figure out the contact info for the others."

For once, Nelda looked confused. Her eyes widened. "Would you repeat what you just said."

"Sure, but first, may I have three blank pages?" He pointed to her yellow legal pad. "And do you have a pen I can borrow until you return?" She tore three sheets out and handed him a pen.

He repeated his instructions and stood. "I'll pay you for the time you've already invested." He waved at all the papers she had before her, and started toward the door.

She looked quizzically at him. "You aren't thinking clearly. You can beat this charge. A guilty plea will mean prison time, maybe twenty years. And even if you plead guilty, you need an attorney to plea bargain for the lowest sentence."

His back still to her, he shook his head and tapped on the door. "Guard."

As the guard opened the door, Philip faced Nelda. "One more thing, when you come again, could you bring three envelopes?"

She nodded, still puzzled.

"Thank you, Nelda. You've been a good lawyer. I like your no-nonsense approach."

Chapter Twenty-Nine

Shortly after sunset. Lupe, Rosa, and Guillermo were driving into Culmine, when Lupe received a call from a strange number.

"This is Nelda Perkins. May I speak with Mr. Lupe Hernandez?"

"Yes, I am Lupe Hernandez."

"My client, Philip Richards asked me to contact you. He said you can give me contact information for his sisters and Edith Strickland."

"Yes, I will text those to you."

"Thank you. Mr. Richards also instructed me to transfer his truck title to you and to document his wish to give you his tools. I'll call you back when I have the paperwork ready in a few days."

"Wait. Why is he doing that?"

She was silent for a moment. "There's a limit to what I can tell you about my client, but if you are his friend, I recommend you see him as soon as possible."

"We are driving into Culmine. I will go to him now. Where is he?"

"County jail." She gave him the address.

By the time Lupe rushed up to the jail clerk's desk, visiting hours were over, and the clerk said Philip Richards had requested no visitors anyway.

"He will see me," Lupe said. "I will be here in the morning at nine." Lupe shoved one hand back across the top of his thick, black hair, puzzling over what to do next.

On the way back to his car, Lily phoned. In a shaky voice, she apologized for leaving the house so abruptly. "Philip's lawyer phoned Dinah and said he wants to sign over his rights to our father's estate to Dinah and me. I don't understand why he would do that."

"I will see him in the morning. I will find out what is going on. Do not worry." Lupe didn't mention Philip also signing away his truck and tools.

Back in the car with Rosa and Guillermo, Lupe said, "Philip is giving everything away, his truck and tools to me and his inheritance to his sisters."

Guillermo said, "These are the actions of a man going to prison... or dying."

"We must do something," said Rosa.

Lupe pushed his hand through his hair again and shook his head. "I am going to call Al. I have to tell him I will not be at work in Vuelta tomorrow, and he knows Felipe well. Let us see what he says."

When Al learned Lupe was in Culmine for the night, he asked him to come to the Hilltop so they could talk, and he recommended the motel next door for their overnight stay. So, Lupe dropped Rosa and Guillermo at the motel office and headed into the café.

At a corner table, Al and Lupe updated each other with what they knew about Philip's arrest. Frank came to their table and shared what he'd told the police about Carmen James on Valentine's night.

Lupe said, "How can I meet this Carmen person?"

"She's here a lot when she's not back in Mexico," Frank said. "Sometimes with a guy, always a different guy. But sometimes alone. She's a talker. Feeds on getting people to listen."

Lupe leaned back in his chair with his arms folded across his chest. "Can you text me if she comes in?"

"Sure thing," Frank said.

Lupe stood. "Good. Then I am going to leave now. If she comes, I do not want her to see me with you guys or to connect me with Philip."

"Makes sense," said Frank. "We're open until midnight tonight, so we've got almost three hours left. Maybe she'll show."

Back in the motel room, Guillermo had sheets of paper from a motel pad spread out on a table. On each sheet he had listed a category of facts they'd collected. While Rosa paced, he moved the sheets around as if stirring facts, looking for connections and patterns.

Lupe scanned Guillermo's work. "At it already, I see. Maybe we should get you a sketch pad."

Even though Lupe was joking, Guillermo nodded solemnly. "I would like to draw Carmen and Ralph. I understand people better when I sketch."

Lupe pulled up a chair. "Okay, here's what Al and the bartender know." He detailed their discussion and his plan to strike up a conversation with Carmen if she came to the bar.

Guillermo looked up from his papers. "We should ask Edith to come here. I think she may have deeper insight, and we must tell her all you have learned about Carmen and about Philip giving away all his property."

Rosa said, "It will upset her." Then she sighed. "But you are right. She must know everything even if it is painful."

———

Edith, with red puffy eyes, still wearing her turquoise sundress, arrived minutes after Lupe called. The four sat around the table, and Lupe filled her in on everything he'd learned. Her face paled and she whispered, "Philip believes he's guilty."

The three, even Guillermo who never seemed shocked, gaped at her. She described Philip's blackouts—how he'd had no memory of the hours they spent together the night they met.

Then she explained about Dinah's childhood rape and the grandfather's denial.

While she spoke, Guillermo continued his notetaking, adding new sheets with categories of information.

She explained the sordid reasons why Philip left home at fifteen. "He lived his whole life carrying guilt over what had happened to Dinah. It wasn't his to bear, but he felt guilty for what happened to her... for not protecting her... for being connected to the men who hurt her. Now someone has accused him of rape at a time when he was blacked out."

Lupe said, "I understand why Philip and his sister had a hard time, but I do not understand what this all has to do with Carmen."

Guillermo's deep calm voice broke the silence. "He believes he is guilty, and he will not do to this woman what was done to Dinah. He will not pretend it didn't happen." He paused then added, "More than guilt, he carries shame."

A text from Frank buzzed in on Lupe's phone: *Carmen.*

Lupe stood, and headed for the door. "Okay, I am going to the bar."

Guillermo said, "I will enter later, so she will not know we are together."

Four people sat at the bar, three men and Carmen. There was an empty stool next to her, so Lupe took it.

Carmen glanced his way as he slid onto the stool.

Lupe smiled and bowed his head slightly, "*Buenos noches, señorita.*"

Frank approached. "What can I get you?"

"Hey," Lupe said with both hands on the bar. "What is good tonight?"

"Just opened a great bottle of Chivas if you're into shots."

"Yes," Lupe said.

"Also have margaritas and mojitos ready."

"Yes," Lupe said.

"And I can make anything you can order."

"Yes," Lupe said again.

Frank grinned. "Yes, to which?"

Lupe angled his head with a crooked smile. "First, a shot. Then a margarita."

Frank set a bowl of pretzels in front of Lupe. "Coming right up."

Lupe scooted the bowl toward Carmen, and switching to Spanish, he said with a boyish grin, "*Señorita*, would you like to share some pretzels?"

She reached for one, returning his smile. "Thank you. I'm not Mexican. How did you know I speak Spanish?"

He angled his head and grinned shyly. "All the most beautiful women speak Spanish."

She laughed like a delighted child and leaned closer to him as if she wanted to whisper.

He dipped his head toward her and lightly put his hand on her back.

She whispered, "Frank's margaritas suck. Mine are much better, like authentic Mexican margaritas." She giggled. "But don't tell him I said so."

He shifted to whisper in her ear. "Yes, there is nothing like an authentic margarita. Do not worry. My lips are sealed. Tell me, *señorita*, how did you learn to make authentic ones?"

She peered up at him through her lashes. "Many, many years in Mexico. I have a home there." Then she offered him her hand. "Carmen. I am Carmen."

He took her hand and held it for a long moment as he locked his gaze with hers. "I am Lupe. The pleasure is mine."

"Lupe, you're not from around here, are you?"

"No. Just got a new job. I am from Vuelta."

Frank set a full shot glass in front of him.

"Oh, thank you, sir," Lupe said. "And the margarita will be here soon? I am very dry. And, please, get this beautiful *señorita* whatever she would like." He turned back to her, pointing at her half-full glass. "Will you have a refill?"

"Yes, thank you," she said to Frank. Then turning back to Lupe, she raised her glass. "*Salud.*"

He picked up the shot glass and clinked it against hers. "And you, *Señorita* Carmen, what brings you to Culmine?"

"I came to visit my sister's family, but now I'm bored with this town."

"Oh no, a beautiful woman cannot be bored."

She leaned toward him again as if to whisper, but at that moment her phone buzzed. She straightened and pulled it out of her purse. "I have to take this." Stepping into a corner she talked quietly.

Frank replaced their drinks.

Quickly, Carmen returned and still standing, gulped her fresh drink. "I'm sorry, Lupe, but I must leave."

Lupe stood. "Ah, so soon? You break my heart."

"I'll be back tomorrow." She giggled and added, "Maybe."

Lupe bowed slightly. "If there is a chance you will be here, then I will come, too."

He stayed standing and watched her leave. Guillermo, seated at a table near the doorway, dropped money on the table and followed her out.

Lupe gave her time to drive away, then he paid Frank and left.

Back in the room, he relayed their conversation word for word. Guillermo, who said she'd been picked up near the doorway by a man in a car, took notes on his *Carmen* page. He included the description of the car and the plate number.

"Thank you, guys, for bringing me into your effort." Edith gestured toward the table with all the notes. "I feel better knowing we're working on this together. We'll prove to Philip that he's innocent." She made her way to the door. "Lupe, I'll see you in the morning at the jail. Let's all talk again after we meet with him."

Chapter Thirty

Lupe, Guillermo, and Rosa arrived at the jail a little before nine. They decided to sit in the waiting area until Edith came, so she could go in first. When she arrived and approached the counter, the clerk gave her the same information she'd given Lupe the day before. "Philip Richards requested no visitors except his lawyer."

Lupe approached. "Please have someone tell him Edith Strickland and Lupe Hernandez are here, and it is very important that we speak with him. It is about his defense. We will wait."

The clerk sighed, pushed up from her chair, and craned her neck to look down a hallway extending from her office area. "Clyde, are you down there?"

A voice answered, "Yep."

"Can you go back and tell the guard Philip Richards has two visitors named..." She looked back at them.

Lupe filled in. "Edith and Lupe."

While they waited, a small, elderly lady, with a towering updo, entered, marched up to the clerk, and in a strong voice said, "I'll see my client, Philip Richards, please."

Edith and Lupe pounced on her, introduced themselves, and asked her to persuade Philip to see them.

She scanned them up and down, nodded once, and marched through a door that had just been swung open by a guard.

Nelda returned about twenty minutes later. All four stood and Nelda approached Lupe and Edith. She had her briefcase in one hand and two envelopes, one addressed to Edith and one to Lupe, in the other. "Mr. Richards asked me to deliver these to you." She handed each one an envelope. "And he said no visitors."

Edith gasped and her eyes clouded with grief. She stared at the envelope in her hand. Silence fell over the group.

Lupe pulled his gaze from Edith's stricken face and ripped into his envelope, scanning the long yellow sheet. "It is about his tools and truck, some instructions for the properties, and..." He paused with his eyes on the page. His voice dropped an octave lower. "...and he thanks me, says he is sorry and... goodbye."

Nelda said, "I'll notify you, Mr. Hernandez, when the truck title is ready to transfer. And I'll give you a signed affidavit declaring his tools are gifted to you." She started to step back.

"Wait, please," said Edith, holding her envelope against her chest, still unopened. "May we talk with you? I know you can't tell us about the case. We understand confidentiality, but could we tell you some things that might help his case?"

Nelda kept her eyes on Edith's face, but her voice boomed, "Pam."

The clerk behind the desk popped up. "Yes, ma'am."

"Is the sheriff's large conference room available?"

"Yes, ma'am."

"Please open it for us." She made an about face. "Follow me."

Inside the conference room with a table large enough for ten people, Edith, Lupe, Rosa, and Guillermo sat across from Nelda.

Edith, holding her sealed envelope next to her heart, told Nelda about Philip's blackouts and their belief that Philip had no memory of Valentine's night. "And," she clarified, "as a result of the family trauma, Philip won't deny the rape."

While she talked, Guillermo laid his notes out on the table. His pages now included a sketch of Carmen and Lupe last night at the bar, another sketch of her getting into the car that picked her up, and a close-up sketch of the man's face looking toward Carmen as she approached the car.

Edith looked at her three cohorts. "Did I leave anything out? Is there anything else we've learned?"

Nelda angled her head toward Guillermo's tablet of blank pages and reached for it. He handed it to her. She ripped out two pages and wrote at the top of the first one, *Gun*. And beneath she listed *stolen, Houston, three years ago, Carmen had it in her car, fired a shot into the ground, Philip took the gun from her*. At the top of the second page, Nelda wrote *linkages to first case*. Then she said, "To fully understand this new accusation, we need to figure out how it links to the first one, which has been dropped even though it had unanswered questions."

She tapped Guillermo's page about Lupe's conversation with Carmen last night. She underlined *margarita*. "And here's a linkage. *Margarita* has come up before. In Carmen's police statement from the first arrest, she made a point of saying Ralph had been at her house, and she'd made margaritas for him with her new blender. She also said she didn't drink any herself because she knew she'd have to drive Ralph home. Those are odd details for her to include."

"How can we speak with Ralph?" Guillermo asked.

Nelda said, "He works out at the bottling plant on the highway just south of town, has a farm on the other side of town that his wife inherited from her parents. His wife is Carmen's half-sister. Carmen stayed with them when she first came to Culmine. Then she moved into a rental trailer near the bottling plant. Doesn't seem to have a job. People say Ralph is an easy-going family man with three children."

Guillermo added this information to his sheet.

Nelda picked up her buzzing phone. "I must take this... Nelda Perkins." She listened then said. "Yes, I just left your brother. He gave me a letter for the two of you that I'll post this morning." More silence. "I'm in a meeting with Ms. Strickland, Mr. Hernandez, and his sister and brother-in-law. Shall I call you back and read it to you after we finish?" Silence. "Very well." Nelda reached into her briefcase and pulled out a letter from Philip addressed to Lily and Dinah. While she opened it and put her phone on speaker, she said, "Philip's sisters are eager to hear this letter—they want me to read it to them."

> Dear Lily and Dinah,
> I left home at fifteen because I was afraid that I was part of the ugliness that had hurt Dinah. Now, I know I am.
> It's too late for me. But two things comfort me. First, the spiral of abuse and denial I was part of not only began generations ago, but it's also a part of a bigger picture. Edith helped me understand our family's story is a microcosm of the whole country's story. Our ancestors abused slaves, and later generations abused their own families.

The other thing I take comfort in is this: I'm not covering up what I did. I own it. I failed to break the pattern of being a blackout drunk and an abuser, but now I break the pattern of denying what I've done. You two and Jacqueline are free of the pattern.

I would never have come back into your lives if I had known what I did Valentine's night. I drank too much and blacked out. Until my arrest at the party yesterday, I didn't know what I had done that night.

Nelda Perkins, my attorney, is drawing up the paperwork to transfer my third of the estate to you two. Lupe will see that the houses are finished and he'll bill me through Nelda. Our father's trunk of papers is still in the master bedroom closet if you want to get them before putting the house on the market.

I'm waiving a trial and pleading guilty. I hope it's resolved fast with as little impact on your lives as possible. This letter is to say I'm sorry, I love you, and goodbye.

    Philip

"No trial," Edith gasped. "He's pleading guilty." Her gaze focused on Nelda.

"Good," Dinah's voice came through the speaker phone.

"No," said Edith. "It isn't good because he's innocent. He didn't rape anyone."

"We all believe he is innocent," Rosa spoke up. "I was close to him for many years. He does not have it in him to... to be an aggressor."

"Dinah," Edith went on. "I've been with your brother, both

when he's drinking and when he's not, and he's never shown any—"

"Edith," Dinah said, mocking the inflection Edith had just used when she said *Dinah*. "Rapists can have normal relationships with selected individuals, but choose to rape other selected individuals. They choose their victims carefully. They also lie and say they don't remember."

"He didn't rape that woman," Edith said, now calm and firm. "And he's not lying about not remembering. Philip is prone to blackouts. Alcohol interferes with his neural transfers of short-term memories to long-term. He can appear sober. He can carry on conversations and complicated actions. On Valentine's Day, Lily had phoned Philip about your father's diagnosis. I think his emotional response to that news was to drink too much."

Lily could be heard faintly in the background. "That's right. That's when I first told him about Daddy."

Edith nodded and closed her eyes. "That night Philip felt stressed, didn't eat, drank, and didn't remember going home. He has blacked out several times in his life, and that night was one of them." She opened her eyes and leaned closer to the phone. "He's pleading guilty because of the twenty-year burden of shame he's carried about what happened to—"

"Enough," Dinah said loudly. "He's lying. If he really didn't remember, he'd request sodium pentothal or submit to hypnosis. Then the truth—"

"No." Edith cut her off. "The events during a blackout never make it into long-term memory. Drugs or hypnosis can't bring back memories that don't exist in—"

"He did it." Now Dinah interrupted Edith. "Accept it. At least he's doing the decent thing now. Ms. Perkins, let us know when the paperwork is ready. Please expedite." The phone connection ended.

Guillermo wrote slowly on a sheet labeled *Dinah*.

Nelda's loud voice broke the silence. "Pam."

Quick footsteps sounded from the reception desk, stopping at the door of the conference room. "Yes, ma'am," she said, sticking her head in the door.

"Is Renfro in the building?" Nelda asked without looking up from her papers.

"Yes, ma'am."

"Ask him to come in here."

After Pam closed the door, Lupe asked, "Who is Renfro?"

"Sheriff," Nelda answered and gestured toward Guillermo's pages. "There's information missing that I think he can give us."

Uneasiness edged into Lupe. "The sheriff? But will he not wish to harm Philip's case?"

Nelda raised her gaze from the papers and looked at the four people across the table. "I know in movies, the defense never trusts law enforcement, but this sheriff is driven by the search for truth, not by the glory of winning prosecutions. Besides, Supreme Court precedent, Brady case law compels all exculpatory evidence to be handed over to the defense. I think he—"

The door opened again. "Morning, Nelda." Joshua Renfro's deep, calm-cadenced voice flowed into the room. He ambled toward the table holding a cup of coffee, introduced himself one by one to the other four, asking their full names, places of residence and connections to the case. Then he settled into an empty chair.

"Renfro, I never received discovery from the first set of charges against my client..." Renfro raised his brows in surprise. "...and new information indicates a strong connection between the two cases. I need that discovery."

Renfro shrugged. "Since the case was dropped, I guess the

DA wasn't required to send you anything. They probably never put anything together."

"Obviously. But I need whatever information you had whether the DA put it together or not. I need to know the background on the gun; Carmen James's prior history, including her time in Mexico; why the charges were dropped for vandalism of her car; and the rationale for dropping the assault charges for Ralph Albertson's injuries."

Renfro nodded slightly indicating he was following her thoughts, but his keen eyes also skirted the sheets spread out on the table and settled on the sketch of the man's face who had picked up Carmen the night before. The face seemed to be of a man in his fifties or sixties, with dark hair hanging past his collar in the back, thick and scruffy around his full face. It was a pleasant face with even features and wide-spaced, serious eyes.

Nelda continued, "I'm wondering if there's significant information from the first case that is being covered up. Maybe that's the reason for the dropping of the original charges and now the creation of these new charges. Shall I file a discovery order based on Brady? Or can you just get the information for me?"

He stood. "Let me see what we have."

Nelda asked, "You recognize this face?" She had picked up on Renfro's attentiveness to it.

He nodded once. "Too bad that's not a photograph. Do you think he's committed a crime?"

Nelda drilled him with her gaze. "If he has, I'll find out."

Renfro scanned the other people in the room. "Edith Strickland, Guillermo Zacatecas, Rosa Hernandez-Zacatecas, and Lupe Hernandez. Pleasure to meet you."

Nelda said, "Would you send Pam back in here? I need some copies made."

Renfro nodded once and left.

"Now," Nelda looked at Guillermo, "with your permission, I'm going to get copies made of your pages." Guillermo nodded and Nelda let her straight shoulders relax against her chairback. She looked pointedly at the four. "You've been very helpful. The insight you've provided makes a difference. Thank you."

"Thank you," whispered Edith, still holding her letter in her hand.

"We will stay in town," Lupe said. "I will try to talk with Carmen again, and maybe we can figure out a way to talk with Ralph."

Nelda looked as if she might object, but then she said, "As long as you don't reveal anything about Mr. Richards' case..." She stood, packing her briefcase as Pam came in to make the copies. "...you're acting on your own." Then, with her gaze locked on Edith, she lowered herself back into her chair.

Everyone else's focus followed Nelda's. Edith slowly moved Philip's envelope away from her chest and started breaking the seal. She pulled out the long yellow sheet. Her honey-colored eyes darkened as she read. No one else seemed to breathe. Rosa, with tears welling in her eyes, put her hand on Edith's arm.

Lupe felt his own throat tighten, and he could not look away from Edith's face.

Finally, Edith said, "I don't think there's anything in here that will help us prove his innocence, but..." Her voice faded to a whisper. "You should read it in case I missed something."

The yellow sheet lay on the table for a moment with no one moving to pick it up. Then Guillermo reached out and in his deep, calm voice read the letter aloud.

Dear Edith,

I love you.

I'm sorry I'm saying this now that everything is

over. I should have said it sooner. You opened up my life.
I'm lucky for the time we had.

I loved you so much that I pushed down my guilt
for not helping Dinah and my shame for being
connected to the Richards men. I've faced the fact
that I'm no different from them. I knew before I met
you that something had happened with Carmen on
Valentine's night. Not telling you about that blackout
was lying, no different from my father and grandfather
and Sabine. I'm a liar.

I promise you if I had known what I did
Valentine's night, I would never have involved you. I'm
sorry for the pain this has caused you. Your pain is my
biggest regret.

I have a small investment portfolio I started years
ago that I've asked Nelda to get transferred to you as
well as whatever's left in my bank account after my bills
are paid. I want you to have this to fall back on in
case you ever need it.

Please forget about me. Move forward. The last
time we were together was one of the best days of my
life—you dancing, laughing with your brothers, and
connecting with Jacqueline and Lily. That was our last
day. We just didn't know it. I don't want you to see me
in jail. It's over for us.

Goodbye,
Philip

When Guillermo's voice stopped, silence held the room. No

one made eye contact. Even Lupe didn't have an upbeat suggestion.

Pam came in with the copies, and Nelda stood again.

Edith, her face expressionless, took Philip's letter from Guillermo and slid a large, thick envelope toward Nelda. "Would you give this to Philip?"

"What is it?" Nelda lifted the flap, slid the manuscript pages out and fanned through them then slipped them back into the envelope.

"Nothing to do with the case, just his old family papers he left with me. He never finished reading them. I thought now that he has time on his hands, he might want them."

"Okay. Edith, could I hold onto Philip's letter to you. It might be useful when I'm building his defense. I promise to return it."

Edith nodded and slowly handed the letter to Nelda.

Nelda added it to her briefcase and said to them all, "I'll be in touch after I have more information. I'm going back in to see him now."

Chapter Thirty-One

Philip didn't expect to see Nelda again in the same day, but less than two hours after their brief mid-morning visit, the guard came to get him.

As usual, Nelda was seated at the table with pages spread out in front of her.

Before he'd settled into his chair she started speaking. "You can't plead guilty under oath unless you actually know you're guilty. It has come to my attention that you have no memory of Valentine's night with Carmen James. If you go before a judge with a guilty plea, he or she will ask you up to eighty-seven specific questions. You must answer all of the judge's questions appropriately before your guilty plea is accepted. You will not be able to answer if you have no memory of the events. Therefore, your guilty plea will be rejected, and we'll be right back where we are now."

Philip, accustomed to her rapid-fire fact citing, nodded with resignation. With no legal training, he hadn't known about hurdles in a guilty plea. He clasped the back of his neck with one hand. "I won't plead not guilty, because I'm guilty."

Nelda was already spreading handwritten sheets in front of

him. "Our task now is to find out what happened. Then we'll decide on a plea."

Pulling back in his chair, away from the table and shaking his head at the array of notes, he said, "I'm not going into any court and saying 'I don't remember.' I won't do that."

Nelda's gaze bore into him. "You don't have an option. You'll be under oath. And the truth is, you don't remember. You've even put it in writing in two of your letters, of which I have the originals. Now, the best way to deflect from divulging your memory loss is to find out what did happen and why this woman has accused you twice. You may not realize this, but you have a cadre of supporters who are already hard at work to get to the truth."

"I don't want my family and friends or..." He started to say Edith. "...or anyone else to deal with this mess."

"Too bad." Nelda was arranging the pages in an order only she comprehended. "They already are, and here's what they've collected. The quickest way to get your friends out of these weeds is to figure out the truth." She tapped on the table with her index finger. "Now focus on these pages. Absorb this information. Then we're going back to the original charge—the night in the parking lot—and we're going over everything again from the day you moved to Culmine, and we'll pick up the pieces you left out the first time."

"Who did these?" he asked, gazing at the handwritten pages.

"Guillermo mostly, but Edith, Lupe, Rosa, and I had a hand in it, too."

Philip's stomach twisted at the thought of these people digging into his ugly quagmire, puzzling over what he did or didn't do to Carmen. He'd rather go to prison than have them, especially Edith, submerged into this.

"Who's this guy?" Philip pointed to the sketch of the man's face.

"Not sure. He picked up Carmen last night in front of the Hilltop."

Nelda plowed ahead, either not noticing or ignoring his angst. The next two hours were spent rehashing information Nelda already had, but, at her repetitive probing for more details, he added facts he hadn't given her before: his first encounter with black-haired Carmen and her odd comments about Valentine's promise and "You're not worth my *escarabajo*" —beetle; her anger at the fact he didn't remember her; the moment in the car after he dragged Ralph out when she keyed something into a phone; Ralph's odd speech pattern alternately slurred and rapid; Ralph's embarrassed grin.

While they talked Nelda added his new information to the sheets. "Fascinating, isn't it?" She cocked one brow and fixed one of her rare smiles on Philip. "I love a good mystery."

Her surprising glint of humor made Philip huff a laugh in spite of himself.

Before he could say anything, she narrowed her eyes and said, "Another thing keeps bothering me. It really has nothing to do with you or Carmen, but I keep wondering if it contributed to the decision to charge you again." She paused, for once unsure.

"What?"

"Well." She leaned forward. "This is an election year, and the district attorney who replaced me when I retired is young, ambitious, and male. In this county's last election, 64% of the voters were women. Get the picture?" She paused for a moment and he nodded. "When your first charges were dropped, there was some grumbling that women weren't being heard by the local male-dominated legal system. There was even a letter to the editor in the local paper. The general public didn't have a way of knowing the whole case against you was groundless."

She started pulling the papers back into her briefcase. "So, my wondering is this. When Carmen came forward with her new accusation, did the DA fear there'd be major repercussions against him if he didn't issue a warrant for your arrest? Is he afraid he'll flounder in the upcoming election?"

She shrugged as if shaking off her own questions and shifted back into her rapid-fire mode. "I've got the sheriff going back to the original case for exculpatory information they have, and I'm leaving you a copy of these notes. I'll get them xeroxed on my way out. Your job for the rest of the day is to go over these sheets again. Figure out what you've left out. "This—" She quickly stood, pulling a thick, large envelope from her briefcase. "—is from Edith. I'll be back tomorrow." Then her volume increased, "Clyde, I'm ready to leave."

He recognized the envelope, his copy of the old manuscript.

Back in his cell, he still felt scraped open. He couldn't let himself think about Edith, what this was doing to her.

He still felt guilty. But Nelda's relentless analysis of the Carmen/Ralph incident and her insistence that there was a connection between his first and second arrest somehow blunted the razor edge of his shame. It still sliced into his core, but now there were distractors around it. And at moments, like a single ray of sunlight breaking through dense forest leaves shifting in a sudden breeze, he wondered if it was possible... that he was innocent. Carmen lied about the parking-lot rape. She could be lying again.

He picked up the manuscript and found the place where he'd told Edith he wanted to stop reading—Russell shot his own father, who'd just murdered Feevah. A rush of memories flooded Philip—not about the manuscript itself, but about the hours with Edith when they read it together. The feeling that for the first time in his life, he'd found home. The scent of her skin, the comfort in her voice, the joy of being one with her. Joy beyond the physical into a zone of spiritual that he'd neither known nor expected.

Gone.

Chapter Thirty-Two

Sabine Richards' manuscript. January–August 1865

In moments, the rope tightened and Seth heard Russell grunting as he ascended the well's wall. When Russell finally pulled himself up over the side of the well, his face was pale and tortured. He stood over his father's body, and Seth thought maybe Russell was going to toss Thomas down the well, too. Instead, Russell retrieved his rifle and started to the doorway.

"Get in the wagon," said Russell's flat voice.

Seth, too stunned to move, stared down into the well.

Russell struck Seth's shoulders with the barrel of his rifle, and said, "Go, get in the wagon. Now."

Somehow, without remembering his walk, Seth crawled into the wagon and lay flat on his back staring up at the night sky.

"What was that shot?" Tenny shouted. "Yankees here?"

"No, it was nothing," Russell said as he climbed into the wagon.

Grandma, wedged on the bench between Russell and Tenny, cried, "Russell, Russell."

"It's all right, Mrs. Richards, we'll take you home, now. Russell's right here and the Yankees won't find us through the hidden right-of-way."

Instead of driving to the house, Russell turned the wagon toward an old Indian trail leading to a dried creek running straight west into the next farm.

"Where do you think you're going?" Tenny demanded.

"Shut up," Russell answered. "The house is full of Yankees. We're going out the back."

"But you just said there's no Yankees here. They haven't even made it to my house yet. My mama said for us to hide at your house until the Yankees pass."

"Shut up," Russell answered.

Seth moved in and out of time as the wagon rolled through the night. Grandma mourning, "Russell, Russell"; Tenny bossing and fussing; and the stars standing still in the black sky. Feevah dead. Seth wished he had died in the barn as well.

Later with the first streaks of dawn, the wagon stopped, and Russell's rough hands shook Seth. "Get up, stupid. You done nothing but lay there all night."

"Your Grandma shit herself," Tenny said. "She stinks."

Seth lay still.

"Get up, I tell you." Russell jerked Seth to a sitting position.

Seth pulled himself up. "I knew you're no match for your daddy's meanness, but I didn't know it'd take you over this quick."

Russell slammed him back down. Seth hoped for an instant that the blow when his head struck the wagon floor would kill him, but it didn't, so he dragged himself up and crawled to the front of the wagon where Grandma was still propped next to Tenny. With Tenny's help, he got her lying down in the back where he had been. Tenny gave him some rags, and he cleaned Grandma.

While Russell slept on the ground near the wagon, Tenny, with her one good arm and partial use of her splinted one, unhitched and tended the horses, fussed through the contents of the wagon, made a small fire, and put together a meal. Seth propped Grandma up and tried to get her to eat. She opened her eyes once and smiled at him, but she wouldn't eat or drink. Seth scooted enough of the stuff around in the wagon to make a place where he could sit now that Grandma was lying, and they waited.

Russell woke with a start and refused the food Tenny had prepared. Within minutes they were rolling again down the dried creek bed. Tenny continued to fuss about the horses needing more rest and Grandma stinking. Seth tilted his head back, so all he could see was the sky. They rolled through the rest of the daylight and into the night again, finally stopping because the creek bed became too narrow, and it was too dark to find a new path. When day broke, they found a passable road leading south.

The road led straight to a burned-out homestead, but the well water smelled good, so they drank and washed and filled their empty containers before moving on. Later that day they were overtaken by a group of about forty Union soldiers.

One called, "Halt." Then the leader and two other men came closer, covering their noses.

"What's that smell?" the lead man asked.

Russell, in a stupor, didn't answer. Tenny, with her terror of Yankees, kept her head down.

"What's in those barrels?" another asked.

Russell was still silent.

"Speak up! I'm asking you a question!"

Seth, seeing Russell wouldn't speak, said, "That stink is sickness coming from Masser's grandma." He put his good arm beneath her shoulders and raised her so the soldiers could see her face. "He ain't talking cause he got the same sickness. We ain't got no medicine, looking to find a doctor."

The three men backed away. The one in charge said, "Move your wagon aside until we pass." Then he added to Seth, "Boy, if you live, you're free. The war is over. The Union won."

After they were out of hearing distance, Tenny said, "Thank you, Seth." Calling him by name for the first time. "You saved me from the Yankees. My mama will be grateful to you."

Hours of silence passed as they moved on. Tenny gradually began her bossing again, telling Russell he needed to eat and the horses needed to rest. Russell remained silent until she said, "Mrs. Richards is dead."

Russell jerked the horses to a hard stop.

Seth checked Grandma and said, "She's just sleeping deep." He could have added that she'd be dead soon judging from the buzzards circling high in the sky.

Time blurred, but within another day or so, the death rattle sounded in Grandma's chest, and Seth kept his hand on her arm until she stopped breathing. "Russell, Grandma has passed."

Russell started toward a grove of trees, but Tenny said, "We don't have a shovel." Without a word Russell continued down the road. Later that day another group of Yankees stopped them. Seth told the same story about sickness, raised up Grandma's dead face, and asked if they had a shovel. Seth wasn't sure if the weary soldiers understood as they covered their faces from the stink and kept moving past them on the road. But when the supply wagon in the rear of the line passed them, a small shovel clanked to the ground.

Russell climbed down, grabbed the shovel, walked to a spot about ten paces off the road, and started digging. Tenny and Seth unhitched and watered the horses and fixed some food.

Seth tried to help with the digging, but Russell wouldn't stop. All day and into the night he dug, and when the grave was even with his forehead, he told Seth to give him an anchored rope so he could pull himself out. Covered with sweaty dirt, he went to the wagon, lifted Grandma out and dropped her into the hole. Without a moment of rest, he started shoveling the dirt into the grave. With Seth and Tenny using pans to help scoop the earth, they filled the grave.

Only then did Russell become still. He lay down on his back on top of the grave. After a time of silence, Tenny said a prayer in German and Seth took his harmonica out of his pocket and played Grandma's beloved, "Are You Washed in the Blood of the Lamb."

Russell lay on the grave the rest of the night and half of the next day. When he finally awoke, he refused food and water and lay in the back of the wagon.

Seeing that Russell no longer cared about what was going on, Tenny ordered Seth to help her get travel ready, and she guided the horses to make a reverse turn to head east back toward the heart of Tennessee. "We're going home."

This time it was Russell instead of Seth lying in the back of the wagon watching the sky, not noticing where they were going. Each time they passed stray travelers, Seth did the talking, and they probably would have made it all the way home had Tenny not decided that night to open one of the barrels on the wagon and dose the two men with her mother's wine.

Tenny gave Seth and Russell each a cupful while she prepared a meal. The tired, dry men immediately mellowed and perked at the same time.

"Seth," she bossed after they had a few minutes of sitting. "Gather up kindling. Russell, set that wine tonic down. Help me cut splints off my arm. I want out."

"What happened to your arm, Tenny?" It was the first time Russell had spoken to her by her name.

She answered while Russell started working loose the leather straps bound around wooden splints. "Papa and I were fixing the barn roof, and my little brother, Otto, let the safety rope slip. We both fell. Papa broke his shoulder and got brain swelling. He's been out of his head most of time since then. That's why we couldn't move him when the Yankees were coming." Russell removed the last of the splint and exposed her bare arm. "Look." She held up both her arms side by side. "The broken arm is smaller than my other arm."

Russell slowly felt both her arms to compare the sizes. Then he rubbed the broken one. "It will fill out in time," he said. "Does it hurt?" Russell rubbed the arm long after he could have stopped.

"No!" She wiggled her arm out of his hands. "Feels good to be free! Here's your prize for freeing me!" Giggling, she filled his cup with more wine. For the first time since their journey began, Russell ate well. After they had finished the meal and had more wine, Seth played his harmonica.

Tenny had spread out blankets beside the fire, so Seth, relaxed by the good meal and wine, fell into a deep sleep.

Pained gasping sounds jolted Seth awake. They were a little like Grandma's death rattles only hard and fast as if someone were being stabbed with a knife. Then he saw the movement beside him—Russell on top of Tenny, rutting into her.

"Take it easy with her," Seth said.

For a moment, both Russell and Tenny were silent and still. Then Russell started again and kept rutting until he finished and rolled off her.

Seth thought he heard Russell say, "Feevah," but he couldn't be sure. The one sound he was sure of was Tenny crying like a hurt child.

The next morning, Russell was silent again. The only change in his behavior was his discovery of the barrels of wine. After a long drink, he lay in the back of the wagon where Grandma had died, still not caring where they went.

Tenny stayed curled up on the ground with blankets wrapped around her.

Seth alone got the wagon loaded and the horses hitched. "Come on, Miss Tenny, let's get you in the wagon. We're going home to your mama."

In a dead voice, Tenny said, "No. Can't go home now. I'm ruined."

Seth became the caretaker. He fed and dosed Tenny with wine. He finally coaxed her into the wagon. With the reins in his hands, he turned the horses back toward the west. "Miss Tenny, if you don't want to go home, we'll go to New York City and find my brother and Feevah's children, and we'll have a new life."

Seth asked travelers along the way for directions to New York City and soon learned they were in Arkansas headed in the wrong direction. However, more than one traveler assured him the best way to get to New York City would be to go south to Parrsville, Texas, cross over to Galveston and take a ship.

As they journeyed farther through Arkansas, the travelers they met were no longer troops but displaced people like themselves. More than one traveler said the Union had won the war, and the slaves were free, but another family claimed the Confederacy had won. Each day the farms they passed looked less like war looted places in Tennessee and more like normal working farms. After they crossed the Arkansas–Texas border, they took the first good road going south.

Each night Seth talked to Russell and Tenny about New York City. "Somewhere in this world are my brother Micah and your boy Solomon. They and Dorcas and Grace are all the people we have left. We'll find them. It's what Feevah said for us to do."

Some nights Russell sat silently, drinking wine, as Seth talked. Some nights Russell cried before he passed out. But night after night, Seth talked about Solomon and New York City. Tenny gradually got her bossiness back and took over the food, the horses, and the schedule. And she didn't cry any more when Russell took her in the night.

"We're out of meat," Tenny fussed one night, and she said to Seth, "We've got to get Russell to go hunting."

Seth and Tenny talked to Russell about hunting, but he was unresponsive. When they reached the Sabine River, Seth picked a campsite with deer signs and found a spot behind some large rocks to hide. Each morning before dawn, he took Russell's rifle and waited. He had luck on the fourth morning and shot a young buck.

Tenny heard the shot and was waiting for Seth when he came back with the news. She started gathering knives and rope. "We'll drag him to this tree to hang. I'll gut and skin and make soup out of the heart and liver. Then we'll cut the meat into strips and dry. I have a bag of salt. Seth, get the big pot to catch the blood —"

"Wait, Miss Tenny, slow down. Let's tell Russell this buck's too heavy for us. Let's get him up and make him see he has to help. Let's don't do everything for him. Maybe this will help him find himself again. It's time he escapes his grieving."

"All right, but I don't like any fur in my meat. He has to do it right," Tenny said.

Seth was right. The change of routine got Russell moving. He still dipped into a wine barrel every day, but at least he was moving around and eating.

They stayed a few weeks before moving and then traveled as long as they could along the Sabine River before veering southwest to cross the Neches River and follow the Trinity River to the gulf coast.

None of them had seen the ocean before. The salty smell, the constant wind, the rolling waves entranced them, and for the first few hours, they found themselves staring, in awe.

Nor had they ever seen so many people before. Although there were not too many soldiers around, some people thought the war was still going on. Other people thought the war was over in every state except Texas. There was bustling, trading, and hundreds of people camped, waiting for ships. Seth found a campsite close to the shore.

Tenny found people to trade with, and within a few days, she replaced her boy clothes with a clean, loose-fitting dress. She also traded for flour, fishhooks, and the abundant fresh fruits and vegetables. Although, she still had a store of dried venison and honey, she traded off the wine first, ending Russell's daily drinks. As soon as the wine barrels were empty, she filled them with crushed fruit, water, sugar, and yeast. From the stores of tools and cookware her mother had packed, Tenny pulled out tubes that fit into the holes in the lids of the barrels. Atop each tube she attached a water-lock device that allowed the fermenting gas to escape without letting air in.

"This is the secret to good wine," she told Seth and Russell. "And one of us must be here all the time to guard. People will steal these water locks; they're very valuable and hard to find. They must stay on until the fermenting stops, twenty, thirty days. Then we'll sell." Soon the scent of fermenting wine filled the vicinity, and people often stopped by to see when she would be ready to sell.

Leaving Russell to guard their campsite, Tenny took Seth to the shore each dawn to fish. One morning, she took him to the market and placed him in a busy intersection with his hat on the ground before him. "Sit here and play your harmonica. People will put money in your hat. I saw a fiddler doing it."

Seth was amazed when people walking by dropped pennies into his hat.

A few days later, Tenny located a busy saloon and ordered Seth to play his harmonica just outside the door late in the evening. Her instincts were right, and he collected even more money at night than he had during the day.

Russell seemed to be rallying with the change of scenery, and Tenny, possibly for lack of a better destination, had taken up the cause for New York City. Knowing it would be hard for a woman to sell the horses and wagon, she urged Russell to find a buyer.

Finally, Russell cleaned himself up and went to the docks where the large boats were anchored. He came back to their campsite with discouraging news. Galveston was blockaded until Texas met all the requirements to rejoin the Union. It could take months to work out. Russell had also learned the best place to make money was in central Texas raising cattle worth five dollars a head and moving them into New Orleans to sell for thirty dollars. He wanted to go to Waco, Texas.

"No," Seth said. "We're doing fine right here. We don't need to go someplace we don't know anything about. Besides, Tenny will be giving birth, and we don't need to be out traveling away from women folks."

Russell looked at Tenny as if he had never seen her before.

For once Tenny was silent.

If she knew she was pregnant, she hadn't talked about it. Seth sensed he'd made a mistake by saying it aloud to Russell, for the notion of taking off to Texas to raise cattle seemed to have rallied his spirit. However, after Seth's speech, Russell fell silent again, and over the next few days, he started disappearing every night and coming home drunk.

One day when Tenny and Seth came back from fishing, Russell was gone. He'd left their wagon unguarded and the bag where Tenny kept their money was also gone.

That night he didn't come home at all. At mid-morning a deputy on horseback led Russell, on foot, to their campsite and asked, "Is this your wagon?"

Seth, seeing that Russell was stuck in one of his silent spells, said, "Yes, suh, this be Masser Russell's wagon."

"I'll be back here before dark," the deputy said to Russell. "If this wagon and these horses are still here, I'm going to confiscate them and put you in jail. And you'll be lucky if the Driscolls don't find you before then because they'll castrate you like a pig. I don't want to see your face again."

As the deputy rode away, Seth scowled at Russell. "What did you do now?"

Russell didn't answer. For once he was the one to start readying the wagon.

Sabine Richards' manuscript. September 1865

The trio was unsure of which direction to go. And maybe because they knew the road that had brought them, they backtracked up the Trinity and across the Neches toward the Sabine River, the same place they had camped and shot the buck. After Russell drove the first day out, he became a stone, lying in the back of the wagon. Tenny and Seth drove the rest of the journey to the Sabine and set up camp. In a couple of days, Seth shot another buck. As before, Russell rallied enough to help them with heavy work.

A couple of weeks later, Tenny was gripped with childbirth pains and started crying the way she had the first night Russell took her.

Seth said, "Don't you worry, Miss Tenny, I helped Feevah when she gave birth to Solomon. I know what has to be done."

He stayed next to her during her labor, bringing her water and helping her squat when she needed to relieve herself. As the contractions grew close and hard, he said, "Russell, it will take more than my one good hand to take care of Tenny and your baby. It's time to be the man Feevah loved. You're no use to anyone the way you are."

Russell followed his orders. And with Tenny yelling and lapsing into what must have been German curses, the head of her baby came into Russell's waiting hands.

"Now, just hold still, Russell. Next push might bring out the rest of it. Be ready to hold on because it'll be slippery."

Seth was right. With the next push the silent baby boy was in Russell's hands, breathing weakly. Seth tied off the chord and started cutting it while Russell gently laid the boy over his forearm and patted his back. Still, the boy was quiet.

Seth said, "Suck his mouth. Must be stuff stuck in there since he's not crying. Lift him upside down to help it flow out."

Russell lifted the baby's body up above his own head. He sucked a couple of times and released some fluid. Then, as if Russell had been doing this his whole life, he cradled the baby and gently blew air into his mouth and nose. After two blows, the baby gave a

Brenda Vicars

strong cry, and Russell opened his shirt, to wrap the baby on his bare chest. He walked down toward the river with him, soothing and talking.

Tenny, finished with her cursing, was silent. After Seth removed the afterbirth, and rolled her off the soiled blankets onto fresh ones, he helped her drink water.

"You have a fine baby boy, and Russell is taking good care of him. Russell is a good daddy. You will see."

"I'm cold," she said. He covered her with another blanket, and she turned her head away. It didn't seem right to Seth that she was so quiet. He remembered Solomon's birth and Feevah's smile when she saw her baby, her need to hold him and to let him nurse. Even though she trusted Dorcas and Seth with her baby, she had to know each thing they did with Solomon from the first moment.

He sat beside Tenny in case she needed anything, and when Russell came back with the baby, Seth said, "You need to let the baby lay by his mama."

"First, I'm going to clean him up. Warm some water."

Seth heated water on the fire, making sure it was just barely warm, and brought it to Russell. Carefully and slowly, Russell kept the baby's body covered except for the part he was washing, and he cleaned him from head to toe. By the time Russell finished, the baby was starting to whimper. Russell took him to Tenny and uncovered her breast.

Seth, remembering Feevah with newborn Solomon, said, "Squeeze the nipple. Let him get a taste of the milk. Then when he opens wide, put the nipple in his mouth."

Russell, carefully pulling the nipple and holding the baby close to Tenny, squeezed a few drops of the clear first milk into the baby's mouth. Immediately, the little mouth opened wide and the baby turned his head from side to side ready to latch onto the source.

Russell chuckled. "What a smart, strong boy you are."

Tenny never moved as Russell held the baby in place for hours

300

throughout the next couple of days and nights, holding him first at one breast then at the other. During the hours the baby slept, Russell lay on his back beside Tenny, with the baby on his chest.

Seth buried the afterbirth, and took all the soiled clothes and blankets down to the river to wash. And each time Russell cleaned the baby, Seth offered Tenny water and food, changed the bloody blankets under her, and helped her squat.

Even after Tenny regained her strength, she had no interest in her baby. She finally started holding him while he nursed, but it didn't seem that she wanted to hold her baby as much as she wanted to avoid the aggravation of having Russell hold him to her breast. Seth hadn't been around a white woman with a newborn, but he remembered Feevah's stories about Mrs. Fuller, who even when she was sick and dying, had strong love for her children.

After a few days, Seth said, "You going to give this boy a name?"

Tenny was silent.

Russell said, "I'll call him Sabine after this river. And I'm carving a notch on my rifle stock each morning since he was born, so when we get somewhere and can find out the date, we can count back to know the date of his birth."

"Why cut the gun?" Tenny asked. "It won't be worth as much."

"It's the one thing I know I will keep," Russell said. "It was handed down to me by my..." He didn't finish, but Seth remembered the day Thomas gave Russell the rifle and the night Russell killed Thomas with it.

Tenny said, "*Sabine* is German for people who leave their home and take hold of a new land." She pronounced it "suh-bean-ah."

"Well, then it must be the right name," said Russell. "He's headed to Waco, a new land. But don't pronounce it the German way."

That night while Tenny was nursing the baby, Seth and Russell were settling the horses, and Seth said, "Sabine being born means Feevah and your daddy have been dead nine months. Doesn't seem possible so much time passed since we ran out of Tennessee."

Silently, Russell turned away and returned to the campsite.

One morning a lone rider came up. "Howdy, folks. Looks like you got a fine camp here. I'm Tom Williams."

"I'm Russell Richards. This is my wife, Tenny, and our son, Sabine."

That was the first time Russell had referred to Tenny as his wife. Her back straightened, and she offered her hand and her smile to the stranger.

"I veered off the road to look for deer tracks along the river and seen your camp."

After some conversation, Russell mentioned his plan to go to Waco.

"Waco," said Williams. "Best place to go right now—got folks there—can't hardly tell there's been a war there. Cattle business is booming. You can camp on the Brazos and live on pecans, wild grapes, and fish. It'll be the biggest town in Texas, the center of trade." He cocked his head toward Seth. "What you gonna do with him?"

Russell frowned and shrugged. "Haven't figured that out yet."

"Well, there's groups of 'em everywhere now, guess no one's got it figured out yet."

Within days Russell, Tenny, and Seth loaded the wagon and left their campsite.

As they headed for the road, Seth said, "I'm going to stay on the coast until I can ride the boat. When I get to New York City, I will look for our people. I'm going leave papers with their names everywhere I go—Feevah taught me how to write the basics. I'm going write that you're in Waco. That way if I can't find Dorcas and Micah, someday they'll get one of my papers and come to Waco to find you."

Sabine had been crying softly since before they got into the wagon. Now, as they approached the main road, he was screaming. "Tenny," Russell said. "Feed him. Can't you hear he's hungry?"

"It's not time for him to feed," she said. "He'll be spoiled if he eats when he wants."

Russell stayed silent, not responding to Seth or Tenny. When they reached the main road, Russell reined to a stop and Seth slid down. He had his pockets full of dried deer meat, corn bread, and his harmonica. Russell paused as if to say something to Seth. Sabine continued to cry.

Seth waited.

Finally, without looking back and without making Tenny feed the crying baby, Russell shook the horses into a trot and headed northwest.

Sabine Richards' manuscript. 1869

Seth had four years of tedious trials and tribulations through his journeys with no noteworthy occurrences before he found his way to Waco. When he arrived, he asked at the post office for Russell's address and drove his carriage to the house.

Philip stopped reading. He stood and stretched and paced around his cell. Since there were no windows and no clock, he had no idea how much time passed while he was lost in this ugly history.

The comment about Seth's insignificance sickened him.

Brenda Vicars

The years after the Civil War were horrendous and dangerous for freed slaves. Sabine's characterization of the four years as *tedious* underscored Philip's suspicion that Sabine was a self-deluded narcissist.

He took a deep breath and returned to the reading.

Even before Seth got close enough to recognize people, he could have guessed which house was Tenny's. The yard was fenced and had vegetables growing in every possible space; dried peppers and spices hanging under the covered porch; chicken coops placed above the root vegetables; two nanny goats staked in a corner. The yard was a miniature replica of her parents' farm in Tennessee.

The only unutilized spot in the yard was a small square area of soil occupied by three dirty little boys. The smallest boy, who looked too young to walk, was sitting naked on the ground, crying; the other two were scratching in the dirt with twigs.

"Sabine," Seth said softly from his carriage.

Sabine, now almost the same age Solomon had been the last time Seth had seen him, looked straight toward Seth. Sabine's resemblance to Solomon fired open the old ache of missing Feevah.

Tenny bustled out the front door with food scraps and orders for Sabine to feed the chickens. Sabine took the scraps, and the middle child started to follow him.

"No," Tenny said, slapping the middle child on the shoulder, pushing him down to the ground. "You stay. You don't know how to walk in the garden without stepping on plants." She went back inside, letting the door slam behind her.

Now two boys sat in the dirt crying.

Seth and his wife, carrying their baby, got down from their carriage and approached the fence. "Sabine," Seth said. This time

Seth was prepared for the wash of memories that Sabine's face brought. "Sabine, please go tell your daddy Seth is here."

Sabine jumped up and ran toward the door, calling, "Daddy, someone is here."

Tenny came out through the open doorway and stopped Sabine. "Don't you come in this house. You're too dirty. I'll tell Daddy." She looked toward the fence and called, "Russell, it's that crippled slave in front of house."

Seth and his wife and daughter waited until Russell stepped out onto the porch.

Russell said, "Well, didn't expect to ever see you again."

"Hello, Russell," said Seth. "This is my wife, May, and my daughter, Feevah. I have news."

Russell, hearing the name Feevah, shifted from the bold man of the house to an empty-eyed shadow.

Tenny said, "You come around to the back, and we'll talk." She pointed in the direction where Seth and his family could enter the back yard. "Sabine, you stay here and watch your brothers." While the visitors walked around to the back, Tenny and Russell went through the house. Tenny stood just outside the kitchen doorway with Russell standing behind her, inside the kitchen.

"What news?" Tenny asked. A faint scent of fermenting wine drifted from the doorway.

"I sailed to New York City, left papers with folks saying, 'To Micah, Solomon, Dorcas, and Grace: Russell and Seth Richards in Waco, Texas.' So, I came to see if you had word from them."

"No," she answered. "That's a question. You said you have news. What is it?"

"I came overland from New York through Chattanooga and stopped at your mama's place. Your papa passed on and your mama married a man with grown sons. Your brothers came back from war. They're all living and working on the place and they took over Richards' place, raising tobacco."

"Too bad Papa died; but he couldn't have gotten any better," Tenny said. "We'll write Mama and tell her she has to pay us for the Richards' place."

"Your mama said she paid Thomas Richards for the place. She said she has the deed with his sign on it. Said she paid $2,000 plus the wagon and four horses you took."

Tenny was silent at this. Seth squinted, trying to see Russell's face in the kitchen as he took in the lie Tenny's mama had told about buying the Richards' place from Thomas. She must have found Thomas's body, and the house deserted.

The kitchen was too dark to see Russell's eyes as he leaned up against a fermenting barrel with a metal tube extending out the top. Russell kept his gaze downward, picking at his nails with a small knife.

"What else did Mama say?" Tenny asked.

"I told her you and Russell married and had a baby boy with a fine German name, Sabine." Seth didn't say that the German mother had scoffed at the name, declaring that *Sabine* is a girl's name, and stupid Tenny gave her boy a girl's name.

"What else did Mama say?"

"She said you and Russell can keep the wagon and four horses, but she would appreciate it if you send back her water locks. She can't make good wine without them, and her papa brought them from France. She can't find them anywhere else."

"I'm keeping the water locks. They're mine. If you see Mama again, tell her she still owes us for the land. The only money she had was Confederate, so that $2,000 she paid was worthless. She has to pay us real money, half to Russell and half to Thomas. What else did Mama say?"

Seth paused, hoping Russell would speak or at least look up. "That's all, ma'am."

Tenny nodded curtly. "Shanty town is south of Waco. You stay there. We'll come find you if we have news."

306

Seth nodded and led his wife, May, back toward their carriage. After they were up in the carriage, Russell, who had followed them, said, "Seth, come here."

Seth climbed down again and walked over to Russell, who leaned against the fence with his gaze downward. Never looking directly at Seth, Russell spoke in a low tone. "The mistake I made is I should've shoved Daddy down in the well. That way Tenny's mama wouldn't have found him dead and she couldn't claim he sold her the place. I thought about doing it at the time. It would have just taken a minute. But he was so bloody, I didn't want to touch him."

Seth started to turn back toward his carriage, but Russell continued. "Damned thing is, that's the same mistake I made the night Daddy tried to kill you in the barn. He told me to throw you down that dried-up well. And I would have done it, but you were so bloody, I didn't want to touch you. I made the same mistake twice."

"Seth?" May called softly. She couldn't hear what they were saying, but Seth's body had jerked as if struck by a rattlesnake. Then he'd slumped forward and something in the curve of his shoulders alarmed her. "Seth, let's go."

Seth, as if in a daze, turned toward her voice. Russell put his hand on Seth's shoulder and stopped him hard. "Get your ass to shanty town and you stay there. Don't come back here again. And if you carry any more tales back to Tennessee, I'll kill you."

Seth looked into Russell's face trying to see his eyes, concealed in shadow. Behind Russell, the three boys were still in their square of dirt. The two smallest ones had fallen asleep.

Sabine stood watching his father.

At last Philip reached the end of Sabine's manuscript. There were no more pages to turn.

The irony wasn't lost on him. The preface of the manuscript

had closed with Sabine turning out as bad as his father by eventually killing his own mother, Tenny.

The Feevah story, with its abuse and murder, ended with the child Sabine witnessing Russell's final evil words to Seth.

Philip had watched his own father and grandfather and now turned out to be as bad as they were—trapped in a fractal spiraling down a black hole.

He looked around his jail cell. Evil goes on and on. His big-swerve clinamen fantasy was just that—fantasy.

Chapter Thirty-Three

Lupe phoned Edith.

"Hey. It's Lupe. Nelda brought us new information from her meeting with Philip." He waited for Edith to say something. Her background noises indicated she was driving. After a pause, he added, "Would you like to come to our room and go over it with us?"

Edith stayed silent. He was about to question their connection, but finally she said, "What's in it?" Her monotone voice made hair twist on the back of his neck.

He gave her the main points, then asked, "Are you still in Culmine?"

"Driving to Austin." She sighed.

Lupe, sensing she might say more, waited.

She let out a shaky breath. "I just talked with Frank. He said Carmen was at the Hilltop the second night Philip and I were together." Her breath shuddered. "Frank noticed that she... she watched us."

"So maybe she was jealous and this is why she is lying about Philip. Maybe this is why she changed her hair color—to be like you." Lupe said. "Maybe she wanted Philip to pay attention to her and when he did not, she made up the story. When will you return to Culmine?"

"Turning around now. I'll come to your room. Bye."

"She's on her way," Lupe told Guillermo and Rosa.

Guillermo, making notes on the papers spread before him, pointed to a new statement Nelda had brought from Philip: "You aren't worth my *escarabajo*" —beetle. Rosa and Lupe stared at it blankly.

Lupe shook his head. "What could it mean?"

Guillermo said, "In some parts of Mexico, extract is taken from the green beetle and used as an aphrodisiac. The Spanish Fly."

"Oh, man." Lupe pushed his hair back off his forehead. "So, she wanted him to take an aphrodisiac. That makes no sense."

"Wait," said Rosa. "It does make sense." She sorted through the pages. "Remember how margarita drinks came up twice. Here." She points to a page. "In the parking lot, she told the police she made Ralph margaritas but she did not drink any. Then she tells you, Lupe, that her margaritas are better than the bar's. Maybe she puts Spanish Fly into her margaritas." Rosa's eyes widened and darted from Lupe to Guillermo. "Maybe she likes to make men lose control. Maybe that is why Ralph was going after her in the car." Then her excitement deflated, and her face saddened. "Maybe she even slipped some to Philip."

"No. Why would a woman do that?" asked Lupe.

"I do not think the extract is powerful enough to make someone lose control," said Guillermo.

Rosa, excited now, raised both hands. "But she could put extra into the margaritas."

Guillermo frowned. "The extract is deadly if someone takes too much."

An incoming text caught Lupe's attention. "Frank says Carmen is at the bar." He moved toward the door.

Rosa clutched his arm. "Wait. What if she puts something into your drink?"

"She cannot do that in a public place."

Guillermo approached Rosa. "After Lupe goes to the bar, we can enter, take a table, and watch them."

"Wait," Rosa said again before Lupe opened the door. "I have plastic bags." She dug into her purse and pulled out some small Ziploc bags. "I keep these for the children's snacks. Put one in your pocket in case she slips something into your drink. Wait until she goes to the bathroom or leaves and pour your drink in here. We can take it to Nelda Perkins to have it analyzed." She gripped his arm. "And whatever you do, do not drink it."

Lupe rolled his eyes. "Rosa, you watch too many movies." But he pocketed the bag.

The moment Lupe entered the Hilltop, Carmen flashed a welcoming smile, but her straight black brows and small, close-set eyes made her smile forced looking.

He grinned and took the stool next to her. *"Buenos noches, Señorita* Carmen. I am the luckiest man in the world to find you two nights in a row."

She smoothed her gauzy skirt across her knees. "Not luck, Lupe. I told you I'd be here."

"Ah, you did. Then I am lucky you kept your word."

"I always..." She caressed his forearm. "...keep my word."

Frank approached, and Lupe ordered a mojito.

With one elbow on the bar, Carmen leaned toward Lupe, reached for his hand on his knee and ran her finger over his wedding band. "Where's your wife?"

"Home with the children in Vuelta." He hoped his ring wouldn't make Carmen less open with him. Somehow the mention of his wife threw him off balance.

Brenda Vicars

"Then we don't have to worry about her, do we?" Carmen lowered her voice. "Ready to be a bad boy tonight?"

Lupe gulped his drink. "It is lonely to be so far from home."

"Lupe, you're blushing." Carmen giggled. "Do I make you nervous?"

"Yes." Lupe grinned at her. "Very nervous." He drank some more. Two couples were dancing in the jukebox corner. One place Lupe was always comfortable, thanks to his mother, was on the dance floor. "Will you dance with me, Carmen?"

"Oh, you're a dancer?" she asked.

"I try."

She pressed her breast against his arm. "I think you just want to hold me."

Lupe tried to return the loaded comment. "Ah, Carmen, you are going to get me into so much trouble." He stood, drained his glass, and took her arm.

She wasn't a strong dancer, but thanks to a lifetime of practice, he knew how to pace himself so anyone could follow. After several songs, they went back to the bar and got refills.

By now Rosa and Guillermo were seated at a nearby table with a clear view of the bar.

Lupe quickly finished his drink and ordered two more, noting she was on her third drink now. "What do you do for fun here in Culmine?"

Her smile twisted into a bitter thing. "This place sucks. There's nothing here."

"Then why stay?"

Her shoulders twitched as if shaking off a weight. "I have a half-sister here. But she's a bitch, and visiting her is a waste of my time. I'll leave as soon as... soon."

"What did your sister do to you?"

"She inherited my father's place. It should have been mine." She pointed to herself. "I'm the first born. My sister should have

312

at least split it with me." She took another drink and put the glass down too hard. "I was also screwed over by my husband. I lived with him over fifteen years—took care of him in his unending, declining years. He lived to be eighty-three. But when he died, I found out all his life insurance and savings were left to his first wife and his kids. All I got is the house in Mexico."

Lupe shook his head in sympathy. "That's awful. Are you staying at your sister's?"

"No. I did for a while, but now I rent a place."

He wanted her to talk about the case. "So, you said you will leave Culmine soon?"

She nodded as she drank. "As soon as my... as soon as I finish some business."

He leaned a little closer. "Sounds mysterious."

She leaned in also, but before speaking, she glanced over her shoulder. "Oh, shit." Her back stiffened and she jerked her face back toward the bar.

"What is it?" Lupe asked, looking back to see what had caused her reaction.

"Don't look," she said. "It's a stupid ex who won't leave me alone." She pulled her purse off the back of her chair. "Come with me. I'll fix you a good margarita." She stood. "Coming?"

"Ah, okay." Lupe, dropping cash onto the bar, had to hurry. She moved fast.

He followed her toward the door. Rosa, with her alarmed-sister expression, almost stood as he passed their table. He shook his head and pantomimed a phone to let her know he'd call.

Outside, Lupe said, "I will follow you."

She kept walking rapidly toward an SUV. "No. Get in. I'll bring you back."

He hesitated an instant, about to insist on driving his own car. Then he remembered his keys were with Guillermo.

She slid in and started her car. "Hurry."

This is a mistake, he thought, but he couldn't pass up the chance to get more information.

She peeled out of the parking lot, sending gravel flying.

Rosa and Guillermo cannot catch up with us even if they try. "Why the hurry?" he asked when they were on the highway headed out of the town.

"Long story." Calmer now, she reverted to her flirtatious tone. "So, what's your wife's name?"

"Josie." Saying her name heightened his discomfort. He wished he were home with her.

"And you leave her often when you work?"

"Yes, I do."

"I bet she worries about you and wonders if you're behaving?" Her eyes sliced toward him and then back to the road.

Lupe hoped her house wasn't much farther. He was a good runner and could take off on foot if necessary.

She flashed him a smile that didn't go with her worried eyes. "Well, Lupe, my handsome man, I want you to relax tonight. I'm going to show you a good time, and let you live in the moment. After you go back to Josie, this night will be a nice memory. You work hard for your family. You deserve a little reprieve. And I'm the right woman to guide you."

Lupe wanted to text Rosa, but Carmen would notice. "Let us stop somewhere. I would like to buy you a drink before we go to your house."

"We're almost there. Besides, I promised you my special margaritas. Tell me, how did you meet Josie?"

"In high school. She was a grade behind me."

"What do you two do for fun?"

"Dance. Go to the kids' soccer games. Visit family. Projects around the house. Garden." He hated sharing family details with this woman.

"Are Josie's parents still living?"

"Yes. They live near us."

"What are their names?"

This question set off alarms, and he decided to invent names.

When they pulled up to a mobile home on a bare lot at the dead end of a dirt road, she said, "*Mi casa es su casa.*"

He followed her up four steps onto a metal porch, that wobbled a little under their weight. It was clearly portable and resting on unlevel ground. She unlocked the door, and when she pushed it open, stuffy heat blasted them. She charged across the room to a window air conditioner. "Motherfucker." She twisted knobs then kicked the wall beneath the window.

"What happened?" Lupe looked around the combination kitchen, dining, living room.

"That bastard installed this air conditioner, and it keeps stopping."

"Who installed it?"

"Never mind." She started opening windows.

Lupe opened windows with her. "Lucky there is a good breeze tonight." Strings of small seashells hung from the curtain rods. "You must like the coast."

"No. I hate sand and grit. These were already here when I moved in." She used the strings of shells to tie back the curtains.

"Well, it is a cozy home. I like the built-in shelves and cabinets."

"Don't lie. It's a dump." She flipped on a radio station playing Mexican music. "But it's temporary. I'll come into money soon. Then I'll go back to Mexico and live like a queen."

"Oh, yeah, a new job?"

She chuckled. "Already did the job, just collecting the payoff."

All the windows were open now, so Lupe stood in the center of the room while she headed to the kitchen counter. "Tell me about this job."

She ignored his request and pointed to the small sofa. "Sit. I'll mix you the best drink of your life."

"Could I use your restroom first?"

"Sure." She was assembling limes, sugar, tequila, orange liquor, and other ingredients next to a blender. "Right there." She cocked her head to the left.

In the tiny restroom he stood in front of the toilet and texted Rosa and Guillermo. A black satin wrap of some kind hung on a hook on the closed door, and the room was so small the slick fabric stroked his arms and back each time he moved. Seconds after he sent the text, an error message flashed—*failed to send*. No bars. He turned on the voice memo app and slipped the phone into his front shirt pocket. *No worries. I will get as much information as I can, pour the margarita into the bag and run back to town as soon as I can make a break.*

The blender *burred* from the kitchen.

Leaving the bathroom, he settled on the small sofa and stretched out his legs. "This is the life. Beautiful Carmen. *La musica*. Margarita. What more can a man ask for?"

She turned toward him with a huge smile and a frosty, stemmed glass, salted around the rim. She carried it high with one hand under the base and presented it to him. He took it from her. Then Carmen, spreading her skirt so wide the fabric splayed onto his knee, sat on the sofa next to him. "Now, Lupe, drink my margarita with gusto or I'll be very unhappy."

He took a drink. *One mouthful can do no harm.* "This is the best margarita I have ever tasted. Too delicious to be gulped. I must savor. Where is yours?"

"I have to drive you back, so no more drinking for me tonight."

"Smart woman. Now, tell me about this business you are wrapping up in Culmine."

Her smile drooped a little. "Why so curious?"

"I am interested in everything about you."

She tilted her head and frowned. "Have you heard about my case?"

"Case? In Culmine?"

"Yes, my legal case. I'm a me-too victim."

"I have been here only a couple of days. What happened to you?"

"This big guy was all nice to me. Pretended to be kind and sympathetic. Then he turned on me. But I have him trapped now. There was an article in the newspaper about how the system is against women. The District Attorney even interviewed me." She paused and shrugged. "I won't get money from this one, but he's going to hurt. Bad."

"Who is this guy?"

Her small dark eyes bored into him. "Why so curious about my case?"

Lupe shrugged, squirming inside. He had to keep her talking. "What is your favorite place you have ever lived?"

"I like big cities. San Antonio, Nuevo Laredo, Houston." She reached the wall switch behind her and flipped off the main overhead light, leaving only the light over the kitchen counter. She circled his ear with one finger. "Tell me the names of your children."

Queasiness surged through Lupe. He hated her probing for his family details. "Bert, Ernesto, and Julia," he lied. "Why do you like big cities?"

"Excitement. Excuse me for a moment." She stood and pointed at his glass. "Finish that while I'm gone, and I'll have a reward for you." She went into the bathroom.

Pulling the plastic bag out, Lupe slipped over to the sink. He poured in a couple of ounces of margarita, sealed the bag and slid it back into his shirt pocket. He poured the rest of the drink down the drain then slipped back to his place on the sofa just as she opened the bathroom door. He set the empty glass on the floor next to the sofa.

Carmen emerged wearing the black satin wrap, slit up one side almost to her waist. The clingy fabric showed she had on nothing underneath. "Oh, you finished. Good boy." She took his glass to the counter and filled it from the blender. "Here you go." She cozied up next to him. "Drink it all."

He took a sip. "I need to slow down a little."

"You need to relax, get more comfortable." She began unbuttoning his shirt. "It's too hot to wear this." She looped a bare leg over one of his and pressed her crotch against his thigh. Almost riding his leg, she started pushing his shirt open with one hand and reached for his zipper with the other. Lupe, hindered by the full drink in his hand, set it on the floor beside the sofa and popped to his feet. His sudden motion propelled her back a little and she grabbed at his shirt in reflex, gripping the pocket with the plastic bag.

She frowned, slid out the bag and peered at it. "What's this?" She flipped on the overhead light.

"Nothing." He reached for it, but she pulled farther back. "Let me have it, please."

"This looks like the margarita." She stood and shoved him surprisingly hard.

"It is a... urine sample. It is embarrassing. I have an infection." He reached for it again. "I must leave."

Opening the bag and sniffing, she glared at him. "You liar." She walked to the sink and dropped the bag in. "What game are you playing with me?"

318

"No game." He buttoned his shirt. "I am trying to learn the truth."

"Truth?"

He took a step toward the door.

She glared at him with her hands on her hips. "What truth?"

With one hand on the doorknob, Lupe glared back. "You accused my friend Felipe of raping you. It is a lie. I want to know why."

Carmen's eyes narrowed, almost closed.

Lupe spoke evenly. "I think you are the one playing games. Why did you accuse him?"

She shouted, surprisingly loud and gruff. "Because he did it. I don't care what that old cripple says. He did it. And he'll pay."

"I do not believe he raped you. And what is with the margaritas and your beetle?" With quick steps, he reached back to the sink and rescued the bag, still containing a couple of tablespoons. He rezipped it. "Did you put Spanish Fly in my drink? In Felipe's drink?" Back at the door he swung it open. "When I get this tested, what will they find?" In his peripheral vision, he caught her hand flying to one of the little cabinets.

Her voice froze him. "I'll tell you what they'll find." She sounded old and hollow.

He met her calm gaze, and his stomach dropped.

She held a pistol pointed at his heart. "Nothing. Because you're putting the bag back into the sink. There will be no testing."

Lupe slowly lifted the bag in front of himself and stepped back to the sink.

"Empty it," she ordered.

He did as she said and made his way back to the door. Through gritted teeth he said, "This proves you put something in my drink." He opened the door. "Otherwise, why not have it tested?"

Her face was blank for a moment. "Looks like I have to kill you now."

"No. People saw me leave with you." Lupe eyed the gun. "If I disappear, they will come looking." He backed out onto the wobbly porch.

Low and calm she said, "Think about what people saw." Now she smiled and nodded, agreeing with her own story. "They saw me, upset, hurry away from the bar—away from you." She laughed, deep and throaty, her shoulders shaking up and down. "They saw you follow me. You followed me home and broke in. Besides you're new in town. No one here cares about you."

Lupe shook his head. "My sister and her husband were in the café watching to see if you put something in my drink like you did Felipe's. And my car is still at the café, so people will know I didn't follow you." He backed down the four porch steps. "We are on to you, Carmen. Your game is over." He gripped the edge of the porch.

She stepped forward until she was standing in the doorway, the gun still aimed at Lupe. "This is perfect. You broke in, got caught, and tried to run away. So, you did all this for nothing." She laughed. "Philip is still going to prison. And you—"

Lupe, still gripping the porch, heaved it up with all his strength, creating a barrier between himself and the gun. The now sideways porch, blocked the doorway, but there was still enough opening at the top of the door for Carmen to stick the gun out and shoot. She fired repeatedly until the gun clicked and stopped.

Lupe ran with his ears ringing from the shots and realized screaming women were in the darkness. He thought he must be dead or dreaming.

Rosa and Edith came running toward him.

"Are you okay?" Rosa ran her hands over his torso.

He propelled Rosa and Edith farther from the trailer. "Yes, she missed. Where's your car?" Then squinting down the road, he saw two cars parked about a hundred feet away. "How did you get here? Where's Guillermo?"

"Guillermo?" Rosa gasped. "Where are you?" Then a gut-wrenching scream.

At the same moment, they all spotted him on the ground, lying still.

Rushing toward him, Rosa cried, "No, no, no." She knelt and touched his face.

Edith felt his pulse. "He's alive."

Guillermo said in his calm voice, "It is not life threatening. Bullet struck ribcage—lower left outside. Broken bones there. No lung involvement."

Carmen's weeping, loud voice rang out from inside the trailer. "Home invasion. People broke in. I shot in self-defense. Hurry, please. I think they're still out there."

Lupe marveled at how convincing she sounded.

"Lupe, you carry my shoulders. Rosa and Edith each can carry a leg. We should get to the cars before she starts shooting again."

After they were about halfway to the cars, Lupe said, "This is good. Let us lower him here. Rosa, bring the car here. Hurry."

"Key in my front right pocket," Guillermo said.

"Not too much bleeding," Lupe said, hoping Guillermo wasn't bleeding internally.

When Rosa pulled up, they lifted Guillermo and stretched him out across the back seat.

Running toward her car, Edith said, "I'll lead you to the hospital, and I'll call ahead."

Rosa sat on the floor in the back next to Guillermo, who had not spoken after he directed Rosa to the car keys.

Out on the highway, Lupe glanced into the backseat. "Why is he so quiet?"

Rosa said, "He's focusing on slowing his heartrate so there's less bleeding. He's doing slow breaths to oxygenate his blood and help his body heal."

"Ah." Lupe turned back to the road. "How did all of you get here?"

"I texted Edith when we went to the café. Instead of coming in, she waited in the parking lot for us because Carmen knows her. She followed you two and called us with directions."

At the hospital, staff came out with a stretcher and wheeled Guillermo into ER. They let Rosa go with him.

In the waiting room, Edith paced while Lupe called Nelda, updating her and explaining he had taped Carmen. "Can you tell the sheriff to test the drink? There is a full glass on the floor next to the sofa and some in the blender on the kitchen counter. If she has not poured them out. It has drugs in it."

Nelda said, "Will do. Text the recording to me and the sheriff. I'll send his cell number. I hope Guillermo is okay. Goodbye."

Stunned by Nelda's quick end to the call, Lupe blinked before hanging up. Then he started texting the recording.

Edith sat beside him and offered a bottle of water. "What are you doing?"

"Sending the recording to Nelda and the sheriff." Lupe drank and shoved his hair back.

Edith clenched her hands together. "I hope Guillermo is

okay." She slumped back into her chair, and said, "Can I hear the recording?"

As they listened to the dialogue, it seemed clear Carmen had put something in the margarita.

Lupe replayed one section twice. "Why does she say *old cripple?* Listen, 'Because he did it. I don't care what that old cripple says. He did it. And he will pay.'"

Rosa came in. "They are going to do surgery to remove bone splinters, just as Guillermo predicted. They think there is no organ damage." She giggled and flopped down onto the sofa.

Edith and Lupe gaped, alarmed by her giggles, as they sat on either side of her.

Rosa giggled again. "I know. It is crazy for me to laugh, but Guillermo said he does not need anesthesia for the surgery. He will self-hypnotize." She laughed so hard tears were streaming from her eyes. "You should have seen the doctor's face." She hugged her stomach, calming herself. "I convinced Guillermo to do what the doctor says. I was afraid for a while he would leave with no surgery." She settled back into the chair. "It will take four or five hours before I can see him."

Then just as abruptly as her giggles had come, gut-wrenching sobs shook her frame. When she caught her breath enough to speak, she said, "What if the anesthesia kills him. It will be my fault for persuading him. What have I done?"

Chapter Thirty-Four

With nothing to do except reread the old manuscript, Philip sank deeper into reality... his own life was another doomed chapter in his ancestors' chronicle.

Thomas murdered Feevah but said, "She weren't much good anyway." Russell raped thirteen-year-old Tenny, then announced to a passerby she was his wife. Sabine killed his mother, Tenny, but deluded himself that it was an accident. Philip's grandfather desecrated Dinah but claimed it didn't happen. Her own father looked the other way. And Philip himself—his stomach churned with this thought—raped Carmen James but didn't remember it. All the men were drunk or hungover or both.

During the long night in jail, while he had accepted his own place in the cycle, the hot blade of focused hatred for his father diffused into a million sharp-edged grains ceaselessly battering him. What had started generations earlier as slave abuse had evolved into sexual abuse. Philip's rage no longer targeted a single man; instead, the whole bloodline, himself included, was equally vile.

His old companion, shame, had ironically weakened. The

old shame he held for his own flaws wasn't gone, but now it was diffused over generations.

A bizarre fragment of him felt relief. He no longer had to dread the truth. There was no truth left untold. And the stain on his family was part of a bigger picture. The whole country shared the history of abuse of slaves. He wondered how many other dysfunctional white families like his own could trace their problems back to their slave-owning ancestors.

He still dreaded prison and grieved losing Edith. But in a twisted way, he was relieved to be punished. No one had punished his ancestors. Instead, Dinah, Feevah, and Tenny paid the price. *So, my going to prison, not my connection with Edith, is my clinamen. I've disrupted the generational fractal pattern and made the big swerve.*

His father's voice taunted. *If you'd been in my shoes, you'd have done the same. You're the same as me.*

"Well, old man, you were almost right, but unlike you, I'm going to prison."

"Talking to yourself?" A guard unlocked Philip's door. "Sheriff wants to see you."

Philip shoved pages back into the envelope. "What time is it?"

"Almost noon."

As they passed through the hallway, a groan escaped from a side room. The door swung open and an officer stepped out. During that instant, Philip saw Ralph inside, slumped in a chair, turning his head from side to side.

"What's going on?" Philip asked the guard.

"Keep walking. Sheriff will fill you in."

Sheriff Renfro, waiting in the hall near the doorway, entered the conference room after Philip. Nelda, crisp as ever, sat next to a young man Philip didn't know. She was explaining the case, using Guillermo's papers spread on the table. Athletic looking, the man wore a tweed jacket and narrow black tie, and with an iPad he was photographing each page Nelda shared.

When the young man looked up, Renfro said, "Mr. Richards, this is Agent Don Holmes of the Texas Rangers. Agent Holmes, Philip Richards."

Holmes stood and offered his hand. In his standing position, the holster and badge on his belt were visible.

Renfro slid into a chair and pointed to the one next to Nelda for Philip. "We had developments overnight. I called in the Rangers because our case is connected to a Houston case, and I think the response from our county has been compromised. My suspicions were first aroused by the sketch Mr. Guillermo Zacatecas provided of the man he observed picking up Ms. Carmen James." Nelda lifted her copy of the sketch. "Then last night, I served a search warrant on Ms. James, and we found incriminating videos of her with several different men, including this one." He cocked his head toward Guillermo's sketch.

Nelda tapped the man's face in the sketch and whispered to Philip. "He's our new DA's father."

Renfro went on as if Nelda hadn't spoken. "There's also a video of Ms. James with Mr. Ralph Albertson in the backseat of her car." He shifted his gaze to Philip. "In the video she pleads with him to stop just as you had reported. Looks like she had her phone secured in the back pocket of the front seat and videoed without him knowing it."

Philip let out a breath he hadn't realized he was holding. Even though his charges for the parking lot incident had been dropped, it was a relief to have proof that he had told the truth.

Renfro placed a page headed *Houston Police Department* on the table. "But the big find is about the gun Ms. James used to shoot Mr. Zacatecas."

Philip jerked forward in his chair. "Guillermo's shot?" He looked from Renfro to Nelda.

Nelda touched his arm. "Don't worry, Guillermo's fine. Already had surgery." Her sympathetic eyes acknowledged Philip's confusion. "It's a long story, but Guillermo and his wife and Edith followed Lupe to Carmen's house. Carmen started shooting, and Guillermo got hit. They'll fill you in on the details later, but the significant finds for your case are the videos and the gun."

"Edith's okay? No one else was shot?"

Nelda faced him, still holding his arm. "Everyone is fine, and there's new evidence proving your innocence." She shifted her gaze to Renfro. "Go ahead, clarify about the guns."

"During the parking-lot incident investigation, Ms. James and Mr. Albertson claimed the gun belonged to you. We were still working on the gun source when the DA dropped the first case against you and filed the new rape charge to have taken place February fourteenth. Now we have this second gun from Ms. James's shooting last night, and the serial number is registered to the same person as the first gun, so it's clear they lied about you bringing the gun to the parking-lot scene."

Renfro cocked his head toward Holmes who picked up the story. "The owner of the guns died three years ago in Houston. The family didn't realize some guns were missing after his death, so no theft was reported. The owner was sixty-seven years old and his autopsy report shows levels of alcohol and sildenafil, a common erectile medication, best known as Viagra." He referred to his iPad as he continued. "The findings weren't questioned at the time since it's not uncommon for a man his age to use sildenafil. The coroner lists a natural cause of death as myocardial infarction, or heart attack, and there was no further investigation. But now we're looking at another odd detail in the autopsy results... a level of cantharidin."

"What's cantharidin?" Philip asked.

Renfro said, "This is where it gets interesting. Cantharidin is a substance secreted by certain beetles. It's used externally to treat warts. But some people believe if you drink it, it's an aphrodisiac. In Mexico it's called the Spanish fly."

Nelda turned to Philip. "Remember I said there was something telling about the way she kept bringing up her margaritas." She faced Renfro and Holmes. "Carmen James was concocting mixtures of margarita, cantharidin, and sildenafil, getting men aroused and intoxicated, making videos without their knowledge, then blackmailing them. She possibly overdosed the deceased man in Houston, and when he died, she helped herself to at least two of his guns."

Nelda hammered her narrative as if she were summing up for a jury. "The night of the parking-lot incident, she had dosed Ralph and was videoing herself pretending to resist him when my client stepped in to save her. Rather than compromise her mark, Ralph, she changed the story to blame an innocent hero who happened to show up. For some reason, maybe fear of his wife finding out, Ralph went along with her lie and has been paying Carmen. As I said from the beginning, my client was simply in the wrong place at the wrong time trying to do the right thing."

She paused a moment giving everyone time to absorb her theory. "And..." She tapped her index finger on the sketch. "... she was blackmailing the DA's father. Got him to use his influence to drop the flimsy parking-lot case and get the Valentine's rape charges placed. Therefore, Sheriff Renfro, I request you release Mr. Richards immediately and move forward expeditiously with expunging all charges against him."

Philip braced for a rebuttal.

Renfro stood and said, "Done."

"Wait," Philip said. "What about February fourteenth? Has she changed her statement?"

Nelda's posture stiffened and she pounced on the question. "Her statement is totally irrelevant and you have no culpability for anything that possibly happened that night. Based on her pattern, she drugged you. If anything, you should be rewarded. Because of your involvement, she won't drug, blackmail, or kill any more men. And as your attorney, I advise you make no further comments."

Renfro backed toward the door. "Your release is being processed. You can clear out in about twenty minutes."

"Where's Carmen now?" Philip asked.

Holmes stood. "In custody transport to Houston. And, we're testing the sample of margarita found at Ms. James's home. If it contains sildenafil or cantharidin, then your attorney's theory will have support."

After Holmes left, Nelda straightened her papers. "We are indebted to your friends. Lupe let himself be lured by Ms. James so he could get a sample of her margarita concoction. And the others followed them out to her house. If they hadn't been so persistent, we'd still be at square one." She snapped her briefcase shut. "Now you're free."

Nelda started to rise, but Philip's low, defeated voice stopped her. "I'm not free."

"What?"

"I'm not free until I know what happened February fourteenth. The statements, Carmen's and Frank's, haven't changed." His voice dropped to a ragged whisper. "I need to know if what she said is true."

"Philip, let go of that." Nelda's normal brisk tone turned soft and gentle. "Legally, you're not responsible for anything that happened if she drugged you. And, I doubt Carmen James will ever tell the truth. She has nothing to gain and even more to lose if she admits trying to have an innocent man imprisoned. Just be glad she's been stopped before she hurt anyone else."

Philip was unmoved by Nelda's encouragement. "There must have been some reason she targeted me."

"You sound like hundreds of crime victims I've encountered. It's not unusual for victims to try to take on blame, especially in cases of sexual assault. Why did she target that poor man in Houston who died? Why the DA's father? Why Ralph?"

The jail attendant came to the door with a paper bag and the envelope containing the manuscript. "Here's your property you came in with and the papers from your cell. Inspect your belongings and sign the receipt." Watching Philip sign, the attendant added, "When you're dressed, an officer can drop you wherever you want to go."

Chapter Thirty-Five

"Can you use me in Dallas?" Philip, talking on his phone, leaned against the wall outside the jail.

"Well, sure," Al said. "You're out?"

"Yeah. All charges dropped. I need to get back to work."

"How about here? Why so far away?"

"Ready for a change." A patrol car pulled up. "Listen, my ride's here, I'll get to the site sometime tomorrow... take whatever work you've got. Bye." Sliding into the car, he asked the officer, "Can you drive me to the hospital?" He wanted to check on Guillermo before leaving town.

"Sure thing."

"I'll be inside a few minutes. Then I'd like to go to Dallas if you can go that far or the bus station if not."

"Let me check with dispatch while you're in the hospital."

During the ride, Philip scrolled through numbers in his phone... Dinah... Lily... Lupe... Edith. His finger hovered over Edith's number. But anything he could say, would only drag out the inevitable. He was out of her life. Being released from jail didn't change Valentine's night. An incoming call vibrated —Edith.

His breath hitched.

A knot formed in his throat.

He powered his phone off.

Taking deep slow breaths, he vowed, *I won't be that man in her life who raped someone but doesn't remember it.*

At the hospital, a nurse sent him to wait in the reception area because Guillermo's doctor was examining him. When she said it was okay to go in, Rosa and Guillermo were both in the propped-up bed watching TV. Seeing these good, truthful people solidified his new reality. Face to face with them, his shame felt more marked.

Rosa leapt up. "You are out of jail." She started toward Philip with outstretched arms. "Thank goodness." But his pained expression must have blocked her. She stepped back without touching him. "We have been so worried."

"Thanks for all you did." Philip's words felt hollow. "How's Guillermo?"

Guillermo clicked off the TV. "Doing well. I should be released tomorrow. The wound is not bad."

"I'm sorry you got shot. Sorry my mess landed you here."

Rosa said, "You have nothing to apologize for. That woman is crazy, poisoning people. Come in, sit with us."

Philip stayed near the door. "Is there anything I can do for you guys? I'll send money for your medical bills."

"Thank you." Rosa pulled a chair close to the bed. "But someone from the county's Victim's Services contacted us. They'll cover the hospital expenses, and Lupe will drive us home tomorrow. We are in good shape. Please sit. Tell us what happened."

"No, thanks. I have to get to a job site."

Guillermo reached toward him with one hand. "But your truck is still in Culmine. You could ride with us tomorrow? We could drop you on our way home."

They didn't seem to know Philip had given his truck to Lupe.

"No, thanks. I'm leaving today. Ride's waiting." He started backing out. "I'm sorry for everything but glad you're okay." He glanced at both of them. "Goodbye."

Down the long hallway at the exit, Philip reached out to push the door.

"Hey, big guy, slow down." Lupe's voice ambushed him from behind. "We have been chasing you all over Culmine. You are too fast."

Philip froze. He braced himself for a renewed rush of shame. Lupe knew of Carmen's statement about Valentine's night.

Before he turned to face Lupe, Edith's soft voice pulsed through him. "Philip."

He squeezed his eyes shut and turned as Edith slammed into him.

She wrapped both arms around him and whispered, "I love you, Philip. I'm never letting you go. Never."

His heart cracked.

He shook his head, took her shoulders, and backed out of her embrace. "No, Edith. I'm sorry." His voice was a rough whisper. "It won't—"

Edith silenced him by touching his lips with her fingers. "You think you assaulted that woman Valentine's night, but you didn't." She pulled close to him again and raised her face to his. "We have proof."

Lupe nudged them. "Let us move out of the doorway. Somebody might want to pass through." He guided them toward some chairs in a waiting area.

Kenneth from the bar sat, smiling, with his walker beside him. "Well, there's Philip."

Before Philip could ask, Edith rushed into an explanation.

"When Lupe was arguing with Carmen, right before she shot at him, she said you raped her and she didn't care what that old cripple says. I wondered if she could have meant Kenneth, so Lupe and I went to his house this morning. On Valentine's night when you left the café, Kenneth's battery was dead. Carmen followed you out, but you didn't leave with her. You and Kenneth left in your truck, bought a new battery, and you installed it for him."

Kenneth pulled himself up on his walker. "That's right. You whispered you needed an excuse to get away from the woman following you. You made me drive, said you'd had too many shots. Then when we got back, you worked on my truck for a long time, said something was wrong with the cables. You let me go into your room and lay down while you finished. Guess I fell asleep cause when I woke up around five in the morning, you were snoring beside me. I slipped out without waking you."

"Are you sure you have the right date?" But even as Philip asked, he realized Valentine's was the only night in Culmine he'd blacked out until the night he met Edith.

"Nope, wasn't sure." Kenneth pulled a folded sheet of paper from his shirt pocket. "But when Edith and Lupe came over, I got out my receipt for the battery. See." He pointed to the date stamp. "February 14, 10.45pm. This is just a copy cause I gave the original to Renfro a while ago when we went to the jail to tell you."

A boulder crumbling let relief fill Philip's chest. He lifted Edith and buried his face against her neck.

Kenneth chuckled. "I'm a sound sleeper but I'd have noticed you raping a woman, even if I am an old cripple."

Philip raised his head and, setting Edith back on her feet, gazed at the three. Choked with emotion, he wasn't sure his voice would work. "You've saved my life."

"Yes!" Lupe clapped his hands once and grinned. "At last, I am a free man."

All eyes focused on him.

"Felipe saved me from a giant rattlesnake. Now, my debt that has weighed me down for twenty years is paid. We are even." He pulled a key from his pocket and slapped it into Philip's palm. "And keep your truck and tools. I do not want to be in debt again."

Amid laughter, Edith said, "Balance is restored."

"Nope, not yet." Kenneth frowned, shook his head, and let them wait several seconds. "I'm still owed a double cheeseburger."

With more laughter of relief, Philip lowered his cheek onto Edith's hair. Then she raised her face toward his, and their eyes could not break their gaze.

For once Lupe didn't have a joke. "Come on, Kenneth. I will take you home."

After a round of farewells, Philip and Edith were alone. He took her shoulders. "Words... can't tell what... this means."

Edith placed her palms on both sides of his face. "You've been in darkness so long that this light you're seeing now is more than you can take in."

"No," he said. "I took in that light the first time we met. You're right, I was in darkness, and after I met you, I could never look away again... Never." His lips found hers and they were both lost in a kiss for long moments. He broke the kiss but stayed so close their lips touched when he spoke. "But now... I'm not just seeing light from a dark place. I'm in the light. I love you."

"I love you, Philip." She kissed him again. "Come on. My car's this way."

"Okay, let's tell the officer I won't need a ride." He led her to the squad car, then still holding on to each other, they turned toward the lot where she had parked.

Inside her car they leaned toward each other, and Philip asked, "Why is it that you never gave up on me?"

"Anyone who really knows you, knows you aren't capable of assault. Rosa, Al, Guillermo, Lupe—no one gave up on you."

He couldn't stop running his hands over her face and hair and arms. "I want to be alone with you."

"So do I, but I have bad news."

"What? Are you okay?"

"I'm fine. It's Dinah. She's admitted herself to a hospital that treats eating disorders."

Philip wasn't sure he heard right. "Eating disorders?"

"Lily said Dinah's in a hospital in Austin. Apparently, she's struggled with anorexia since her teen years."

He leaned back in the seat and raked his hand over his hair. "I didn't know that, but it makes sense. She seems to shrink every time I see her."

"Lily thinks what triggered this episode, aside from your father's death and your arrest, is all the trouble she's having at her job and with Jack. He wants a divorce and full custody of Jacqueline."

"But he hardly sees Jacqueline."

Edith turned on the ignition. "Lily believes he's trying for custody to snag a bigger divorce settlement. Jack wants his and Dinah's home as well as half of Dinah's inheritance."

"What a lowlife," Philip muttered. "Can we see Dinah?"

Edith pulled out of the parking lot. "Yes, we can go there now."

Dinah, at a small table by a window, sat gazing out at the brick wall of the next building.

"Hey," Philip said as they slowly entered her silent room.

Dinah continued to look out the window. The bones in her face were more pronounced than the last time he'd seen her.

Edith walked to the edge of the bed and sat.

Noticing pages of the original copy of the manuscript spread across the table top, Philip sat in the chair across from Dinah. "Talk to me. You know the police dropped all charges, right? I'm not like our grandfather."

Still facing the window, Dinah said in a low monotone, "Other than the fact you're an alcoholic who conveniently doesn't remember things."

Philip took a deep breath. "You're right. I am an alcoholic. I own that."

Eyebrows lifting in surprise, Dinah faced him.

"I want to quit. I want never to black out again. And I know how lucky I am to be bailed out of my blackout, that Edith and the police have evidence that my accuser lied. She's been poisoning and framing men. She killed one man."

"What happened to her?" Dinah asked.

"Jail—Houston."

"No." Dinah glared at him. "I don't mean now. I mean what happened to her that she's so damaged that she's poisoning and framing men."

Philip nodded thoughtfully. "From what I read in the police statements, she felt betrayed by her father and her sister. Her mother died when she was a little girl. Her husband also died. That's all I know about her but sounds like she had a hard time." He carefully lifted a brittle, yellowed page from the manuscript. "You read it?"

"Every word."

Philip gently set the page down. "Think about this story,

337

Dinah. We were born into a family with generations of abuse, going back to slave masters. It's like a fractal. It goes on and on, and what happened in our family line, happened in the whole country. The ugliness is not just about us, it's about the whole country. We were snared in something bigger than us."

Dinah gazed back out at the brick wall. "Isn't it odd that we never knew our ancestors owned slaves."

Philip said, "Yeah. I guess white people like to... to... unremember that."

Dinah's voice was so low Philip had to strain to hear. "For me, it's never been just about what Granddaddy did to me." She turned to him as if a veil had lifted from her face. She was clear eyed, her skin almost translucent. "It was that people didn't believe me... that people told me to get over it. Even—" Her voice cracked as it had that night in their grandparent's kitchen twenty years earlier. "—Mama. But I needed everyone to admit the truth and stop expecting me to act like nothing happened."

Philip reached for her hand. "Mama truly believed it was better that way. Back then people weren't tuned in to the 'no means no' culture we have now. She thought it would be hard on you to have to confront people."

Dinah pulled her hand back. "Our grandparents knew the truth. Daddy and Aunt Loraine knew the truth. They just didn't want to deal with the ugliness of a man raping his granddaughter. They protected... him... and themselves."

Philip nodded. "And don't you see, it's the same thing our ancestors did. They knew the truth, that the masters should have owned up, apologized. Instead, they pretended the abuse never happened. They expected everyone to just shut up and get over it. But we don't have to be like our ancestors, and I'm going to help you get your life back on track."

The door opened and Lily entered. "I finished going through Daddy's trunk." She reached into her large bag, and pulled out a folder holding old pages, creased with multiple fold lines. "These three pages were folded into a small square and must have fallen from that stationery box." She sat on the edge of the bed next to Edith. "Listen." She kept the pages on the folder and didn't touch them while reading.

Addendum to Sabine Richards's manuscript. 1955

I am ninety-one years old. I have lived too long. Yesterday I opened my stationery box to conclude my self-serving monologue. Rereading, I wonder how I could have been so blind.

My first impulse was to burn the pages, but Seth's story of Feevah should not be destroyed. If I had the energy to rewrite with my own views expunged, I would do so.

I had convinced myself through my extensive reading and my enlightened understanding of human nature, I was outside this cycle that created the monster my father became. In a pathetic attempt to distance myself from my family's history, I adopted a written dialect, which I fancied differed from that of my community. All I accomplished with my rhetoric was spectacular self-delusion because I, who have no slaves or wife or children to abuse, killed my own mother. When the institution of slavery ended, the innate hatefulness that enables a man to victimize innocents did not end simply because the victims had been removed. Instead of victimizing their slaves, the Richards men victimized their own wives and children; indeed, they victimized their own souls.

At least my father's and Feevah's bastard son Solomon will never be cursed with the burdens I carry. Yesterday, much to my surprise, two coloreds stopped their fancy car in front of my home. Costumed in gentleman's suits, they walked boldly toward my door. I stepped onto the front

porch to give a strong presence before they achieved
excessive proximity.

Lily gently shifted the top page to the bottom and started
reading from the next sheet. Heavy silence gripped the room.

Philip waited with dread. He had hoped when the opening
admitted to the killing of Tenny that Sabine had finally
recognized his own bias. But he worried about what new
atrocities might be revealed, and he carefully watched Dinah.
She seemed so fragile. He hoped nothing in these pages would
cause her additional pain. Her skin was even paler now as her
gaze locked on Lily.

"Good day, Mr. Richards," began the taller of the two men.
"My name is Solomon Richards and this is my son Russell
Richards." He offered his hand to shake, but I was too
shocked to reciprocate. After an uncomfortable pause, he
continued, "We are searching for descendants of Russell
Richards and his slave Seth. Both left Tennessee at the
close of the Civil War."

I was so moved by this golden man, this physical
manifestation of Seth's chronicle, that I was momentarily
stunned. And, his name! His name! Of course, freed slaves
were able to keep their masters' surnames, but I was
dismayed at Solomon's brazen choice of Russell, my own
father's name, for his son. This bastard, Solomon, who
based on Seth's memory was four years my elder, had the
straight back and square shoulders of a much younger man,
and he exhibited a self-assurance, which could have
evolved only from his belief that he was sired by a
white man.

"Sir," he repeated. "You are Mr. Sabine Richards?"

He could have easily verified my name with neighbors.

"Yes," I answered tersely. "I am Sabine Richards, but I have no knowledge of the people whom you reference."

"I see." He frowned. "I have been searching for these people and their descendants for most of my life. I had great hope you might be able to direct me to their whereabouts."

Philip's face had grown hot when Lily read the line saying Solomon's self-assurance came from his assumption that he had a white father. Sabine, at ninety-one, was still blind to his own narcissistic view.

Once more Lily shuffled the pages. The final sheet must have been on the outside of the folded bundle. It was the most damaged, and she was careful not to touch it. Everyone in the room held deadly still as if movement might frighten these ghosts away while Lily read on.

In spite of his gentleman's appearance, I marveled at the ignorance with which he would approach this subject in the full light of day with numerous inquisitive neighbors obviously taking note. As I turned to go back into my home, I said in my most benevolent tone, "You and your son need to leave. There is no business for coloreds in my neighborhood."

Then, even if I had not known Feevah's three children and Micah had escaped to New York City after the war, I would have guessed the location of Solomon's home in the next few moments. In an act, which only an uppity New York City Negro would execute, Solomon boldly pranced onto my porch, opened my letterbox, and deposited a folded sheet of blue paper. He said, "Mr. Richards, in case you encounter someone who does know these people, this is my name and address. Any information you could mail will be most appreciated. Good day."

My life's effort has been to know the truth and be graced with the Divine blessing promised in John 8:32: *And ye shall know the truth, and the truth shall make you free.* I now have mastered truth as only an old man can, and the knowledge has served to secure my solitary, regretful misery: enlightenment came too late for me.

As progenitor, my grandfather never acknowledged the truth that the institution of slavery was evil. My father never had the courage to speak the truth to his own father, and as a result Feevah was slaughtered like an animal, an evil act that destroyed the humanity in my father. If only the truth had prevailed, I could have lived life whole instead of contorted by burdens spawned by my ancestors' blindness.

ad infinitum, Sabine Richards, 1956

Edith, in a soft voice, said, "He tries to express the same thing you do, Philip, except he was too damaged. If only he would have told Solomon the truth. What a gift that would have been."

Dinah stretched her hands, palms up, toward Lily, requesting the pages.

"They're pretty fragile." Lily passed the folder to Dinah.

Dinah flung the folder aside, grasped the pages, and her hands jerked.

Rip.

Lily and Edith gasped.

Dinah tore the three pages in half and then in half again.

Philip laid his hands over Dinah's. "You don't have to—"

"Don't touch me." Yanking away, she grabbed several pages of the manuscript still scattered on the table and ripped them.

Lily started grabbing the pages and pulling them away. "Dinah, don't."

Dinah stood with fists clenched at her side. "What a self-righteous bigot... so full of himself." She laughed. "Sabine had the nerve to question Solomon's use of the name *Russell* when Russell was just as much Solomon's father as he was Sabine's." Her white cotton robe hung loose on her thin, trembling frame. "And all that preaching about truth." She narrowed her eyes at the three stunned onlookers. "Truth. You are just as deluded as Sabine. You think you're all woke now. You've identified the interconnectedness of sexual abuse with slave abuse. You're all part of an endless fractal." She glared at Philip, mocking his theory. "The stain bleeds down for generations."

She pointed at the manuscript pages, now safely out of her reach. "Well, that means nothing. Nothing. I. Am. Screwed. Get it? Screwed. It doesn't matter whether it's just some fluke in my lifetime or it came down—" She jerked both arms upward. "—through the ages. I'm still screwed. I'm about to lose my daughter. My divorce is a cliché. My career is crashing. I'm losing my property. And you know what's the most hysterical? Ironic and insane?"

She glared at them, eyes wide and crazed. "Do you?" She pointed at the pages now in Lily's hands and said in a scratching whisper, "I'm just like them. Remember my infamous rant at the barbeque. Open your eyes and see. Nothing. Nothing. Nothing has changed."

Her face wet with tears, Lily said, "Don't. Stop and think about all you've accomplished... your daughter, your students."

Dinah ignored the encouragement. "I do the same thing Sabine did. I go to work every day thinking..." With a fake-clownish smile, she rocked her head from side to side. "...I am not a racist. But you know what I do. I tell all children to just move on." For the first time, she faced Philip, locking her gaze with his. "I ignore what happened and tell them to get over it. Just like everybody told me to do when our grandfather raped me." She shifted her gaze to Lily. "Rebuttals?" Then to Edith. "Wise advice?"

Her talk had been so rapid that her sudden stop left the listeners dumbstruck.

Dinah laughed sarcastically. "I thought not. So now you can all go home and continue your new woke lives, and rest assured I've faced reality. I'll force my weight up. Find a new job that doesn't get me near people. I'll keep myself on a controlled calorie intake. I'll drag myself through this life and be glad I don't have to witness what the next generation does." Dinah dropped into her chair as if exhausted.

Blotting her tears, Lily pulled another folder from her bag.

Philip focused on Dinah. "No. You aren't going to do this on your own. If I have to move into your house, I will, but you are going to get better. I don't care what it takes. I wasn't there for you when you were twelve. But I'm here now, and I'm not leaving."

Lily opened the folder. "I'm going to find our cousins."

Everyone turned toward her, questioning.

"Cousins?" Dinah melted farther back into her chair as if she might slide down to the floor. "Why would you want to see them again? They all denied what Granddaddy did to me."

On the folder in Lily's hand lay a small, obviously old square of blue paper. "No, not them. I mean the cousins we've never met. Descendants of Feevah and Seth. We've got a name and address to start with." She tilted the folder so they could read a neatly printed name and address: *Solomon Richards, 6th Street, Bedford-Stuyvesant, New York City, New York.* "This was folded inside Sabine's addendum... the address Solomon left. I'm going to search for his descendants, and this is the first clue."

Philip stood and stepped closer to Dinah. "We can never make up for Thomas maiming Seth and killing Feevah or all the years people said just get over it. But maybe this story in the manuscript will mean as much to them as it does to us. They deserve the truth. Dinah, remember that day at the barbeque when I told you I'm sorry for everything that happened to you? It was the first time I'd seen you smile since you were a child. Remember how much my simple acknowledgment meant to you?"

Dinah, with a soft gasp, reached for the folder.

Lily pulled back. "No. I don't want it torn."

Philip gently gripped Dinah's shoulders. "Think about the one thing you wanted your whole life. The one thing you needed, for everyone to own the truth about what our grandfather did to you. This is our chance to give Feevah's and Seth's descendants the truth about their past. It can help them."

A new glow emanated from Dinah's face. A peacefulness overpowered all the rage she'd expressed moments earlier. "This is real," she whispered to the blue slip of paper. "Not just woke bullshit. We'll find them and give them Seth's story. We'll admit how Thomas crippled Seth and killed Feevah."

Lily said, "And, Dinah, doing this will help you... help all of us... let go of the pain that our hatred is causing us." Then Lily turned to Edith. "Where do we start? How did you find all that stuff about our ancestors?"

Edith, nodding, already had her phone out.

Epilogue

Three years later

The large painting of a Black man holds my gaze. Alive and enticing, it's painted in oils, but the rustic browns and granular texture evoke the look of wood. The man's face, while not intricately detailed, is unforgettable, like a wood carving. His expression makes me breathe more deeply. He's sitting in a rocking chair under an awning outside a small house. There's a table beside him with what looks like a bottle of wine and two glasses. Mottled shadows across the scene suggest sunlight filtering through leaves. I want to hear his music, taste the wine, and sniff the air.

For the past ten minutes, I've been waiting in the school's reception area to interview Dr. Dinah Richards. Her new private school, Seth Richards Academy of Grace, will be the topic of my first article for my journalism internship with the *Gire Gazette*. I'm worried about how to make the article stand out because *school* is not a thrilling topic.

Again, the painting pulls my gaze and pushes aside my nagging concerns about the article. Next to the portrait is a framed document. The frame is recessed, so the page, clearly very old, is a couple of inches away from the glass cover. I approach to read it. One corner of the yellowed paper is torn. The fancy, loopy handwriting is done in ink, faded to gray:

> When I finally inquired whether the melody he had played as I approached him that first day was "Amazing Grace," his simple answer stunned me.
>
> "My song ain't 'Amazing Grace.' It just 'Grace' cause them that knows grace, knows there's no need to put 'amazing' in front of it."
>
> By Sabine Richards, 1935

The words express... a mystery bigger than my ability to articulate. I'm captivated, intrigued. Who is this man in the painting? Who is Sabine Richards?

Enough.

I must focus on my article.

Here's what I know so far. About three years ago, Dr. Richards' brother, a construction contractor, rehabbed their deceased father's home into a school. She started this private, tuition-free school a year later with eleven students. Then she received an exorbitant funding boost from a New York philanthropic group, the Feevah Foundation, that specializes in setting up and supporting non-profits led by Blacks. However, while I've been waiting for the interview, I've noted that the students are not solely Black but seem to represent a variety of races. The school now has over a hundred students. And, I've heard construction is planned for an addition with projected population for next year to be more than two hundred students.

Finally, two ladies approach.

Even though they are both white and can't be the head, I stand and introduce myself. "Dr. Richards? I'm Mia Hart."

"No," the dark-haired one says. "I'm Lily, a social worker. I come in twice a week to conduct symbolic restorative circles with the students. This is my sister-in-law, Edith. She comes in to teach advanced placement English and social studies classes. Dinah just phoned and asked me to tell you she's five minutes out. Sorry for her delay."

I nod, greeting them both. "No problem. What's a restorative circle?"

Lily says, "Students select a conflict, either contemporary or historical, research it, and role play the differing sides. Then they mediate a resolution."

"What types of conflicts?"

"All kinds. This month the middle school students are doing the January 6 insurrection." She smiles. "They're determined not to repeat the mistakes of our generation."

A bell sounds.

The blonde woman, Edith, says, "That's our signal for class. Sorry to leave you alone. Dinah will be here soon."

"Thanks," I say as they leave.

Maybe I could focus my article on a restorative circle. Before I can finish the thought, there's a loud racket from outside. Through the window I see a man at the tree line that edges the large playground. He's peering up into the trees where the sounds seem to be coming from. There are large, chicken-sized birds up in the trees. Dozens.

A little boy with thick glasses passing through the reception area notices my gaping. "Those are our guineas. They scare the snakes away."

"Oh?" Before I can ask him for more information, he scurries down the hallway. *Snakes and guineas*, I wonder, peering back out. That might be an interesting slant to the article. Although, the playground is immaculate with seemingly no place for snakes to hide, the forest beyond the tree line is dense.

The man moves toward a staked-out area that seems to be

framed for a foundation—most likely for the new addition. He takes some measurements then approaches the building. It's hard to stop staring at him. He's strong and graceful at the same time. Nearing the entry, he stomps his feet as if to clean off any dirt.

When he enters the reception area, he spots me. "Hello. Has anyone helped you?"

"Yes, I'm Mia Hart waiting for Dr. Richards. We have an appointment."

Coming closer he offers his hand. "I'm Philip—just checking the foundation frame for tomorrow's pour. Dinah should be here soon."

"Thanks. Uh, can you tell me about those guineas. Do they really keep snakes away?"

He grins. "That's the folklore. But for sure they remind the students to watch for snakes."

"Do you have a lot of snakes here?"

"No. We haven't seen one in three years. But this is Texas, so we need to be on guard."

At that moment the door opens and a slender, dark-haired woman enters.

"Mia Hart?" she asks as she approaches.

"Yes." We shake hands.

"I'm Dinah Richards. Sorry to be late." She turns to Philip. "Here are the checks you need for the contractors."

"Thanks, I'll be on my way." And to me as he goes to the door, "Nice to meet you."

Hmmm. Dinah Richards appears to be white. How did she get funding from a philanthropic group that supports Black-led non-profits?

After introductions we settle in for the interview.

"Why did you start this school?"

"I had spent nine years in public education trying to make

students fit the system. I realized three years ago that a fairer approach would be to make the school fit students. In the beginning we targeted a few students who were clearly falling through the cracks in the public system."

Now for the big question. "Why is a New York foundation funding a Texas school directed by a white person?"

She smiles. "Three years ago, our family discovered that some of our ancestors were slaves—"

"I'm sorry to interrupt. Your ancestors were slaves? Are you saying you are Black?"

She smiles. "No, I'm not Black. My great-great-great grandfather had a son who was a slave. We tracked down his descendants, and those of another slave, Feevah. It turned out after the Civil War, Feevah's daughter, who could read and write, started educating newly freed Blacks in New York. Her work attracted funders, and the foundation expanded and diversified and still exists today. When we met the descendants and told them about the school we were trying to start, they wanted to be involved." She pauses as if to emphasize her next words. "We couldn't have done it without their guidance, financial support, and political clout."

"This is fascinating. How did you learn about your ancestors?"

"An old manuscript that our great-great uncle Sabine wrote."

"Could I read it? It would enrich my article to have this background?"

"Yes. We copyrighted and published it as a limited edition."

My pulse speeds up. *There's my story!* "Why did you name the school the Seth Richards Academy of Grace?"

She turns toward the large painting of the Black man with a harmonica. "That's Seth, my great-great-great uncle, as imagined by our artist friend Guillermo Zacatecas. Seth provided the oral history that Sabine used to write the manuscript. Without Seth's words, we would still be trapped in our short-sighted view of the world. I would still be trying to mold children into contrived patterns without first acknowledging their truths."

Peering at the painting again, I'm at a loss for words. I should ask more questions, but I can't find them.

Dr. Richards puts a brochure into my hands. "I think the students say it best."

I pull my gaze away from the painting down to the brochure entitled, 'What Seth Richards Academy of Grace Means to Me.'

Scanning the student testimonials, key words jump out: "a safe place... reparations... healing ... reconciliation... fairness... even-playing fields... escape from a spiraling trap... new chance at life."

One student's simple statement ends the list: "When the teachers at Seth Richards Academy of Grace heard my truth, for the first time, I heard it, too."

THE END

Discussion Questions

1. Philip Richards has obvious flaws (alcoholism, risky rattlesnake handling, alienation from family), but why are characters such as Edith, Lily, Rosa, and Lupe drawn to him anyway?

2. How do you interpret Philip's two differing responses to scents?

> A whiff of cotton-candy perfume alerted him that someone was approaching. The scent triggered dread in his gut. His thigh muscles tensed ready to run.

> A faint, warm scent—lavender he thought—launched a hum throughout his body. He inhaled deeply and tilted toward the scent...

3. In the wooden wagon, after Feevah and her daughters are purchased, the little girls find peaceful moments imagining a house by drawing in the layer of flour dust that coats the rough floor. How is their game ironically symbolic of their real world?

Discussion Questions

4. The first night Feevah is at the Richards' home, she is attracted to Russell.

> *This most beautiful and compelling emotion was too precious to pray away. She had never felt more alive.*

Is the reader conflicted between accepting her almost-instant attraction to Russell versus believing her arousal is Sabine's romanticized version of Seth's story?

5. When Brother Tune questions Feevah about where everyone sleeps, Feevah's speech patterns change.

> *This here be Grandma's room. Masser done told me and the children to sleep with her cause she get scared in the night and run off. We watches her and keeps her company.*

Why does she speak in differing dialects?

6. To what would you attribute Tenny's style of mothering?

7. How does Sabine explain his own "literary" dialect?

8. Why does Feevah do something so out of character in this scene with her son?

> *She slapped him [Solomon] hard and shook him by the shoulders. Mrs. Richards started crying. Solomon gasped in shock, and Feevah slapped him again. "I told you, put your head down... down!"*

354

9. Mrs. Richards is furious about the work that Mrs. Schmidt did.

With a high pitched, angry drawn-out grunt, Mrs. Richards began jerking the clothes out of the water and throwing them around the room. The four onlookers dodged to avoid the propelled clothes, but everyone in the room was wet with flying water by the time the wash tub was emptied.

However, almost immediately Mrs. Richards accepts Feevah's interventions calmly. Why the difference?

10. How would you interpret the novel's use of truth as relayed by different characters:

- Sabine claims to be tormented by his search for truth, and he ultimately declares he discovers the truth only to say later that it didn't save him.
- Feevah believes: "a story's strength came not from the teller but from the ring of truth."
- Philip reacts to Edith's journal entry about the night they met. "The truth in the words he didn't remember saying found home within him."
- Philip avoids the truth of what happened during his Valentine's night blackout.
- Lily, as a four-year-old child, is sheltered from the truth of Dinah's molestation.
- Dinah says, "Truth. You are just as deluded as Sabine. You think you're all woke now. You've identified the interconnectedness of sexual abuse with slave abuse... The stain bleeds down for generations... Well, that means nothing..."

- Tenny says moments before the fall that kills her: "Truth!... I tell the truth, but you don't hear!"

11. How does Philip equate fractal patterns with multigenerational behaviors?

12. How does Guillermo compare Mandelbrot's fractals with Toltec timelines?

13. In the beginning of the novel, Philip is a high-functioning alcoholic who occasionally blacks out. By the end of the novel, he seems to be free of his blackout issue. Is his progress believable? Why or why not?

14. Consider this passage from Chapter 35:

> Dinah gazed back out at the brick wall. "Isn't it odd that we never knew our ancestors owned slaves."
>
> Philip said, "Yeah. I guess white people like to... to... unremember that."

How is forgotten time different from unremembered time? What role does time, forgotten or unremembered, play in the novel?

15. Do you agree with Sabine's statement that men damaged their own souls?

> Instead of victimizing their slaves, the Richards men victimized their own wives and children; indeed, they victimized their own souls.

16. What does Seth's statement tell you about him?

> *My song ain't 'Amazing Grace.' It just 'Grace' cause them that knows grace, knows there's no need to put 'amazing' in front of it.*

Acknowledgments

Bloodhound Books

First, thank you for reading and accepting my manuscript. Your team's passion and professionalism are the magic that every writer seeks to bring a book into the world. Special thanks to three members who directly interacted with me during the publishing process: Betsy Reavley (Director and Founder), Tara Lyons (Editorial and Production Manager), and Clare Law (Associate Editor). Their dedication to their work is a gift to a novelist. And, Clare Law. What can I say? She understands my characters and the saga's timeline better than I do. Clare is an amazing editor who elevated my work. Thank you, Clare.

Melissa Rupert

I can never talk about writing without acknowledging my friend, Melissa. She offers support every step of the way, usually through daily texts.

Dr. Cynthia de las Fuentes

When working toward my Ph.D., I needed an elective credit and serendipitously, Dr. de las Fuentes's course at Our Lady of the Lake University was one that fit my schedule. Her brilliant illumination of ancestral influence planted the seed for this novel. I'll be forever grateful that I accidentally landed in her treasure of knowledge.

Jose Del Valle

Jose, thank you for introducing me to swerve.

John Burt

John Burt, Paul Prosswimmer Professor of American Literature, Brandeis University, and Literary Executor for Robert Penn Warren, graciously granted permission to quote "Bearded Oaks." His response to my request to use Warren's poem was encouraging and timely.

Texas

I lived in Texas when I started this book and workshopped drafts with fellow authors: Claire Ashby, Elizabeth Buhmann, Ron Seybold, Jasmine Patterson, Nancy Warren, Shannon Stewart, Druzelle and Rob Cederquist, Adam Carduff, Debbie Eynon Finley, Julie Rennecker, and Chris Cervini. Their input in the early stages helped me begin.

Vermont

I moved to Vermont before finishing the book and found a rich community of writers who provided support during the final phases: Vicki Disorda, Erin Bodin, Natalie Coe, Shirley Oskamp, Patty Wheeler (deceased), Erika Bodin, Sue Priest, Brigid Brown, Angelia Mae, Kamala Rose, Rose Moody, Yvonne Daley (deceased), Jean Beatson, Gemma Lury, Monda Kelley, Deb Levesque, Hilary Appelman, Ruth Ann Castillo, Dr. Barbara D. Parks-Lee, Arlinda Vaughn, Deborah Klee, Haley Kenyon, Norma Murphy. These writers not only offered recommendations on my writing, but they also shared their own work with me. I learned by being a part of their processes.

Three poets

One of the characters in the book is the poet, Edith. Three lovely Vermont poets helped me shape Edith and her work: Penelope Weiss, Victoria Crain, Linda Wigmore.

Claire Ashby

A special call out to this author whose book *When You Make It Home* taught me that literature is at its best when it tugs the heartstrings.

Family

When your mother or any relative publishes a book, like it or not, you're stuck being a part of it. Parts of this story are raw and ugly. They will strike nerves with readers. I apologize in advance for negativity that may touch you.

Readers

Dear Reader, thank you. Your precious time spent reading this novel is appreciated. I hope *Echoes of Our Ancestors* has value for you.

A note from the publisher

Thank you for reading this book. If you enjoyed it please do consider leaving a review on Amazon to help others find it too.

We hate typos. All of our books have been rigorously edited and proofread, but sometimes mistakes do slip through. If you have spotted a typo, please do let us know and we can get it amended within hours.

info@bloodhoundbooks.com

9 781917 214094